ROSS THOMAS

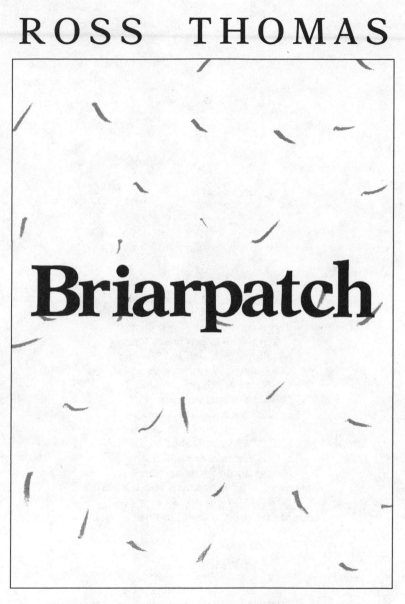

Briarpatch

Simon and Schuster New York

Briarpatch

THE redheaded homicide detective stepped through the door at 7:30 A.M. and out into the August heat that already had reached 88 degrees. By noon the temperature would hit 100, and by two or three o'clock it would be hovering around 105. Frayed nerves would then start to snap and produce a marked increase in the detective's business. Breadknife weather, the detective thought. Breadknives in the afternoon.

The door the detective stepped through led out onto the second-floor landing of a two-story yellow brick duplex with a green copper roof. The detective turned back, made sure the door was locked, and started down the outside staircase. The yellow brick duplex was in the still-fashionable Jefferson Heights section and had been well built fifty-two years ago on a nicely shaded sixty-foot lot on the southeast corner of 32nd Street and Texas Avenue. By dint of some rather dubious creative financing, the homicide detective had bought the duplex seventeen months back, lived alone in its upper two-bedroom apartment, and rented the lower floor for $650 a month to a thirtyish home-computer salesman and his girl friend, who were usually late with the rent.

It was 7:31 on the morning of August 4, a Thursday, when the detective reached the bottom of the outside staircase, turned left, stopped at the salesman's door, and rang the bell. After thirty seconds or so the door was opened by an unshaven, sleepy-looking Harold Snow who tried his best to seem surprised and almost succeeded.

"Oh-my-God, Rusty," Snow said. "Don't tell me I didn't pay it again."

"You didn't pay it, Harold."

"Oh-my-God, I forgot," Snow said. "You wanta come in while I write the check?" Snow was wearing only the stained Jockey shorts he had slept in.

"I'll wait out here," the detective said. "It's cooler."

"I already got the air-conditioning on."

"I'll wait out here," the detective said again, and smiled a small, meaningless smile.

Harold Snow shrugged and closed the door to keep the heat out. The detective noticed a suspicious-looking gray blister, about two inches in diameter, on the brown molding that framed the door. With the aid of a fingernail file, the detective gently probed the blister, suspecting termites. I cannot afford termites, the detective thought. I simply cannot afford them.

The gray blister turned out to be only that, a paint blister, and the detective let out a small relieved sigh just as Harold Snow, now wearing a blue polo shirt, but still no pants, opened the door and held out the rent check. It was one of those brightly tinted checks with a pretty picture on it. The detective thought such checks were silly, but accepted it and studied it carefully to make sure Harold Snow hadn't postdated the check or forgotten to sign it, or even, as he had once done, written in differing amounts.

"Damn, I'm sorry it's late," Snow said. "It just clean slipped my mind."

The redheaded detective smiled slightly for the second time. "Sure, Harold."

Harold Snow smiled back. It was a sheepish smile, patently false, that somehow went with Snow's long narrow face, which the detective also found to be rather sheeplike, except for those clever coyote eyes.

Still wearing his smile, Harold Snow then said what he always said to the homicide detective, "Well, I guess you gotta go round up the usual suspects."

And as always, the detective didn't bother to respond, but said only, "See you, Harold," turned, and started down the cement walk toward the dark-green two-year-old five-speed Honda Accord that was parked the wrong way at the curb. Snow shut the door to his apartment.

The detective unlocked the two-door Honda, got in, put the key in the ignition, and depressed the clutch. There was a white-orange flash, quite brilliant; then a loud crackling bang, and a sudden swirl of thick greasy white smoke. When it cleared, the Honda's left door was hanging by one hinge. The detective sprawled halfway out of the car, the red hair now a smoking clump of fried black wire. The left leg below the knee ended in something that looked like cranberry jelly. Only the greenish gray eyes still moved. They blinked once in disbelief, once again in fear, and then, after that, the detective died.

Harold Snow was the first to race through the door of the downstairs apartment followed closely by Cindy McCabe, a thin tanned blond woman in her late twenties, who wore her hair up in green rollers. Snow had his pants on now, but no shoes. Cindy McCabe, also barefoot, wore a man's outsized white T-shirt and faded jeans. Snow held out a cautioning hand.

"Stay back," he said. "The gas tank might go."

"Jesus, Hal," she said. "What happened?"

Harold Snow stared at the sprawled body of the dead homicide detective. "I guess," he said slowly, "I guess somebody just blew away the landlady."

CHAPTER

1

THE long-distance call from the fifty-three-year-old chief of detectives reached Benjamin Dill three hours later. By then, because of different time zones, it was almost half-past eleven in Washington, D.C. When the phone rang, Dill was still in bed, alone and awake, in his one-bedroom apartment three blocks south of Dupont Circle on N Street. He had awakened at five that morning and discovered he was unable to go back to sleep. At 8:30 A.M. he had called his office and, pleading a summer cold, informed Betty Mae Marker he wouldn't be in that day, Thursday, and probably not even Friday. Betty Mae Marker had counseled rest, aspirin, and plenty of liquids.

Dill had decided to forsake work that morning, not because he was sick, but because it was his thirty-eighth birthday. For some inexplicable reason he had come to regard thirty-eight as the watershed year in which youth ran down one side, old age the other. He had spent the morning in bed wondering, with only mild curiosity, how he had managed to accomplish so little in his more than three dozen years.

True, he told himself, you did manage to get married once and divorced twice—no mean feat. A year after his ex-wife had slipped quietly out of his life on that rainy June night in 1978, Dill had filed for divorce in the District of Columbia, charging desertion. Apparently convinced that Dill would never do anything right, she had filed in California, charging irreconcilable differences. Neither divorce was contested and both were granted. The two things Dill now remembered best about his former wife were her long and extremely beautiful blond hair and her unforgivable habit of sprinkling sugar on her sliced tomatoes. As for her face, well, it was fading into something of a blur—albeit a heart-shaped one.

During that long morning of reevaluation, which turned out to be both depressing and boring, Dill wisely ignored his financial balance sheet because it was, as usual, ridiculous. He owned no insurance, no stocks or bonds, no vested pension, no real property. His principal assets consisted of $5,123.82 in a non-interest-bearing checking account at the Dupont Circle branch of the Riggs National Bank and a recently paid for 1982 Volkswagen convertible (an unfortunate yellow) that was parked in the apartment building's basement garage and whose sporty demeanor Dill now found disconcerting. He assumed this new attitude was yet another symptom of galloping maturity.

Dill gave up on his morning of pointless introspection when the long distance call from the fifty-three-year-old chief of detectives began its seventh ring. It was then that he picked up the phone and said hello.

"Mr. Dill?" the voice said. It was a stern voice, even harsh, full of bark and bite, gravel and authority.

"Yes."

"Have you got a sister named Felicity—Felicity Dill?"

"Why?"

"My name's Strucker. John Strucker. I'm chief of detectives down here and if your sister's name is Felicity, she works for me. That's why I'm calling."

Dill took a deep breath, let some of it out, and said, "Is she dead or just hurt?"

There was no pause before the answer came—only a long sigh, which was an answer in itself. "She's dead, Mr. Dill. I'm sorry."

"Dead." Dill didn't make it a question.

"Yes."

"I see."

And then, because Dill knew he had to say something else to keep grief away for at least a few more moments, he said, "It's her birthday."

"Her birthday," Strucker said patiently. "Well, I didn't know that."

"Mine, too," Dill said in an almost musing tone. "We have the same birthday. We were born ten years apart, but on the same day—August fourth. Today."

"Today, huh?" Strucker said, his harsh voice interested, overly reasonable, and almost kind. "Well, I'm sorry."

"She's twenty-eight."

"Twenty-eight."

"I'm thirty-eight." There was a long silence until Dill said, "How did—" but broke off to make a noise that could have been either a cough or a sob. "How did it happen?" he said finally.

Again, the chief of detectives sighed. Even over the phone it had a sad and mournful sound. "Car bomb," Strucker said.

"Car bomb," Dill said.

"She came out of her house this morning at her regular time, got into her car—one of those all-tin Honda Accords—threw out the clutch, and that's what activated the bomb—the clutch. They used C4—plastic."

"They," Dill said. "Who the hell are they?"

"Well, it might not've been a they, Mr. Dill. I just said

that. It could've been only one guy, but one or a dozen, we're gonna get who did it. It's what we do—what we're good at."

"How quickly did she—" Dill paused and took a deep breath. "I mean, did she—"

Strucker interrupted to answer the incomplete question. "No, sir, she didn't. It was instantaneous."

"I read somewhere that it's never instantaneous."

Strucker apparently knew better than to argue with the recently bereaved. "It was quick, Mr. Dill. Very quick. She didn't suffer." He paused again, cleared his throat, and said, "We'd like to bury her. I mean the department would, if it's okay with you."

"When?"

"Is it all right with you?"

"Yes, it's all right with me. When?"

"Saturday," Strucker said. "We'll have a big turnout from all over. It's a nice ceremony, real nice, and I'm sure you'll want to be here so if there's anything we can do for you, make you a hotel reservation or something like that, well, just let—"

Dill interrupted. "The Hawkins. Is the Hawkins Hotel still in business?"

"Yes, sir, it is."

"Make me a reservation there, will you?"

"For when?"

"For tonight," Dill said. "I'll be there tonight."

CHAPTER

DILL stood at one of the tall, almost floor-to-ceiling windows that lined the north side of his living room and watched the old man with the Polaroid take a photograph of the blue Volvo sedan that was illegally parked near the corner of 21st and N Streets.

The old man was the owner of a vacant four-story apartment building across the street from Dill's windows. At one time the old man had leased his bile-green building to a District program that had filled the apartments with drug addicts who were trying to break their habits. After the program's funds ran out, the addicts moved away, no one quite knew where, leaving behind a sackful of drawings that fell off the garbage truck and blew about the neighborhood.

Dill had picked up one of the drawings. It had been done with crayons in harsh primary colors and seemed to be a self-portrait of one of the dopers. There was a purple face with round eyes that had crosses in them and a big green mouth with fangs for teeth. The drawing was on the level of a bright first- or second-grader. Underneath the face was the laboriously printed legend: I AM A NO GOOD FUCKING DOPE FEIND. Dill sometimes wondered if the therapy had helped.

After the addicts moved out of his building, the old man lived in it alone, refusing either to sell or rent the property. He kept busy by taking Polaroid snapshots of the cars that parked illegally in front of it. He angled his shots so that they included both the No Parking sign and the offending car's license plate. Evidence in hand, the old man would then call the cops. Sometimes they came; sometimes they didn't. Dill often watched the old man at work and marveled at his rage.

Dill turned from the window, looked down, and discovered he was holding an empty cup and saucer. He could not remember either making or drinking the coffee. He crossed the room to the kitchen, moving slowly, a tall man with the lean, planed-down body of a runner, a body he had done virtually nothing to acquire, but had inherited from his dead father along with the carved-out, almost ugly face that male Dills had handed down to their sons since 1831 when the first Dill stepped off the boat from England.

The most prominent feature of the face was its nose: the Dill nose. It poked out and then shot almost straight down, not quite curving back into a hook. Below it was the Dill mouth: thin, wide, and apparently remorseless, or merry if the joke were good, the company pleasant. There was just enough chin, far too much to be called weak, but not quite enough for determined, so many settled for sensitive. The Dill ears were large enough to flap in a high wind and grew mercifully close to the head. But it was the eyes that almost rescued the face from ugliness. The eyes were large and gray and in a certain light looked soft, gentle, and even innocent. Then the light would change, the innocence would vanish, and the eyes looked like year-old ice.

At the stainless steel kitchen sink, Dill absently let water rinse over the cup for a full two minutes until he realized what he was doing, turned off the tap, and put both cup and saucer on the drainboard. He dried his wet right hand by running it through his thick dark coppery hair, opened the refrigerator door, peered inside for at least thirty seconds, closed the door, and moved back into the living room, where he stood, totally preoccupied with his sister's death, as another part of his mind tried to remember what he should do next.

Pack, he decided, and started toward the bedroom only to notice the tan leather one-suiter standing near the door that led out into the corridor. You already did that, he told himself, and remembered the suitcase open on the bed, and his robotlike taking of socks, shirts, shorts, and ties from the drawers, the dark-blue funeral suit from the closet, and then his folding them all into the suitcase, and closing it, and lugging it into the living room. Then you made the coffee; then you drank it; and then you watched the old man. He glanced down to make sure he had actually got dressed. He found he was wearing what he thought of as the New Orleans uniform: gray seersucker jacket, white shirt, black knit silk tie, dark-gray lightweight slacks, and black pebble-grain loafers, nicely polished. He could not remember polishing the loafers.

Dill checked his wrist for his watch and patted his pockets for wallet, keys, checkbook, and cigarettes, which he couldn't find, and then remembered he no longer smoked. He glanced once more around the apartment, picked up the airline-scuffed suitcase, and left. On the southwest corner of 21st and N he hailed a cab, agreed with the Pakistani driver that it was cooler than yesterday, but still hot, and asked to be driven first to the bank, and then to 301 First Street, Northeast: the Carroll Arms.

15

At one time the Carroll Arms, hard by the Capitol, had been a hotel that catered to politicians and to those who worked for them and lobbied them and wrote about them and sometimes went to bed with them. Now it had been taken over by Congress, which housed some of its spill-over activities there, including an obscure three-member Senate subcommittee on investigation and oversight. It was this same subcommittee that paid Benjamin Dill $168 a day for his consultative services.

Dill's patron and rabbi, or perhaps abbot, on the three-member subcommittee was its ranking (and only) minority member, the Child Senator from New Mexico, who had been called the Boy Senator from New Mexico until someone wrote an apparently earnest letter to *The Washington Post* charging that Boy Senator was sexist. A syndicated columnist had seized on the issue and got a column out of it by suggesting that Child Senator might be far more fitting in these troubled times. He also had consoled the Senator with the observation that he would all too soon outgrow the appellation. However, the new nickname had stuck and the Senator wasn't at all unhappy about the space and the air time it had earned him.

The Child Senator's name was Joseph Ramirez and he was from Tucumcari, where he had been born thirty-three years ago. His family had money and he had married more. He also had a law degree from Harvard and a B.A. from Yale, and he had never worked a day in his life until he was named assistant county attorney a year out of law school. He made a local name for himself by helping send a county commissioner to jail for accepting a bribe that allegedly amounted to $15,000. And although everyone had known for years that the commissioner was bent as bobwire, they were still surprised and impressed when young Ramirez actually sent the old coot to jail. The kid's a comer, they had agreed, and it was generally conceded that with all that Ramirez money (and don't forget the wife, she's got money too) the kid might go far.

Ramirez went to the State Senate and then leapfrogged into the U.S. Senate in his thirty-second year. He now made no secret of his desire to be the first Latino President of the United Staes, which he figured would be around 1992 or 1996 or maybe even 2000, when "we beaners will make up the majority of the electoral vote anyhow." Not everyone thought the Child Senator was kidding.

To Benjamin Dill the corridors of the Carroll Arms still reeked of old-style tag-team politics, and of its cheap scent and loveless sex and hundred-proof bourbon and cigars that came wrapped in cellophane and were sold for a quarter one and two at a time. Although he considered himself a political agnostic, Dill liked most politicians— and most laborskates and consumer fussbudgets and civil rights practitioners and professional whale watchers and tree huggers and antinuke nuts and almost anyone who would rise from one of the wooden folding chairs at the Tuesday night meeting in the basement of the Unitarian church and earnestly demand to know "what we here tonight can do about this." Dill had long since despaired that there was not much anyone could do about anything, but those who still believed there was interested him and he found them, for the most part, amusing company and witty conversationalists.

Dill walked through the door marked 222 and into the cluttered reception room where Betty Mae Marker ruled as major domo over the subcommittee's limited pre-cincts. She glanced up at Dill, studied him for a moment, and then let sympathy and concern flood across her dark-brown handsome face.

"Somebody died, didn't they?" she said. "Somebody close passed on."

"My sister," Dill said as he put down his suitcase.

"Oh, Lord, Ben, I'm so sorry. Just say what I can do."

"I have to fly home," Dill said. "This afternoon."

Betty Mae Marker already had the phone to her ear. "American okay?" she asked as she started punching the number.

"American's fine," Dill said, knowing if a seat was available, she would get him on the flight and, in fact, would get them to bump someone off if it was full. Betty Mae Marker had worked on Capitol Hill for twenty-five of her forty-three years, almost always for men of great power, and consequently her reputation was impressive, her intelligence network formidable, and her fund of political due bills virtually inexhaustible. Bidding for her services was often spirited, even fierce, and many of her cronies had wondered why she let the Child Senator lure her over to that do-nothing subcommittee stuck way off down there in the Carroll Arms.

"Coattails, sugar," she had replied. "That man's got the longest, fastest-moving set of coattails I've seen up here since Bobby Kennedy." After Betty Mae Marker's assessment got around, the Child Senator's political stock crept up a few points on the invisible Capitol Hill index.

Dill waited while Betty Mae Marker murmured softly into the phone, giggled, scrawled something on a scrap of paper, hung up, and handed the scrap to Dill. "Leaves Dulles at 2:17, first class," she said.

"I can't afford first class," Dill said.

"They're overbooked on coach, so for the same price they're gonna stick you up there in first class with all the free liquor and the youngest stews, which I thought might cheer you up a little." The genuine sympathy again swept across her face. "I'm so sorry, Ben. You all were close, weren't you?—I mean, real close."

Dill smiled sadly and nodded. "Close," he agreed, and then gestured toward one of the two closed doors—the one that led into the office of the subcommittee's minority counsel. "He in?"

"Senator's with him," she said, picking up the phone again. "Lemme break the news and then all you've gotta do is poke your head in, say hello, and be off about your own sad business."

Again, Betty Mae Marker murmured into the phone in that practiced contralto, which was pitched so low that Dill, standing only a yard away, could scarcely make out what she was saying. She hung up, nodded toward the closed door, smiled, and said, "Watch."

The door banged open. A big blond man of around thirty-six or thirty-seven stood there in his shirtsleeves, loosened tie, and a belt that he wore down almost below hip level so his gut would have room to hang out over it. On his face he wore an expression of pure Irish grief.

"Goddamnit, Ben, I don't know what the hell to say, except I'm goddamn sorry." He wiped hard at the bottom half of the plump, curiously handsome face, as if to wipe away the display of grief, although it stayed firmly in place. He then shook his head sorrowfully, nodded toward his office, and said, "Come on in here and we'll drink about it."

The man was Timothy A. Dolan, the subcommittee's minority counsel and a furloughed lieutenant late of one of Boston's frequent political wars. His share of the spoils had been the job of minority counsel. "Two years down in Washington there, that won't spoil the lad none," it was decided up in Boston. "And then we'll see. We'll see." Dill had long been convinced that Boston was to American politics what the Aberdeen Proving Grounds were to armaments.

As Dill followed Dolan into the office, the Child Senator rose and held out a hand. The expression on the young-looking face was one of deep concern. And again Dill thought what he always thought when he saw Ramirez: Smart as a Spaniard.

Senator Joseph Luis Emilio Ramirez (D.-N.M.) looked taller than he really was, probably because of his plumbline posture and the beautifully tailored pin-striped suits he favored. Dark-brown hair swept down in a lock over a high forehead, and he kept brushing it away from glittering black eyes that sometimes seemed a mile deep. He had a perfect nose, light olive skin, and a wide mouth with a touch of overbite. His chin had a deep cleft that made most women and some men want to touch it. He was actor handsome, not quite genius smart, extremely rich, and at thirty-three he looked twenty-three, possibly twenty-four.

The voice went with the rest of him, of course. It was a low baritone with a memorable husk. He could make it do anything. He now made it offer his condolences.

"You have all my sympathy, Ben," the Senator said, taking Dill's right hand in both of his, "even though I can only guess at your sorrow."

"Thank you," Dill said, discovering there was really nothing more to say when condolences were offered. He sat down in the chair next to the one the Senator had been sitting in. Dolan, back behind his desk now, began pouring three drinks from a bottle of Scotch.

"She was a policewoman, wasn't she?" the Senator said as he sat down next to Dill. "Your sister."

"A homicide detective," Dill said. "Second grade. She'd just got her promotion."

"How'd it happen?" Dolan said, leaning over the desk to serve the two drinks.

"They say it was a car bomb."

"*Murdered!*" the Senator asked, more surprised than shocked.

Dill nodded yes, drank his whisky down, and put the glass on Dolan's desk. He noticed the Senator only sipped a small swallow and then put the glass down. Dill knew he wouldn't pick it up again.

"I'm going to be gone a week or ten days," Dill said. "I thought I'd better stop by and let you know."

"Need anything?" the Senator asked. "Money?" It apparently was all he could think of.

Dill smiled and shook his head. Dolan, still standing,

stared down at him thoughtfully, cocked his head to the left, and said, "You say you'll be down there for a week, maybe ten days?"

"About that."

Dolan looked at the Senator. "Maybe we could put Ben on the expense since Jake Spivey's still holed up down there."

The Senator turned to Dill. "You know Spivey, of course."

Dill nodded.

"Hell," Dolan said, "Ben could take Spivey's deposition, save us from flying him back up here, and then we could charge Ben's expenses off on the Brattle thing."

The Senator nodded, almost convinced. He turned to Dill again. "Would you be willing to do that while you're down there, take Spivey's deposition?"

"Yes. Sure."

"You know the Brattle thing? What a question. Of course you do." The Senator looked back up at Dolan. "Then it's settled."

Dill rose. "I'll get a copy of Spivey's file from Betty Mae."

The Senator also rose. "Spivey could help tremendously in resolving this...problem. If he isn't entirely forthcoming, be—well, you know—firm. Very firm."

"You mean threaten him with a subpoena?"

The Senator turned to look at Dolan. "Yes, I think so, don't you?"

"Shit, yes," Dolan said.

Dill smiled slightly at Dolan. "Could we get it out of the committee?"

"Never," Dolan said. "But Spivey doesn't have to know that, does he?"

CHAPTER

IT was a little more than ten years since Dill had been back to his native city, which was also the capital of a state located just far enough south and west to make jailhouse chili a revered cultural treasure. Wheat grew in the state, as did rattlesnakes, sorghum, broomcorn, cotton, soybeans, blackjack oaks, and white-faced cattle. There were also oil, gas, and a little uranium to be found, and the families of those who had found them were often wealthy and sometimes even rich.

As for the city itself, it was said that the parking meter had been invented there back in the thirties along with the supermarket shopping cart. Its international airport was named after an almost forgotten pilot-navigator, William Gatty, who had helped guide Wiley Post around the world in 1931. There were not many Jews in either the city or the state, but plenty of blacks, numerous Mexicans, two tribes of Indians, a world of Baptists, and 1,413 Vietnamese. According to the U.S. census, the city's population was 501,341 in 1970. By 1980 it had risen to 501,872. There were, on the average, 5.6 homicides a week. Most of them took place on Saturday night.

When Dill came out of the Gatty International Airport terminal shortly after 4 P.M., the temperature had dropped to 101 degrees and a hard hot wind was whipping down from Montana and the Dakotas. Dill couldn't remember when the wind hadn't blown almost constantly, either up from Mexico or down from the Great Plains, searing in summer, freezing in winter, and nerve-racking always. It now blew hot and dry and laden with red dust and grit. Sudden gusts of up to thirty-five miles per hour snatched at Dill's breath and tore at his coat as he leaned into them and plodded toward a taxi.

Dill's native city, like most American cities, was laid out on a grid. The streets that ran east and west were numbered. Those that ran north and south were named, many after pioneer real estate speculators, and the rest after states, Civil War generals (both Union and Confederate), a governor or two, and a handful of mayors whose administrations were thought to have been reasonably free of graft.

But as the city grew, imagination had faltered, and the newer north-south streets were named after trees (Pine, Maple, Oak, Birch, and so on). When the trees were at last exhausted—ending with Eucalyptus for some reason—the names of presidents had been brought into play. These expired with Nixon Avenue a far, far 231 blocks west of the city's main street, which, not surprisingly, was called Main Street. Main's principal intersecting thoroughfare was, inevitably, Broadway.

As the taxi neared the city's center, Dill discovered that most of the landmarks of his youth had vanished. Three downtown motion picture theaters were gone: the Criterion, the Empress, and the Royal. Eberhardt's pool hall was gone, too. Located just two doors down and one floor up from the Criterion, it had been a wonderfully

23

sinister place, at least to thirteen-year-old Benjamin Dill when he had first been lured into it one Sunday afternoon by evil Jack Sackett, a fifteen-year-old acquaintance who had gone on to become one of the premier pool hustlers on the West Coast.

The post–World War Two building boom had not reached the city's downtown section until the mid 1970s, some thirty years late. Until then, downtown had remained much as it was when it had been caught flatfooted by the crash of '29 with two thirty-three-story skyscrapers nearly completed and another one halfway up.

The two thirty-three-story skyscrapers had been built across the street from each other, one by a bank and the other by a speculator who was later wiped out by the crash. There was a race to completion—a dumb publicity stunt, critics said—and the bank had won. The day after the ruined speculator's building was completed by a syndicate of oil men who had bought it for a song (some said less), the speculator rode the elevator up to the top of his broken dream and jumped off. The third skyscraper, the one that was only halfway up when the crash came, was never finished and they finally tore it down in the mid-fifties.

By 1970, the city's downtown section still looked like 1940, except there weren't as many people. The big department stores had long since fled to the outlying malls along with their customers. Other firms followed; urban decay set in; the crime rate shot up; and nobody came downtown. The panicked city fathers hired themselves an expensive Houston consulting firm that came up with a redevelopment plan and then pried a huge federal grant out of the Department of Housing and Urban Development in Washington. The redevelopment plan called for the leveling of most of the downtown area and erecting in its place one of those cities of tomorrow. They razed almost everything and then the money ran out, as it usually does, and downtown was left looking rather like downtown Cologne after the war. But the demolition had not really begun until mid-1974, and by then Benjamin Dill was gone.

Dill was surprised to discover he didn't really mind the changes that had taken place—not even the glossy new buildings that were beginning to poke up out of the erased landmarks of his youth and childhood. You should be old enough to distrust change, he told himself. Change marks time's passage and only the young with very little past willingly embrace the new without argument—only the very young and those who stand to profit from it. And since there's absolutely no way you're going to make a buck out of it, maybe you're not so old after all.

The taxi driver, a morose black in his early forties, turned right on Our Jack Street, which separated the two old skyscrapers. Originally, Our Jack Street had been named Warder Street during the second term of Jack T. Warder, the only governor ever to be impeached twice, the first time for graft, which he beat by generously bribing three state senators, and the second time for the bribes themselves. He had resigned in 1927, but not before pardoning himself. The disgraced governor had ended his final press conference with a sly grin and a long remembered, often quoted quip: "What the hell, fellas, I didn't steal half what I could've."

Forever after he was Our Jack, fondly and ruefully remembered by old-timers who still liked to quote his quip, smirk, and shake their heads. They finally changed the street's name to United Nations Plaza, but everybody still called it Our Jack Street, although few now knew why and the rest seldom bothered to ask.

The Hawkins Hotel was located at the corner of Broadway and Our Jack Street in the heart of the downtown section. It was a somber gray eighteen-story sixty-year-old building, as steadfastly Gothic in design as the University of Chicago. For a time, the Hawkins had been virtually the only hotel in town—at least downtown—

the rest having been felled by dynamite and the wrecker's ball. But then a new Hilton had gone up, followed quickly by a Sheraton and, as always, a huge Holiday Inn.

The fare for the seventeen-mile taxi ride from the airport was a dollar a mile. Dill handed the morose driver a twenty and told him to keep the change. The driver said he by God hoped so and sped off. Dill picked up his bag and entered the hotel.

He found it not much changed. Not really. It had retained those soaring vaulted ceilings that gave it the hushed atmosphere of a seldom-visited out-of-the-way cathedral. The lobby was still a place to sit and watch and doze in reddish leather easy chairs and plump couches. There were also low tables with convenient ashtrays and a lot of fat solid lamps that made it easy to read the free newspapers that still hung on racks: the local *Tribune*; the *News-Post*, published in the rival upstate city that prided itself on its eastern airs; *The Wall Street Journal*; *The Christian Science Monitor*; and the pony edition of *The New York Times*, whose contents were transmitted by satellite, printed locally, and delivered by mail the same day, sometimes before noon if you had the right postman.

The Hawkins' big lobby was far from crowded: a half-dozen middle-aged men who looked like crack salesmen; several couples; a young woman who was more than pretty; and an older woman, in her mid-sixties, who for some reason stared at Dill over her *Wall Street Journal*. He thought she had the look of a permanent hotel guest. The temperature in the lobby was a chilly 70 degrees, and Dill felt his sweat-soaked shirt begin to cool and dry as he moved toward the reception desk.

The young male clerk at reception found Dill's reservation and asked how long he might be staying. Dill said a week, possibly longer. The clerk said that was fine, handed Dill a room key, apologized for not having a bellman on duty (he had called in sick), but added that if Dill needed any help with his luggage, they would somehow get somebody to bring it up later. Dill said he didn't need any help, thanked the clerk, picked up his bag, turned and almost collided with the more than pretty young woman he had noticed earlier.

"You're Pick Dill," she said.

Dill shook his head, smiling slightly. "Not since high school."

"In grade school they used to call you Pickle Dill. That was at Horace Mann out on Twenty-Second and Monroe. But all that ended one afternoon in the fourth grade when you beat up on three of your what?—tormentors?"

"My finest hour," Dill said.

"After that they called you Pick instead of Pickle right through high school, but stopped when you went down to the university, although your sister always called you that. Pick." The young woman held out her hand. "I'm Anna Maude Singe—like in scorch—and I'm—was, damnit—a friend of Felicity's. I'm also her attorney and I thought you might like the family counselor on hand when you got here in case there's something you want done."

Dill shook Anna Maude Singe's hand. It felt cool and strong. "I didn't know Felicity had a lawyer."

"Yep. Me."

"Well, I do want something—a drink."

Singe nodded to the left. "The Slush Pit do?"

"Fine."

The Slush Pit's name originally was the Select Bar, but oil men back in the early thirties had started calling it the Slush Pit because of its darkness, and the name had stuck until finally, in 1946, the hotel made it official with a discreet brass plaque. It was a smallish place, extremely dark, very cool, with a U-shaped bar and low heavy tables and matching chairs that were more or less comfortable. There were only two men drinking at the bar and another couple at one of the tables. Dill and Anna Maude Singe took a table near the door. When the waitress came over, Singe ordered a vodka on the rocks and Dill said he would have the same.

"I'm very sorry about Felicity," the Singe woman said almost formally.

Dill nodded. "Thank you."

They said nothing more until the waitress came back with the drinks. Dill noticed that Singe had a little trouble with her R's, so little he really hadn't noticed until her "sorry" came out almost like "sawwy," but less pronounced than that. Then he saw the faint white scar on her upper lip, barely visible, that had been left by the skilled surgeon who had corrected the harelip. Her R's were the only letter that still seemed to give her any trouble. Otherwise her diction was perfect with not much trace of a regional accent. Dill wondered if she had had speech therapy.

The rest of her, in the straight dark skirt and the candy-striped shirt with its white collar and cuffs, seemed well tanned, nicely put together, and even athletic. He tried to decide whether she went in for running, swimming, or tennis. He was fairly sure it wasn't golf.

He also noticed that she had very dark-blue eyes, as dark as blue eyes can get without turning violet, and she squinted them up a little when looking at things far off. Her hair was a taupe color that had streaks of blond running through it. She wore it in what Dill thought was called a pageboy bob, a style that he understood from someone (who? Betty Mae Marker?) was making a comeback, or had made its comeback, and was now on its way out again.

Anna Maude Singe's face was oval in shape and her eyebrows were just a little darker than her hair. Her nose tilted up a bit, which gave her an air of being either shy or slightly stuck-up—or both. Dill thought they often went together. Her mouth was full and reasonably wide and when she smiled he noticed her teeth had had a good dentist's loving care. She had a long slender neck, quite pretty, and Dill wondered if she had ever danced. It was a dancer's neck.

After the drinks came, he waited until she took a sip of hers, and then asked, "Did you know Felicity long?"

"I knew her just a little down at the university, but when she graduated, I went on to law school, and then when I came back up here and opened my practice, she was one of my first clients. I drew up her will. I don't reckon she was more'n twenty-five or six then, but she'd just transferred into homicide and—well, she just thought she'd better have a will. Then about—oh, I'd say sixteen, seventeen months back—she bought her duplex and I helped her with that, but in the meantime we'd become good friends. She also sent me some clients—cops needing divorces mostly—and she talked about you a lot. That's how I knew they called you Pickle in grade school and all."

"She ever talk about her work?" Dill said.

"Sometimes."

"Was she working on anything that might've caused someone to plant a bomb in her car?"

Singe shook her head no. "Not that she ever told me about." She paused, took another drink, and said, "There is something I think you should know."

"What?"

"She worked for a man called Strucker."

"The chief of detectives," Dill said. "He called me this morning."

"Well, he's pretty upset about Felicity. Two hours after she died he called me and the first thing he wanted to know, even before he told me she was gone, was whether I was the executor of her estate, except he didn't say executor, he said executrix."

Dill nodded his appreciation of the fine Liberationist point.

"I told him yes, sir, I am, and then he told me she'd

died and before I could ask how or why or even say oh-my-God-no, he asked me to meet him down at Felicity's bank."

"Safety deposit box?"

She nodded. "Well, I was there when they opened it, me crying and mad at the...the goddamned waste. They brought it all out of the box, one thing at a time. There was her birth certificate, then her will, then some pictures of your parents, and then her passport. She was always talking about going to France, but she never got around to it. That's what she majored in, you know, French."

"I know."

"Well, the last thing they brought out of the box was the insurance policy. She took it out just three weeks ago. It was a term policy naming you as sole beneficiary."

Anna Maude Singe stopped talking and looked away.

"How much?" Dill said.

"Two hundred and fifty thousand," she said and looked quickly back at Dill, as if to catch his reaction. There was none, except in the eyes. Nothing else in his face changed except the large soft gray eyes that suddenly iced over.

"Two hundred and fifty thousand," Dill said finally.

She nodded.

"Let's have another drink," he said. "I'll buy."

CHAPTER

4

AT 5:45 P.M. Benjamin Dill was hanging his dark-blue funeral suit in the closet of room 981 in the Hawkins Hotel when they knocked on the door. After he opened it he automatically classified them as policemen. Both wore civilian clothing—well-cut, obviously expensive clothing—but the carefully bored eyes, the practiced intimidating carriage, and the far too neutral expressions around the mouths betrayed their calling.

Both were tall, well over six feet, and the older one was wide and thick, while the younger one was rake-lean, tan, and just a trifle elegant. The wide one stuck out his hand and said, "I'm Chief Strucker, Mr. Dill. This is Captain Colder."

Dill shook Strucker's heavy freckled hand and then accepted the one offered by Colder. It was slim and exceptionally strong. Colder said, "Gene Colder, homicide." Dill said, "Come in."

They came into the room a little warily, the way

policemen do, sweeping it with their eyes and classifying its contents and occupant, not out of curiosity, but habit. Dill waved them to the medium-sized room's two easy chairs. Strucker lowered himself carefully with a sigh. Colder sat down like a cat. Strucker took a cigar from his pocket, held it up for Dill to see, and said, "Mind?"

"Not at all," Dill said. "Would you like a drink?"

"I think I would, by God," Strucker said. "It's been a hard one."

Dill took a bottle of Old Smuggler from his suitcase, removed the plastic covers from two glasses on the writing desk, fetched another glass from the bathroom, and poured three drinks. "Water?" he asked. Strucker shook his head. Colder said no thanks. Dill handed them their drinks, took his own into the bathroom, ran some water into it, came back out, and sat down on the bed. He waited until Strucker got his cigar going and had swallowed some of the Scotch.

"Who did it?" Dill asked.

"We don't know yet."

"Why did they do it?"

Strucker shook his big head. "We don't know that either." He sighed again—that long, heavy, despairing sigh. "We're here for a couple of reasons. One is to try and answer your questions and the other is to offer you the city's and the department's official sympathy. We're goddamned sorry. All of us."

"Your sister," Colder said and paused. "Well, your sister was one exceptional...person."

"How much did she make a year?" Dill said.

Strucker looked at Captain Colder for the answer. "Twenty-three-five," the Captain said.

"And the annual premium on a two-hundred-and-fifty-thousand-dollar term life-insurance policy for a twenty-eight-year-old woman in good health is how much?"

Strucker frowned. When he did the cap of thick wiry

32

gray hair moved down toward black eyebrows that guarded
the already guarded eyes whose color was more nearly
green than hazel. The eyes were set close to a wandering
nose that had been broken once. Perhaps twice. Well below the nose was the tight, thin-lipped mouth that seemed
to disapprove of almost everything, and below the mouth
was the doorstep chin. It was a worn, lined, highly in-
telligent face that at fifty-three might well have been on
its third owner.

Strucker was still frowning when he said, "You heard
about that, huh?"

"I heard about it."

Colder smiled slightly, not enough to display any teeth,
but just enough to register mild disapproval and a touch
of regret. "Her lady lawyer, right?"

Dill nodded.

Strucker finished his glass of whisky, put it down on
a table, and turned back to Dill. "According to the Ar-
buckle Life Insurance people, the annual premium was
$518 and she paid it in a lump sum, all cash, on the
fourteenth of last month."

"Not a very wise investment for someone with no de-
pendents," Dill said. "No surrender value. She couldn't
ever borrow against it. Of course, if she knew she was
going to die, she might've wanted to leave something to
a loved one—me, in this case. You don't think it was
suicide, though, do you?"

"It wasn't suicide, Mr. Dill," Colder said.

"No, I didn't think it was." Dill rose, walked over to
the window, and looked down nine stories at Broadway
and Our Jack. "Then there's her house."

"The duplex," Captain Colder said.

"Yes. When she wrote me about it seventeen months
or so back she said she was buying herself a little house.
I assumed it was an old bungalow, around sixty or seventy
thousand dollars. You can still buy them for that here,
can't you?"

"Around in there," Colder said, "but they're getting scarce."

"Okay, so how much would she have to put down on a sixty- or seventy-thousand-dollar house? Twenty percent? That would be twelve to fourteen thousand. I had a few bucks to spare, not many, so I called and asked if she could use a couple of thousand to help out with the down payment. She said she didn't need it because it was being creatively financed. She sort of laughed when she said creatively. I didn't press. I just assumed she was putting five or maybe ten down, taking out a first mortgage of around fifty or less, and a balloon payment for the rest. On twenty-three-five a year she could just about've managed it." Dill paused, drank some of his Scotch and water, and said, "But that's not what she did, was it?"

"No, sir," Strucker said. "It wasn't."

"What she did," Dill said, "was to buy a fine old duplex out on Thirty-second and Texas for one hundred and eighty-five thousand. She put thirty-seven thousand cash down and took out a first mortgage of one hundred thousand at fourteen percent, which meant her monthly payments were going to be around thirteen hundred—except she was getting six-fifty a month from the guy she rented the ground floor to, so that meant she'd only have to come up with six-fifty a month, maybe seven hundred. You say she was making nineteen hundred gross a month so that would be what?—fourteen, fifteen hundred take-home?"

"Around in there," Colder said.

"Which left her about six or seven hundred a month to live on. Well, figuring in the tax break it could be done, I guess, with supermarket coupons and Junior League thrift-shop clothes and library books and TV for entertainment. But then there was that balloon payment—the creative financing. Her lawyer says it's due the first of next month, which will be exactly eighteen months after she bought the place. That balloon payment is for forty-eight thousand dollars—plus interest."

Dill turned from the window and looked down at Strucker. "How much did my sister have in her checking account?"

"Three hundred and thirty-two dollars."

"So how do you figure she was going to come up with fifty thousand or so by the first of next month?"

"That's what we need to talk about, Mr. Dill."

"Okay," Dill said, moved back to the bed, sat down, and leaned against the headboard. "Let's talk."

Strucker cleared his throat, puffed on his cigar, waved some smoke away, and began. "Detective Dill had a fine record, an exceptional one. For her age, none better—male or female. Now I gotta be the first to admit we transferred her outta bunco into homicide as sort of our token woman, along with three coloreds and a couple of Mexicans. It was either that or lose some federal grant money. But by God she was good. And we jumped her up to second-grade over a raft of other guys, some of 'em with a hell of a lot more seniority. In two more years, maybe less, she'd've made sergeant easy. So what I'm saying, Mr. Dill, is your sister was one damn good cop, a fine one, and she got killed in the line of duty—at least, that's what we believe—so we're gonna bury her on Saturday just like I told you and then we're gonna find out just what the hell went wrong."

"You mean why she went bad," Dill said.

"We don't know that she did, though, do we?" Captain Colder said. Dill looked at him. Colder's half-smile was back in place—an almost hesitant smile full of diffidence. Or deception, Dill thought, for there was absolutely nothing diffident about Colder other than the smile. It's his disguise, Dill decided. He wears it like a false beard. The smile failed to hide the true skeptic's face with its inquisitive nose, wise forehead, cold blue doubting-Thomas eyes, and the chin that almost said, "Prove it." It was a face that, with a slightly different coloring, might have found happiness in the Inquisition. Dill felt its owner was reasonably content as a homicide captain.

When Chief Strucker cleared his throat again, Dill turned back to him. "We're gonna get to the bottom of this, Mr. Dill," he said. "Like I told you over the phone: it's what we do. It's what we're good at."

Dill nodded, rose, and held out his hand, first for Colder's empty glass, then for Strucker's. Both men hesitated. Then Strucker sighed and said, "I shouldn't, but I will, thanks."

After Dill poured the fresh drinks and served them, Colder said, "What exactly do you do in Washington, Mr. Dill?"

"I work for a Senate subcommittee."

"Doing what?"

Dill smiled. "Getting to the bottom of things."

"Must be interesting."

"Sometimes."

Strucker drank half an inch of his Scotch, sighed his pleasure, and said, "You and Felicity were close."

"Yes. I think so."

"Your parents are dead." It wasn't a question either.

"They were killed in a one-car crash up in Colorado when I was twenty-one and she was eleven."

"What'd your daddy do?" For the first time, Strucker asked as if he didn't already know the answer.

"He was an army fighter pilot during the war," Dill said. "And after that he was a professional student for four years, which was as long as his GI Bill lasted. He studied at the Sorbonne, the University of Mexico, and at the University of Dublin. He never got a degree. When all that finally ended, he became a crop duster, then a Kaiser-Frazer salesman, and once in a while he would be Mr. Peanut—you know, for Planter's Peanuts. Then he turned promoter—junk-car racing, donkey baseball, stuff like that, and finally he bought out an almost bankrupt foreign-language correspondence school. He was still running that when he went up to Colorado to see about investing in a ghost town. That's when the accident happened. It killed them both. I sometimes think my mother must've been relieved."

Strucker nodded sympathetically. "Didn't leave much then."

"Not a dime."

"You must've almost raised Felicity."

"I was in my first year at law school down at the university. I dropped out and got a job with UPI covering the state House of Representatives. Felicity was eleven and I tried to make sure she went to school and did her homework. By the time she was twelve she was doing the shopping and the cooking and a lot of the housework. At eighteen she won a full scholarship to the university and I got an offer to go to Washington. After that, she was pretty much on her own."

"Well, sir," Strucker said, "I'd say you did a real fine job of bringing her up. Real fine."

"We always liked each other," Dill said. "We were— well, good friends, I guess."

"Did you stay in close touch?" Colder asked.

"I usually called her every week or ten days. She almost never called me. She wrote letters instead. Letters from back home, she called them. She thought everyone who moved away should get letters from back home and that's what hers were. Gossip. Base rumors. Mild scandal. Who went broke and who got rich. Who died. Who got divorced and why. It was a kind of diary, I suppose, not about her so much, but about the city. She actually loved this place for some reason."

"I take it you don't," Colder said.

"No."

"You didn't happen to save those letters, did you?" Strucker asked.

"I wish I had."

"Yeah. So do we. She didn't save copies either. We went through her place today. Nothing."

37

"What about cancelled checks?"

"Another zero," Colder said. "Utilities, house payments, phone bills, groceries from Safeway, car payments, a couple of department store charge accounts. The usual."

"No record of that down payment she made on the duplex?"

"The thirty-seven thousand in cash?" Colder said. "All we know is that it was all in hundred-dollar bills, which are getting to be about as common as twenties used to be."

"No trace, huh?" Dill said.

"None."

"Who holds the mortgage?"

"The former owner, who didn't object in the least to all that cash money," Colder said. "She's a sixty-seven-year-old widow who sold the place to Felicity and then moved down to Florida. St. Petersburg. I talked to her today. She's got no complaints. The monthly payments were almost always on time, but she is a little worried now about that balloon payment."

"I don't blame her," Dill said.

Strucker fished around in his pants pockets and came up with a key. He offered it to Dill.

"What's this?" Dill said.

"Her house key. The upstairs is sealed off right now, but our people will be all through before noon tomorrow so there's no reason you can't go in after that and, well, look around—stay there, if you want to."

Dill rose, took the key, and sat back down on the bed. He looked first at Strucker and then at Colder. "What was she working on?"

This time Colder's smile wasn't his diffident one. It was the sardonic kind that lifted the left side of his mouth up and displayed three or four very white teeth. "You mean the one where the town's major coke dealer got whacked out—or the one where they found the oil millionaire down at the bottom of his indoor-outdoor pool?"

"I don't know what I mean," Dill said. "But either one would do."

Colder shook his head almost regretfully. "She was working on a liquor store owner who was shot and killed late one slow Tuesday night for thirty-three dollars. She also had the one where the wife over on Deep Four came home hot and tired from cleaning up after the white folks and found her husband in bed with their fifteen-year-old daughter. She killed 'em both with the breadknife. That one's pretty well wrapped. Then there's that other one Felicity was on where this guy who worked out in Packingtown pulls up for the light at Thirteenth and McKinley? And this other guy, who's been twiddling his thumbs on the bench at the bus stop there, gets up, goes over, sticks his twenty-two target in the window, plinks the guy in the car four times, then turns and sort of ambles away. We gave that one to Felicity, too. She told me the other day she might be getting somewhere on it."

"She had to be messed up in something," Dill said. "Or by something."

Strucker sighed again and heaved himself up out of the chair. "Well, maybe yes and maybe no. But right now we've got to find out who killed her. We find that out, we'll find out the rest. You know, Mr. Dill, homicide is usually the easiest crime there is to solve because the guy will call you up and say, 'Hey, you'd better get over here on account of I just killed my girl friend with this here baseball bat.' And when you get there he's sitting on the edge of the bed, her next to him, with the bat still in his hands probably, and crying like a two-year-old. That's your run-of-the-mill homicide. But then, every once in a while, you'll get a tricky one. Like this one."

Again, Strucker brought up one of his sighs from deep down in his chest. "They're gonna hold the services at

Trinity Baptist at ten A.M. on Saturday. There'll be a limo for you or, if you like, you can ride with me and the Captain here."

"I don't know," Dill said. "I guess I'd rather do it alone."

"Sure."

Dill frowned. "Why Trinity?" he said. "Felicity wasn't a Baptist. In fact, she wasn't much of anything."

"I am," Colder said. "I'm a deacon."

"You?"

The sadness came then to Colder's face, edging aside the chronic skepticism. "Your sister and I," he said, "well, when my divorce comes through a couple of months from now, we were going to get married." He studied Dill's face. "She never told you, did she?"

"No," Dill said. "She never told me."

CHAPTER

5

DURING the past ten years Dill had lived for varying lengths of time in New York, Los Angeles, London, Barcelona, and twice in Washington. He rarely dreamed about any of them, not even Washington, where he had lived the longest. But occasionally he did and his dreams of the far-off, sometimes foreign cities invariably melded themselves into the city of his birth. Wilshire Boulevard and Third Avenue and the Edgware Road and even the Ramblas somehow ran dreamily past the houses he had lived in as a child, the schools he had attended, and the bars he later had frequented.

Many years ago, some said in 1926, an immense milk bottle had been erected in the city atop a one-story building that sat on a small triangular plot of land formed by the juncture of Ord Avenue, 29th Street, and TR Boulevard, which was what the locals called the winding thoroughfare named for the first Roosevelt. It was a gigantic milk bottle, at least thirty feet high, with the risen cream clearly visible in its neck. It had perched for almost sixty years on top of the tiny convenience food store that Dill remembered as having been owned by a dairy. Springmaid Dairy. He assumed 7-Eleven had taken over both bottle and store by now. For some reason the giant milk bottle was always popping into Dill's dreams of foreign climes. Something Freudian there, he thought, something Freudian, funny, and phallic, pleased as always by alliteration's artful aid.

At 7:15 that evening, the evening of the day his sister had died of a bomb, Dill was driving the big rented Ford along TR Boulevard, one of the three thoroughfares that broke up the metropolitan grid as they curved and wound their way across the city from south to north. At one time streetcars had zipped along TR Boulevard's center divider, but they had been abandoned in the late forties. Everyone now acknowledged what a dumb mistake that had been and hinted darkly of the plot by General Motors and the oil companies to scrap the trolleys in favor of buses. It was a conspiracy theory that had endured for nearly forty years.

Dill had rented the big Ford from Budget. It was the biggest Ford they had and he would have rented a Lincoln had one been available. Dill, the VW owner, always rented large Detroit cars with power everything, because he felt it was an opportunity not to be missed—something like renting your own dinosaur.

Just around the long curve of 27th and TR the giant milk bottle finally came into view, but it was no longer white. It was flat black instead. Dill slowed to stare. The little building was vacant except for some empty glass display counters that looked dusty. Over the entrance was a large sign in fading psychedelic colors: Nebuchadnezzar's Head Shop, but it looked as if Neb had long since gone bankrupt. Dill decided the failed shop was yet another nail driven into the coffin of the sixties and the seventies.

Three blocks past the black milk bottle, on the corner of 32nd and TR, stood a large frame three-story Victorian house tarted up in two shades of pastel green paint that already had begun to peel. The house was home to what was alleged to be either the third- or fourth-oldest press club west of the Mississippi. For its first sixty years or so the club had shared a building at a convenient downtown location with the Benevolent and Protective Order of Elks. But the Mayor was mad at the media (with reason) just as the city's redevelopment plan got under way, and the downtown press and Elks Club building had been inked in as the first to fall.

The club had never really offered much other than a bar that frequently stayed open after the legal closing hour, steaks of a remarkable quality from a mysterious source over in Packingtown, and a long-running table-stakes poker game that began promptly each Saturday at noon and ended just as promptly at 5 P.M. on Sunday so everybody could go home and watch the eager victims go through their weekly self-immolation on *60 Minutes.*

Members of the working press actually belonged to the club. At least thirty percent of the membership had something or other to do with the news business. The rest were in advertising, the law, politics, or public relations. These were called associate members and their dues were five times as high as those of the working press. The minority felt that if the voteless majority wanted to hang out with members of the press, they could damn well pay for the privilege. The club's unofficial motto was engraved on a brass plaque that had hung behind the bar for years: I Used to Be a Newspaperman Myself.

Dill had not been in the club since it moved to its new location. He had been almost an habitué of the place when it shared the five-story downtown building with the Elks—the press club up on the top two floors, the benevolent and protective order down below. In fact, when

43

he worked nightside for UPI, Dill had often closed the place up.

He parked the Ford as near to the Victorian house as possible—a block away—and tried to remember whether he had ever paid his final bar tab. If not, he was sure there would be someone to remind him. The Greek, if no one else.

There was still an hour of daylight left when Dill walked up the six steps to the screened wraparound porch. He crossed the porch to the locked door and rang the buzzer. A tinny voice, as irascible as ever, asked its usual one-word question: "What?"

"Ben Dill."

"Jesus," the voice said. A moment later the buzzer sounded, unlocking the door. A small foyer led into a room that, except for the kitchen in the rear, seemed to occupy the entire first floor of the large old house. Tables and banquettes were to the right. Near the foyer was a lounge area that focused on a huge bay window where, Dill thought, you could sit just like you could sit in private clubs all over the world and, as someone once said, watch it rain on the damn people. He felt it might even be why private clubs were invented.

Dill headed for the L-shaped bar that was to the left of the lounge area. He noticed it was the same mahogany bar they had used in the downtown location. They had even brought along the old brass rods that ran up above the bar. From them hung the salvaged leather trolley straps, providing convenient support for those who had nipped too long at the gin.

The man who stood behind the bar, leaning on it with both hands, had stood behind it for thirty years as both club manager and head bartender. His name was Christos Levides, or Christ, the Greek! or usually just the Greek. He was in his mid-fifties and looked not much different than he had at twenty-five. The black eyes were still as full of guile, the elegant mustache as trim, and the expression of faint disdain as crafty and Ulysses-like as ever. There were some new lines, of course, running in deep trenches down from the remarkable nose and in horizontal creases across the forehead. It was a carefully bored face that obviously had heard most of life's lies and all of its excuses.

Levides didn't move or speak until Dill settled himself on a stool and looked around to see if there was anyone else he still knew. There wasn't. Two men were at the bar's far end, but they looked like lawyers. A dozen or so diners were seated at tables.

"Well," Levides said finally. "You're back."

"I'm back," Dill agreed.

Levides nodded thoughtfully, as if Dill looked as awful as he had expected him to look. "I heard about your sister." There was a long pause as Levides seemed to consider carefully what he should say next. "I'm sorry."

"Thanks."

"Hell of a thing."

"Yes."

"I remember when you used to bring her down to the old place, when she wasn't more than yea-tall." He held up a hand at shoulder height to show how tall Dill's dead sister had been. "Ten, maybe eleven then?"

"About that," Dill said. "Not much older anyway."

Levides nodded somberly and, his brief mourning over, said, "What'll you have?"

"A beer. Beck's, if you've got it."

Levides nodded again, spun, whipped a bottle out of the case, snapped its top off, spun back around, and set it down on the bar along with a frosted glass. "Two bucks," he said, "and you still owe thirty-eight eighty-two on your tab, which you sort of forgot about paying when you took off for Washington—when was it? Ten years back?"

"Around in there," Dill said, took a fifty-dollar bill from his wallet, slid it across the bar, and told Levides to take it all out of that.

Levides turned to the cash register, rang up the sale, and turned back with Dill's change. "How've you been?" Dill said.

"Same old shit."

Dill glanced around. "Looks pretty nice."

"Yeah, if you like dry rot."

"The steaks still passable?"

Levides shrugged. "I ate one day before yesterday and I ain't dead yet." He looked away. "Who did it?"

"They don't know."

"Who they got on it?"

"I talked to the chief of detectives," Dill said. "Strucker."

"Him I know."

"And?"

The Greek shrugged. "Smart. Not college smart exactly, but smart-cop smart. Been on the force twenty-five years at least. Maybe more. Went to night law school. Took Dale Carnegie public speaking lessons. Married a whole lot of money the second time around. Lives good, dresses nice. And not a blot on him."

"Captain Colder," Dill said. "Gene Colder."

"Him."

"Him."

"Well, him I don't know hardly at all. They brought him in a couple of years ago from back east—Kansas City or Omaha, I think, someplace like that. They're grooming him, I hear."

"For Strucker's job?"

"If Strucker goes, and there's talk about him running for something, Colder might take it, but he won't even hardly get the seat warm. Colder's going all the way up when old man Rinkler finally retires."

"Rinkler's still chief of police?" There was more than a touch of incredulity in Dill's tone.

"Still."

"Hell, it's been thirty years. At least thirty."

46

"Almost," Levides said. "They tapped him for it when he was thirty-five and he's at least sixty-four now. Anyway, he'll go when he's sixty-five. It's the rule."

Drill drank some of his beer and asked, "Who's the *Trib* got on the police run now?"

"Who else?" Levides said. "Freddie Laffter."

"Jesus, doesn't anything change around here?"

The Greek seemed to give it some thought and then shrugged. "Not a hell of a lot."

"Laffter still come in every night?"

"Eight on the dot—right after the bulldog."

"He'd know about Colder, wouldn't he?"

"If anybody does." The Greek looked away before asking his next question. Dill remembered it as an affectation designed to make Levides' questions seem offhand, even indifferent. "How come you're so interested in Colder?" he asked in a bored voice.

"Because he claims he was going to marry my sister."

The Greek looked back at Dill and smiled. "Yeah," he said, "that's a pretty good reason. You want another beer?"

"Why not?" Dill said.

Dill was still husbanding his second beer when the old man came in, seventy now at least, Dill thought, and perhaps even more. He was moving with a deceptively quick shambling gait that sped him toward the rear of the dining room. His eyes were fixed straight ahead behind steel-rimmed bifocals. On his head was a hat, a soiled Panama with a rippling brim, perhaps one of the four real Panamas in the city, or even the state, and he wore it with the brim turned down all the way around.

The old man's striped summer suit appeared to be made out of bed ticking. He wore a white pongee shirt that was yellowing with age and whose collar was at least two sizes too large. His tie was old and gray and looked greasy. A reporter's notebook peeped out of the suitcoat's left-hand pocket. The bulldog edition of the *Tribune* was stuck down into the right-hand one. On the old man's feet were a pair of new Gucci loafers. Dill assumed they were counterfeit.

"Hey, Chuckles," the Greek called.

Fred Y. Laffter stopped his headlong flight toward the rear, turned, and looked at Levides with contempt. "What the fuck do you want?"

"Somebody here'd like to talk to you."

"Who?"

The Greek nodded at Dill. "Him."

Laffter turned his head. It was an egg-shaped head, the large end fortunately up, and pale pink in color, except for the nose, which was a button of near crimson. The brows were white and almost invisible above eyes that had faded from blue into something almost colorless. The mouth was a thin mean line and surprisingly prim. A fine web of old age had etched itself across the face, but the pale, pale eyes were still alert, curious, and they now examined Dill with interest.

"Dill," Laffter said. "Ben Dill."

"Right."

"Used to be with UP."

"UPI."

"What the fuck, I still call it UP. What'd you wanta talk about, your sister?"

"If you've got a few minutes."

"I haven't eaten yet."

"Neither have I. Maybe we could have dinner together. My treat."

"I was gonna have a steak."

"Chuckles," the Greek said. "You haven't bought a steak here in five years."

Laffter ignored Levides. "I was gonna have a steak," he said again. "A big thick steak with fresh asparagus and maybe a shrimp cocktail to start."

"Fine," Dill said. "I'll have the same."

Laffter turned to Levides. "Hear that, you ignorant pederast? Tell Harry the Waiter that the gentleman and I're gonna have two big steaks, porterhouse, I think. Medium rare. Shrimp cocktails to start. Asparagus. A pair of vodka martinis first though to spark the appetite. Doubles, I'd say. And also a bottle of wine—something sound for a change. A Burgundy perhaps. Cognac afterward, of course, and maybe even a cigar, although I'll decide about that later."

"Eat all that shit and you're gonna wind up right back in intensive care," Levides said.

Laffter had already turned to Dill. "He missed his true calling, you know," the old man said with a small backward nod toward the Greek. "He should've been a pimp in Piraeus, selling the behinds of little Greek boys to sailors off of Turkish ships."

In a bored voice, Levides said something rank about the old man's mother and moved down the bar to see if the two lawyers wanted a refill.

CHAPTER

THEY sat at a corner table in the dining area. After the double vodka martinis came, Laffter took the folded edition of the *Tribune* from his pocket and handed it to Dill. "Page three," he said.

Dill turned to page three and the 36-point flush-left one-column headline at the top on the right that read:

CAR BOMB
KILLS CITY
DETECTIVE

Dill read the bylined story quickly and found it contained little he didn't already know. He refolded the paper and handed it back to Laffter. "She was twenty-eight, not twenty-seven," Dill said.

"They told me twenty-seven."

"Today's her birthday. She's twenty-eight today."

"Oh."

"Tell me about Captain Colder."

"Your almost brother-in-law."

"You know about that then."

The old man shrugged. "They weren't exactly trying to hide it."

"Had they set a wedding date?"

Laffter looked at Dill with interest, but it died quickly. "He wasn't divorced yet and so they were seeing each other socially, as they used to put it back in the dear dead days beyond recall. But I don't think they'd set up light housekeeping. At least not so anybody'd notice." The interest flared again in the old man's pale eyes, but again died away. "She didn't tell you about Colder, did she."

"No."

"Well, she must've had her reasons."

"Such as?"

"How the hell would I know? Ask Colder."

"He says he thought she'd told me." It wasn't quite what Colder had said, but Dill was interested in the old man's reaction.

"Called her a liar, did he?"

"In a way."

"That's wasn't very nice, but who pays for nice nowadays?"

Laffter finished his martini in a gulp and looked around for Harry the Waiter. Dill picked up his own untouched martini and set it down in front of the old man. "Here," he said. "I haven't touched it."

"Jesus, if there's one thing I can't stand, it's a controlled drinker."

Laffter raised his new drink in a mock toast. "To our most enduring myth—the bibulous newspaperman." He swallowed some of the drink, put it back down, took out a package of unfiltered Pall Malls, offered them to Dill, who refused, and lit one with a new Zippo.

"Guess how long I've been in this business," the old man said.

"A hundred years?"

"Fifty come September the third. Half a century, by God. I was twenty-two and outa work and outa college for more'n a year when old man Hartshorne hired me for seventeen-fifty a week—and that was a forty-eight-hour week back then. One day off. I got Tuesday. Who the fuck wants Tuesday off? He's still there, you know."

"Who?"

"Hartshorne."

Dill shook his head. "Couldn't be."

The old man grinned. Dill saw that he had some very shiny new teeth. "Walks to work every morning, ninety-seven years old. Swings along Grant to Fifth and then cuts south on Our Jack, the Cadillac creeping along just behind with old Pete, that colored chauffeur of his at the wheel who's gotta be at least eighty himself. Ninety-seven and Hartshorne's at work every morning by eight. That's why I'm still there. He thinks of me as Young Laffter."

"What about Jimmy Junior?"

"Hell of a thing, isn't it, to be sixty-seven years old and have everybody still calling you Jimmy Junior? He's editor and president and the old man's still chairman and publisher and owns sixty-two percent of the stock so you can guess who calls the shots."

Harry the Waiter came over and served the two shrimp cocktails. Harry the Waiter, whose real name was Harold Pond, was black, forty, and fat, and had started at the Press Club as a skinny dishwasher when he was sixteen. He had turned himself into what may well have been the city's finest waiter. The Cherry Hills Golf & Country Club had tried to hire him at least a dozen times, but Harry the Waiter always refused and stayed on at the Press Club, where he pretended to despise news people. Or pretended to pretend. He reviled their product, mocked their intelligence, and scoffed at their pretensions. The members regarded him as a treasure and repeated his insults with pride.

After he set the shrimp cocktail down in front of Laffter, Harry the Waiter began one of his harangues: "You eat that shrimp, old man, and you're gonna be up around two or three reaching for the Gelusil like always. Can't for the life of me see how anyone old as you and with the gumption God gave a goose'd eat and drink stuff the doctor says is gonna kill 'im. One of these days I'm gonna serve you your chili-mac like you always eat, instead of that nice porterhouse you went and promoted yourself this evening, and you're gonna dip your spoon in and shovel it into that big ugly mouth of yours and swallow it, and then your eyes're gonna bulge out like this, and you're gonna get all red in the face, even redder'n the drink's done made it, and then you're gonna keel over dead and guess who's gonna have to mop it all up? Me. That's who. The Greek said you wanted a French Burgundy. You don't know nothing about French wine. I'm gonna give you a nice old Napa pinot noir that ought be just about right." Harry the Waiter turned to Dill. "How you, Ben? Sorry to hear about your sister. Terrible thing. I was gonna say something about it before, but I didn't get the chance."

"Thanks, Harry," Dill said.

"Go away," Laffter said. "Go back in the kitchen and spit in the soup or whatever you do."

"Spit in the soup?" Harry the Waiter said. "Goodgawd-almighty, I never thought of that! Lemme go tell the other niggers."

After he left, Laffter asked, "How come he treats you like a white man?"

"Harry and I go back a long way."

"How long?"

"Fifteen, sixteen years. We were both broke back then and we'd lend each other money. Sometimes he'd give me a ride home."

"Why?"

"Why'd he give me a ride home?"

Laffter nodded, interested.

"Because I didn't have a car," Dill said.

"Oh." Laffter speared one of the large Gulf shrimp, dipped it into the Tabasco-ketchup-and-horseradish sauce, bit off half, and chewed it thoroughly. "Your sister moved up pretty quick in the PD," he said around what was left of the shrimp.

"They tell me she was good."

Laffter shrugged. "She was all right. How come she ever became a cop anyhow?"

"It was either that or teach French to junior high school kids who didn't much want to learn French. Also the pension. She liked the idea of retiring at forty-two or three."

"She like homicide?"

"She said it was better than bunco."

The old man licked some sauce from his fingers. "I did a little feature on her about a year ago—maybe a bit more—but they never ran it."

"Why?"

"I don't know. It was a pretty good piece. Homicide's new female whiz kid and all that good shit. I somehow managed to avoid calling her the new Sherlock Holmes, but it was a struggle. She'd just made a couple of collars, one of them kind of spectacular, and I thought she was worth a feature, but they killed it."

"Who?"

"I don't ask anymore. I don't ask because I don't care. I think I quit caring back around 1945. After they shipped me back to New York from *Stars and Stripes*."

After several moments, Dill sighed and finally asked, "What happened in New York?"

Laffter paused in his eating to stare at something over Dill's left shoulder. "You ever hear of *PM?*"

"It was a New York tabloid that leaned a little left until it fell over."

Laffter nodded and shifted his gaze back to his shrimp. He picked one up with his fingers and bit it in two. "Well, in France I'd run into Ralph Ingersoll, who'd practically founded the thing, *PM*, and he'd seen some of my *Stars and Stripes* stuff, so he made arrangements for me to see this guy on *PM* when I got to New York. It was my first time there." He paused. "Last time, too."

The old man waited for Dill to say something. After almost a minute went by, Dill said, "And?"

"Oh, the guy offered me a job at about three times what I'd been making down here. Even talked about a column, but that was just 'maybe' talk—about the column, I mean. Well, I went back to my hotel and thought about it. It was my chance at the big time. That's what we called it back then. The big time. I didn't think *PM* would ever go anywhere, but I could've bounced over to the *News* or even the *Times*. I wrote pretty good back then. Well, I never called the guy back. Instead, I tried to get on the next plane out, but it was full up, so I took the train. Chair car all the way back down here."

The old man paused and waited for Dill to say something. He wants me to ask him why, Dill thought. "Chuckles," he said.

"What?"

"I didn't really believe that story the first time I heard it fifteen years ago when I was twenty-three and you'd run out of anybody else to tell except me. But back then you were stirring in a blond New York actress who begged you to stay and when you wouldn't, she either killed herself or went to Hollywood. I don't remember which."

The old man stared at Dill coldly. "I never told that story to anyone else in my life."

"Never told who what?" Harry the Waiter said, materializing at the table with two large pewter steak platters on his left arm. He skillfully whisked away the shrimp cocktail bowls, placed them on another table, and served the two large steaks with a small flourish. Laffter stared at his hungrily.

"*PM*, Ingersoll, and last chance in New York," Dill said and picked up his fork and knife.

"Shoot, I must've heard that one about two dozen times myself. He put the blond actress in?"

"He left her out."

"He's been doing that lately, but two, maybe three weeks ago, he cornered that new little old AP gal and had her in tears and buying him drinks half the night with his blond-actress tale and all."

Laffter glared at Harry the Waiter. "You forgot the wine."

"I don't forget nothing," Harry the Waiter said, reached behind his back, produced a bottle as if by magic, drew the cork, and poured a small measure into Dill's glass. Dill tasted it and smiled.

"Good, huh?" Harry the Waiter said, filling the two glasses.

"Very."

Harry the Waiter surveyed the table carefully, nodded his satisfaction, and left. Laffter cut into his steak, forked a piece into his mouth, and said, "I've paid for a lot of suppers and drinks with that story." He paused to chew and then swallow. "I never did go back to New York though. Maybe I should've. What d'you think?"

Dill was surprised at the request for advice. "I don't know," he said. "Maybe you should've."

Laffter nodded and went back to work on his steak, his salad, his asparagus, and his baked potato, which he slathered with six pats of butter. He didn't speak again until he had finished. Holding up the almost empty wine bottle, he looked questioningly at Dill, who shook his head. Laffter poured the last of the wine into his own glass and drank it. He belched softly, lit a cigarette, and settled into a new position that had him leaning forward slightly, both forearms on the table. It was a posture that invited confidences, even secrets. Dill wondered how many thousand times the old man had sat just like that.

"Okay," Laffter said, "what d'you really want to know?"

Dill stared at him thoughtfully for a moment and then went back to carving the final morsel of tenderloin from the steakbone. Dill always ate the tenderloin last. For some reason, he distrusted those who didn't. His ex-wife, he remembered, had eaten it first. "My sister," he said. "Who do you think killed her?"

"The generic who, you mean?"

"Right."

"Somebody with money."

"Why?"

Laffter blew some Pall Mall smoke into the air. "That bomb. It was done by a pro. The C4 plastic. The mercury fulminator. Very classy. That probably means out-of-state talent and that costs money. Ergo, somebody rich."

"Okay," Dill said. "That's who. What about why?"

"A guess?"

"Sure."

"She'd found out something that could stop whoever hired the bomber from being rich anymore."

"What?"

"You mean, what'd she find out?"

Dill nodded.

"Well, she was in homicide, so maybe she found out who killed John—our generic John, of course." He paused. "I heard about the duplex and the money and all. I didn't use it. Not yet anyway. But I might have to."

"You think she was on the take?" Dill said, carving the very last sliver of tenderloin from the bone.

"I don't know," Laffter said.

"Neither do I—and she's my sister." Dill put the last

small piece of steak into his mouth, chewed, swallowed, and then arranged his knife and fork on his plate.

"You always eat the tenderloin last?" Laffter asked.

"Always."

"Huh," the old man said. "I always eat mine first."

CHAPTER

7

THE computerized time and weather sign on the First National Bank read 11:12 P.M. and 86 degrees as Dill walked into the lobby of the Hawkins Hotel after parking his rented Ford in the basement garage. The elderly woman who looked to Dill like a permanent guest was still seated in the lobby reading a book. Dill tried to catch its title as he walked past. It was something he always did. She caught him at it, lowered the book quickly, and glared. Dill smiled at her. The title on the book's spine had been *The Oxford Book of English Verse*.

A new male clerk was behind the reception counter. Dill paused long enough to see if there was anything in his box. There wasn't, so he smiled reassuringly at the clerk and stepped over to the bank of four elevators. He touched the button, looked up at the floor indicator, and saw that the nearest descending elevator was on five. Something tapped him on the shoulder and a man's voice said, "Mr. Dill?"

The voice was a deep, deep bass with a softened Southern R in the mister. When Dill turned he saw how nicely the voice fitted the owner, who looked as though he needed the bass to go with his size, which was as tall and wide as a garage door. He was also extremely ugly. Christ, Dill thought, he's even uglier than I am. But then the big man smiled and he was no longer ugly. That's not true either, Dill decided. He's still ugly, but that smile is so glorious it blinds you.

"I bet you smile a lot," Dill said.

The big man nodded, still smiling. "All the time. If I don't, grown men pale and little children flee." He stopped smiling and went back to being ugly and either mean or extremely hard.

"Clay Corcoran," the big man said, and watched Dill's face hopefully.

Dill shook his head. "No bell rings."

"I was hoping it would. Then I wouldn't have to explain how ridiculous I am."

"Ridiculous?"

"Jilted lovers are always ridiculous. That's me. Clay Corcoran, the jilted lover. Maybe even the cuckold, which is even more ridiculous, except I'm not sure you can be a cuckold if you're not married."

"We could look it up," Dill said.

"By now you must've figured out I'm talking about your sister."

Dill nodded.

"I'm more than sorry about Felicity," Corcoran said. "I'm fucking well shattered." And as if to prove it, a tear rolled down the tanned cheek from the corner of the left eye. Both eyes were green, although the left one had some yellow flecks in it. They were small eyes, set too far back in the skull and too far away from a nose that seemed to have been clumsily remodeled. The head itself was a squared-off chunk topped by a thinning hank of tow-blond hair that was almost white. It was hair so fine that it wafted about at the slightest movement of the big body. Even the bass voice made it float a little. Below the hair was a scant inch or so of forehead that had wrinkled itself into a permanent scowl. And far below that was the chin resembling a broken plow. The total effect could bother the brave and frighten the timid, until that blinding white smile came and bathed everything in its warm, reassuring glow.

Corcoran reached up for the single tear and absently wiped his finger off on the white short-sleeved sailcloth shirt that covered his massive shoulders and chest. "Well, I just thought I'd come by and pay my respects," he said.

"Thank you," Dill said.

The big man hesitated. "I reckon I'd better let you go get some sleep."

"Would you like to talk about her?"

When the smile came back again, Dill thought he had discovered the right word for it: angelic. The huge head nodded eagerly and twisted around on the eighteen-inch neck as the eyes searched for something. "Slush Pit's still open," Corcoran said.

"Fine."

They started for the bar and Corcoran said, "This is real decent of you, Mr. Dill."

"How old are you?" Dill asked.

"Thirty."

"Thirty and above calls me Ben."

"Felicity was what—ten years younger'n you? Twenty-seven?"

"Twenty-eight," Dill said. "Today was her birthday."

"Aw Christ," Corcoran said and stopped smiling.

They chose the same table Dill had sat at earlier that day with the lawyer, Anna Maude Singe. He ordered a cognac from the cocktail waitress. Corcoran asked for a bourbon and water. When she asked him what brand of bourbon, he said he didn't care. Dill liked the big man's indifference.

After the drinks came and Dill had his first sip, he said, "Where'd you meet Felicity?"

"Down at the university. I was a senior and she was a junior and I was having a little trouble with my French One-O-Two because I'd redshirted the year before and—"

"Redshirted?"

"A sports fan you're not."

"No."

"I dropped out of school for a year because my knee went snap and by dropping out I maintained my eligibility."

"To do what?"

"Play football."

"When the knee got better. I see."

"Well, there was a one-year gap between my French One-O-One and the One-O-Two that I needed to graduate, so I asked the head of the French department to suggest a tutor. He suggested Felicity. We went out a few times, but there was no big romance or anything, and after I graduated the Raiders drafted me and I went out there."

"There being Oakland, right?"

"Oakland then, L.A. now."

"They moved?"

Corcoran scowled. Despite himself, Dill wanted to draw back. Corcoran noticed and smiled. "Don't mind me, that's just my professional puzzled-rage scowl. Is there something about football you don't like?"

"Nothing. It's just that I don't follow team sports closely, probably because I never played any."

"Never?" Corcoran seemed almost shocked. "Not even baseball—Little League?"

"Not even that. It takes some conniving, but you can actually go through life without playing on a team."

"You're sort of bullshitting me, aren't you?"

"A little."

Corcoran smiled. "That's okay. Not many people do. I kind of like it."

"You were playing for Oakland."

"Right. And this time the knee went snap-crackle-pop instead of just snap and that was the end of my career as a promising linebacker. Well, I had my degree in philosophy, a brand new Pontiac GTO, two suits, and no trade—unless I wanted to be a philosopher, which I'm really not too good at. So I came back home and signed on with the cops and there Felicity was. And then it really got started with us and it was very, very good. In fact, it was goddamn near perfect."

"What happened?"

Corcoran snorted. "Captain call-me-Gene Colder is what happened. Felicity and I'd been, well, you know, going together—"

"Seeing each other socially," Dill said, remembering the old police reporter's phrase.

"That's one way of putting it, but it was a hell of a lot more than that. We'd even talked about getting married—or something close to it anyway." He looked at Dill curiously. "She never said anything at all about me?"

"No. Not once. For all I know, she lived like a nun. I never asked because it was none of my business. She never asked about my lady friends for the same reason, I suppose. Otherwise we were fairly close. At least, I thought we were."

"She talked about you a lot," Corcoran said.

Dill nodded. "So what happened between you two?"

"That's just it. Nothing happened. One day everything was great and the next day it was over. She said she needed to talk to me, but we had conflicting shifts that week and she didn't get off till eleven. So we met at this place we used to go to a lot, this bar, and she said I'm sorry, but I've met someone else and I won't be able to see you anymore. Well, I just sat there for a minute or two trying to get used to the shock and the pain—and don't let 'em kid you, there's real pain—and finally I knew I had to say something so I asked her who. She said that wasn't important and I said it was important to me. She just shook her head as if she was really sorry about everything. Well, I just sat there like a fool and couldn't think of anything to say. She got up, leaned down, and kissed me on the forehead—on the forehead, by God!—and said, Thank you, Clay. Then she left and that was the end of it."

"When did all this happen?" Dill asked.

"At six minutes until midnight on February twelfth a year and a half ago. Eighteen months. It was a Friday."

"She was with homicide by then."

"Been there for two or three months. Transferred in from bunco."

"Did you give up?"

Corcoran shook his head. "I got drunk and tried to see her once and made a mess of it. Then I called her three times. The first time she said, 'I'm sorry, Clay, I can't talk to you,' and hung up. The second time I called her I said, 'Hi, it's me,' and she said, 'Don't call me anymore,' and hung up. The third time I called and said it was me she didn't say anything. She just hung up. I stopped calling."

"I don't blame you. Were you in bunco with her?"

"We never worked together or anything like that. She did a lot of undercover stuff when she was in bunco. I was in public affairs and about all I did was go around and talk to school kids—real little kids—about what wonderful folks policemen are. I'd worked up this funny kind of talk with slides. Public affairs figured if the kids could get used to me, they'd never have any hangups about normal-looking cops. I kind of liked it. But then I started seeing Felicity around with Captain Colder and I couldn't stand that, so I quit."

"What do you do now?"

"I'm a frightener." Corcoran scowled and once again Dill wanted to shrink away. The big man smiled and chuckled a little. "What I am now is almost as ridiculous as being a cuckold. I'm a private detective and you're gonna ask me how the hell can anybody my size stay private."

"I was really going to go upstairs and think about it."

"Yeah, well, I do a lot of bodyguard work, for oil companies mostly, who're in places where the politicians are a little weird—Angola, Indonesia, places like that."

"You go there?"

"No, they use me when those folks come here, and my job is to make sure none of the native nuts get close. They keep me on a retainer—the oil companies—and that pays the overhead, which isn't all that high except for the phone. As a frightener, I do a lot of work on the phone."

"Who do you frighten?"

"Deadbeats. Say some guy loses his job out in Packingtown and falls behind on his car payments. Well, he's a deadbeat, right? Now some folks would say he's a victim of an outmoded economic system that scraps people the way it scraps old cars, but you and I know better, don't we? You and I know that anybody in this grand and glorious country of ours can go out and find himself a job if he'll just put on a clean white shirt and go look. I mean a guy who's fifty-four years old and has been wrapping bacon for seventeen years for Wilson's out in Packingtown and gets laid off, well, hell, he can go wrap bacon somewhere else. I'd hire him if I needed some bacon wrapped, wouldn't you? Sure you would.

"So this guy, this skilled ex-bacon wrapper, falls behind on his car payments and the finance company turns him over to me. And if his phone hasn't been cut off, I call him up and say in my real deep scary voice, 'My name's Corcoran, pal, and you owe us money and if you don't pay up, something's gonna have to be done about it—

understand?" I'm really a pretty good frightener. Well, sometimes the guys pays up—I don't know how, but that's not my worry. If he doesn't, I get hold of this kid who used to steal cars for a living and we go out and repo the car so the guy can take the bus when he goes out looking for a job wrapping bacon." Corcoran paused. "Like I said, I'm a little ridiculous." There was another, longer pause. "I think I'll have another drink."

Corcoran had only to glance over his shoulder to bring the waitress hurrying over. After she left with the order, he said, "There're some days I just want to go out and break something, know what I mean?"

Dill nodded. "I think so." He took a sip of his cognac. "The services are going to be at ten on Saturday in Trinity Baptist."

"Why there? Felicity was a real let's-not-fuck-around atheist."

"The last I heard," Dill said, "she was sort of a well-intentioned agnostic."

"That was before homicide. After about two or three Saturday nights down on South Broadway she had this sudden leap of faith and went all the way. We were still together then. I remember she called me up one Sunday morning about six. I said hello and she said, 'There is no God,' and hung up. I found out later some guy had just wiped out his family with a Boy Scout hatchet. There were six of them, not counting his wife. Six kids, I mean. The oldest was eight. Felicity was first through the door."

"They're sending a limousine for me," Dill said. "You like to ride along?"

The big man thought about it for at least fifteen seconds and then slowly shook his head no. "I don't intend any disrespect—hell, that's not the word. Indifference is the word. I'm not indifferent, but I don't want to go to Felicity's funeral. Funerals are awfully final and I don't want to say goodbye yet. But thank you for asking me."

"Is there anyone else I should ask—anyone close?"

Corcoran thought about it. "Well, you might ask Smokey."

"Who's Smokey?"

"Anna Maude Singe—singe, burn, scorch—Smokey. Felicity's lawyer. Mine too. They were close. It was Smokey who told me you were staying here."

"You talked to her today?"

Corcoran nodded.

"Did she tell you about the two-hundred-and-fifty-thousand-dollar life-insurance policy Felicity took out naming me as sole beneficiary?"

"No. When?"

"When did she take it out?" Dill said. "Three weeks ago."

"Smokey didn't tell me about it." The big man's expression grew thoughtful as he stared down at his drink. When he looked up Dill saw that the slightly mismatched green eyes had changed. Before they had been too small, too recessed, and too far apart, but clever. There was still too much wrong with them, but now they were more than clever. They had become smart, perhaps even brilliant. He tries to hide it behind all that size and ugliness, Dill thought, but occasionally it just seeps out. "There was no reason Smokey should've, was there?" Corcoran said. "Told me, I mean."

"I guess not."

"But it means Felicity knew, doesn't it?"

"Knew?"

"That somebody was going to kill her."

"Suspected."

"Right. Suspected. If she'd known for sure, she would've done something."

"What?"

Corcoran smiled, but it was a small smile that only made him look sad. "She was a cop. There were a lot of things she could've done and she knew 'em all."

"Unless she was doing something a cop shouldn't do."

This time there was no pretense to the scowl. Corcoran leaned across the table, the green eyes angry now, the expression quite terrible. Dill sat very still, determined not to flinch. "You're her brother," Corcoran said, almost whispering the words, which somehow made them even more awful. "If you weren't her brother and said that, I'd have to twist your fuckin' head off. Maybe you'd better explain."

"Let me tell you a story," Dill said. "It's about a brick duplex, a down payment made in cash, and a fifty-thousand-dollar balloon payment that's due on the first."

Corcoran, his expression still suspicious, leaned back in his chair. "All right," he said. "Tell me."

It took Dill ten minutes to tell what he knew. When he was done, Corcoran remained silent. Finally, he sighed and said, "That doesn't sound too good, does it?"

"No."

"Maybe I'd better look into it. You know, I really am a pretty fair snoop. It's like research. I always liked research. Any objections if I look into it?"

"I don't really care what's she done," Dill said. "I just want to find out who killed her."

"And why."

"Right," Dill said. "And why."

8

ON Friday, August 5, Dill awoke a little after seven, rose, and went to the window. Nine floors below he could just make out the First National's time and weather sign. The time was 7:06 A.M. The temperature was 89 degrees. As he watched, the temperature clicked over to 90 degrees. Dill winced, turned from the window, and went to the phone. He dialed room service and ordered breakfast, a meal he rarely ate. He ordered two poached eggs on whole-wheat toast, bacon, and coffee.

"What kind of juice?" the woman's voice asked.

"No juice."

"It comes with the breakfast."

"I don't want any, thanks."

"Hashbrowns or grits?"

"Neither."

"They're free, too."

"I'll pass."

"Well," the woman said reluctantly, "okay."

While waiting for his breakfast, Dill showered and shaved. Because he had no choice, other than the blue funeral suit, he again put on the gray seersucker jacket and the dark-gray lightweight trousers. He noticed the overnight air-conditioned humidity had ironed most of the wrinkles out of the trousers. When dressed, Dill went to the door, opened it, and picked up the free copy of the local *Tribune*, fattened nicely by ads for the weekend sales. He counted four sections and 106 pages.

The *Tribune* had always (and always to Dill was as far back as he could remember, which was either 1949 or 1950) devoted three-quarters of its front page to local and state news. National affairs and foreign news fought over the rest. Murders, crimes of passion, interesting battery, and other spicy items not deemed fit for breakfast reading were shunted off to page three. Dill turned to page three and saw that his sister's murder still occupied its upper-right-hand one-column position.

Dill flipped through the rest of the paper, noting a couple of two-paragraph wire service stories on pages five and nine that would have made the front pages of both *The New York Times* and *The Washington Post*. He paused at *The Tribune*'s Op-Ed page to see what had changed and was perversely gratified to discover that nothing had. They were all still there: Buckley, Kilpatrick, Will, Evans and Novak—like some old law firm forever arguing its dismal case before the bar of history.

As he turned the pages, Dill saw that the *Tribune* no longer contained a Society section—at least it was no longer called such. It was now called Home instead—but it still meant six pages of parties, weddings, engagements, recipes, and Ann Landers. Dill decided that on the whole the *Tribune* was still the same rotten prosperous newspaper it had always been.

There was a knock at the door and Dill let in the room-service waiter, who put the breakfast tray on the writing table and smiled when Dill tipped him two dollars, instead of the one dollar he usually got. Dill dawdled over breakfast until nine o'clock, drinking coffee from the large silver Thermos carafe even after the coffee had grown cold. At nine he rose, went over to his suitcase, took out the Jake Spivey file that had been handed to him by Betty Mae Marker, opened it, noted a telephone number, crossed back to the desk, and dialed the number. It was answered at the beginning of the third ring by a woman's voice that gave only the phone number's last four digits. Dill had always found the practice irritating.

"Mr. Spivey, please."

"Mr. Spivey isn't available at the moment, but if you'll leave your name and number, I'm quite sure he'll return your call." She had a young voice, Dill thought, cool and professional and faintly Eastern, from up around Massachusetts somewhere.

"Would you do me a favor?" Dill said.

"I'll try."

"Would you please tell Mr. Spivey that this is Mr. Dill and that unless he comes to the phone right this very minute he's going to be the sorriest son of a bitch who ever lived."

The woman said nothing. It sounded over the line as if she had pressed the hold button. And then the big loud voice came roaring joyously over the phone. "That you, Pickle, no shit?"

"I whipped your ass in the fourth grade for calling me that and I expect I can still do it."

The laugh came then, a marvelous honking hoorah so infectious that Dill felt it should be quarantined. It was the totally uninhibited laugh of a man who found life an all too brief passage made up of rainbows, blue skies, bowls of cherries, plus a long head start in the pursuit of happiness. The honking hoorah belonged to John Jacob Spivey. Suddenly the laughter stopped. "I didn't watch the news last night, Pick. Was it on?"

"I don't know," Dill said.

"I just read about it five minutes ago in the *Tribune*. I was stunned. By God I was. I just sat there and read it and then I thought, No, they gotta be talking about somebody else. Not Felicity. Then I read it again, real slow, and, well, I had to believe it. I was just fixing to call you in Washington when you called me. Goddamn, I'm sorry."

Dill said thank you. It was all there was to say. Apparently, no one ever expected him to say anything else.

"Felicity," Spivey said, stretching the name out, pronouncing each syllable with care and affection. "Talk about your hog on ice. She was one independent little old gal even when she was real little right after your folks died. One minute she was ten or eleven and then all of a sudden she was acting eighteen, well, sixteen anyway." Spivey sighed. "Where you at, boy?"

"The Hawkins."

"Shoot, Pick, nobody stays there."

"I do."

"You would. When'd you get in?"

"Last night," Dill lied. "Late."

"How soon can you get yourself out here?"

"Well, I don't know, Jake. I'm—"

Spivey interrupted. "Lemme guess. Except it ain't no guess, at least it'd better not be, not with all the money I'm paying those jackass lawyers of mine up in Washington. You're down here on business for the kid Senator, right? Goddamn if that ain't just like you, Pick, mixing business with sorrow. Well, we can tend to all that later. Right now you oughta be with your friends and you ain't got any friend older'n me, right? None older and none better, for that matter."

"You're a brick, Jake."

"Don't you still use old-timey words though. Brick! Sure you got that spelled right? I ain't heard anyone say brick in twenty years. Maybe thirty. Maybe ever. But then you're the only man I ever heard, white or colored, who called somebody Toots. You used to call Lila Lee Cady

that back in what?—the eleventh grade? You remember
Lila Lee."

"I remember her."

"Went and got fat as Pat's pig. Saw her going down the
street week before last. Waddling—know what I mean?
I ducked down so she wouldn't see me." There was the
laugh again followed by a question. "You want me to
send for you?"

"I rented a car."

"How soon can you get here?"

"I don't even know where you are, Jake. All I've got is
your phone number and a post-office box."

"My God, we have been out of touch. Well, at least I
won't have to give you directions. Guess what I went and
done?"

"No telling."

"About six months back I went and bought the old
Dawson place."

"Jesus God."

"Something, idn't it? Little old Jake Spivey living in
Ace Dawson's place."

"The Dawson mansion," Dill said.

"Yeah, that's right—that's what they always called it
in the *Tribune*, wasn't it? The Dawson Mansion with a
capital M. Goddamn place had termites, can you imagine?
Cost me a fortune to fix it up livable."

"You can afford it, Jake—and enjoy it. I can't think of
anybody who'd enjoy it more."

Spivey again laughed his marvelous laugh. Dill smiled.
It was impossible not to. Still chuckling, Spivey said, "It's
got thirty-six rooms. Thirty-six, by God! What in hell do
I need with thirty-six rooms?"

"You can hide in them."

"You mean when they come looking for me."

"Sure."

"It'll never happen."

"Let's hope not," Dill said.

"How soon you gonna get out here?"

"About an hour. I've got to stop and pick up something."

"What?"

"A tape recorder."

"You won't need it," Spivey said. "You can use one of mine. I got a dozen tape recorders."

"All right," Dill said. "We'll use one of yours."

CHAPTER

IN 1915, two years before America's entry into the First World War, a prosperous dentist who went by the name of Dr. Mortimer Cherry bought seven sections of scrub land 6.7 miles north of the city limits and proceeded to lay out what eventually would become the state's most exclusive suburb. He called it Cherry Hills.

There would be, Dr. Cherry decided, no straight streets—only gently curving drives, twisting lanes, and perhaps two or three sweeping boulevards. Furthermore, all street names would have a pronounced English lilt: Drury Lane, Sloane Way, Chelsea Drive, and so on. The minimum lot—for the merely affluent—would be 100 feet wide and 150 feet deep. The rich could build on parcels as large as ten, even fifteen acres.

By 1917, the lots were plotted, the streets surveyed, and grading was about to start when the country entered the war. Dr. Cherry wisely decided to postpone further development until after the war's end.

In early February 1919, the *Tribune* ran a front-page story revealing that Dr. Cherry had been born into what it called the Hebrew faith as Mordecai Cherowski in either Poland or the Ukraine. The *Tribune* never did pinpoint the exact location. But it managed to convince nearly everyone that Dr. Cherry was no real dentist. True, the *Tribune* admitted, he had pulled a lot of teeth down in Texas, but that had been when he was a medical-orderly trusty in the Huntsville State Prison, serving two years for fraud. Released in 1909, Dr. Cherry had changed his name and moved to the city where he set up practice. His credentials consisted of a diploma from a Wichita Falls dental college that hung proudly in his reception room. His practice thrived and almost everybody agreed he was an awfully good dentist. The *Tribune* revealed that the diploma was a fake. On March 1, 1919, Dr. Cherry drove home from his now nonexistent practice, locked the bathroom door, and shot himself in the head. He was forty-nine years old.

In the late summer of 1919, the development known as Cherry Hills was acquired for next to nothing by the oil millionaire Philip K. "Ace" Dawson, an ex-bootlegger and card sharp from Beaumont who had once done a six-month stretch in Huntsville himself. Ace Dawson held a two-thirds interest in the development. The remaining third was owned by his silent partner, James B. Hartshorne, the twenty-nine-year-old editor and publisher of the *Tribune*.

By 1920, the streets of Cherry Hills were paved, the utilities in, construction of the Cherry Hills Golf & Country Club was nearing completion, and Ace Dawson's thirty-six-room prairie Tudor mansion was rising on fifteen acres of prime land where only blackjack oak and bois d'arc had stood before. Ace Dawson lived in the mansion until Christmas Day 1934, when he was kidnapped by the twins, Dan and Mary Jo McNichols, who demanded and got a $50,000 ransom and then shot Ace

Dawson nine times in the back. Dan and Mary Jo were themselves shot to death in Galveston by Texas Rangers on June 3, 1935, shortly after the twins' twenty-fifth birthday and long after they had spent all the money.

The widow Dawson had had a ten-foot-high serpentine brick wall built around the entire estate after her husband's body was eventually found just outside Liberal, Kansas, in the back of an abandoned 1929 Essex Super Six sedan. She and her seventeen-year-old son, Ace, Jr., lived in the mansion alone except for the servants. She died at the age of eighty-five in 1973, leaving everything, including the thirty-six-room mansion, to Ace, Jr., who had long since fled to Marin County in California. Ace, Jr., tried for years to unload the old home place without success until Jake Spivey came along and took it off his hands for an undisclosed price that some said was less than two million and some said more. Much more.

Dill knew most of the history of Cherry Hills and the suicide dentist and Ace Dawson and the rest. It was part of the folklore he had grown up with. He even thought about some of it as he drove north on Lee Boulevard. Lee—along with TR and Grant boulevards—were the three winding thoroughfares that broke up the city's boring grid. As he drove automatically, not needing to think about where he was going, Dill tried to remember if he had ever heard anyone express sympathy for the ill-fated Dr. Cherry. He thought his father might have done so once, almost in passing, but then Dill's father had been a sentimental soul who, despite his lengthy foreign education, drew most of his day-to-day philosophy from the popular songs of the thirties and forties. The senior Dill had considered the lyrics of "September Song" to be especially profound and poignant. Son was glad Dad had died before hard rock really got going.

When he turned off North Cleveland Avenue, which also ran south all the way to Packingtown, Dill saw they had finally torn down the gatehouse. The gatehouse had been built at the Grand Boulevard entrance to Cherry Hills shortly after Ace Dawson was kidnapped. Up until 1942, uniformed private guards had made random spot checks of all cars entering the suburb. But then the war came along and the guards all quit and either joined the army or went out to Lockheed and Douglas in California. The old gatehouse, which looked as if it might have been designed by a Disney disciple, had stood vacant after that, but now it was gone, and Dill guessed it must have been torn down recently because the land still looked raw.

The trees along Grand Boulevard had thrived, he noticed. They were taller, ten years taller. The poplars had shot up the most, followed more slowly by the elms, the pecans, the persimmons, and the sycamores. As he crossed Cherry Hill Brook, which once was called Split-Tail Creek, he saw that the cottonwoods had also flourished and this, for some reason, pleased him most of all.

Dill turned east off Grand Boulevard into Beauchamp Lane. The lots were larger here, beginning with three acres and rising to five, eight, and finally, fifteen acres, which was what the old Dawson mansion stood on. The houses along Beauchamp Lane (pronounced the way it looks: beau as in bo and champ as in champion) were an eclectic bunch, ranging from sprawling ranch to plains Mediterranean and having almost nothing in common other than their size, which was uniformly immense.

Dill drove alongside the Dawson estate's serpentine brick wall, now capped with shards of glass, until he came to a locked iron gate. He pushed a button on a speaker and a woman's voice said, "Yes." Dill said, "Ben Dill." The gate swung open. Dill drove through and up the curving asphalt drive past the sprinklers that were keeping the rolled bluegrass lawn green even in the August heat that the radio said had already reached 98 degrees and was expected to hit 100 by noon. There were enough tall leafy trees to make the huge old mock Tudor look almost cool. None of its mullioned windows was open, and Dill knew Spivey would have the air-conditioning going full blast.

As he drove past the open six-car garage he counted a Rolls, a Mercedes 500 SEL coupe, a high-sprung Chevrolet pickup, an old open Morgan, a Mustang convertible, and a big Country Squire Ford stationwagon. None of the cars, except the Morgan, looked more than six months old.

Dill stopped his own car in front of a wide carved-oak front door with hammered black metal hinges. He came out of the 75-degree Ford into the 98-degree sunshine and immediately shed his seersucker jacket. He draped it over the left arm that also pressed the manila envelope to his side. The envelope contained the file on Jake Spivey. With his right forefinger, Dill rang the doorbell. Somewhere, far inside, chimes played "How Dry I Am." Dill wondered who had put them in, Ace Dawson or Jake Spivey, and finally decided it could have been either.

To Dill the woman who opened the door would have looked unattainable, if his ex-wife hadn't looked much the same. He had since concluded that all such unattainable appearing women are not quite lean, not quite rangy, and not quite beautiful. They do look smart and easily bored. They also look rich, or as if they had once been that way. And, he was nearly convinced, they all gave off a certain faint scent, which, if only he could bottle it, he would have called Class Distinction.

This one, who seemed to be mostly long tanned legs and bare tanned arms, stared at Dill for several seconds and finally said in a drawl that sounded both Eastern and expensive, "You are Mr....Dill, right?"

"Right."

"You were awfully rude over the phone."

Dill smiled. "I was trying to get Jake's attention."

"Yes, well, you certainly did that." She opened the big door all the way. "I suppose you'd best come in." Dill went in.

She was wearing brief white shorts, a blue-and-white

striped sleeveless top with scooped-out armholes, and nothing else as far as Dill could see, not even shoes. Her toenails were done in a quiet coral. She had sun-streaked, honey-colored hair, appraising brown eyes, a faintly amused mouth, and a slightly sunburned nose. She wore no makeup. Dill guessed she never did because she never needed any. She turned to look at him again and he stared back, deciding that she had the look of old money long gone.

"You're staring," she said.

"Yes."

"I remind you of someone?"

"Of my ex-wife—a little."

"Was she nice?"

"She sighed a lot and sprinkled sugar on her sliced tomatoes."

"Yes, I can see why she would—sigh a lot, I mean. I'm called Daffy." She didn't offer a hand.

"As in Duck or in Daffodil?"

"As in Daphne. Daphne Owens."

"Of course. I should've known."

"I work for Mr. Spivey."

"I see."

"I'm his executive assistant, if you dote on titles."

"It must be pleasant here—the informal atmosphere and all."

"Yes. It is. I live here, too, of course."

"Of course."

"Well, I suppose we'd best go find Jake." She turned and started down a long wide paneled hall lined with long narrow tables that held unused glazed vases. It was a very long hall, and if rest were needed, there were a dozen straight-back, dark wood chairs with faded red plush seats. On both walls were hung nicely done oil portraits of bearded men in nineteenth-century dress. The men all looked extremely proper and Dill was quite sure none of them was related in any way to either Ace Dawson or Jake Spivey.

"Do you know the house?" Owens asked over her shoulder.

"Jake and I were here once a long time ago."

"Really? When?"

"Every Christmas up until 1959, I think. Mrs. Dawson used to throw a party for the city's hundred neediest kids. Jake and I talked our way onto the list." He paused. "It was Christmas, 1956."

"But you weren't really, were you?"

"What?"

"Two of the one hundred neediest."

"Who's to say?"

"It makes a charming story anyway."

"Ask Jake about it," Dill said.

She stopped and turned. Surprisingly, Dill found that she looked older out of the sun. Nearer to thirty than to twenty-five. "I'd like to ask you another question," she said.

"Go ahead."

"Do you intend to cause him any trouble?"

"I don't know," Dill said. "I might."

CHAPTER

10

Aᴛ the end of the long hall Daphne Owens stopped before
an eight-foot-high pair of double doors and slid them back
into the walls. Dill followed her into a large room, which
obviously was the mansion's library, with shelves of books
lining three sides. Six tall leaded windows at the room's
far end were rounded into fan tops. The windows overlooked a garden, rather an elaborate one, where three
Mexicans were digging something up. As Dill watched,
two of them stopped digging, wiped their dripping faces,
and started supervising the third man. Beyond the Mexicans and through some fading white roses could be seen
the blue of the pool.

John Jacob Spivey rose from behind the large old-fashioned black walnut desk that was placed in front of the
tall windows. He leaned forward, palms flat on the desk,
his big head cocked slightly to the left, his shrewd blue
eyes fixed on the approaching Dill. He's still round and
plump and pink, Dill thought, and from here he still looks

like the neighborhood bully who's bigger and smarter than anyone else. Then Jake Spivey smiled and chuckled and transformed himself into the most likable man in the world.

There was warmth in the smile, genuine interest in the expression, and keen anticipation in the eyes once they abandoned their calculating blue stare and began twinkling. He hasn't got a shred of self-consciousness left, Dill thought. He's no more aware of himself than he is of his big toe. It's you he's interested in, Dill. What would you like? he wants to know, and how do you feel? And what do you think? And where in the world have you been?

Spivey had begun nodding as Dill neared the desk. It was a nod of pleased confirmation. "You know what we did, Pick?" he asked. "We went and got older on each other."

"It happens," Dill said as he accepted the hand that Spivey extended over the desk.

"You met Daffy."

"I met Daffy."

"She's from back East," Spivey said. "Massachusetts. Went to school back there."

"Holyoke," Dill guessed, and smiled at Daphne Owens.

"Not even close," she said.

"Sit down, Pick. You're gonna stay for lunch, aren't you?"

"All right. Thanks."

Now settled back into his old wooden swivel chair, Spivey looked up at Owens. "Sugar, would you mind letting Mabel know there's gonna be three of us for lunch?" He turned to Dill. "Mabel's the cook."

"Anything else before I go?" Owens asked.

Spivey looked solicitously at Dill. "You wanta do a little coke or something?"

"What about a cold beer?"

"I got beer right down here in this little old built-in

icebox," Spivey said as he reached down, opened the door of a small desk refrigerator, and brought out two cans of Miller's.

"No coke, then?" Owens asked.

"Don't believe so, sugar," Spivey said and popped open the beer cans. "Not right now anyway."

"I'll see you at lunch, Mr. Dill."

"I hope so," Dill said.

She turned and started walking toward the double doors. Spivey watched her go with obvious appreciation, then smiled, turned to Dill, and handed him one of the cans of beer. "I think I might haul off and marry that one," he said.

"You two've got a lot in common, Jake: background, taste, education, age."

"Don't forget money," Spivey said. "She ain't got any and I got a bunch."

"That should make it a perfect match."

Spivey leaned back in his swivel chair and examined Dill carefully. "Haven't done all your mourning yet, have you?"

"No. Not yet."

"Takes time, Pick. Lord, it takes time." He sipped some of his beer. "How long's it been now?"

"Seven years, almost eight."

"Genoa, right?"

"Right."

"I was with Brattle and you were with, what was her name? Lorna, Lana? Lena?"

"Laura."

"That's right. Laura. You all split up?"

"You heard, huh?"

"Nope. You just look sort of split up. Divorced. What happened?"

Dill shrugged. "Terminal boredom, I guess. She went out one night to see a play—Chekhov, I think—and never came back."

Spivey grinned. "No shit? Chekhov?"

"*The Cherry Orchard.*"

Spivey shook his head in either amusement or commiseration. "She was one handsome woman. Know who reminds me of her?"

"Your Miss Daphne. I noticed it, too." Dill drank from the can of beer. "Let me tell you why I'm here, Jake."

Spivey nodded, interested.

"The Senator wants a deposition from you."

"No problem there, but you're gonna be plowing up the same old cotton. I've already talked to Justice more times than I can count. The IRS has got me on permanent audit. Even Treasury sent some tall drink of water down here, and he and I went round and round for three days. The only ones who haven't dropped in on me is the fucking CIA, and I expect they'll come sneaking over the wall one of these nights just to find out what I've been telling everybody else."

"They've located Brattle, Jake."

The blue eyes opened a little wider and the wide mouth split into a charming but skeptical grin. "Found Clyde? Clyde Brattle? Where was he this time, Cape Town? Rangoon? One of the Tripolis? Downtown Tulsa maybe? Shit, Pick, they been spotting old Clyde here, there, and over yonder for months now. You know what I think?"

"What?"

"I think old Clyde's dead."

"You hope so anyway."

"Well, I can't say I'd be in the front rank of mourners."

"But you would be off the hook."

"I ain't exactly wiggling on one now. Where'd they claim to have spotted him?"

"London."

"When?"

"Two months ago."

"Whyn't they pick him up? Hell, he's extraditable."

"They lost him."

"Who the fuck are they?"

"The Brits."

"Well, no wonder. Look, let's get this thing over with. You say you want a deposition for the Senator? Let's do her."

Dill looked around the room. "Where's the tape recorder?"

Spivey shook his head sadly. "Pick."

"What?"

"It's been running from the second you walked in."

Drill grinned. "I should've known. I'll just start then."

"You start and then Daffy'll give the tape to one of the girls to get typed up and Xeroxed and sworn to and all."

"Okay," Dill said, "here we go." He paused, counted silently to fifteen, and then began. "This is the sworn deposition of John Jacob Spivey given freely on this day of August whatever it is, ladies, at his home at the right address on Beauchamp Lane and so forth."

Dill put his beer on the desk and opened the file on Jake Spivey. He looked at the file and then up at Spivey.

"Your name is John Jacob Spivey."

"Yes."

"Your age?"

"Thirty-eight."

"You are an American citizen, living permanently at the above address."

"Yes."

"Your occupation?"

"Retired."

"Your previous occupation?"

"I was engaged in the purchase and sale of defensive weaponry."

"For how long?"

"Seven years, almost eight."

"And before that?"

"I was a contract employee of a government agency."

"Which agency?"

"The Central Intelligence Agency."

"Where were you employed?"

"You mean where did they hire me or where did I work?"

"Both."

"I was hired in Mexico City and I worked in Thailand, Vietnam, Laos, and Cambodia."

"For how long?"

"From 1969 to 1975."

"What was the nature of your duties?"

"The oath I took when employed by the CIA precludes me from revealing the nature of my duties unless I request and am given written permission by the Central Intelligence Agency."

"Have you sought such permission?"

"Yes."

"Was it given?"

"It was refused."

"When was the last time it was refused?"

"On June fourteenth of this year."

"Why did you ask for the permission?"

"I did so at the request of the Federal Bureau of Investigation."

"And the permission was denied?"

"Yes."

"Are you willing to violate your oath at this time?"

"No, sir, I'm not."

"Why not?"

"On the grounds that it could be self-incriminating, and I cite the Fifth Amendment."

"When did you first meet Clyde Tomerlin Brattle?"

"In 1970, around March or April. I'm not exactly sure of the date."

"Where was this?"

"Bangkok."

"How did you meet him?"

"He was my supervisor."

"Your case officer?"

"My supervisor. He instructed me in the duties I performed in Vietnam, Laos, and Cambodia whose exact nature I am prevented by my oath from disclosing."

Dill grimaced and drew a finger across his throat. Spivey, smiling broadly, reached beneath the desk and cut off the tape recorder.

"Jesus Christ, Jake."

"What'd you expect?"

"It's canned."

"You goddamn right it's canned—by Dump, Diddle and Squat, which is what I call those jackass lawyers of mine up in Washington who're sucking me dry. When's the last time you got a bill from a lawyer?"

"It's been a while."

"Well, here's some advice. Sit down before you open it—or better yet, lie down, because sure as green apples give gripe you're gonna faint dead away."

"But all that crap about an oath."

"I took an oath just like I said. Does Langley deny it? Hell, no, they don't. They just deny I ever worked for 'em."

"They don't deny that either," Dill said. "They just refuse to confirm it."

"Pick, I don't really give a fuck about any oath I took for those fuckers. I was twenty-three years old then and when I quit 'em I was thirty and an old man. I mean old up here." Spivey tapped his forehead. "Up here, I was a hundred-and-two. They paid me one thousand bucks a week, which back then was serious money, and I did stuff I wouldn't do now and stuff I don't even let myself think about much anymore. But what I did I didn't do for God, flag, or country. I did it for one thousand bucks a week cash money and believe it or not, I paid a price. What price, you're thinking, right? Well, old buddy, I never got to be twenty-four or twenty-five or twenty-six or any of those good years, because one day I was twenty-three and six months later I was a hundred-and-two going on a hundred-and-three."

"Poor old Jake."

Spivey shrugged, suddenly indifferent, even bored.

"So what would happen if you violated your so-called oath?" Dill said. "I mean, what do you think would happen?"

"Not much," Spivey said. "There might be some juicy headlines for a day or two, but there'd never be any trial or anything because Langley'd slam the lid down tight. Just like they did before—all in the interest of national security. Hell, Pick, Vietnam's old hat now. You got a generation coming of age that thinks of Vietnam, if they think of it at all, like you and me used to think of World War Two. Ancient history. When you and me were twenty-one, the war'd been over for twenty-two years. Twenty-three maybe." He paused. "You want another beer?"

"Sure."

Spivey took two more cans of Miller's from the desk refrigerator and popped their lids. Dill took a long swallow and said, "Okay, you want to start again?"

"What now—Brattle?"

"Brattle."

Spivey moved his hand underneath the edge of the desk. "Okay, we're rolling. Now."

Again, Dill counted silently to fifteen and asked his first question: "Clyde Brattle worked for the CIA how long?"

"Twenty years."

"He was a career employee?"

"Yes."

"When did he resign?"

"He didn't resign. He was fired in seventy-five."

"Why?"

"I'm not sure."

"Can you guess?"

"I'm no lawyer, but I don't think a guess would be admissible."

"Did it have something to do with funds under his control?"

"That would be pure speculation on my part."

"Were the funds misappropriated?"

"I heard they were, but that's only hearsay."

"Your disclaimer is noted. How much money was involved?"

"Somewhere around five hundred thousand, I heard."

"Dollars?"

"Dollars."

"When did you leave the employ of the CIA?"

"In April of seventy-five just after Saigon fell."

"Where were you then?"

"When it fell? In Saigon."

"Where was Clyde Brattle?"

"He was there, too."

"Neither you nor Brattle made any attempt to escape?"

"No."

"Why not?"

"Because we were no longer in the spook trade. We were by then simple businessmen."

"Describe the nature of your business, please."

"We formed a company that bought surplus equipment from the new Vietnamese government and sold it on the open market to whoever wanted to buy it."

"What kind of equipment?"

"Defensive weaponry, transportation, communications."

"What kind of weaponry?"

"Small arms. Mortars. Light artillery. Some rolling stock—jeeps and trucks. Field communications gear. Some helicopters. Whatever they wanted to get rid of. They needed money bad and we had some and knew where we could get a whole lot more."

"You and Brattle put up the money to form your company?"

"Yes."

"How much did he put up?"

"Close to four hundred thousand."

"And you?"

"All I had. One hundred thousand."

"And the profits were shared how?"

"A quarter for me, three-quarters for Clyde. That's because I had the contacts."

"The Vietnamese contacts."

"*North* Vietnamese. Except by then it was all one big happy country, North and South alike."

"And who did you sell the surplus American weaponry to?"

"It wasn't American. It was Vietnamese. They fought a war. They won the war. The spoils were theirs."

"But it was of American manufacture?"

"That's right."

"So who did you sell it to?"

"Whoever would buy it."

"For instance."

"People in Angola, Ethiopia, Lebanon, Yemen, both South and North, Bolivia, Ecuador, and a little, but not much, to some folks in Uruguay."

"How much of this American-made, Vietnamese-acquired equipment did you sell?"

"About a hundred million dollars' worth."

"And your share of the profits?"

"You mean just mine?"

"Yes."

"I cleared a little over four million after expenses, which ran sort of high."

"And Brattle. How much did he net?"

"I'd say around sixteen million after expenses."

"And this went on for how long?"

"You mean Brattle and me?"

"Yes, your association, your partnership."

"For about five or six years."

"Then what?"

"Then he wanted to get into some funny stuff and I got out."

"What kind of funny stuff?"

"Computer technology, sophisticated weaponry, guidance systems, all kinds of new stuff you could get hold of in the States, but could never get the okay to sell. Clyde said we could sneak 'em out. I said fuck it and quit."

"Strike the 'fuck it' and substitute 'no thanks,' please. And so that's what you did—you quit?"

"That's right."

"Was Mr. Brattle upset?"

"Well, he wasn't exactly humming 'Blue Skies.'"

"Was there any unpleasantness?"

"I had to get some lawyers and he got his and they all hemmed and hawed at each other and I came out with a net of about thirteen million, which was all reported to the IRS, where I'm under permanent audit, like I told you."

"When's the last time you saw Mr. Brattle?"

"About a year and a half ago."

"Where?"

"Kansas City. He had some routine papers for me to sign. I flew up there, signed them, and had a drink with him. Then I flew back here."

"Have you seen him since?"

"No."

"It was shortly after your meeting with him that he fled the country, right?"

Spivey laughed his loud hoorah laugh. "Yeah, I guess you'd have to say old Clyde was sort of forced to flee."

"Strike the laughter," Dill said. "You know why he skipped, of course."

"Because they wanted to arrest him for doing business with the wrong folks."

"Where do you think he is now?"

"Dead," Spivey said.

"Let's assume he isn't dead," Dill said. "Let's assume he's arrested and brought to trial. Would you be willing to testify against him?"

"I have no comment to make at this time," Spivey said, moved his left hand underneath the edge of the desk, and switched off the tape recorder. He studied Dill for several moments. "You offering me immunity, Pick?"

Dill nodded slowly.

"Put it in writing?"

Dill shook his head no.

"Give me a few days to think about it?"

Again, Dill nodded.

Spivey grinned. "You think I got another tape recorder going, don't you?"

Dill smiled and nodded.

CHAPTER

11

THEY had lunch in the "family" dining room, which was large enough to hold a carved oak sideboard, a matching china closet, and a table that seated twelve—or up to sixteen with all the leaves in. To get to the family dining room, Spivey led Dill through the "company" dining room, whose table could easily seat thirty-six, although Spivey said he never used it because he didn't know three dozen people he'd actually want to sit down and eat with.

They sat at the end of the table farthest from the kitchen or—as Dill later observed—the pantry. The family dining room overlooked the pool, which was oblong in shape and had been added as an afterthought in the early thirties just before pools started taking on the forms of kidneys and boomerangs. It was a big pool, at least forty by seventy, and Dill thought it resembled the municipal one he and Spivey had learned to swim in at Washington Park.

Spivey was seated at the head of the table with Dill on his right when Daphne Owens came in. She had changed

into a skirt and blouse. Dill rose when she came in. Spivey didn't. She gave Dill an amused look that made him feel a trifle gauche for some reason.

"Who taught you your manners, Mr. Dill," she asked, "your mama or the Phi Delts?"

"My mama," he said.

"She was one nice lady," Spivey said. "A little—" He looked at Dill. "What's the word I want—distant?"

"Vague," Dill said.

"That ain't it either. Ethereal's the word. But I expect it saved her a lot of heartache considering what she had to put up with, with your old man."

Dill smiled and nodded slightly.

"What did your father do, Mr. Dill?" Owens asked.

"He was a professional dreamer."

"What's wrong with that?"

"It implies he should've been paid for them. He seldom was."

"Pick and me were the poorest kids in Horace Mann grade school," Spivey said proudly. "And we would've been the poorest kids in junior high school, but they integrated it along about then and brought in some colored and Mexican kids who were even poorer'n Pick and me, but we were still the poorest *white* kids in Coolidge Junior High. Right, Pick?"

"Absolutely."

Before Spivey could dredge up further memories, one of the Mexicans who had been out digging the garden came in wearing a starched white jacket and nicely pressed jeans. Everyone ordered drinks and the gardener/houseman left through the swinging door that Dill noticed led into a pantry. He also noticed that the tablecloth was Irish linen; the silverware English; the china from France—Limoges, he thought—and the two wineglasses at his plate were heavy leaded crystal and possibly Czech Knowing Spivey, he was almost certain lunch would be Tex-Mex.

"Then you two really were out here back in the fifties when you were kids," Daphne Owens said to Spivey.

He grinned at Dill. "You tell her about that?"

"She asked me if I'd ever seen the house before."

"Me'n Pick were two of the city's hundred neediest kids—at least, that's how we promoted ourselves. We were what then, Pick—ten?"

"Ten," Dill agreed.

"Well, sugar, we'd heard tales about old Ace's mansion. My God, everybody had. Solid-gold bathroom fixtures. Stuff like that. And we just *had* to see it. So Pick came up with the idea that if we got dressed up in our oldest clothes—and there really wasn't one hell of a lot of difference between our oldest and our best—and then went down and saw the principal, old lady McMullen—how old you reckon she was then, Pick?"

"Old," Dill said. "At least forty."

"Older'n God to us," Spivey said. "So that's what we did."

"Jake gave the spiel," Dill said. "I just looked wistful. Very poor; very wistful."

"And the next thing you know me'n Pick're on a hired city bus with about fifty-eight cute little colored kids and thirty-five even cuter little Mexicans and five other poor whites heading out to Cherry Hills and old Ace Dawson's mansion for a Christmas party."

"Weren't you embarrassed?" Owens asked. "I mean, didn't you find it—well, for God's sake, demeaning?"

"What's demeaning about curiosity?" Dill asked. "Ace Dawson was a myth. We wanted to see how a myth had lived."

"And we sure as shit didn't lie, sugar," Spivey said. "We *were* poor, although Pick here was sort of shabby genteel poor and I was just plain dirt poor." He turned to Dill. "Remember what I told you that night in the bus on the way back home?" Before Dill could reply, Spivey

96

turned back to Daphne Owens. "What d'you think I told him?"

"That some day you were going to own it, of course. The Dawson mansion."

Spivey shook his head as if both puzzled and disappointed. "Daffy, you got a romantic streak in you I never suspected." He turned to Dill. "Tell her what I told you that night on the bus home."

Dill smiled. "That being rich sure looked a lot easier than being poor, and you thought you might as well take the easy way out."

Owens stared at Spivey with almost equal amounts of awe and suspicion. "You really said that at ten?" she asked, the awe winning out in her tone.

Spivey grinned. "Well, maybe not word for word," he said, still grinning. "But almost."

As he pulled up in front of his dead sister's yellow brick duplex at the corner of 32nd Street and Texas Avenue, Dill could still taste the quesadillas and green corn tamales he had had for lunch. And the avocados, too. Dill didn't much like avocados and there had been too many pieces of them in his salad. He had eaten them out of politeness and now wished he hadn't.

He sat in the Ford sedan, the engine idling, the air-conditioning on as high as it would go, and examined the duplex. He remembered it now, not because he had ever been inside, but because he had passed it scores of times and, by merely passing, had absorbed it into his memory.

The radio was on and turned to the all-news station. Dill was waiting for a Delta Airlines commercial to end and the weather girl to come on. She had a low breathy voice that was supposed to make the weather sound lascivious. When the commercial ended, she breathed the time, which was 2:49 P.M.; the temperature, which was

97

104 degrees Fahrenheit; the humidity, which was just 21 percent, and the wind which, for a change, was blowing gently out of the southwest at 5 miles per hour. When she began to suggest cute ways to beat the heat, Dill switched the ignition off and silenced the radio.

Before getting out of the car, he locked the file on Jake Spivey in the glove compartment. The file now included the sworn deposition, whose contents Dill felt were almost worthless. It had been transcribed by Spivey's unseen typists—word processors, actually—and witnessed by Daphne Owens, who had turned out to be a notary public whose commission expired on June thirteenth of the following year.

When Dill got out of the Ford, the dry scorching heat almost made him gasp. With his seersucker jacket slung over his left shoulder, he hurried toward the inviting tall green elms with their promise of cool shade. The promise was broken and the invitation proved false, for there was no respite in the shade, and Dill's shirt was soaked and his chin dripping sweat as he started slowly up the outside stairs. At the landing, he used the key the chief of detectives had given him, unlocked the door, pushed it open, and went inside.

He looked for the air-conditioning first and found a set of controls on the near wall. The controls were for both heating and cooling. He switched the system on, moved the cool indicator from medium to high, stepped to the center of the living room, glanced around, and found that there was nothing to indicate his sister had ever lived there. Nor, for that matter, had anyone else with a shred of personality.

There was furniture in the living room, of course: a dark-green boxy couch, a matching chair, and a chrome-and-glass coffee table with nothing on it except last week's copy of *TV Guide.* On the floor, because there seemed no place else for it, was a small black-and-white Sony portable television set. There were no books, not one, which Dill found strange because he knew Felicity had despised television and as a child had read eight or nine books a week, sometimes ten, although they had been young-adult books, which at eleven she finally had dismissed as "mostly crap." During the summer of her twelfth year she had turned to the Russian novelists and, having disposed of them, picked up Santayana's *The Last Puritan* from somewhere. She had spent an entire week in August reading it, a frown on her forehead and a pitcher of Kool-Aid within easy reach. She said she found Santayana both "stuffy and dull" and devoted the rest of that same August to Dickens.

Dill could still remember her seated at the card table, *Little Dorrit* open in front of her, the Big Chief tablet to her right for notes and annotations, and on another corner of the table, the seldom-used *Webster's Collegiate Dictionary*. Opposite the dictionary was the pitcher of Kool-Aid. Grape, as Dill recalled. Dickens, Felicity had informed her brother, was pretty good stuff (high praise) but a "little soupy." Dill sometimes felt his sister was the least sentimental person he had ever known.

He examined the living room carefully, trying to find some hint of her personality, a trace of her habits. There was a rug of a neutral sand shade on the floor, a few pictures on the wall that appeared to be cheap mail-order prints of Dufy, Cézanne, and Monet, and in one corner an inexpensive-looking Korean stereo so new it looked unused. Dill didn't bother to examine the two dozen or so records. He knew if they were Felicity's, they would be Beethoven, Bach, the early Beatles, plus every song Yves Montand had ever recorded.

The living room blended into a dining area where four chairs surrounded a drop-leaf maple table that looked as if it had been ordered by catalogue from Sears. A fake Tiffany lamp hung by a heavy golden chain over the table. That's not Felicity either, Dill thought.

In the kitchen he peered into the refrigerator and found

four bottles of Perrier, a stick of butter, three eggs, a jar of Dijon mustard, and a loaf of whole-wheat bread with three or four slices gone. He remembered that his sister had always kept her bread in the refrigerator. He took out one of the Perriers, twisted its top off, and drank from the bottle.

With the bottle in his left hand, Dill opened the doors to the kitchen cabinets. There were a set of dishes—fairly good Japanese imitations of Dansk—a half-dozen glasses, and a few bowls. Nothing else. Where the canned goods, the spices, and the staples should have been were only two cans of Van Camp's pork and beans, a jar of Yuban instant coffee, almost empty, a round box of Morton's salt, a small box of Schilling black pepper, but no other spices, not even tarragon, which Dill remembered his sister had dumped into virtually everything.

To cook with there was only a frying pan, nearly new, and a couple of battered aluminum pots that would do to boil the eggs and heat up the beans. In one of the drawers, Dill discovered enough stainless steel knives, forks, and spoons for two. He opened the rest of the drawers, but found nothing except a few kitchen odds and ends. He wondered what Felicity had done with their mother's silver.

Still carrying his bottle of Perrier, Dill went from the kitchen back into the living room and then down a short hall. The second door on the left led into what apparently had been his sister's bedroom. There was a double bed, neatly made up, a chest of drawers, and a dresser with a mirror. It was a matched set made out of walnut veneer, and it looked both cheap and fairly new. A small table by the bed's left-hand side held a Tensor reading lamp. Dill opened the table's drawer. It contained only a round shallow plastic box of birth-control pills.

Dill opened the closet next. Hanging there were a few dresses, some slacks, several blouses, a light trench coat, but no winter coat. Five pairs of shoes were lined up primly on the closet floor. There was one pair of black pumps and the rest were sandals, loafers, and a scuffed-up pair of green jogging shoes.

In the drawers of the dresser and the bureau Dill found only a couple of sweaters in plastic dry cleaner's bags, a few folded shirts and blouses, some underwear, panty-hose, and not much else. There was just enough clothing, he decided, to last someone a month or two, possibly three. But there were no keepsakes or mementos or sou-venirs or anything, for that matter, that would attest to character, personality, or bad habits—except that whoever had lived there was obsessively neat and apparently de-spised either cooking or eating.

Dill left the large bedroom and went down the hall into the second, smaller bedroom, which turned out to be the den of someone who had run out of money. There were a card table, a bridge lamp, and on the card table a very old Remington portable typewriter. A canvas director's chair was drawn up to the table. To the table's right was a gray two-drawer metal file. Dill stooped, opened the file's top drawer, and then the bottom one. Both were empty. He assumed the police had removed the contents. There was nothing at all in the second bedroom's closet except three wire coathangers.

From the smaller bedroom/den, Dill went into the bathroom and opened the medicine cabinet. He found aspirin, Tampax, Crest, makeup, a razor, but no prescrip-tion drugs. The soap dish held a cake of Yardley's and the toothbrush holder held two toothbrushes and a small con-tainer of green waxed dental floss. There was nothing else in the bathroom other than some towels and washcloths and a plastic shower cap. There was not even, Dill noted, a bathroom scale. He thought that might be significant; that it might even be a clue.

Dill left the bathroom and started back to the kitchen to see if he could find where Felicity had kept her liquor. He thought under the kitchen sink would be the most likely place. He was almost to the kitchen when the doorbell rang. Dill turned, crossed to the door, and opened it. Standing there in skimpy yellow shorts and an equally skimpy blue polka-dot halter and no shoes was a well-tanned, long-legged woman whose limp blond curls seemed to be gasping for air. She had large blue eyes, too large really, a shiny pink nose, and a wide mouth coated with dark-red lipstick that was exactly the wrong shade.

"You're the brother, aren't you?" the woman said.

"I'm the brother," Dill agreed.

"You got the same hair she had—sort of copper-colored. But you don't look much like her, except for the hair."

"She was pretty; I'm not."

"Well, men aren't supposed to be pretty, are they?" the woman said, and for a moment, Dill was afraid she might simper, but she didn't.

"You're what—a friend, a neighbor?" Dill asked.

"Oh, I'm Cindy. Cindy McCabe. Me and Harold live downstairs. We're, you know, the tenants."

"Harold is Mr. McCabe." Dill didn't make it a question.

"Well, no, not exactly. I mean we're not exactly married. Harold's last name is Snow. Harold Snow. We've been together for, oh, I guess, two years now. At least two." She paused. When she spoke again her voice was low, her tone important. "Harold saw it happen to Felicity—well, almost."

"You'd better come in," Dill said.

"I guess it would be a little cooler than out here, wouldn't it?"

12

CINDY McCabe came in and sat down in the easy chair that matched the green couch. She stuck out her lower lip and blew upward, as if to blow away the light film of sweat that coated her forehead and upper lip. "Isn't this heat something?" she said, obviously expecting no answer.

"I was about to have a drink," Dill said. "Like to join me?"

"Well, a cold beer *would* be nice."

"Sorry. No beer. Unless I find where Felicity keeps the booze, it'll have to be plain Perrier."

"Under the kitchen sink," McCabe said.

"That's what I thought," Dill said and headed for the kitchen.

There were two bottles of green-label Jim Beame under the sink next to the liquid Ivory and the Easy-Off and the Comet. One of the bottles was still sealed. The level of the other one was down two inches. Dill remembered

Felicity had always drunk bourbon, when she drank at all, because she claimed it had a more honest taste than Scotch. He also remembered that she thought vodka was a soak's drink and gin was for those who had run out of Aqua Velva. Rum, however, was okay, especially if mixed with Kool-Aid. As Dill poured whiskey over the ice and added the Perrier, he wondered why he had found no Kool-Aid. Once again, Watson, he told himself, the dog doesn't bark.

He carried the drinks back into the living room and handed one to Cindy McCabe, who nodded her thanks and rubbed the chilled glass across her forehead. "Gosh, that feels good." She took a long swallow, smiled, and said, "That feels even better."

Dill, seated on the couch, tried some of his own drink. "You're right," he agreed.

"Harold and me are awful sorry about Felicity, Mr. Dill. It was just so—well, awful. One minute there she was ringing our doorbell and the next minute she was gone."

"How long've you lived here?"

"About a year and a half. A little less maybe. We moved in right after Felicity bought the place. She sure was a nice landlady. Some of them, you know, will raise your rent every six months, but Felicity didn't even raise ours once because Harold helped her around the place fixing anything that went broke. He's good at that—fixing stuff."

"What's Harold do?"

"Well, he's selling home computers right now and doing okay, but he says it's going to peter out this month or next the way they're flooding the market again. What he really wants to do is get back into electronics. He had two years down at the university, you know, studying electrical engineering, but had to drop out. Harold's real good at that stuff. Electronics. He likes it a lot more'n selling."

Cindy McCabe, apparently made thirsty by talk, took

a long pull at her drink. Dill watched her almost invisible Adam's apple move up and down three times. She lowered the drink and smiled, if not nervously, at least uncomfortably. "I sorta hate to bring this up right now," she said.

"What?"

"Well, yesterday, just before it—you know, happened, well, Felicity stopped by and reminded Harold he'd forgot to pay the rent again. Sometimes I don't know about Harold. Things just slip his mind. He's sorta like the absentminded professor, you know?"

Dill nodded that he did.

"Anyway, it's embarrassing. So he wrote the check out yesterday and gave it to her and then it happened, right out front, and, well, we don't exactly know what to do. You think we oughta stop payment on that one and write another one? And who do we make it out to? It's sorta tacky, I guess, bothering you with this now, but we don't want anyone coming around later and claiming we didn't pay the rent."

"Forget about it until the end of the month," Dill said. "By then things should be straightened out, and Felicity's lawyer will call and tell you where to send the rent and who to make the check out to."

"And we'll just stop payment on the one we gave Felicity?"

"Yes, I think so."

"Well, that's a relief." As if to prove it, she finished off her drink in three swallows. Dill rose and held out his hand for her glass.

Cindy McCabe frowned. "I don't think—oh, well, one more, I guess."

When Dill returned with the fresh drinks he saw that the blue polka-dot halter had either slipped or been tugged down an inch or so, revealing the top quarter of Cindy McCabe's perky breasts, which seemed to be as well

105

tanned as the rest of her. Dill handed her the drink, smiled down at her breasts, or what he could see of them, and said, "You have a nice tan."

She giggled and looked down. "I work on it hard enough." She gave the halter a tug up, but it was only a half-hearted tug. "There's this hedge out back?" she said, making her statement a question.

Dill nodded that he believed it.

"Well, it goes all the way around the backyard and it's about nine feet tall and real thick. Nobody can see through it. So this summer I just laid out there in nothing at all until the middle of last week when it got so godawful hot. I mean, it was just like lying in an oven, even with nothing on. Earlier this summer, when it was cooler, Felicity'd come out and join me sometimes when she was working nights or on the swing shift."

"In nothing at all?" Dill said.

"Oh, no, it wasn't anything like that."

"Like what?"

"Well, when she came out I'd put something on. I mean, after all."

"Did you and Harold see much of Felicity?"

"To tell the truth we didn't, because she worked those funny hours. One week days, one week nights, and the week after that it'd be the swing shift. Sometimes we didn't even see her for weeks at a time. In fact, we wouldn't even hear her up here. I mean, if she was working nights, she'd get home in the morning before we got up, and then she'd usually leave while Harold was still at work and I was out back. She never made a sound up here. I told her once we never heard her and she just smiled and said she went barefoot most of the time. But anytime anything went kaflooey she'd leave a note asking me to ask Harold to take care of it. And when he did she'd be so happy and ask us both up to have a drink. But we never went out anywhere together, and like I said, we hardly knew she was up here. The only time we ever heard anything was when that big guy came around yelling and banging on her door."

"What big guy?" Dill asked.

"I guess he was her ex-boyfriend. He sure was big, I know that. Harold said he used to play football down at the university, but if he told me his name, I forgot it because I think football sucks."

"How often did the big guy come around?"

"You don't think he had something to do with what—well, with what happened, do you?"

"No. I'm just curious about Felicity and who her friends were—even her ex-friends."

"Well, he was blond and big as a barn and young, not over thirty anyway, which I still think is young and I'm twenty-eight and don't care who knows it."

"You don't look it," Dill lied.

"Well, I am."

"How often did he come around yelling and banging on the door?"

"The big guy? Oh, that just happened once, the very first month we moved in. I thought, What in the world have we got ourselves into? It got so bad I asked Harold to do something about it, but he wouldn't. Harold said it was none of our business what a cop did, even a lady cop. I think he was a little afraid of the big guy—and he really was big. Of course, Felicity wasn't so little her-self—five-ten at least. But I still don't know how she and the big guy ever—well, you know." Her expression grew a bit dreamy and Dill wondered how often she had had fantasies about the big guy.

"So what happened?" Dill said.

"Oh, I went up the next morning and saw her and told her all that fuss'd kept Harold awake, which was a lie, because he'd slept right through most of it, and it was me they'd kept awake. She was nice as pie. But then she always was, even when Harold got the rent checks fucked up—oops. Sorry. Must be the bourbon." She giggled. Dill smiled.

"The big guy didn't come back?" he asked.

"Nope. Never. Felicity said it'd stop and it did. Never a sound after that. She didn't even play her TV hardly any, not even in the morning for *Good Morning America*, and that's what I always watch. She'd sometimes turn it on for the evening news, but not loud."

"Did Captain Colder come around much?" Dill said.

"Who?"

"Captain Colder. Gene Colder."

"Oh. Him. He was here yesterday. Asking me and Harold questions and kind of pretending we'd never seen him before."

"But you had?"

"Oh, sure. He used to come around and pick Felicity up, maybe once or twice a week."

"Did he always bring her back?"

"Sometimes he did. But sometimes she didn't come home at all."

Dill thought that the look she gave him over the rim of her glass was meant to be smoldering. Instead, it was a bit glazed. He realized she was a little drunk.

"You're saying she sometimes didn't come home at all after going out with Colder?" he asked.

"Does that bother you?"

"No."

"I mean, when two people are all grown up and everything, it's the natural thing to do, right?"

"Right."

"Take me and you, for example."

"Okay."

"Okay what?"

"Okay, let's take you and me."

"Yeah, well, if you and me had a sudden yen for each other and decided to do something about it, who'd care?"

"Harold?"

"He wouldn't mind. He had a yen for Felicity, but he never got anywhere. Shoot, I wouldn't have minded if he had. He was always answering the door when she knocked in his Jockey shorts and a half hard-on. That's why I think he was late with the rent sometimes. So he could open the door for Felicity in his Jockey shorts and his half hard-on."

"Harold sounds like quite a guy."

"He's about what you'd expect. Any more bourbon out there?" She waved her glass a little and Dill decided she was even drunker than he had thought.

"Sure," he said, rose, took her glass, and went back into the kitchen, where he mixed her another drink, but filled his own up with the last of the Perrier. When he came back into the living room, the halter was all the way off. Dill handed her the drink, smiled, and said, "Looks a lot cooler that way."

"What d'you think of them?" she asked, cupping her left breast and offering it for display.

"Nice."

"Just nice?"

"Extremely nice."

"This is sort of a pass I'm making at you."

"I know."

"Well?"

"Well, it's a shame I have to be downtown in fifteen minutes."

"No kidding."

Dill nodded regretfully.

Cindy McCabe drank a third of her new drink. When the glass came down, her eyes were still glazed and also a little crossed. They stared at Dill anyway. "You know something?" she said.

"What?"

"I made a pass at Felicity once—out there in the back-yard."

"What happened?"

Cindy McCabe laughed. It was a brief harsh laugh, more sad than merry. "She brushed me off real nice." McCabe paused, frowned, looked down at her bare breasts, looked up, and added, "Almost like the way you're brushing me off right now."

CHAPTER

13

AFTER he finally got rid of Cindy McCabe, Dill drove downtown, parked the rented Ford in the basement garage, and at 3:46 P.M. walked into the nicely cooled Hawkins Hotel. The temperature outside, according to the First National Bank sign, was 104 degrees Fahrenheit. There was no wind. Dill could not remember when there had been no wind.

The elderly woman, whom he took to be a permanent resident, was seated in her usual chair in the lobby working on an intricate piece of needlepoint. She looked up as Dill approached, but this time she didn't frown or glare. Nor did she smile. She merely stared. Dill smiled and nodded. She nodded back and said, "Tornado weather."

Dill said, "You could be right," and continued on until he came to the reception desk, where he paused to see if there were any messages in his box. There was one on a slip of pink paper. He asked the clerk for it. The clerk, the same one who had checked Dill in, looked at his watch first, took the slip from the box, and leaned across the counter, his manner suddenly confidential or conspiratorial. Or both, Dill thought.

"Captain Colder," the clerk said, barely moving his lips.

Dill liked melodrama, especially in the afternoon. "Where?"

"The Slush Pit."

"How long?"

The clerk shrugged his thin shoulders. "Fifteen, maybe twenty minutes."

"And?"

"He's looking for you."

"There a back way out?"

"You can go—" The clerk stopped. The tips of his ears grew pink. "Aw hell, Mr. Dill, you're kidding me."

"Not really," Dill said, turned, and headed for the Slush Pit. As he walked he read the message slip. It asked him to "please call Mr. Dolan, Washington, D.C., before 6 P.M. EDT." Dill looked at his watch again. It wouldn't be six in Washington for another hour. But there was really no hurry. Timothy Dolan never left the subcommittee office before seven anyhow, not even on Friday nights.

The Slush Pit, living up to its name, was as oil-black as always. It took Dill's eyes several moments to adjust. He finally located Captain Gene Colder at a table near the north wall. Colder sat with his back to the wall, a glass of beer in front of him. The beer looked untouched. Dill suspected Colder of not really being much of a drinker despite the two Scotches he had put away up in Dill's room the previous afternoon. Dill thought those two drinks might well have used up Colder's ration for the week.

Dill crossed to the table. Colder looked up at him and nodded. It was not a friendly nod. Neither was it unfriendly. It was the cool nod one stranger might give another, reserving all judgment until the second stranger does something strange.

"Sit down," Colder said.

Dill nodded back his own stranger-type nod, pulled out a chair, and sat down.

"Drink?"

Dill didn't really want anything. But he said, "Sure, I'll have a beer. A draft."

Colder raised his hand. The cocktail waitress hurried over. Lately, Dill told himself, you've been drinking with people who command instantaneous service.

"He wants a beer, Lucille," Colder said to the waitress.

"You okay, Captain?" she asked.

"I'm fine."

Lucille went away. Colder took out a package of Salems and offered Dill a cigarette. Dill shook his head. "I quit."

"If I keep on smoking these things, so will I." Colder lit the cigarette with a throwaway lighter and leaned forward, his elbows on the table. "I thought we could have a talk without the chief breathing down our necks."

"Okay."

"Felicity," Colder said. "I'd like to talk about her."

"All right."

"It may not show, Dill, but I'm almost falling part."

Dill nodded in what he hoped was a sympathetic way. It apparently wasn't, because Colder stared at him as if expecting something more.

"So am I," Dill said. "Falling apart. Almost."

That was better, Dill saw. Not much, but some. Colder looked away and said, "I'm married to a bitch."

"It happens."

"She's the daughter of an ex-deputy chief back home. In Kansas City." He ground the scarcely smoked cigarette out. "And that's why I married her—because she was a deputy chief's daughter." He went on carefully grinding out the cigarette. "I made a mistake."

"I make them all the time," Dill said because he saw that Colder expected him to say something. The waitress came over, put the glass of beer down in front of Dill, and went away. Dill took an experimental swallow. Colder still hadn't touched his.

"I'm thirty-six years old and if I play it right, I can be chief by the time I'm forty. Maybe even before. And I don't mean chief of detectives like Strucker. I mean chief of police—the *queso grande.*"

"But," Dill said.

"What d'you mean, but?"

"That's why you're telling me all this, because there's a but."

Colder stared at Dill. It's his Grand Inquisitor's stare, Dill decided, the one that says: Confess. Reveal. Disclose. Spill.

"Just what kind of but do you think it is?" Colder said.

Dill shrugged. "I won't even try to guess because you're going to tell me." In fact, he thought, you're dying to tell me. The Inquisitor becomes the Inquisitee, although I suspect that whatever the revelations are, Captain, they will leave you blameless.

"My wife," Colder began, "well, my wife was giving me a rotten time long before I ever met Felicity. In fact, I moved out on her."

"Before you met Felicity."

"Well, right after anyway."

"I see."

"I don't want you to get the idea that Felicity broke up any happy home."

"I'm sure she wouldn't've."

"My wife and I don't have any kids. So the only hassle I had when I moved out was with her."

"She's here?"

"Right. She's here."

"How old is she?"

"A little older'n I am. Thirty-eight."

"Almost too late for kids anyway."

"I don't think she really ever wanted any," Colder said and took a glum sip of the beer that Dill thought must be flat by now. Colder didn't seem to think so.

"So what happened then?" Dill said. "I mean after she found out about Felicity?"

"You've already heard, haven't you?"

"Heard what?"

"That my wife threatened to kill Felicity."

"No, I didn't hear that."

"You will."

"Did she?"

"Threaten to? Sure."

"No," Dill said. "That's not what I mean."

"You mean did she kill Felicity?"

"Yes."

"No," Colder said. "She didn't."

"How'd your wife threaten her?"

"She'd call her up and yell at her. She'd call her up at home and say, 'If you don't keep away from my husband, I'll kill you.' She'd call her up at work, too. If Gertrude— that's her name—couldn't reach Felicity, she'd leave a message with whoever answered. Messages like 'This is Captain Colder's wife. Tell Detective Dill I'll kill her if she doesn't leave him alone.' That went on for a couple of weeks."

"Then what?"

Colder lit another one of his menthol cigarettes. He inhaled and made a face at what he tasted. Or at what he was about to say. "In this state, two doctors can commit. The department has two of them sort of on standby— guys that could have a little trouble with the state medical board, if we wanted to do something about it. We keep them on tap." He paused. "Isn't that awful?"

Dill nodded. "Yeah," he said. "It is."

"So I tucked her away for a month."

"Gertrude."

"Yeah. Gertrude."

"When was this?"

Colder ran time through his head. "A year ago in September."

"So she's been out—what? Ten or eleven months?"

"Right."

"And?"

"She's calmed down. They've got her on Valium. She's even seeing some guy she met in that place. I checked him out. He's an on-again, off-again juicer and they were drying him out when she met him. He's got a trust fund, which is what every juicer ought to have, so he doesn't have to worry about money. It brings him in a couple of thousand a month and sometimes he sells a little real estate. But what he does mostly is hang around Gertrude. He brings her flowers and takes her to the pictures and the plays, whenever one of them gets here, and she likes that kind of thing. He's older. In his early fifties, and I imagine he's fucking her, but not too often, and that'd sure be all right with her, too."

"She's agreed to the divorce then?" Dill said.

"Oh, yeah. She finally agreed to that after she got out."

"Where was she?"

"Millrun Farm. Ever hear of it?"

Dill nodded. "It used to be old Doc Lasker's place when he was the resident abortionist here. They'd come from all over back then—from New York, L.A., Memphis, Chicago. It used to be a pretty nice place, but that was years ago."

"It still is," Colder said. "Lasker died, you know."

Dill shook his head. "I didn't."

"He was old and his business had gone to hell anyway when they legalized abortion, so he sold it to a couple of young shrinks and they've made a go of it. God knows they charge enough."

Dill finished the last of his beer. "I wonder why Felicity never told me she was going to be married."

Colder shook his head as though bewildered. Dill didn't believe the gesture. Bewilderment had no more room in Colder's makeup than did humility. And whatever you are, Captain, you are not humble.

"She said she wrote you about it," Colder said.

"She didn't."

"Maybe it was because of Gertrude and everything."

"Maybe." Dill decided he wanted another beer. He looked toward the bar, caught the eye of Lucille, the waitress, and made a circular motion over the table with his forefinger pointing down. Lucille nodded her understanding. Dill turned back to Colder and smiled his most pleasant smile.

"Let me ask you something," Dill said, his smile now almost ablaze with warmth, understanding, and compassion.

Colder apparently didn't believe the smile for a moment. He took his elbows off the table and leaned back in his chair. It was a defensive position. When he replied his voice had resumed its utter-stranger tone. "Ask me what?"

"Where did Felicity live?" Dill carefully kept his smile alight.

"Thirty-second and Texas," Colder said without hesitation.

The smile went out and Dill shook his head regretfully. "I guess I didn't phrase it right."

"You asked where she lived. I told you. Thirty-second and Texas."

"That's where she camped out," Dill said. "I was there this afternoon. I poked around. Nobody lived there. Nobody. Somebody kept some clothes there. Somebody had a cup of coffee there once in a while. Now and then, somebody even slept there. But nobody lived there. At least, nobody named Felicity Dill. So what I'm asking, I guess, is where did Felicity really live? Your place? Is that where she spattered the stove with her rémoulade sauce, and read nine books at once and left most of them open on the floor, and smoked her two packs of Luckies a day, and weighed herself at least twice, and kept her kitchen stocked with enough food to last two months even if she knew she'd throw a lot of it out? That was my sister, Captain. That's how she lived. She wasn't obsessively neat. She didn't hang mail-order Impressionist prints on her wall. Give Felicity five minutes in a room, any room, and she made it look like she'd lived there forever. She was a nester, Captain, and she built her nests with things—odd things, funny things, even dumb things like the fire hydrant she bought when she was fifteen, welded the cut-down washtub on top of, and turned into the frontyard birdbath." Dill took a deep breath, held it for a long moment, then let it out and asked in a quiet, reasonable voice, "So where did she live, Captain?"

Lucille the waitress arrived with two beers and served them. She started to say something to Colder, but changed her mind when she saw his expression, and hurried away. Colder, still staring at Dill, put his left hand in his pants pocket, picked up his beer with his right hand, and drank several swallows.

After Colder put the beer down, he said, "Fillmore and Nineteenth. Know it?"

Dill ran the map of the city through his memory. The map proved to be indelible. "Fillmore dead-ends at the park, Washington Park, and then picks up on the other side. There're some old houses on the corner there. Very large old houses."

"Southwest corner. Seventeen thirty-eight Fillmore. An architect bought it and turned it into apartments. There's a garage apartment out back. On the alley. That was Felicity's." His left hand came out of his pocket and placed a single key on the table next to Dill's beer. "That's the key."

Dill looked at the key and then up at Colder. He thought that for a second he saw something in the other man's

eyes. Perhaps pain. But it went away almost immediately.
"Why two places?" Dill asked.

"I don't know."

"But you knew about both places."

"Christ, yes, I knew. Look, friend, maybe you should try to get something straight: I was going to *marry* her. Not because she could do my career any good. Not because she was rich. Not because she—aw hell. I loved her. That's why I was going to marry her."

The pain, Dill saw, was back in Colder's eyes. It didn't go away this time. "What'd she say—about having two places?"

"She said the other one, the duplex, was an investment for you and her. She said you were thinking of coming back here to live. She said you'd helped her buy it."

"She said that?"

Colder nodded, the pain in his eyes threatening to spread across the rest of his face.

"She lied," Dill said.

"Yeah," Colder said. "We both know that now, don't we."

CHAPTER

14

AFTER leaving Captain Colder, Dill went back down into the hotel's basement garage, retrieved the file on Jake Spivey from the Ford's glove compartment, and took the elevator from the garage up to the ninth floor. He planned to call Timothy Dolan in Washington and read him some of the more relevant passages from Spivey's deposition.

Dill unlocked the door to 981, pushed it open, and entered the room. He turned to close the door and the arm went around his neck. It was a thick arm, very muscular, very strong. Dill just had time to think chokehold and to notice that the arm's owner was neither panting nor breathing hard. Maybe he does it for a living, Dill thought, and then, with his oxygen and carotid artery shut off, and without enough air going down into his lungs and not enough blood flowing up into his brain, Dill lost consciousness and came to nine minutes later.

He found himself lying on the floor beside the bed. The first thing he did after opening his eyes was swallow.

Nothing had been crushed. Nothing even hurt very much—only a slight soreness in his throat that he felt would soon disappear. It's not much worse than it was when Jake and I found out how to do it to each other in the fifth grade, Dill thought. Except we didn't know it was called the carotid then. We just thought it was a neat way to pass out.

He sat up slowly, even warily, and looked around to see if the chokehold expert was still present. He wasn't. Dill patted his jacket breast pocket for his wallet. It was there. He took it out, looked inside, and counted the money. None had been taken. His watch was still on his left wrist. Dill got to his knees, then to his feet, and looked around for the file on Jake Spivey. It was only a brief glance, devoid of hope. He knew the file would be gone and it was.

Dill sat down on the bed and gingerly explored his throat with his right hand. The slight soreness was already going away. The brain damage would be minimal, he told himself, a few hundred thousand cells lost at most, but there are millions more and since you don't use them very much anyway, you're just as smart as ever, which means you can still cross wide streets by yourself.

He tried to remember all he could about the attacker. He remembered the forearm. It was one hell of a forearm, the right one probably, because the left hand would have been locked around the right wrist, exerting the pressure. Then there had been that easy, normal breathing. He didn't exactly panic while waiting for you to show up. His nerves, if he has any, are in fine shape. And his pulse rate probably shoots up to around seventy-two when he gets excited— if he ever does. Dill didn't need to feel his own pulse to know it was racing.

And since his attacker had done it so smoothly and with so little apparent effort, Dill decided he must have done it frequently in the past, which possibly indicates, Inspector, that before turning to his life of crime, he may well have been an honest policeman, or even a dishonest one, possibly from Los Angeles, where all chokehold champions are said to dwell. And this one could easily have qualified for the chokehold Olympics. There was the chance, of course, that he could have picked up his craft elsewhere. He could be a slightly crazed veteran of the Special Forces, a graying Green Beret, who'd learned all about chokeholds and silent killing down at Bragg, practiced them to perfection in Vietnam, and now peddled his hard-won skills to whoever would buy. Learn a trade in the army, they'd advised him, and he had.

Dill rose from the bed, crossed to the bottle of Old Smuggler that still sat on the writing desk, opened it, sniffed its contents suspiciously (for what? he asked himself. Cyanide?), poured slightly more than two ounces into a glass, and drank it down. It burned slightly and made him shudder, but no more so than usual.

After putting the glass down, Dill picked up the telephone, closed his eyes, remembered the number he wanted, and dialed it. It was answered on the third ring by the voice of Daphne Owens, who again recited the phone number's last four digits.

"This is Ben Dill again. I'd like to speak to Jake for a minute."

"Just a moment," she said, and ten seconds later Spivey was on the line, brimming with his usual good cheer. "I was about to call you, good buddy."

"What about?"

"Sunday. You're still gonna be in town Sunday, right? Well, the weatherman says it's gonna be another scorcher so I thought you might like to come out here and barbecue some ribs and jump in the pool and goggle some half-naked ladies. Spend the day."

"Sounds goods," Dill said. "Maybe I'll bring one."

"A half-naked lady?"

"Right."

"I sure admire the way you smooth city boys operate."

"I've got a problem, Jake."

"Big or little?"

"Little. I lost your deposition."

Spivey was silent for several moments. "Lost it?"

"Through carelessness."

"I guess I should ask where you lost it, and then you could say if you knew where you lost it, you'd go find it. So where'd you lose it?"

"I had it in my attaché case," Dill lied. "I put the case down at the newsstand here in the hotel to look at some magazines and when I reached down for it, it was gone."

"Lot of that going on downtown," Spivey said. "What else was in your case?"

Dill decided to embroider his tale. "My airline ticket, some papers, but nothing important. I was wondering if you could come up with another copy of your deposition."

"Nothing to it. All I have to do is ask one of the girls to push a button and the printer'll spit out another one. Goddamn computers are something, aren't they?" Before Dill could reply, Spivey went on, his tone musing. "Nothing in that deposition anyway. I mean nothing I gotta worry about. Tell you what, I'll have 'em print up another copy, get Daffy to notarize it, and send it down by one of my Mexican folks. Should be there in about an hour in case you've gotta call your people back in Washington and tell 'em what a fine job of work you're doing down here."

"You're a brick, Jake."

"Sure wish I knew how you spelled that. Now Sunday, why don't you come on out here about noon, you and your lady friend?"

"That sounds fine."

"See you Sunday then."

Dill thanked Spivey again and hung up. He stood, staring down at the phone, carefully memorizing the lies he had told Spivey, picked up the phone again, dialed eleven numbers, listened to the long-distance crackles and beeps, the ringing phone, and then the voice of Timothy Dolan saying, "Dolan."

"It's Ben, Tim."

"I've got some news. Clyde Brattle's back."

"Back where?"

"In the States. He crossed over from Canada."

"But they didn't spot him, right?"

"Not until two days later when one of them finally decided, hey, that guy looked kinda familiar, went through his mug book, and recognized Brattle."

"Where was this?"

"Detroit."

"When?"

Dolan either sighed or blew out some cigar smoke. "Ten days ago, but nobody ever got around to letting us know until this afternoon. The Senator'd already taken off for Santa Fe and some weekend politicking and I haven't been able to reach him yet. He's gonna raise all kinds of hell. I've raised my fair share already."

"Why do you think Brattle came back?"

"I'd say he might need to clear up a few loose ends."

"Like Spivey?"

"Maybe. You talk to him yet?"

"This afternoon."

"He agree to give you a deposition?"

"He already gave it to me, fully sworn."

"Anything in it?"

"It's what's not in it that's interesting."

"What's he want for what's not in it—immunity?"

"Right."

"What'd you say?"

"I nodded."

"Well, he can't get a nod on tape."

"There's something else," Dill said.

"I don't like your tone, Ben. It hints of calamity and unmitigated disaster."

"I got mugged."

124

"Jesus. When?"

"About fifteen minutes ago in my hotel room. They got the file on Spivey."

"What else?"

"That's all they wanted."

"They?"

"He was big enough to be a they. He used a chokehold on me, and no, I'm not hurt, but it was kind of you to ask."

"I'm thinking," Dolan said. "The file itself isn't important. We've got copies."

"And Spivey's going to send me another copy of his deposition. I told him somebody'd stolen my attaché case."

"You haven't got an attaché case."

"Spivey doesn't know that."

There was silence from the Washington end until Dolan said, "I was thinking some more. What was in the deposition—between the lines?"

"Between the lines, if I heard and read it right, Jake Spivey could hang Clyde Brattle, if he wanted to, and if we'd grant him immunity so he wouldn't hang himself at the same time."

"After Detroit," Dolan said slowly, "I wonder where Brattle went."

"You're not wondering, you're suggesting he's right here and that he wanted a quick peek at Spivey's file."

"It's a possibility."

"Maybe I'd better warn Jake."

"Go ahead, but if Clyde Brattle wants him dead, he's dead. Our problem is to keep Spivey alive long enough to—" Dolan broke off. "Look, if I can get it cleared up here, talk to the chairman and to that shit, Clewson, well..." His voice trailed off. Clewson was Norman Clewson, the subcommittee's majority counsel. Dolan despised him. "I can do it," he said suddenly.

"Do what?"

"Schedule a subcommittee hearing down there for next

Tuesday or Wednesday. The Senator can chair it. Hell, it's on his way back. I'll come down and we'll hold it in the federal building, give Spivey immunity, and let him talk his head off while he's still alive."

"They'll never clear it," Dill said.

"They'll clear it," Dolan said, his tone confident. "They won't have any fucking choice after I tell 'em if they don't, they'll never get Jake Spivey's unvarnished testimony because he'll goddamn well be dead."

"You really believe that?"

Dolan paused a short moment before answering. "Sure. Don't you?"

"You don't know Jake as well as I do."

"You mean Brattle might be the dead one?"

"He might."

"What the hell, Ben. If you're right, we still come out ahead."

CHAPTER

15

AT three minutes to six that Friday evening, Anna Maude Singe, the lawyer, answered her office phone with a crisp and businesslike "Anna Maude Singe."

"This is Ben Dill."

"Oh," she said. "Well. Hi."

"I wasn't sure I'd catch you."

"I was just leaving."

"The reason I'm calling is that they—they being the cops—are sending a limousine for me tomorrow, and I was wondering if you'd care to go with me to the services and then on out to the cemetery."

There was a brief silence until Singe finally said, "Yes. I'd like that." There was another pause and then she said, "I need to talk to you anyway."

"What about tonight?" Dill said.

"Tonight?"

"Dinner."

"You mean like a real date?"

"Reasonably close."

"With real food."

"That I can promise."

"Well, it sounds better than Lean Cuisine. Where'll I meet you?"

"Why don't I pick you up?"

"You mean at home?"

"Sure."

"Christ," she said, "it really is like a real date, isn't it?"

Anna Maude Singe lived at 22nd and Van Buren in a seven-story apartment building that had been built in early 1929 by that same syndicate of oil men who later bought the bankrupt speculator's skyscraper. Ostensibly, the oil men built the faintly Georgian building to house the parents of the new oil rich who didn't want the old folks underfoot anymore. It was a well-thought-out, carefully designed building, and the new oil rich promptly snapped up long leases—only to discover that their parents balked at the idea of apartment living (most thought it wicked) and refused to set foot in the place.

The syndicate members, stuck in 1930 with what seemed to be a white elephant, had shrugged and lodged their own girl friends and mistresses in what came to be known derisively as the Old Folks Home, although its real name was the Van Buren Towers.

It was a solid, extremely well-built structure that employed a lavish amount of Italian marble, especially in the rather gaudy bathrooms. Later, as the oil men and their paramours aged, parted, and died, the apartments began commanding premium rents, with two-bedroom units going in late 1941 for as much as a hundred dollars a month. To the delight of the lucky tenants at the time, it was there that rents were frozen by wartime controls until late in 1946.

Dill had been in the building only once, and that was back in 1959 when evil Jack Sackett had invited him and Jake Spivey up to meet Sackett's "Aunt Louise," a thirty-three-year-old beauty who turned out to be the well-kept girl friend of Sackett's father, then the Speaker of the state House of Representatives. Aunt Louise had served her young gentlemen callers Coca-Cola and bourbon and later led them one by one into her bedroom. Dill and Spivey were not quite fourteen. Sackett, the future premier pool hustler of the West Coast, was fifteen. It remained for Dill a memorable summer afternoon.

As he waited in the Van Buren's marble lobby for the lone elevator that would lift him up to the fifth floor, Dill noticed how the lobby's rugs were now a bit frayed, its walls soiled by sticky fingers, and its thick glass door in need of washing. In the elevator, which smelled of dog urine, he tried to remember Aunt Louise's apartment number, but couldn't. Dill knew better than to hope Anna Maude Singe's number would be the same.

She was wearing a striped, nubby cotton caftan when she opened the door after he pushed the ivory-colored button. She smiled and stepped back. As he went in, she said, "Welcome to faded splendor."

Dill looked around. "You're right. It is."

"You know its lurid history? The building, I mean."

He nodded.

"Well, this particular apartment was occupied from 1930 till early last year by one Eleanor Ann Washburn, but then Miss Ellie up and died, leaving it all to me—furniture, clothing, books, paintings, everything—including her memories. It went condominium, you know."

Dill said he didn't.

"Back in seventy-two," she said.

"Why'd she leave it to you?"

"I helped her straighten out the royalties on some oil leases that old Ace Dawson gave her back in the early thirties. She was Ace's fancy lady. He gave her what she called a slop jar full of leases that played out in the fifties, but when the oil crisis came along—not the one in seventy-three, but the one in seventy-nine—well, it became profitable to start stripping those old wells. So after the oil-company man came around, Miss Ellie sent for me because she said she never met a land man in her life who wasn't crooked as cat shit and she claimed she ought to know. I got her the best deal I could, which wasn't bad, and then she went to another lawyer and changed her will and left me her condo and everything in it."

"And she was Ace Dawson's girl friend?"

"One of them. She told me he had a half-dozen or so scattered all over the state."

"I know the guy who bought his house."

"Jake Spivey," she said.

"You know Jake?"

"Everybody talks about him, but not too many seem to know him."

"Like to meet him?"

"You're serious."

"Sure."

"When?"

"Sunday. They're going to barbecue some ribs and jump in his pool."

"Sunday," she said.

Dill nodded.

"What time?"

"We'd start out there about noon."

"All day then?"

"Probably."

"Well, I'm no star-fucker, but I'd kill to see the inside of that house."

Dill grinned. "You think Jake's a star?"

She shrugged. "In this town he passes for one." She glanced around the room and frowned. "What're you standing up for anyway? Sit down." She indicated an easy chair that was covered in an unworn but faded floral fabric. The flora seemed to be intertwined red and yellow roses with sharp thorns and very pale green stems. Dill sat down. Anna Maude Singe smiled. "Like I said, faded splendor." She turned and moved toward the hall entrance. "I'll be back."

While she was gone, Dill examined the sizable living room and its ten-foot ceiling. The walls were of thick combed cream plaster. The furnishings all smacked of the thirties and forties. There was even a Capehart record player, the automatic kind that picked up the 78-rpm records after they were played and dropped them gently down a padded slot. Dill remembered seeing one in operation at a friend's house in Alexandria, Virginia. The friend had called it an antique.

The rest of the furniture had sharp angular lines, and it all seemed to be either seldom used or recently upholstered. The colors, except for the faded floral easy chair, were muted shades of brown and tan and cream and off-white, although there were a lot of bright red, yellow, and orange pillows scattered about. Dill thought the pillows went nicely with the large Maxfield Parrish print of "Daybreak." He got up to inspect it more closely, trying to figure out whether the teenage figures in it were boys or girls. He was still undecided when Anna Maude Singe returned wearing a cream silk dress whose hem ended just below her knees. Dill thought the dress looked both elegant and expensive. He smiled and said, "You look awfully nice."

She glanced down at the dress, which had a scooped neck and very short sleeves. "This old thing. I can honestly say that because it's either forty-eight or forty-nine years old and it's real Chinese watered silk. Miss Ellie and I were just about the same size—at least, way back then she was. Later, she got a little fat."

On the way down in the elevator, Anna Maude Singe laid out in succinct fashion what steps Dill should take to collect on his dead sister's two hundred and fifty thousand-dollar insurance policy. On the way to his parked car, she outlined the obstacles he might encounter if he tried to sell the yellow brick duplex. Dill found her review both concise and objective. As they got into the Ford, he said, "I think I might need a lawyer."

She shrugged. "You might."

He put the key in the ignition and started the engine. "You can be my lawyer."

She said nothing. Dill pulled away from the curb. After driving a block, he said, "Well?"

"I'm thinking."

"About what?"

"About whether I want to be your lawyer."

"Christ, I'm not asking you to marry me."

"It's not you," she said. "You'd make a nice dull client. It's Felicity."

"Felicity's dead."

"I still represent her estate."

"So?"

"There might be a conflict of interest."

"My one year of law school, though dimly remembered, tells me that's just so much bullshit."

She turned to look at him, resting her back against the door and tucking her feet up beneath her on the seat. "Felicity used to talk to me—confide in me, actually, as both her friend and attorney. Sometimes it's hard to decide where legal confidentiality begins and ends."

"You're not making sense."

"That's because I don't think I should say anything else."

Dill glared at her and returned his attention to the road ahead. "I'm her goddamned brother," he said, "not the fucking IRS. My sister's been killed. She was leading a pretty strange life before they blew her away. She bought a duplex she hardly lived in with money she didn't have. She took out a two hundred and fifty thousand dollar life insurance policy, paid cash for it, and died three weeks later—right on schedule. Doesn't anyone wonder—you, for instance—where the hell the money was coming from? Doesn't anyone, for God's sake, think the money and the killer might be connected? But all you do is sit there and talk about confidentiality. Jesus, lady, if you know something, go tell the cops. Felicity's dead. She won't mind if you reveal her confidences. She won't mind about anything at all."

"That's a red light," Singe said.

"I know it's a red light," Dill said, jamming on the brakes and locking the Ford's wheels.

They sat at the red light silently until she said, "Okay. I'll be your lawyer."

Dill shook his head dubiously. "I don't know if you're even smart enough to be my lawyer. After all, I've got some awfully complicated affairs that need untangling. I've got to sell a house and collect on an insurance policy. That might require some pretty fancy legal footwork. It might even involve writing one letter and making two, maybe even three phone calls."

"The light's green," she said.

"I know it's green," Dill said, and sent the car speeding across the intersection.

"Well?" she said.

"Well what?"

"You want me to be your lawyer?"

Dill sighed. "Aw, hell. Why not. What d'you want to eat?"

"Sweetbreads."

He looked at her and grinned. "Really?"

"I crave sweetbreads," she said.

"That means Packingtown. Chief Joe's?"

"Where else."

"Jesus," Dill said happily. "Sweetbreads."

•   •   •

Everything south of the Yellowfork was called Packingtown even though Armour had long gone, as had Swift, and now only Wilson remained to butcher the hogs and the steers and the occasional lamb—occasional because eating lamb was generally held to be kind of a sissy thing to do. The Yellowfork, of course, was the river that everyone described as being a mile wide and an inch deep—not a very original description, but the city had never placed much of a premium on originality.

Sometimes there was water in the Yellowfork, quite a lot of water, but at other times, like now, it was only a wide meandering river of bright yellow dry sand lined with willows and cottonwoods.

For years the Yellowfork had served the city as a convenient line of economic and social demarcation. South of it lived the poor white and the other, variously colored poor. Although the lines became somewhat smudged after World War Two, it was largely out of convenience and habit that everything south of the Yellowfork was still called Packingtown. JFK High School actually called its football team the Kennedy Packers. And even though all but one of the abattoirs were now gone, there were times, Dill knew, when on a hot summer evening with the wind from the south just right, you could still smell the stench of the doomed and dying cattle. You could even smell it as far north as Cherry Hills.

Dill felt he was almost on automatic pilot as he drove south on Van Buren, east on Our Jack, then turned south again at the Hawkins Hotel onto Broadway. South of the hotel, Broadway maintained its respectability fairly well until it reached South Fourth Street, or Deep Four, as the natives called it. After Deep Four, South Broadway was a mess. South Fourth, Third, Second, and First Streets had once comprised almost the only black enclave north of the Yellowfork. The former ghetto was now fully integrated and populated largely with the dregs of all races, creeds, and sexes—the last being sometimes rather ambiguous. Both the respectable and the not-so-respectable blacks had long since moved as far uptown as they could afford, abandoning the Deep Four area to the lowlife and their often grisly pursuits. Dill remembered his sister had worked the South Broadway-Deep Four area shortly after she transferred into homicide. The area was mostly bars, dives, liquor stores, porno flicks, and small cheap hotels with fancied-up names like the Biltmore, the Homestead, the Ritz, and the Belvedere. There were also a large number of elderly tacked-together frame houses with wide front porches. The people who sat out on the porches looked hot, mean, sullen, and desperate enough to revolt, if only it would cool off some. The temperature shortly after 7 P.M. was 95 degrees. The sun had not yet gone down. A lot of the front-porch sitters drank beer from cans and wore nothing but their underwear. There was no breeze.

"Where'd all the whores come from?" Dill asked as they neared South First Street.

"From the unemployment office," Singe said. "Felicity used to talk to them sometimes. They all told her it was either fuck or starve."

They stopped at a red light. A man staggered off the curb, made his way around the front of the Ford, and halted at Dill's window. The man was about thirty-five. He wore a soiled green undershirt and khaki pants. Dill couldn't see his shoes. He had blue eyes that seemed to float on small ponds of pink. He needed a shave. Something white and nasty was caked around his mouth. He tapped on Dill's window with a large rock. Dill rolled the window down.

"Gimme a quarter, mister, or I'll bust your goddamn windshield," the man said with absolutely no inflection.

"Fuck off," Dill said, and rolled up the window. The man stepped back and took careful aim at the windshield with his rock. Dill sped off, running the red light.

"I should've given him the quarter."

"You shouldn't even have rolled down your window," Singe said.

Just past South First Street, Broadway started curving right to where the bridge over the Yellowfork began. The four-lane concrete bridge had been built in 1938 and named after the then Secretary of the Interior, Harold F. Ickes. When Truman fired MacArthur in 1951, the city council—almost alight with patriotic glow—had renamed the bridge after the five-star general, but nearly everybody still called it what they had always called it, the First Street Bridge.

As they started up the bridge's steep approach, Dill asked, "Why didn't they tear down Deep Four and South Broadway when they were tearing down everything else?"

"They thought about it," Singe said. "But then they got scared."

"Of what?"

"Scared all the creeps and weirdos would move someplace else—maybe even next door."

"Oh," Dill said.

CHAPTER

16

FOR dinner they had sweetbreads and okra and black-eyed peas and cole slaw and cornbread, buttermilk to drink, and for dessert, lemon meringue pie. They sat under the bearded head of a bison that had been dead for thirty-nine years. The walls of Chief Joe's were covered with the stuffed heads of bison, deer, elk, moose, bobcat, mountain lion, coyote, wolf, bighorn sheep, and three kinds of bear. After Dill and Anna Maude Singe finished their dinner they agreed it would be what they'd both order if ever they had to order the last supper.

The restaurant had been started by Joseph Maytubby, who was part Cherokee and part Choctaw with a little Kiowa thrown in. Everyone had called him Chief because that's what all Indians were called. Maytubby had been an army cook in France during the First World War. He stayed on after the war, married a twenty-three-year-old Frenchwoman, brought her back to the city, and together they started Chez Joseph in 1922. It was only a counter and four tables to begin with, but the food was superb, and once the cattlemen discovered what Madame Maytubby could do with mountain oysters, it became one of the two most popular restaurants in Packingtown. The other was Puncher's, which specialized in steaks. You could also order a steak at Chief Joe's, but few ever did, and asked instead for such specialties as sweetbreads, mountain oysters, brains and eggs, lamb stew, real oxtail soup, and the wonderful no-name dish the restaurant prepared from wild duck when it was in season.

The mounted animal heads had begun when a cattleman customer shot a grizzly up in the Canadian Rockies in 1927. He had the head stuffed and presented it to Chief Joe. Not knowing what else to do with it, Chief Joe hung it on the wall. Then everyone else who shot anything started presenting him with their prey's mounted heads until the walls were covered with glass-eyed animals. Chief Joe died in 1961; his wife in '66. Their only son, Pierre Maytubby, took over and a few old customers tried to call him Chief Pete, but he wouldn't stand for it. Under Pierre, the restaurant's quality remained the same as did the sign outside, which still read Chez Joseph, although no one had ever called it that except Madame Maytubby.

When the coffee and cognac came, Dill leaned back and grinned at Anna Maude Singe. Their table was in front of one of the banquettes, and Singe was seated against the wall directly under the dead bison, who was beginning to look a bit motheaten.

"You like buttermilk with your dinner," Dill said. "I'm not sure I ever went out with a woman who liked buttermilk with her dinner."

"I've even been known to drink it for breakfast."

"That takes a certain amount of guts."

"What do you have for breakfast?"

"Coffee," Dill said. "It used to be coffee and cigarettes, but I quit smoking. Remarque called coffee and a cigarette the soldier's breakfast. I read that at an impressionable age."

"Were you ever a soldier?"

"Why?"

She shrugged. "You were about the right age for Vietnam."

"I wasn't in Vietnam."

"But you were overseas."

"I was abroad. Civilians go abroad; soldiers go overseas."

"So you weren't a soldier."

"No."

"Some guys say they feel guilty now about having missed out on Vietnam."

"Middle-class college-educated white guys?"

Singe nodded. "They feel they missed out on something they'll never get another chance at."

"They did," Dill said. "They missed out on getting their butts shot off, although I don't think they would have. You didn't find too many middle-class college-educated white guys in the line companies."

"You don't seem to feel guilty," she said.

"I had a deferment. I was the sole support of an eleven-year-old orphan."

"Would you have gone?"

"To Vietnam? I don't know."

"Suppose they said, 'Okay, Dill, you're drafted. Report down to the Post Office for induction next Tuesday.' What would you've done?"

"I would've either gone down to the Post Office or up to Canada. One out of conviction; the other out of curiosity."

She studied him for several moments. "I think you would've gone down to the Post Office."

Dill smiled. "Maybe not."

"What'd you do overseas? I mean abroad?"

"Didn't Felicity tell you?"

"No."

"I thought she used to talk about me."

"About when you all were growing up. Not about when you were in Washington or overseas."

"Abroad."

She smiled. "Right. Abroad. What'd you do over there?"

"I poked around."

"Who for?"

"The government."

Anna Maude Singe frowned, and when she did, Dill smiled. "Don't worry, I wasn't with the agency, although I used to bump into them from time to time."

"What're those CIA folks really like?" she said. "You read about them. They make picture shows about them. But I never met one. I don't think I ever came close to meeting one."

"They were..." Dill paused, trying to remember just how they really had been. He recalled sharp noses and close-set ears and bitten fingernails and prim mouths with self-important expressions. "I guess you'd have to say they were sort of...like me. Stuffy."

"Stuffy?"

He nodded.

"All of them?" she asked.

"I didn't know all of them. But Sunday you get to meet one who wasn't very stuffy."

"Who?"

"Jake Spivey."

"*Jake Spivey* was with the *CIA*. Good Lord!"

"They won't admit it, but he was. Maybe Jake'll tell you some stories. He went to Vietnam and Laos and Cambodia, but he didn't go out of patriotism, or because he got drafted, or even out of curiosity. Jake went because at twenty-three they were the only outfit around who'd pay him a thousand bucks a week to do whatever he did."

"What'd he do?"

"Jake? I guess Jake probably killed a lot of people."
"Does it bother him?"
"You mean does he feel guilty?"
She nodded.
"Jake never felt guilty about anything."

Dill chose another route back to Anna Maude Singe's apartment building. He took South Cleveland Avenue until it turned into North Cleveland just on the other side of the Yellowfork. He followed North Cleveland for a little more than two miles until he reached 22nd Street, and then cut east to Van Buren and the Old Folks Home.

Singe didn't wait for him to open the car door for her. As she got out, she said, "All I've got is some California brandy."

Dill took that for an invitation and said he thought California brandy had a lot going for it, especially the price. Up in her apartment Dill resumed his inspection of the large Maxfield Parrish print while she went for the brandy. When she returned with the bottle and two balloon glasses, Dill had almost decided the two figures in the painting were girls. He also noticed Singe had changed back into the striped nubby cotton caftan. From the way her breasts moved underneath the fabric, he was sure she was wearing nothing else. He took this for yet another invitation of sorts, and wondered whether he would accept or send regrets.

Singe sat down on the off-white couch, put the glasses on the free-form glass coffee table, and poured two brandies. While she did that, Dill took out his checkbook, quickly wrote a check for five hundred dollars to Anna Maude Singe, added "legal retainer" in the memo space, tore it out, and handed it to her.

She read the check, put it carefully down on the table, looked at him coldly, and said, "That was a pretty goddamned rude thing to do."

He nodded. "Yes, I guess it was."

"This isn't my office. This is where I live—my home. Where I carry on my social life and also my sex life, such as it is. I was thinking that tonight I might even enrich both of them a little, but I guess I was wrong."

"You accept the check?" Dill said.

She hesitated before answering. "What the hell is this?"

"You accept the check?" Dill said again.

"All right. Yes. I accept it."

"Then you really are my attorney—retained at a modest fee, I'll admit—and if I get into trouble with the law, you'll come running, right?"

"What kind of trouble?"

"That's another question, not an answer."

"Okay. I'll come running. What kind of trouble?"

"When I was overseas—"

"Abroad," she interrupted.

He didn't smile. "Right. When I was over there poking around, I developed a kind of instinct. I don't know what else to call it. But I learned to depend on it. It was a kind of warning system."

"Hunch," she said.

"Okay. Hunch is good. But it kept me out of trouble a few times because I made sure I had both backup and a fallback position. Well, ever since I got here I've been getting those same faint signals."

"You're talking about Felicity and all that."

"Partly."

She drank a little of her brandy. "You said trouble with the law."

"So I did."

"So what're we really talking about—plot, conspiracy, paranoia, what?"

"Let's try paranoia," Dill said. "At around five o'clock this evening I went up to my room in the hotel. A very large arm went around my neck in a chokehold. I passed out for about nine minutes. When I came to, I still had my watch, my wallet, and all my money."

"What was gone?"

"The file on Jake Spivey."

"What file?"

"I work for a Senate subcommittee. It's investigating Spivey."

"Your friend."

"My oldest."

"Does he know?"

"Sure he knows."

She frowned. "You call getting mugged a hunch." She shook her head. "No, of course you don't. That was the two-by-four somebody slammed you across the nose with to grab your attention." Her eyes widened, not much, but just enough to make Dill relax as he congratulated himself on his choice of lawyers. She senses it, he told himself, but she's not quite sure just what it is. But neither are you.

"What else?" Singe said.

"What else," Dill repeated, picked up his glass, and drank some of the brandy, noting that the California vintners still had a way to go before overtaking their French competitors. "Well, 'what else' includes an old reporter on the *Tribune* who already has the whole story on Felicity's funny finances, except he's holding back on it until he gets the word."

"From whom?"

"He didn't say and I knew better than to ask. Then there's Felicity's ex-boyfriend, the frightener and one-time football great."

"Clay Corcoran," she said.

"I thought he gave up on being jilted too easily, but Felicity's tenant, the female one, more or less confirms his story. The tenant's name is Cindy McCabe. She took off her halter to let me admire her bare bosom. She also claimed she'd once made a pass at Felicity, but got turned down."

"Did you turn her down?"

"I'm afraid so. I was late for my next appointment, which I didn't know I had at the time, but which turned out to be with Captain Colder, the bereaved fiancé. Captain Colder gave me the key to a garage apartment where Felicity really lived." Dill reached into his jacket pocket, brought out the key Colder had given him, and placed it on the glass table. "The apartment's over on Fillmore and Nineteenth, not too far from here."

"Across from Washington Park," she said.

"You know it?" he said. "I mean did you know she had an apartment there?"

Singe slowly shook her head. "No. I didn't."

"And you were her lawyer, her confidante, her friend. Didn't she ever invite you over?"

"Just to the duplex. I was over there quite a few times. I told her I thought it looked a little bare, even a little sterile. That it didn't look like her. She said she wasn't there much because she was spending most of her free nights with Colder."

"Felicity tell you about Mrs. Colder?"

Singe nodded and looked away. "He committed her."

"You know why?"

"Because she drank too much."

"That's not quite it. He committed her because she threatened to kill Felicity, not just once, but often."

"Felicity never told me that," Singe said in a voice that was almost a whisper.

Dill picked up the key Colder had given him. He held it up for Singe to see. "I want to use this tomorrow after the funeral. I want to go see where Felicity really lived. I want you to go with me."

"You want a witness."

"Right."

"Okay. Fine." She finished the rest of her brandy, put the glass down, and looked at her watch. "It's late," she said. "You want to stay here or go home?"

Dill didn't answer for several seconds. "I think I'll go home."

She nodded and rose quickly, as if to speed the parting guest. Dill also rose. She stood looking at him, a bemused half-smile on her face. He took her in his arms and kissed her. It was a long greedy kiss that neither seemed willing to end. Dill's hands went exploring and discovered a remarkable body. Just before they both reached the sexual terrain from which there could be no retreat, she tore her lips and tongue away, stepped back, and said, "Something's happening, isn't it?"

"You mean with us?"

She shook her head. "That'll happen or it won't. I mean something else, something lousy."

"Yes," Dill said. "I think so."

She gave her head a small puzzled shake and then went with him to the door, where they kissed again. This time it was more definitive than before. Questions were asked and answered. Needs and proclivities stated. Mild aberrations noted. When it was over Dill felt they knew and even liked one another much better. He smiled at her, and instead of murmuring something tender, asked, "Where did Felicity say she got all the money?"

Singe didn't seem to expect anything tender. It was as if they had already gone past all that and were now approaching absolute intimacy. She frowned and said, "For the down payment on the duplex and everything?"

Dill nodded.

"From you." She added a small wry smile. "She said you'd got rich."

"Too bad she was lying."

"Yes," Anna Maude Singe said. "Isn't it though."

CHAPTER

17

DILL parked the Ford sedan in the basement garage of the Hawkins Hotel, got out, locked it, and headed for the elevator. As he passed the second large square concrete pillar a man stepped out from behind it and said, "How's the neck?"

Dill stopped short. His right hand moved almost involuntarily to his neck. "Still a little sore," he said.

Another man joined the first man. The second man was thin the way a knife is thin and about six feet tall. He looked short and frail next to the first man, who was well over six-three and built like a weight lifter who had given it up when he reached forty, which Dill guessed was three years back, possibly four. The weight lifter had thinning gray-blond hair, still blue eyes, and a wide happy mouth. The knifelike man had dyed black hair the color of coal, dead blue eyes, and a tight mouth that looked either sad or mean. Mean, Dill decided.

Both men wore rumpled summer suits of tan poplin.

The weight lifter wore a blue shirt; the skinny man had chosen white. Neither wore a tie. The suitcoats were buttoned and seemed a trifle large. Dill assumed that the coats concealed the pistols, since neither man looked as if he'd bother with a jacket once the temperature rose above 80 degrees. As Dill had driven down Our Jack Street on his way to the hotel, he noticed that the First National Bank sign was claiming a temperature of 87 degrees at 1:17 A.M.

"Says his neck's still a little sore," the weight lifter said.

The other man nodded regretfully. "I'm sorry." He studied Dill for a moment. "We don't want any trouble, Mr. Dill."

"Neither do I," Dill said.

The lean man nodded toward the far end of the garage. "We're down there in the van," he said and started walking toward a large blue Dodge van that was parked head-out against the wall. Dill hesitated. The weight lifter smiled pleasantly and opened his coat. The pistol was there. Dill got only a glimpse of it, but it seemed to be a short-barreled revolver. The weight lifter nodded toward the van. Dill turned and fell into step behind the lean man.

When they reached the van the lean man slid the side door back, revealing a customized interior. Dill could see the small sink, propane stove, refrigerator, and the floor which was carpeted with tan shag. The walls were paneled with what seemed to be wood, although Dill suspected it was some kind of grained plastic. There were no windows in the rear of the van.

"You'll find a nice comfy chair on your left," the lean man said.

"Where're we going?" Dill asked.

"Nowhere."

The weight lifter touched Dill's shoulder lightly and nodded at the van's interior. Dill stepped up and into the van, turned left, saw first the chair, and then the man who was seated at the rear of the van behind a table. On the table were some glasses, a bottle of Smirnoff vodka, a Thermos bucket of ice, three bottles of Schweppes tonic, and the file on Jake Spivey. The last time Dill had seen the man behind the table had been in Genoa. In the Hotel Plaza on the Piazza Corvetto. There had been four persons gathered in the living room of the suite on the fifth floor. Suite 523, he recalled, surprising himself with his memory. There had been Dill, the then Mrs. Dill, Jake Spivey, and the man who now sat behind the table, Clyde Brattle.

Brattle smiled. "Well," he said. "Ben."

"Well, Clyde," Dill said and indicated the contour swivel chair that was covered with a very good imitation leather, "This mine?"

"Please."

Dill sat down in the chair and found it to be quite comfortable. The two men came into the van. The lean one sat down across from Dill in a twin contour chair. Dill couldn't see where the weight lifter sat. On the floor maybe. Dill turned to look. The weight lifter was seated on a hinged stool that swung out and down from the kitchen unit. It was for sitting on while you scrape the carrots, Dill thought.

"Remarkably compact units, aren't they?" Brattle said after Dill turned back.

"Remarkably."

"That's Sid across from you and behind you is Harley."

"Harley and Sid," Dill said.

"It's been a while, hasn't it?" Brattle paused. "Seven years?"

"Closer to eight. Genoa. Hotel Plaza. Suite five-twenty-three. Your suite."

Brattle smiled in appreciation of Dill's memory. "I believe you're right. And how's the charming Mrs. Dill?"

"She's fine and we're divorced."

"Really. I didn't know, or if I did, I guess I forgot." He

frowned. It made him look thoughtful, solemn, almost sincere. "I read about your sister, Ben." Brattle paused exactly long enough. "I'm sorry."

Dill nodded.

"Funeral's tomorrow, I understand."

"Yes."

"I assume that's the real reason you're down here." Brattle tapped the file on Jake Spivey with a forefinger. "And not because of this garbage." He smiled warmly. "How is Jake, anyway?"

"Jake's fine."

"Old Jake." Brattle shook his head, still beaming in evident appreciation of that old rapscallion Jake Spivey's many endearing qualities. The head that Brattle shook was handsome in the way that busts of long-dead Roman statesmen are often handsome—but not too handsome. The features are never too regular. The expressions are never too remote. The blank eyes never betray anything. Dill had once spent a long rainy Spanish afternoon studying a roomful of such busts in Merida. He had seen on those long-dead faces what he now saw on the face of Clyde Brattle: worldliness, cool detachment, and utter cynicism. He felt it must have been a useful mind-set back in Roman times, what with the Visigoths on the way down from the east and the north.

Now fifty-five, Brattle could easily have passed for one of those banished Roman consuls who had served too long in some dreary distant province. There were that same faint curl of lip, that same thin haughty nose, and those same illusionless eyes of no particular color unless winter rain has color. The shortish hair finally had gone gray—gray-sky gray—but it was still thick, unparted, and combed with the fingers only, if at all. The voice was still that scratchy overeducated drawl from which any regional trace had long since been excised.

"What would you say to a drink?" Brattle asked.

"I'd say fine."

"Good."

Sid, the lean one, rose and silently mixed two vodka-tonics. He set one in front of Brattle and handed the other to Dill. Brattle took a swallow, sighed, and smiled. "I suppose you heard I was back," he said.

Dill nodded. "They say you crossed at Detroit."

"It's rather tedious, as you well know, Ben, being on the dodge like this." He looked at the man called Sid. "Mr. Dill used to be with Jasper, Sid."

"No shit," Sid said. "Who's Jasper?"

"It's a what, not a who," came the voice of the weight lifter from his perch on the stool.

"You're right, Harley," Brattle said. "It *was* a what. The Ford White House set it up shortly after Mr. Nixon's rather sodden farewell. How much do you think he'd put away that day, Ben? The best part of a fifth?"

"I don't know," Dill said. "I don't know how well he could handle it."

"So why'd they call whatever it was Jasper?" Sid asked.

"It's my understanding," Brattle said, "and Ben can correct me if I'm wrong, that when the negotiations were going on for Mr. Nixon's pardon, Mr. Ford was shocked to learn that, in his words, 'Some Jasper's made off with three million fucking dollars.' From all that money that was floating around back then. The Committee for the Re-Election of the President. The CREEP money."

"Sure," Sid said. "I remember that. I always did wonder who got well off of that deal."

"So they set up Jasper," Brattle continued, "and brought some people in, outside people, untainted people, like Ben here, and set them off in pursuit of the missing swag. All extremely sub rosa. Not even Langley knew about it. Or the FBI. In fact, both were rather high up on the list of suspects, right, Ben?"

"Right."

"So Ben here and a few other patriots spent the years of the Ford administration roaming over Europe looking for the Jaspers who'd made off with the three million fucking dollars. You had nearly a year in London, didn't you, Ben, and then almost two years in Barcelona?"

"About that."

"So what happened?" Harley asked from the van's galley. "I never did hear what happened."

"Nothing happened. Although you did come close, didn't you, Ben?"

"Very close."

"I like to think that Jake and I were of some help."

"You helped, Clyde."

"But not quite enough." Brattle sighed. "They were dead by then—the Jaspers, I mean. There were three of them as I recall." He looked at Dill for confirmation.

"Three," Dill agreed.

"Two men and a woman. A messy combination when you think about it. Doomed to failure."

"So who finally got the money—the three million?" Sid asked.

Dill looked at him. "The people who killed them."

"Oh," Sid said with a look of total understanding. "Yeah, well, sure. I can see that." He nodded as if it all made perfect sense.

"And Ben here had a perfectly splendid three years or so in Europe." Brattle looked at Dill and smiled. "They were good years, weren't they, Ben?"

"As you say, Clyde, they were splendid."

Brattle was wearing a white polo shirt which made his deep tan look even deeper. The shirt had no identifying brand on its pocket. Dill suspected Brattle would gladly have paid bespoke prices for the shirt as long as it bore no trademark. He now reached into the shirt's pocket, produced a gold Swiss gas lighter, picked up a pack of Gauloises from the table, and offered them to Dill, who refused with a shake of his head. Brattle lit one of the cigarettes, inhaled gratefully, and blew the smoke out. His fifth smoke of the day, Dill thought. Maybe his sixth.

"You've been with the subcommittee how long now—three years?" Brattle asked.

"About that."

"As a consultant."

"Right."

"Pay anything?"

"Enough."

"Spartan habits, simple needs, right?"

"Absolutely."

"You and young Senator Ramirez have a good working relationship, I presume."

"Based on warm mutual respect."

Brattle smiled at Dill's answer and its edge of sarcasm. "And then there's the minority counsel, young Mr. Dolan. Timothy, isn't it?"

"Timothy."

"Schooled by the Jesuits and the old pols of Boston. Who could wish for a sounder or more practical education? He is a man of some ambition, I suppose—young Tim?"

"He's a professional Boston Democrat, Clyde."

"It goes without saying then." Brattle had another swallow of his drink and another deep drag on his cigarette, which Dill envied him. "As you no doubt suspect, Ben, I have a proposition for the Senator—and young Dolan, too, of course."

Dill nodded.

"I'm willing to take my medicine, you might say."

"How much medicine, Clyde?"

"Perhaps two years in one of the more relaxed federal hoosegows and a reasonable fine of, well, not more than two or three hundred thousand." He smiled. It was a warm smile that spoke of unshakable self-confidence.

"Two years instead of life, right?" Dill said.

"Life is such an indeterminate sentence. Once the prison gates clang shut behind me—they do clang, don't they?—I could be dead in a week, and think how cheated everyone would feel then."

"In some joints I know," Sid said, "you might not even last the week, Clyde, once the boogies get a look at your sweet ass."

"What does the Senator get?" Dill asked.

"A tidy package. He could go to the Justice people with three, plus me, which equal four, if my arithmetic still serves."

"Which three are you willing to shop?"

"Dick Glander for one and also Frank Cour. They could drop the net on both of them within twenty-four hours."

"Glander and Cour and you go back quite a long way, don't you? Nineteen years, twenty?"

Brattle nodded, a slight sad smile on his lips. "Nineteen." He shrugged and the slight sad smile went away. "But the time comes in a man's life when even the oldest friendships must be sacrificed to serve the common good. Fortunately, I have everything on them—good solid stuff—and they have virtually nothing on me. Were the roles reversed, well, I'd expect them both to make the same hard choice I've made. In other words, I'd expect them to do me before I did them." He smiled again, this time with genuine amusement. "My sanctimony isn't getting to you, is it, Ben?"

"It's refreshing," Dill said. "I'm a little worried though about your arithmetic. You said three. Glander and Cour only add up to two."

Harley chuckled from his stool in the galley. "You forgot somebody, Clyde."

Sid made a noise deep down in his throat, which Dill interpreted as a kind of merriment. Still making the noise, Sid winked at Dill and nodded at Brattle as if to say, Old Clyde.

Brattle himself shot his eyebrows up to register fake amazement. "My God, don't tell me I forgot Jake?"

"You forgot Jake, Clyde," said Sid, still making the merry noise down in his throat.

Brattle lowered his eyebrows and again smiled at Dill. "And Jake makes three, plus me, which is four, as I said."

"What've you got on Jake?" Dill asked.

"On Jake?" Brattle said. The smile faded. "In all candor, Ben—in all earnestness—I've got enough on Jake Spivey to land him three consecutive life sentences without hope of parole."

"Three at least," Harley said. "Maybe even four."

"Jake is my prize package," Brattle continued. "My ultimate quid pro quo. My gilt-edged annuity. My irresistible bait. My ticket to the golden years of well-earned rest and retirement. Jake's done terrible things, Ben—terrible, awful, shocking things."

"Jake's bad all right," Sid agreed.

"Unspeakable deeds," Brattle told Dill with a new and cheerful smile. "And I can prove them all. Tell the Senator that—and young Dolan, too."

"Okay," Dill said.

"Good," Brattle said. "Oh," he added as if just remembering something. "You might want this back." He picked up the file on Jake Spivey and held it out to Dill, who rose, put his drink down on the table, accepted the file, and sat back down. "There really is nothing in it but garbage," Brattle said, his tone carefully disappointed.

"It's what's not in it that's important, Clyde."

"I'm not quite sure I follow that."

"Sure you do. Jake claims he can hang you from the highest tree. I sort of believe him."

Brattle adopted a new expression of utter sincerity that Dill couldn't remember having seen before. The old boy's acting's improved since we last met, Dill thought. He was good then, now he's superb.

"I'm going to give you a word of advice, Ben," Brattle said. "Some counsel. What I'm going to tell you has taken me—" He paused to compute the years carefully. "—sixteen years to learn. It's really quite simple and it's simply this: don't believe one fucking word Jake Spivey says."

"Not one fucking word," Sid agreed.

"If he said he was breathing, I wouldn't believe him," Harley said.

"Not...one...fucking...word," Brattle said, spacing his own words for emphasis. "Tell the Senator that."

"Okay."

"When d'you think you might be talking to him?"

"The Senator?" Dill said. "Right after I talk to the FBI and tell them where I saw you."

"Of course," Brattle said. "How stupid of me." He held out his hand. Dill didn't hesitate. He rose and accepted it, turned, and moved toward the sliding door. Harley came off the folding stool to slide the door back.

"Sorry about the neck," Harley said.

Dill looked at him and nodded. "You bet," he said and stepped down from the van. Before Dill reached the elevator, he heard the van's engine start. He pushed the elevator button, turned, and watched the van speed up the ramp and out of sight. He didn't bother to memorize its license number.

CHAPTER

18

Up in his room, Dill stood at the window and stared down at the nearly deserted two-in-the-morning streets. He could see the First National Bank's digital sign claiming the temperature had dropped to 86 degrees, and that the time was 2:09 A.M. It was also Saturday now, August 6, the day they would bury Felicity Dill, the homicide detective, second grade, deceased.

Dill was trying to decide which telephone call to make first. He thought there was a possibility that the calls, and especially the order they were made in, might affect the lives of those called in years to come. Because he was having trouble deciding on the order, Dill accused himself of philosophical flabbiness—of letting mere friendship get in the way of duty and responsibility and other such moral obligations. You've come down with a bad case of the qualms, he told himself, and the best cure for that is logic, the cold and implacable kind.

He went to the writing desk, where the whisky was,

sat down, and took out a sheet of hotel stationery. Using the hotel ball-point pen he listed four names:

FBI
Sen. Ramirez
J. Spivey
T. Dolan

Dill stared at the four names for several moments, trying to decide which to call first. He reached for the bottle of whisky and poured a measure into his glass. A shot of Old Implacable blended logic should help, he thought, drank the whisky down in two gulps, and wished for perhaps the thousandth time that he still smoked.

He continued to stare at the list until he again picked up the hotel pen and wrote a single digit after each name. When done, he put the pen down, leaned back in his chair, and stared at what he had written:

FBI—4
Sen. Ramirez—3
J. Spivey—1
T. Dolan—2

You should cover your ass, he thought. You should go down to the lobby and use the pay phone because someday, maybe even years from now, a neat blue suit with a shiny plastic government-issue briefcase will drop by the hotel and demand the records of the phone calls made by a certain Benjamin Dill on that morning of August sixth—on that same hot August morning when he buried his sister and tipped off the notorious international fugitive John Jacob Spivey. Ask yourselves, ladies and gentlemen of the jury, did Dill do this for gain, for personal profit—or for any motive that you or I could possibly understand? He did not. He did it out of something he describes as friendship, out of something he calls loyalty. And just what was the basis of this alleged loyalty?

Why, Dill would have you believe that he and Spivey were once pals, mates, boyhood chums—even asshole buddies. Now I ask you, members of the jury, what kind of sociopath would be asshole buddies with the likes of John Jacob Spivey, the most wanted man in the world? And so forth and so on, Dill thought as he sighed, picked up the telephone, and dialed a number.

The phone rang nine times, then ten, and finally, on the eleventh ring, was answered with a gruff, sleepy "Who the fuck is this?"

"Your asshole buddy, Benjamin Dill."

"You drunk?" Spivey asked.

"You awake?"

"Lemme get a cigarette."

In the background, Dill could hear the voice of Daphne Owens asking, Who is it? and Spivey replying, Pick. What does he want at this hour? she demanded in a half-awake, half-querulous tone. How the fuck do I know what he wants until I talk to him? Spivey said, and came back to the phone with "What's up?"

"I am."

"Yeah, I know you are, but what else?"

"Brattle's back."

There was a silence that lasted several moments before Spivey finally said, "So?"

"Back here, I mean."

"Here in town?"

"Right."

"Well." Spivey was again silent for perhaps a dozen seconds. "Who's with him?"

"Somebody large called Harley and somebody with dyed black hair called Sid."

"Those pricks."

"He's going to shop you, Jake. He's going to serve you up in a neat package to Ramirez along with Dick Glander and Frank Cour. He says he can drop the net over them both in twenty-four hours. He also says he's got enough on you for three consecutive life sentences—with no parole. Ever. Clyde says he'll do all this in exchange for a two-year stretch in some federal rest home and a fine of no more than two or three hundred thousand."

"How'd he look?" Spivey said.

"Confident."

"He always looks like that. Where'd you see him?"

"In the hotel basement. In a van."

There was another lengthy pause and then Spivey said, "Well, thanks for calling, Pick. I appreciate it."

That's not the right reaction, Dill thought. Where's the panic, the fear, the voice that quavers? He's thanking me for telling him where I last saw his lost dog. "That it?" Dill asked.

"I can't think of anything else."

"Clyde sounded awfully sure of himself, Jake."

"That's the business he's in—the trust-me business."

"He sounded more sure of himself than usual."

"Look, he wants a deal, that's all. You say he's willing to do two years to get it. Well, I want a deal, too, but I'm not doing any fucking two years. I want immunity. Now I suggest you go talk to that kid Senator of yours and find out who he and Justice would rather nail—me or Brattle. I got the feeling he's going to say Brattle. Well, I can give him Brattle on a platter. Tell him that. See what he says. If he agrees that he'd rather nail Brattle than me, then that's when I'm gonna have to start worrying about old Clyde because that's when Clyde'll try and—well, do something."

"I have to call the FBI first and tell them where I saw Brattle."

"Yeah," Spivey said, his tone completely uninterested. "You do that." He chuckled. "You mean you haven't called them yet?"

"No."

Spivey chuckled again. "You know what you are, Pick? You're all mush."

"Could be."

"Lemme know what the Senator says."

"All right."

"And we can still count on you for Sunday."

"Sure, Jake," Dill said. "You can count on me."

After he hung up, Dill felt as if he had spent the past hour or so wandering through a vast and largely uncharted land with one of those ancient maps that read: Here There Be Monsters. Dill knew the map was right. He had come this way before. Yet, you still don't believe they really exist—the monsters. No, that's wrong. You believe they exist all right, but after fifteen years of watching them, writing about them, and even tracking them down, you still think they're normal, harmless and domesticated. Even housebroken.

But what if they, after all, are the norm and you are indeed the aberration? The thought enchanted Dill. Its simplicity was compelling, its implicit offer of absolution irresistible. He was so pleased with the whisky-inspired notion that he poured the last of the Old Smuggler into a glass and drank it down. He then reversed the previous order he so carefully had decided on (goodbye, cold logic) and called all three telephone numbers at which Senator Ramirez might be reached in New Mexico.

Later, some were to claim that if Senator Ramirez had been where he said he would be, at any one of the three numbers, he might have prevented it from happening—or prevented at least some of it. But those who claimed this were mostly professional partisans and the Senator's political foes. Tim Dolan always argued that it didn't really matter who Dill called that morning because nobody could have stopped what eventually happened from happening. Dill himself never claimed anything at all, and it was he who made the three calls to New Mexico and reached the three different answering machines that said, in two languages, that the Senator was not available, but would return all calls if only the caller would leave both name and number after the tone. Dill left his name and number three times and then woke Tim Dolan up in Washington.

After Dill reported on his conversations with both Jake Spivey and Clyde Brattle, he stopped talking and waited for Dolan's reaction. It didn't take long for that political mind to reach the conclusion Dill knew it would reach.

"They both want to slice each other up, don't they—Spivey and Brattle?" Dolan said in a pleased tone from which all sleepiness had fled.

"So it would seem."

"Then we've got 'em both."

"Tim," Dill said, "I'm not sure you really understand these guys."

"What's to understand? We'll let them slice each other up and then we'll serve 'em on toast to Justice. The Senator will get ninety seconds on the network news, and be a hero back home for three days, maybe even a week."

"I think you'll have to settle for one or the other," Dill said.

"Not both, huh?"

"No."

"Okay," Dolan said. "Which one?"

"That's not my choice to make."

"You're weaseling, Ben."

"I know."

"Okay, I'll tell you what we'll do. We'll toss it to the Senator and let him decide. What d'you say?"

"Fine," Dill said.

"That's settled then. He and I'll be down there late Monday or Tuesday morning."

"The hearing still on?"

"Not exactly," Dolan said. "We decided we don't want to go public too soon. What the Senator wants to do is meet privately with Spivey. Can you fix that?"

"Yes."

"What about Brattle?"

"I have the feeling he'll be in touch," Dill said.

"With you?"

"With me."

"See if you can fix up a session for him and the Senator."

"What about the FBI?"

"What about them?"

"Somebody has to call them. About Brattle."

"Let me do it here," Dolan said. "I know a couple of guys over there who're halfway reasonable."

"You'll take care of it then?" Dill said.

"I'll take care of it," Dolan promised. "You better get some sleep. You sound bushed."

Afterward, no one but Dill ever had a very good answer for the question that puzzled members of the federal grand jury asked most frequently: "Why didn't you guys just call the FBI or something?"

"I thought somebody did," Dill always replied.

CHAPTER

19

THE limousine the police department sent for the somewhat hungover Benjamin Dill at 9:15 that Saturday morning was a black 1977 Cadillac, which its driver said had
163,000 miles on it and formerly belonged to the mayor.

"It didn't really belong to him, you understand," explained the middle-aged police sergeant in dress suntans
who said his name was Mock, "but it was assigned to
him, and then when they bought him his new one, this
one went back into the pool. You say you wanta pick
somebody up?"

"A Miss Singe over on Twenty-second and Van Buren."

"The Old Folks Home, right?" Sergeant Mock said,
holding the rear door open for Dill, who climbed into the
air-conditioned car and sank into its soft cushions. "That's
what they used to call it—the Van Buren Towers, I mean,"
Mock added as he got behind the wheel. "I don't know
why they called it that, but they did."

The sergeant pulled the large car away from the curb

in front of the Hawkins Hotel and drove north up Broadway. He glanced in the rearview mirror at Dill, who sat slumped in the right-hand corner, staring out at the light Saturday-morning traffic.

"I'm sorry about your sister, Mr. Dill," Sergeant Mock said. "She was one real nice little old gal—although I reckon Felicity wasn't so little at that—five-nine or ten, around in there."

"Five-ten," Dill said.

"Tall for a woman."

"Yes."

"You want me to shut up?"

"It might help."

"A little hung?"

"A little."

"Look in that compartment right in front of you—you gotta slide it open. I put three cans of cold Bud in there, just in case."

"You're a saint," Dill said, opening the cabinet and removing one of the still frosty cans. He opened it and drank gratefully.

The sergeant grinned into the rearview mirror. "I always do that on funeral details," he said. "First thing I do when I get up in the morning is head for the kitchen and pop three or four cans in the freezer—you know, get 'em good and cold. Lotsa people need a little something when they go to a funeral. Sad things, funerals." He paused. "Well, I'll shut up now."

"Thank you," Dill said.

Anna Maude Singe wore black—simple expensive unrelieved black—except for the white gloves, which she carried. She came out of the Van Buren Towers escorted by Sergeant Mock, who had volunteered to fetch her. Dill slid over into the left-hand corner of the limousine as Mock opened the right-hand door for Singe. She came

164

into the car gracefully, her rear first, followed by her long dancer's legs, which she swung in with one smooth motion. She turned to examine Dill, who was wearing his dark blue suit, a white shirt, and the knitted black silk tie. Singe nodded both her greeting and her approval. "You look nice," she said, "and that hangover you're trying to hide lends a certain sad credence."

"I somehow knew you'd talk in the morning," Dill said.

She smiled. "Doesn't everyone?"

Again behind the wheel, Sergeant Mock started the engine, turned his head, and said, "The lady doesn't look like she's gonna need a beer, Mr. Dill, but if she does, you know where it is. Now I'm gonna roll up the divider so you all can have your privacy. People going to funerals always like their privacy."

"Thanks," Dill said. Mock pushed a button, the glass divider rose out of the back of the front seat, and the large car pulled away from the curb.

"You want a beer?" Dill asked.

Singe shook her head no. "Where'd you get the hangover?"

"Up in my room alone."

"I didn't think you'd drunk that much with me."

"I had a visitor."

"Up in your room?"

"Down in the hotel garage. We talked in his van."

"Who?"

"Clyde Brattle." Dill paused. "I didn't tell you about Brattle, did I?"

Again, she shook her head no.

"Maybe I'd better."

"Where do they keep that beer?" she asked.

"The cabinet in front of you—just slide it open."

Singe opened the cabinet, brought out a beer, pressed its top down, and handed it to Dill. "Okay," she said, "Tell me."

Dill took a long swallow of the second beer and then told her about his meeting in the blue Dodge van with Clyde Brattle and the two men called Harley and Sid. When he was finished, they were nearing Trinity Baptist Church, which was located at Thirteenth and Sherman, a little more than fifteen blocks from the Van Buren Towers.

Singe looked thoughtful for a moment or two after Dill finished his account. Then she frowned and said, "I'd feel better if you'd called the FBI yourself."

"Yes," Dill said. "So would I."

There were far more Baptists in the city and state than anything else, followed—not too closely—by Methodists, Presbyterians, Christians, fundamentalists of various stripes and hues, Catholics, and a surprising number of Episcopalians, whom most people thought of as prosperous, stylish, Eastern, and not nearly so given to strange ritual as the Catholics with their suspect allegiance to Rome. In 1922 a rumor had circulated that the Pope was due in at Union Station on the 12:17 MKT from Chicago and an estimated three thousand persons turned out to see if it was true. Most had come merely to gawk, but others had thought to bring along asphalt and feathers. All were disappointed when Pius XI failed to step down from the train.

Trinity Baptist had been built in the mid-fifties from plans drawn by a professor of architecture down at the university who was noted for his extreme taste in design, women, and politics. The state legislature didn't necessarily think a man's womenfolk, or what kind of bricks he favored, were any of its business, but it did know, as one member put it, "right smart about politics." The members also knew they didn't want any pinkos teaching the kids down at the university. So they hauled the professor up in front of a state House of Representatives subcommittee on subversive activities and grilled him mercilessly about his crackpot political theories, and after they tired of that, about his women and his draftsmanship.

One seventy-two-year-old representative from an area of the state known as Little Dixie brandished a rendering of a rather free-form piece of statuary that was destined to grace the church grounds. He wanted to know if that was what the professor really thought John the Baptist looked like. The professor replied that he thought it indeed did look a great deal like John. Smiling sweetly, he then asked if the committee had yet found any pink in the beard of the saint, but none of its members could quite figure out what he was getting at. The hearings ended shortly thereafter. The professor wrote a four-word letter of resignation ("Fuck it. I quit.") and went off to teach at the University of California at Berkeley. The Baptists went ahead and built the church he had designed for them. Almost everybody now liked it immensely.

Dill was surprised by the number of cars that filled the church parking lot and were double-parked out front. He counted twenty-four police motorcycles—all bone-jarring Harley-Davidsons, he noted, and not the infinitely superior Kawasakis. Made in America still counts for something down here, he decided, pushed the button that lowered the dividing window, and asked: "All these people aren't here just for my sister's funeral, are they?"

"They sure are," Sergeant Mock said. "Your sister was a cop, Mr. Dill, and when cops get themselves killed, other cops turn out. I saw the list. Why, we got cops here from as far off as Denver and Omaha and Memphis and all the way up from New Orleans."

"Where else?" Singe asked.

"Lemme think. Dallas, Fort Worth, Houston, Amarillo, Oklahoma City, Tulsa, Kansas City, Little Rock, Santa Fe, Albuquerque, and—oh, yeah—the one who said he was coming down from Cheyenne. They're gonna witness, Mr. Dill, that's what. They're all gonna witness."

It was a few minutes before ten when Mock pulled the limousine into the chief mourner's reserved space, got out, and opened the door for Singe and Dill. Fifty or sixty weaponless policemen were still standing around outside, all wearing their neat dress suntans. For some reason, Dill had expected them to wear blue. He could sense their pointing him out to each other as the brother of the dead Felicity Dill.

A smooth-looking, olive-complexioned lieutenant introduced himself as Lieutenant Sanchez, graciously expressed his sympathy, and offered to escort Dill and Singe. He led them through the police and into the church. It was the first time Dill had been inside and he was impressed by the architect's wit. It looks like a Baptist church all right, he thought, but like one where they really do make a joyful noise unto the Lord and have just one hell of a good time doing it.

The interior was of granite (with just a blush of pink) and it soared up eagerly, almost happily, as if indeed bound for glory. Dill found the stained-glass windows to be of an interesting, not quite abstract design. He decided that if you got bored with the sermon, you could always stare up at the windows and make up your own stories. If his sister had to be prayed over in a church, Dill thought it might as well be this one. She would've liked the architecture, if nothing else.

Lieutenant Sanchez ushered Singe and Dill to the center aisle and turned them over to the waiting Chief of Detectives John Strucker. It was the first time Dill had seen Strucker in uniform. He was impressed with how well the chief wore it and with the uniform itself, which had been meticulously tailored out of what appeared to be tan linen, although it didn't wrinkle enough for linen. Under his left arm Strucker had tucked his garrison cap, which had a lot of gold braid on its bill.

"We're all the way down front," Strucker murmured

and led them down to the front row on the right. A man rose from the left front row and moved toward them. He was an older man, in his sixties at least, and Dill finally recognized him as Dwayne Rinkler, the chief of police. It had been years since Dill had last seen him and the chief's long narrow face seemed to have lengthened; the frigid blue eyes appeared to have grown even colder, and the thin lips had finally disappeared, leaving only a wide straight ruled line. Rinkler also had lost most of his hair and acquired a deep tan. He wore his uniform almost as well as Strucker. There was even more gold braid on his cap.

Strucker made the introductions and Chief Rinkler shook hands first with Singe and then with Dill. "We're deeply sorry, Mr. Dill," he said in his rasping bass, "all of us."

"Thank you," Dill said.

"She was a fine woman," Rinkler added, nodding as if to reconfirm his own assessment. Still nodding, he turned and went back to his seat. Strucker joined him. Dill and Singe took their places across the aisle.

When seated, Dill examined the casket for the first time. He really couldn't see the casket itself because it was draped with a large American flag. On either side of the casket, six tall stalwart policemen in immaculate summer uniforms stood at motionless parade rest. Dill wondered how long they had been standing like that.

Somewhere, a mixed choir began to sing. Dill followed the sound, turned, and looked up. In the choir loft twelve very young male and female police officers were lifting their unaccompanied voices in a slow somber rendition of "The Battle Hymn of the Republic." They apparently intended to sing all four verses as the church filled up. Dill thought they sang quite well and wondered if Felicity would have objected to the hymn. She might have once, he concluded, but she doesn't now.

When the hymn was over there was the usual amount

of rustling and throat-clearing and half-stifled coughs. The young-looking minister made his appearance and mounted slowly to the pulpit, where he surveyed the gathering with sad eyes from behind earnest horn-rimmed spectacles.

"We are here today," he said, "to mourn the death and pray for the soul of someone who was not of this church or of this faith, but one who chose a life of public service that protected both this faith and this church. We are here to mourn and pray for Detective Felicity Dill and to thank her for her all too short life of dedicated service to this community."

He went on like that for another five minutes—a deadly dull young man, Dill thought, apparently devout and obviously sincere. When the young minister uttered the inevitable words "in vain," Dill quit listening as he always did when anyone spoke those words. They always came right after "sacrifice," another word that sent Dill's attention wandering. Someone murdered my sister, he thought, as the young minister's voice rose and fell. If Felicity didn't die in vain, I don't know who did.

There was a new sound and Dill realized the young minister had finished and the police choir was singing yet another hymn. The dozen fresh-scrubbed young policemen and women were giving out with "Amazing Grace," a hymn that Felicity Dill had particularly detested. "Read the words sometime, Pick," she had written him shortly after Jimmy Carter let it be known that "Amazing Grace" was his favorite hymn. "I mean really read them and then you'll understand why people still put up with all the shit they put up with." Dill listened to the words now, really listened, but they meant absolutely nothing to him, although he thought the police choir sang them very well indeed.

After the hymn was over, Dill assumed the services were too, but they weren't. The young minister had already descended from the pulpit and now someone else mounted it. The someone else was Gene Colder, Baptist deacon and homicide captain, looking neat and melancholy in a dress uniform that seemed as finely tailored as the chief of detectives'. Colder gripped the lectern, not out of nervousness, but with the air of an experienced orator who has something important to say. His eyes examined his audience, beginning with those in the back and ending with Dill in the front row, to whom he nodded slightly. Colder then picked out the mourner he intended to talk to—who seemed to be about halfway back—and began.

"I have been asked to say a few words about Detective Second Grade Felicity Fredricka Dill (God, how she hated Fredricka, Dill thought), not only because she was in my division, homicide, but also because we were friends." Colder paused and added, "Very good friends." Now everybody knows they were sleeping together, if they didn't know before, Dill thought.

"Detective Dill was what I would call a cop's cop," Colder continued. "She won her promotions, and they were indeed rapid promotions, because of her hard, often brilliant work. I do not hesitate to predict that had she lived and pursued her career with this same determination and brilliance, she could've become this city's first female chief of detectives and, it is not at all inconceivable, its first female chief of police." Captain Colder smiled slightly. "It goes without saying that she would have made captain."

After that, Colder talked about what a wonderful person Detective Dill had been. He praised both her mind and her bravery. He had nice things to say about her sound common sense and her uncommon compassion. He described her loss as tragic and her legacy as everlasting, although Dill didn't know what he meant by that. Colder failed to mention the dead detective's two hundred and fifty thousand dollar life insurance policy and the yellow brick duplex, which were also part of her legacy, but not

171

an especially everlasting part, in Dill's opinion.

Finally, Colder said, "I can only repeat the highest compliment we can pay her: she was a cop's cop, and we shall miss her. All of us."

The deacon now gazed out over his congregation, for that was how Dill had come to think of it, and asked them to join him in the Lord's Prayer. Dill watched as the honor guard's heads snapped down and they prayed together at parade rest.

When the prayer was over, the police choir burst into song again. Dill, no churchgoer, thought this one was "Abide with Me." He glanced at Anna Maude Singe, who reached for his hand and squeezed it. "Think of it this way," she said in a low voice. "Somewhere she's laughing."

"Sure," said Dill, who didn't at all believe it. He turned to meet the approaching Captain Colder, who shook hands first with Singe and then with Dill. "I appreciate what you said, Captain," Dill said.

"I meant every word of it."

"It was very moving," Singe said.

"Thank you." He looked at Dill. "Everything work out all right—the limousine and all?"

"It's been perfect. I want to thank you very much."

"Well, I'll escort you back out to your car. It'll be right behind Felicity." Not behind the hearse, Dill noticed, but behind the still uninterred Felicity. Colder smiled reassuringly. "The graveside services are very brief, very formal. Shall we go?"

As they walked up the aisle, Dill looked for someone he knew—for some old family friend he could nod to or smile at—but there was none. She has friends here, he thought, but you don't know them because that ten-year gap between your ages was almost unbridgeable. He did notice the section of out-of-town policemen who sat together, spruce and correct in their varied uniforms, and eyed him curiously and with sympathy as he walked past.

And that's who came to bury Felicity, Dill realized. Cops and the wives of cops. The cops themselves were young and middle-aged. I guess there aren't any old cops anymore, except for the chief of police. I guess they put in their twenty or thirty years, take their pension, and get out. Detective Dill. Sergeant Dill. Captain Dill. Chief of Detectives Dill. Chief of Police F. F. Dill. Well, who knows. It might have happened.

On the aisle seat in the next to the last row sat Fred Y. Laffter, the ancient police reporter. He rose and sidled up to Dill and in a hoarse whisper said, "We're gonna go with the stuff on your sister's insurance policy and the money she paid down on her duplex and all that crap. Any comment you wanta make?"

Dill stopped. "What d'you mean 'we'?"

Laffter pointed a finger skyward and shrugged. "They tell me upstairs they wanta go with it, so we go with it. I can still work you in a graph, if you want, although that's my idea, not theirs."

"No quote," Dill said. "Nothing."

"For God's sake, Laffter, not now," Colder said and inserted himself between Dill and the old man.

"I'm doing him a favor," Laffter said.

"Not now, damnit," Colder said.

Laffter stared at him coldly. "It's my job, sonny," he snapped, stepped nimbly around Colder, and again confronted Dill. "No hard feelings, kid."

"Get the fuck out of my way," Dill said.

CHAPTER

20

LED by the two dozen Harley-Davidsons, which were themselves led by a green-and-white squad car with its bar flasher on, the mile-long funeral procession rolled at a stately fifteen miles per hour toward the Green Glade of Rest cemetery that once had been a hardscrabble farm on the eastern outskirts of the city.

The centerpiece of Green Glade was a none-too-complicated maze about one-quarter the size of a football field. The maze was composed of swamp privet hedge eight feet tall and a couple of feet thick. There were also gravel paths for strolling and stone benches in convenient nooks where mourners could sit and rest and think long thoughts about life and death and what it all meant. However, the gravel was hard to walk on, the stone benches uncomfortable, and the maze was usually shunned by those who visited the cemetery.

In the past five years the police department had buried seventeen of its slain officers at Green Glade of Rest.

Detective Felicity Dill would make it eighteen. Before the department had bought its own cemetery plot, KOD policemen were buried all over town. KOD stood for Killed on Duty.

Virtually all of those who had been at the church service also attended the graveside ceremony. As promised, the ceremony was brief. A police chaplain read the Twenty-Third Psalm. A squad of sharpshooters fired a rifle volley. A bugler played "Taps" on a cornet. The stalwart honor guard, doubling as pallbearers, folded the American flag covering the casket into a neat triangle and presented it to Dill, who had not the slightest idea of what to do with it. And then it was over, the dead sister buried, and the time was not yet noon.

The police department's KOD plot was up on a slight knoll. With the services over, the mostly uniformed mourners began to walk slowly back down to their cars, skirting the maze. A few lingered on to shake Dill's hand and murmur their sorrow. As Dill and Anna Maude Singe slowly made their way to the waiting limousine, he shook the offered hands and politely thanked the murmurers.

Dill and Singe found themselves almost alone not far from the maze when someone tapped Dill on the shoulder. He turned, as did Singe. They found themselves bathed in the angelic glow of the smile that belonged to Clay Corcoran, who had loved the dead sister.

"I just couldn't keep away, Mr. Dill," Corcoran said.

"Ben," Dill said.

"Ben," Corcoran agreed and turned his warm smile on Singe. "How you, Smokey?"

Singe said she was fine. The big man's dazzling smile went away and he turned serious. "I thought it was a swell funeral," he said. "I think Felicity might've giggled a little here and there, but everything went off real nice."

Corcoran seemed to be soliciting Dill's confirmation, so Dill said that he, too, thought it had all gone very well. Corcoran glanced over the heads of Dill and Anna Maude

Singe. Behind them the police in their summer uniforms were moving past the maze toward their cars, although at least a fourth of them, mostly those who had brought wives, were now gathered in small gossipy groups.

Corcoran dropped his deep voice down into what he must have hoped was a confidential mutter. "I told you I was going to snoop around a little?" He had made it a question, so Dill nodded in reply.

"Well," Corcoran went on in the same tone, "I think I might've come up with something." Again, he glanced over their heads as if afraid of being overheard. Apparently satisfied, he added, "But I've got to ask you a couple of questions first."

"Okay," Dill said.

"There's this guy called Jake Spivey who—" Corcoran never finished his sentence, and later Dill thought the big man's reflexes had been incredible. Corcoran threw a hip into Dill that sent him sailing. He landed four feet away. It was Dill's first brush with contact sports and he found it strangely exhilarating.

Before Dill had even landed, Corcoran used his left arm to clothesline Anna Maude Singe and send her sprawling. The pleasant look had fled and Corcoran's frightener's scowl was back as he dropped to one knee and clawed at something beneath his right pants leg.

Dill looked where Corcoran was looking. He saw the large fist and the small gun poking through the thick swamp privet hedge thirty-some feet away. Or perhaps, Dill later thought, the smallness of the gun made the fist look large. He saw the gun fire. He heard the sharp nasty crack of a single shot. Dill turned and saw that it had caught the kneeling Corcoran low in the throat. The big man dropped the small flat .25-caliber automatic he had just snatched from the ankle holster on his right leg. He pressed both hands against the wound in his throat. A moment later, he removed his bloody hands and stared at them in amazement.

Corcoran knelt there on one knee for two seconds, three seconds, four seconds, then sighed, and slowly lay down on the grass. Blood pumped from his throat. Dill, rising, looked around. The only persons still standing were the wives of the policemen. The policemen themselves had dropped to the grass. Some had dropped flat. A dozen others knelt, their right or left pants legs up, revealing white hairy calves and the small leather holsters that were strapped to them.

A dozen pistols, mostly flat little automatics much like Corcoran's, had suddenly blossomed in big fists. The cops with the pistols were swiveling their heads, searching for someone to shoot, someone to arrest. But all they found was other cops—and a lot of them strangers—who were also waving pistols around.

Dill later thought the silence after the single shot had lasted no more than three or four seconds and not the hour it seemed at the time. One of the policemen's wives finally screamed at the sight of Corcoran lying on the grass, his knees drawn up almost to his chest, the blood still pumping from his throat. After the scream, the shouting and confusion began.

Dill was the first to reach Corcoran. The big man's green eyes were still open, but not quite focused, although he seemed to recognize Dill. He tried to speak, but instead blew a large pink bubble which burst with a tiny plop. Corcoran's lips moved again and Dill bent to listen. Those watching later said they thought Corcoran managed only three or four words before the blood finally stopped pumping from the wound. Out of Corcoran's mouth came one last sigh. It formed another pink bubble that popped almost immediately. Then the heart ran out of blood, stopped, and Corcoran was dead.

Dill slowly rose to his feet. A policeman who seemed to have had medical training knelt quickly by Corcoran and used deft fingers to search for any signs of life. He found none and sat back on his heels, shaking his head.

Dill helped the trembling Anna Maude Singe to her feet. When he asked if she was hurt, she slowly shook her head no, her eyes fixed on the huge curled-up body of Clay Corcoran. Dill put an arm around Singe to lead her away. He found their path blocked by Captain Gene Colder. A moment later, Chief of Detectives John Strucker rushed up. Colder glanced at Strucker, as if for permission. Strucker granted it with a nod.

"Tell us quick, Dill," Colder said in a crisp hard voice. "They say he said something. Could you understand what he said?"

"Dill nodded. "Sure. He said, 'It hurts. It hurts.' He said it twice."

"That's all?" Strucker said, the disbelief in his tone, if not on his face.

"That's it."

Strucker turned to Colder. "You know what to do, Captain. You'd better get at it."

"Yes, sir," Colder said, turned, and hurried away, pointing first at this policeman and then beckoning to that one. It was the only time Dill could remember having heard Colder say sir to Strucker.

The chief of detectives took a cigar from his breast pocket and slowly stripped away the cellophanelike plastic, not taking his eyes from the body of the dead Corcoran. He wadded the cellophane up into a small ball and flipped it away. Still staring down at Corcoran, he bit off one end of the cigar, spat it out, and lit it with a disposable lighter.

"You knew him, huh—Corcoran?" Strucker said, still staring at the dead man.

"He said he used to go with my sister."

"That's right," Strucker said, finally shifting his gaze to Dill. "He did."

"He said he used to be a cop."

"He was. Not bad either, although he was a hell of a lot better linebacker. He say what he was doing now?"

"He claimed he was a private detective," Dill said. "A frightener, he called it."

Strucker smiled, but it was a small grim one that vanished almost immediately. "He wasn't bad at that either, although he was better at football than anything else. He just came down and introduced himself to you where—at the hotel?"

"Right."

"What'd you talk about?"

"My sister, what else?"

"He tell you how she'd dropped him sudden-like?"

"Yes."

"He still steamed about it?"

"He seemed more resigned than anything else—resigned and sad, of course."

Strucker turned to Anna Maude Singe. "You knew him, too, didn't you, Miss Singe?"

"Yes. Quite well."

"What happened here—a few moments ago?"

"I'm not absolutely sure."

Strucker puffed on his cigar, blew smoke up into the air and away from Singe. He nodded at her encouragingly. "Just tell me what you saw and what you remember."

She frowned. "Well, Clay came up to us and said he thought it was a nice funeral and everything seemed to have gone off quite well. Mr. Dill agreed and then Clay said he'd been looking around, or poking around, maybe, and that he needed to ask Mr. Dill something. But then, well, then I guess he saw something behind us—behind Mr. Dill and me—because after that everything happened awfully fast. He bumped Mr. Dill—"

Dill interrupted. "He gave me a hip shot."

Strucker nodded and again smiled encouragingly at Singe.

"Then his arm snapped out like this," she said, demonstrating how Corcoran's arm had moved. "And the next thing I knew I was flat on my back."

"Clotheslined her?" Strucker asked Dill.

"Apparently."

"Then I heard the shot," Anna Maude Singe went on, "and I looked up and saw Clay, except he was down on one knee by then, kneeling, and he had his pants leg up and a little gun in his hand. But he dropped the gun and his hands went up to his throat and came away bloody. After that, he just decided to lie down. It looked like that anyway. He lay down and his knees came up to his chest and he just—he just curled up and died."

She looked away then. "You all right?" Strucker asked.

She nodded. "Yes. I'm all right."

Strucker turned to Dill. "What'd you see?"

"The same thing—except I also saw a hand poking a gun through the hedge right about there." Dill pointed to where a knot of policemen were down on their hands and knees in their dress uniforms making a careful search of the cemetery grass near the spot in the privet hedge Dill had indicated. He assumed they were looking for a spent cartridge.

Strucker watched them for a moment and dolefully shook his head. "Look at 'em," he said. "All in uniform and alike as peas in a pod. He could've got himself an out-of-town uniform somewhere, gone to the funeral, come out here, shot Corcoran, and ducked out the other side of the maze. Could've happened like that."

"Maybe," Dill said.

Strucker looked at him with renewed interest. "What d'you mean, maybe?"

"The one time I talked to Corcoran, he told me he did a lot of bodyguard work. Maybe that's what he did here—almost by reflex. He got Anna Maude and me out of the way and then went for the shooter—except it didn't work out too well."

Strucker puffed thoughtfully on his cigar, coughed twice, and then nodded—a bit grudgingly, Dill thought. "And the shooter was after who?" Strucker said. "You?"

Dill looked at Singe. "Or her."

Singe's eyes went wide for a second and her mouth dropped open, but snapped shut so she could form the M in her startled *"Me?"*

"Maybe," Dill said.

"Why the hell me?"

"For that matter," Dill said, "why the hell anyone?"

CHAPTER

21

AT police headquarters, Sergeant Mock waited outside in the limousine while Dill and Singe made brief statements into a tape recorder. He then drove them back to the Hawkins Hotel. The question Dill had been expecting didn't come until he and Singe rode the elevator down to the basement garage and were seated in the rented Ford with its engine idling and its air-conditioning turned as high as it would go. Outside, the First National Bank's time and temperature sign was reporting 101 degrees at 1:31 P.M.

"Why didn't you tell them what Clay said about Jake Spivey?" Anna Maude Singe asked.

"What'd he say?"

"He said, 'There's this guy called Jake Spivey who—.'" She paused. "That's verbatim."

"There's this guy called Jake Spivey who what?" Dill said.

"I don't know."

"Neither do I, and that's why I didn't tell them. Why didn't you?"

"You're my client."

"That's not it," Dill said and backed the Ford out of its parking slot.

"Maybe," she said, "maybe I didn't because Clay could've been about to say, 'There's this guy called Jake Spivey who asked me to come out to his house Sunday for barbecue and a jump in his pool and I understand you all are coming, too.' Or..." She fell silent.

"Or what?" Dill said as he drove up the ramp.

"I don't know."

They came out on Our Jack Street, drove to a red light at the corner of Broadway, stopped, and turned right on red—a logical practice the city had come up with in 1929, which later was borrowed without acknowledgment by California.

After driving north for two blocks on Broadway, Dill said, "You hungry?"

"No."

"Finish your 'or' then."

"Or," she said, " 'There's this guy called Jake Spivey who asked me to be his bodyguard and keep somebody from killing him.' "

"That's not bad," Dill said.

She shook her head, rejecting all suppositions. "The variations are endless," she said. "And meaningless."

"You sure you're not hungry?" he asked.

"I'd like a drink."

"Okay, we'll stop somewhere and you can have a drink and I'll have a sandwich and a drink."

"Then what?"

"Then," Dill said, "well, then we'll go see where Felicity really lived."

Anna Maude Singe changed her mind and had a bacon, lettuce and tomato sandwich along with a Bloody Mary in Binkie's Bar and Grille. The "e" on the end of Grille had troubled Dill, but inside the place was inviting enough despite too much butcher block and too many plants. He ordered a beer and a cheeseburger. The cheeseburger turned out to be superb. Singe said her BLT was also excellent.

After she ate the last of the sandwich and licked a little mayonnaise from a finger, she said, "What do you expect to find?"

"In her garage apartment?"

Singe nodded.

"I don't know," he said.

"Haven't the cops already been there?"

"Yes. Sure."

"Then what're you looking for?"

"For some small trace of my sister," Dill said. "So far, there doesn't seem to be any."

The big house sat just across the street from Washington Park. The park was composed of a deeply sunken twenty-five acres that had got that way because it once had been a brickyard. The clay that had been dug out of the yard had gone into the red common brick used in the construction of most of the city's houses prior to 1910. After that, the city grew in a sudden spurt, land prices rose, and the area around the brickyard became economically attractive to real estate speculators—except nobody wanted to live next to where bricks were made. The city quickly decided progress and profit were far more important than bricks. It condemned the brickyard and turned the twenty-five-acre hole in the ground into Washington Park. It was in the park's public pool that both Benjamin Dill and Jake Spivey had learned to swim.

The old brick house was a sprawling, three-story affair built in 1914 with wide eaves and a huge screened porch. Its sixteen rooms sat on a choice corner lot that was two hundred feet deep and one hundred fifty feet wide. For trees there were elms, dogwood, locust, two apricots, and a peach. At the rear on the alley was the two-story carriage house where the dead detective was said to have lived.

After parking the Ford on 19th Street, Dill and Anna Maude Singe walked along the sidewalk to the alley. There Dill fished out the key Captain Colder had given him and used it to unlock the downstairs door. Inside was a steep flight of narrow stairs. There were no windows in the stairwell, which made it both dark and stifling. Dill felt around, found a wall switch, and turned it on. A forty-watt bulb provided light. He started up the stairs, followed by Anna Maude Singe.

At the top of the stairs was a small landing, no more than three by four feet. Dill used the same key in the lock of the second door. It worked. He pushed the door open, went in, found the light switch, flicked it on, and knew immediately that Felicity Dill had indeed lived there.

For one thing, there were the books: two solid walls of them, plus neat piles on the floor and in the deep sills of the four dormer windows that looked out over the alley. A GE air-conditioning unit was also wedged into one of the windows. Dill went over and switched it on. He picked up one of the books and noticed it had been published by a state university press. As he flipped through it he read the title aloud to Singe: *"Beekeeping in Eighteenth Century New England."* The pages were underlined and annotated. Dill put the book back and turned to inspect the rest of the room.

Near where Singe stood was a large deep winged armchair with an ottoman. A curved brass floor lamp was arranged so its light would come over the left shoulder of the seated reader. Dill remembered being taught that in grade school. The reading light should always come over the left shoulder. He had never understood why and tried to remember if he had passed on the curious notion to Felicity. He didn't think it was still taught in school.

"It's her room all right," he said.

Singe picked up a glazed blue-and-yellow vase from the coffee table, examined it, and put it back down. "I remember when she bought this," Singe said. "We went to a garage sale. That's where Felicity bought a lot of her things—at garage sales. She said it gave everything a desperate air—even dramatic."

"That's my sister," Dill said.

"You notice something?"

"What?"

"There's no dust."

Dill looked around, ran his finger over the edge of the highest bookshelf, and examined it for dust. "You're right. I guess they went through every book."

"The police?"

He nodded.

"They were awfully neat."

"Gene Colder probably saw to that."

Dill again looked around. There really wasn't much more to see: a worn Oriental rug on the floor that he guessed was machine woven; some paintings on the walls—Felicity-type paintings, Dill thought—which meant they contained more emotion than art. One was of a sad-faced woman in eighteenth-century European dress leaning on a window ledge. Dill thought her expression was what a suicide might wear. Another was of a fat, uproarious drunk seated on a three-legged stool with a stein of beer on one knee and a plump simpering barmaid on the other. It appeared to be early nineteenth century. A third was an abstract of such harsh colors that it almost screamed of rage. A couch stood against a wall. The coffee table was in front of it. There were also some chairs, a magazine rack (full), and a whatnot stand in one corner. None of the furniture matched, yet none of it seemed out of place.

A short hall led from the living room. Dill moved down

it and noted that the bathroom was on the right and a small kitchen on the left. He switched on the kitchen light and saw the spices. There was a six-tier spice rack that held at least thirty or forty kinds. There was also a four-foot shelf crammed with cookbooks. He opened one of the cabinet doors and found it full of canned goods, plus a generous supply of Kool-Aid. As usual, Dill thought with a smile, there were enough canned goods to last the winter. An inspection of the refrigerator revealed that someone had cleaned out all the perishables—the police probably—leaving only six bottles of Beck's beer. No one had turned off the refrigerator and the beer was still cold.

"You want a beer?" he asked Anna Maude Singe, who was opening and closing kitchen drawers.

"A beer would be good," she said.

"You see an opener?"

"Here," she said, took one out of a drawer and gave it to him.

He opened the two beers and handed her one. "You want a glass?" he asked.

"It'll stay colder in the bottle." She drank from the bottle, moved back to one of the drawers, and pulled it open. "Her silver is all here."

"That was her inheritance when our folks died. All of it."

"She kept it polished," Singe said, and closed the drawer. "What next—the bathroom?"

"Okay."

It was a large, old-fashioned bathroom that was covered halfway up its walls with square white tiles. On the floor were small white hexagonal ones. Both the tub and sink had separate faucets for hot and cold water. The medicine cabinet held nothing of interest.

"No prescription drugs," Dill said, closing the cabinet door.

"Felicity was pretty healthy." Singe looked at him curiously. "Find what you were looking for?"

He nodded. "She lived here. And she seemed to like it. That's all I was after really."

"Shall we try the bedroom?"

"Sure."

The bedroom was not quite as large as the living room because its size had been reduced by the addition of a large closet. There were pretty yellow curtains on the windows and a cheerful white-and-brown rug on the floor. The bed was of the three-quarter kind, quite large enough for one and even for two, providing number two didn't plan to stay the night.

The bedroom also contained an old-fashioned chaise longue, which gave it the air of a boudoir. A card table, bridge lamp, portable electric typewriter, and director's chair gave it the air of Felicity Dill.

Dill crossed to the closet and slid one of its doors back. The closet was filled with women's clothing, all neatly hung on hangers with winter clothes in plastic bags and summer clothes ready to hand. Dill shoved the hung clothing to one side to see if there was anything else worth noting and discovered the man at the back of the closet. The man had a long narrow face that wore a foolish smile. His eyes were a yellowish brown and looked trapped. Dill thought they also looked clever.

"Who the hell are you, friend?" Dill said.

"Lemme explain," the man said.

Dill stepped back quickly, looked around for something hard, spotted the windowsill, and smashed the beer bottle against it. It left him with a weapon formed by the bottle's neck and three or four inches of sharp jagged green glass.

"Explain out here," Dill said.

The man came out of the closet carrying a small tool-chest and still wearing his fool's smile.

"I'll tell you exactly what I want you to do," Dill said. "I want you to put that chest down very carefully, then reach into a pocket just as carefully—I don't care which one—and come out with some ID. If you don't, I'm going to cut your face."

"Take it easy," the man said, still smiling his fixed smile. He put the toolchest down as instructed, reached into a hip pocket, and brought out a worn black billfold. He offered it to Dill.

"Give it to her," Dill said.

The man offered the billfold to Anna Maude Singe. She approached him warily, almost snatched the billfold from his hand, and hurriedly stepped back. She opened it and found a driver's license.

"He's Harold Snow," Singe said. "I remember that name."

"So do I," Dill said. "You're Cindy's roomie, aren't you?"

"You know Cindy?" the man said, his tone puzzled, the fool's smile still trying to please.

"We met," Dill said.

"Harold's the tenant," Singe said. "At the duplex. His name was on the lease."

"I know," Dill said.

Harold Snow's foolish smile finally went away. The yellowish-brown eyes stopped looking trapped and began looking wily instead.

"You guys aren't the cops then," he said in a relieved tone.

"I'm worse than that, Harold," Dill said. "I'm the brother."

HAROLD SNOW obeyed Dill's instructions exactly. He squatted down, his hands behind him, groped for the handle of the toolchest, found it, and rose, holding the toolchest just below the seat of his chino pants.

"Now we're going into the living room, Harold, where it's cooler," Dill said. "But when I say stop, I want you to stop or I'll slice off an ear. Got that?"

"I got it," Snow said.

"Let's go."

Snow went first into the hall followed by Dill. Anna Maude Singe came last. When they reached the door to the kitchen, Dill said, "Stop, Harold."

Snow stopped. "You know where the knives are?" Dill said to Singe.

"What kind d'you want?"

"Something that'll impress Harold."

"Right."

"You don't need any knife," Snow said.

"Shut up, Harold," Dill said.

Dill could hear Singe open and close a drawer in the kitchen. A moment later she was saying, "What about this one?"

Dill turned to look. She was holding up a wicked-looking breadknife. "Fine," Dill said, took the knife and handed her the broken neck of the beer bottle.

"Okay, Harold, into the living room."

Still carrying the toolchest behind him, Snow moved into the living room followed by Dill and Singe. She tossed the neck of the beer bottle into a wastebasket.

"You can put the chest down, Harold," Dill said.

It was awkward going down with the chest behind him, but Snow managed it and then stood up again. "Now what?" he said.

"Sit down over there."

"Over here?" Snow said, moving to the large easy chair with the ottoman and the brass floor lamp.

"That's the one."

Snow sat down in the chair. "Is your toolchest unlocked, Harold?" Dill asked.

"It's unlocked."

"Let's open it and see what's inside." Snow started to rise. "Not you, Harold," Dill said, motioning him back down with the breadknife.

Anna Maude Singe knelt by the toolbox and opened it. She lifted up a tray of assorted tools and inspected the bottom of the chest. "He's either the telephone man or the man who comes to fix the hi-fi," she said. "Except I don't think either one would have this in his toolchest."

Dill looked quickly to his left and then back at Harold Snow. "Is it loaded?" he asked Singe.

"It's loaded."

"Let's have it." Singe rose, moved over to Dill, and handed him the short-barreled five-shot .38-caliber Smith

191

& Wesson revolver. He gave her the breadknife. Dill aimed the pistol at Snow and smiled. The smile made Snow swallow nervously.

"We're going to tell the cops, Harold, that we surprised you in a burglary, you pulled this on us, I took it away from you, and then shot you in the knee. The right knee, I think." Dill moved the gun so that it was pointed at Snow's right knee.

"You wouldn't do that," Snow said.

"Why wouldn't he?" Anna Maude Singe said.

"Christ, lady, people don't just go around shooting people."

"He's the brother, Harold—remember? The death of his sister's made him sort of crazy."

"Harold," Dill said.

Snow looked at him. "What?"

"I'm going to ask you what you're doing here. If you lie to me, I promise I'll shoot you—in the knee. Understand?"

"You're not gonna shoot me," Snow said, his tone as defiant as he could manage.

Dill squeezed the trigger of the pistol. The gun fired. The .38-caliber slug tore into the ottoman in front of Snow's knees. Snow yelped and shrank back in the chair. Dill wondered if anyone had heard the shot. Probably not, he decided, not back here in the alley at the rear of a two-hundred-foot lot. He also decided he didn't really care.

"Sorry, Harold," Dill said and carefully aimed the pistol, with both hands this time, at Snow's right knee.

"The tape!" Snow shouted. "That's all. Just the tape."

Dill lowered the pistol. "What tape, Harold?" he said pleasantly.

"The last one," Snow said.

"The last one. And where is this last tape?"

Snow pointed toward the ceiling. "In the crawl space. It's sort of an attic. You get to it by going up through the trap in the closet ceiling in the bedroom."

"How did you know the tape is up there, Harold?"

"I put the recorder in."

"The tape recorder?"

Snow nodded. "It's voice-activated and I ran it off of house power so I wouldn't have to fool with batteries."

"When did you do all this, Harold?" Anna Maude Singe asked.

Snow looked at her, then back at Dill. "Who the hell's she?" he said.

"She's my witness for when I shoot you in the knee, Harold. But if you answer our questions, maybe I won't have to."

"Can I smoke?" Snow said.

"No," Dill said. "When did you put the tape recorder up in the attic?"

"About six months ago." Snow sulked. "Why can't I smoke?"

"Because," Dill said. "Why'd you put the recorder up there?"

"I got paid to, that's why."

"Who paid you, Harold?"

"Some guy."

"I'll bet some guy's got a name."

"I can't tell you his name," Snow said. "He's a...a client."

"Harold," Anna Maude Singe said softly.

He looked at her. "What?"

"You're not a lawyer, Harold, or a doctor, or a priest, or even a private detective, so there's no rule of confidentiality involved here. You don't have clients, Harold. All you've got are slippery customers, and if you don't tell us who some guy is, Mr. Dill is going to shoot you in the knee. Right, Mr. Dill?"

"Absolutely," Dill said.

Snow looked at Dill, then at Singe again, and then once more at Dill. He ran his tongue over his upper lip as if trying to lick away the sweat. His forehead was also covered with it. He used the sleeve of his soaked blue T-shirt to wipe it away. After that, he dried his hands on the legs of his chino pants. Finally, he lowered his gaze until his eyes rested on the ragged hole the .38 bullet had made in the ottoman. He spoke to the ottoman in a low, almost inaudible voice. "His name's Corcoran. Clay Corcoran." He looked up at Dill. "He used to be gone on your sister and he's gonna tear my fuckin head off when he finds out I told you."

Dill shook his head. "He won't tear your head off, Harold."

"You don't know him."

"Sure I know him. But he won't tear your head off because somebody shot him. Around noon. Today."

Snow's surprise was obviously real. His mouth sagged open and his eyes widened. Disbelief was written across his face. He finally managed to say, "Shot him?" and there was nothing but doubt in his voice.

"Shot him dead, Harold," Anna Maude Singe said. "In the cemetery."

"Tell us, Harold," Dill said almost gently. "Start way back there at the beginning and tell us all about you and my sister and Clay Corcoran."

"Can I smoke?"

"Of course you can."

Snow fished a package of Vantage menthols out of his pants pocket and lit the cigarette with a paper match. He blew the smoke out and looked at Dill. "You sure he's dead?" he said.

"He's dead, Harold. I saw him die."

Snow's yellowish-brown eyes narrowed thoughtfully. "You killed him?"

Dill only smiled and said, "From the beginning, Harold."

Snow looked around for an ashtray. Anna Maude Singe found one and gave it to him. He didn't thank her. Instead, he flicked some ash into the tray and said, "We moved in right after your sister bought the place—the place over on Thirty-second and Texas. We didn't see much of her, me and Cindy. Then one night Corcoran came around when she wasn't there and started raising hell up on the second floor landing."

"When my sister wasn't there, right?"

"Yeah. Right. He'd been there once before raising hell, but your sister'd been home that time. This time she wasn't. Neither was Cindy. Just me. So I went up to see what the trouble was. He was drunk and talkative and he said he and your sister'd split and now she was shacking up with somebody else. He didn't say who the other guy was but I already knew. Well, what the hell, it smelled like an easy dollar or two, so I made him a proposition. I told him I could run a spike mike up through the floor and get everything your sister and the other guy said on tape. Corcoran wanted to know who the fuck I was. I told him my name and how I was into electronics. He wanted to know how much it would cost. I told him and he said we had a deal. I told him we didn't have no deal until I saw some money. He said come by his office the next day and we'd settle everything. So that's what I did. I went by his office. Turns out he's a private detective. I remember when he played football, but I didn't know he was any private detective."

"He had an office," Dill said. "Where?"

"The Cordell Building, know it?"

Dill nodded.

"He was sober though when you saw him in his office," Singe said.

"Stone sober, lady. And all business. He told me exactly what he wanted. He wanted the spike up through the bedroom floor and he wanted a tap on her phone, too. And he wanted it voice-activated. Well, that was gonna cost and I told him so and how much. He pulled out a roll and paid me in hundreds—no receipt, no questions, no nothing. So that's what I did."

"How often did Corcoran pick up the tapes?" Dill asked.

"Once a week," Snow said and ground his cigarette out in the ashtray.

"What was on the tapes?" Dill said.

Snow stared at Dill for a moment, and Dill thought he saw the apprehension and fear leave Snow's eyes. They were replaced with something that Dill finally identified as greed. He believes that somehow he's going to make a few bucks out of this after all, Dill thought.

"You wanta know what was on the tapes, huh?" Snow said. "Well, the sound of fucking was on the tapes, I guess, but I don't really know because I didn't listen to them. I've done a lotta this kind of work and when I first got into it, I used to listen to the tapes, but after a while, you don't because it's just the same old crap."

"So you didn't listen to them?" Singe said.

"No."

"Not even once."

"I listened to a little bit of the first one to check the quality, but after that I just dropped 'em in an envelope."

"Then what?" Dill said.

"Well, then Corcoran calls and says he wants to see me. And once again, he's all business. I mean it was like doing business with IBM or somebody. He says your sister's got another place where she spends a lotta time and he wants that wired, too. Well, he meant this place here. So I drove by and took a look and I didn't like the setup, so I went back and told him so. You wanta know what he said? He said, How much? That's all. How much? Well, I had a problem here. He wanted both the bedroom and the phone. Now I could do that okay and feed it all up into the attic there. But how was I gonna get the tapes? I mean, I could break in here once and install my gear, but I couldn't bust in every week just to pick up the tapes, could I?"

"So what'd you do, Harold?" Dill said.

"Bursts," Snow said.

"Bursts."

"Yeah. I rigged up a sender, something like a CB?" Dill nodded.

"I used this voice-activated low-ips tape, right? I mean, you can get hours on that stuff. So every two or three days I'd drive by in the van, park, and send the radio up there in the attic a signal. It'd rewind the tape and shoot it back to me in a burst—maybe two, three, four seconds. Never more'n five. I'd record it on my stuff in the back of the van, then rerecord it at normal speed and give it to Corcoran."

"And it worked?" Dill said.

"Sure it worked."

"Sounds expensive."

"It was."

"How expensive, Harold?" Anna Maude Singe asked.

Instead of answering, Snow again tugged the package of Vantage menthols out of his pants pocket and lit one. "You know, I've been thinking," he said as he waved out the match and dropped it into the ashtray. "All this oughta be worth a little something to you guys."

Dill sighed, bent forward, and cracked Snow across the right knee with the barrel of the revolver. Snow wailed, dropped his cigarette, and grabbed the struck knee with both hands. Dill bent down, picked up the cigarette, and stuck it between Snow's lips. "Don't be dumb, Harold," Dill said. "You're not real smart, but you're not dumb either. How much did Corcoran pay you?"

The cigarette was still between Snow's lips and he was still massaging the struck knee when he said, "One thousand a week."

Anna Maude Singe whistled softly. "How did he pay you, Harold?" she asked.

"What d'you mean how'd he pay me?" Snow said and took the cigarette from his mouth. "With money."

"Cash?"

"That's right, cash."

"You think it was his money, Harold?" Dill said.

Once again, the shrewdness crept back into the eyes. "You know, that's kind of an interesting question. I think it was his money all right when I did the first stuff. But later I think he started using other people's money. I think there was other people who wanted to find out what your sister was up to."

"He found himself a client, huh?" Dill said.

"Yeah. A client."

"Who?"

"How should I know? Somebody hands over a grand a week in tens and twenties to you, you ain't gonna ask too many questions."

"Or listen to the tapes?" Anna Maude Singe said.

"I didn't listen to 'em, lady. What little I did hear was mostly fuck talk and that doesn't do a thing for me." He paused. "But I will tell you this."

"What?" Dill said.

"He wanted me to tap in on somebody else."

"Corcoran did?"

"Yeah. He said name your price. So I went out and took a look at it and came back and said no way. I mean, this guy was set up just like he was expecting somebody to make a move on him."

"What'd Corcoran say when you said you wouldn't do it?" Dill asked.

"What could he say? I didn't tell him I wouldn't do it; I told him I couldn't. If you can't, you can't."

"Who was it, Harold?" Dill said.

"Some guy in a big house out in Cherry Hills is all I know."

"Was his name Jake Spivey?"

Harold Snow no longer bothered to look surprised at anything Dill said. "Yeah," Snow said. "Jake Spivey. How the hell did you know?"

CHAPTER

WITH his own pistol aimed at him, Harold Snow used the
kitchen stool to go up into the crawl space above the
bedroom closet and bring down the recording and sending
equipment. It was smaller than Dill had expected—not
much larger than a cigar box—and enclosed in a green
metal case.

"That's it?" he asked Snow.

"That's it."

"What about the microphones?"

Snow pointed to something in the ceiling above the
bed. "See that?"

"What?"

"Looks like a nail hole."

"I see it."

"That's the spike mike. I'm gonna leave it. It's not
worth the trouble to take it out. I patched in the phone
up there, too."

"You don't think the cops found it when they went over this place?"

Snow shook his head. "Not unless they went up into the crawl space, and they didn't."

"How do you know?"

"Talcum powder. I blew some talcum powder around after I installed it. It was still there."

Anna Maude Singe moved over and looked down at the small green metal box Harold Snow still held. "You said there's a final tape on there."

"That's right."

"Can you play it?" she said. "I mean, can you play it so we can hear it?"

Snow looked at Dill, who had let the pistol drop to his side. "Can I keep my stuff if I do? Can I keep this?" He moved the green box around a little. Dill brought the gun up. Snow hurried with his explanation. "Look, I put it together myself and it's worth a couple of thousand. I know where I could get at least a couple of thousand for it."

"You can keep it, Harold," Dill said.

They had to go back into the living room, where Snow had left his toolkit. It took him less than two minutes to splice a wall plug onto the cord that led from the green metal box. He plugged it into the wall socket and said, "This thing's only got an inch-and-a-half speaker on it, so you're not gonna get any quality."

"Just play it, Harold," Dill said.

"There's not much on it," Snow warned.

"Just play it, Harold," Dill said again.

The first thing they heard was a muted click. "That's the phone being picked up," Snow explained.

"Why doesn't it ring?"

"It don't pick up on rings."

"Hello," the woman's voice said. It was the voice of Dill's dead sister. Dill felt a small cold shudder. A *frisson*, he thought, surprised that the word had come to him.

A man's voice said: "Well?"

"I think the same time and place," Felicity Dill said.

"Right," the man said. There was a slight click. A brief silence. Another click. And Felicity Dill again said, "Hello."

"Another phone call," Snow said.

MAN'S VOICE: It's me.

FELICITY: Hi.

MAN'S VOICE: I can't make it tonight, damn it.

Dill recognized the voice. It belonged to Captain Gene Colder.

FELICITY: I *am* sorry. What happened?

COLDER: Something came up that the Troll says he needs me on.

FELICITY: You'd better not let him hear you call him that.

COLDER: (laughter) I caught it from you, didn't I?

FELICITY: Just don't let Strucker hear you.

COLDER: Will you miss me?

FELICITY: Of course I'll miss you.

COLDER: What're you going to do?

FELICITY: Well, since you won't be coming over here, I think I'll go over to the duplex and wash my hair.

COLDER: I'd like to help.

FELICITY: Wash my hair?

COLDER: Wash you all over.

FELICITY: (laughter) Next time.

COLDER: I've gotta go. Love you.

FELICITY: Me, too.

COLDER: 'Bye.

FELICITY: Goodbye, darling.

There was a click and after that, nothing, until a man's voice said: "Looks like she read a lot."

Snow switched off the machine. "That's the cops. You wanta hear it?"

Dill said he did and Snow played it, but there was nothing much on it other than an occasional "Whaddya think of this, Joe?" And finally, there was only silence.

"Can you play it once more for us, Harold?" Dill said.

"*All* of it?"

"Just the first phone call."

FELICITY: Hello.

MAN'S VOICE: Well?

FELICITY: I think the same time and place.

MAN'S VOICE: Right.

Then a slight click and Dill said, "One more time, Harold." Snow again rewound and replayed the four lines of conversation.

"Again," Dill said.

Snow played them again. Dill looked at Anna Maude Singe.

"Two words are all," she said. "'Well' and 'Right.'"

"Not enough?"

She frowned. "Not for me."

"Me either," Dill said and turned to Harold Snow. "Harold, you can keep your wonderful machine, but I want the tape."

"You mean I can go?"

"After I get the tape."

Snow quickly rewound the tape, removed it, and handed it over. He unplugged the recorder-sender, wound the cord around it, and tucked everything under his left arm. "You didn't have to hit me," he said as he bent down for his toolbox.

"Sorry," Dill said.

"Can I have my gun back?"

"No."

"You can take out the shells and give it to me."

"Goodbye, Harold."

Harold Snow started toward the door. "That tape oughta be worth something to you. A hundred bucks anyhow."

"Go home, Harold."

Snow stopped at the door. "You wanta get the door at least?"

Dill moved over and opened the door that led to the stairs. "Lemme ask you something," Snow said. "She was on the pad, wasn't she—Felicity?"

"I don't know, Harold."

"You oughta've looked after her better."

Dill nodded. "Probably." He paused. "One last thing, Harold."

"What?"

"That tape we just heard. Can you put a date to it?"

The greed popped back into the coyote eyes. "For a hundred bucks, I can."

Dill shook his head in defeat, took out his wallet, removed two fifties, and stuck them down into Snow's pants pocket.

"It was this Wednesday," Snow said.

"How do you know?"

"Because I cleaned the tape off on Tuesday. It had to be Wednesday because on Thursday—well, you know what happened on Thursday."

"She died on Thursday," Dill said.

Snow nodded, started to say something, changed his mind, and started down the stairs. When he was halfway down, he stopped, turned, and looked back up at Dill.

"I'm sorry," he said. "I mean, I'm sorry she got killed."

"Thanks, Harold."

Snow again nodded, again turned, and continued on down the stairs.

CHAPTER
24

DILL was seated, drink in hand, on the couch in Anna Maude Singe's living room. He again was staring at the large Maxfield Parrish print when she came in from her shower wearing a short white silk robe that was transparent enough to see through. She sat down on the couch. The couch's large center cushion separated them.

Dill put his drink down on the coffee table and said, "I can see through that."

"I know."

"You got a built, as they say in Baltimore."

"Part's inherited, part's acquired."

"Dancing?"

"How'd you know?"

"The way you move mostly."

"They thought it would help me with this," she said and touched the slight scar on her upper lip.

"What's that?"

"It used to be a harelip. Until I was seven I talked funny—or peculiarly, I suppose. Then I had the operation and a lot of speech therapy, and I didn't talk funny anymore. But I thought I still did. So I was given dancing lessons—to increase my confidence."

"Did it?"

"Not really. But at thirteen I turned pretty. It was almost overnight. It seemed that way anyhow: all of a sudden. So I decided I wanted to do something where looks didn't much count. I decided to become a lawyer."

"At thirteen?"

"Sure. Why not?"

"At thirteen," Dill said, "I wanted to be ambassador to the United Nations."

"Whatever for?"

"You got to live in New York. You didn't have to stand up when you worked. There were always people seated behind you, whispering secrets into your ear and handing you important slips of paper. It looked like a steady job. I was very impressed by people with steady jobs when I was thirteen."

He picked up his drink from the coffee table, swallowed some of it, put it back down, and moved over next to Anna Maude Singe. He touched the small scar on her lip. "I still have a little trouble with my R's," she said.

"I didn't notice," Dill lied and kissed the scar.

"You know why I really gave up dancing?"

"Why?"

"Because it was therapy. They said I was very good, but I figured that meant I was just good at therapy—at curing myself. So when I got to be thirteen I decided I was cured and gave it up."

Dill's hand went to her waist and began to untie the loosely knotted sash. She bent her head to watch. "Your robe," he said. "It looks something like the ones in the Parrish print."

"I know. When I was taking my shower, I thought about you and got all excited. I thought the robe might help things along."

He slipped the robe from her shoulders. Her breasts were several shades lighter than the rest of her skin, which was nicely tanned. The nipples were erect. He touched first the right one, then the left. "In the Parrish print," he said, "I never could figure out whether they're boys or girls."

"I hope you like girls or we're going to a lot of bother for nothing."

"I like girls very much," he said and kissed the right nipple.

"Strawberry," she said. "The other one's vanilla."

He kissed the left one. "So it is."

As he straightened up, she said, "You've got too many clothes on," and started loosening his tie. Dill worked on the buttons of his shirt. Seconds later, his clothes were on the floor. She examined him with frank interest and said, "I like looking at naked men."

"Women are better."

"They're okay, but men are better—I don't know—engineered. Take this, for example."

"You take it."

"All right," she said. "It's the most remarkable thing in the world."

"Not quite," he said, his hand and fingers now exploring the wet softness between her legs.

She closed her eyes and smiled, her head thrown slightly back. "We can begin on the couch and then move to the floor."

"Where there's more room."

"Right. Then you can carry me into the bedroom, throw me on the bed, and have your way with me."

"Sounds like a hell of an afternoon."

"I hope so," she said.

They came together then in a hot hungry frantic kiss. They remained on the couch for a while and then somehow found themselves on the floor. They were there for a long time. They never did make it to the bed.

Dill was still lying on the carpeted floor, his arms folded beneath his head, when Anna Maude Singe came naked into the living room carrying two cans of beer. She knelt beside him and put one of the ice-cold cans on his bare chest. Dill said, "Christ!" and grinned, removed his right hand from behind his head, and snatched the beer from his chest.

Singe raised her own beer in a mock toast and said, "To one hell of an afternoon."

"It was that," he said and raised himself up so he could lean on his left arm.

"Do you run?" she said, examining his body again. "You look like you run."

Dill looked down at his body. "No, I don't run. It's my inheritance, and it's just about spent. It's all my old man left me—a remarkably sound metabolism. He left me his nose, too, but he could've kept that."

"It's a fine nose," she said. "It makes you look like Captain Easy, Soldier of Fortune."

"You don't remember Captain Easy."

"He had a sidekick named Wash Tubbs. I had a case once involving copyright infringement of an old comic strip. During the research I learned just one heck of a lot about what they used to call the funnies—more than I wanted to learn probably. But then that's really why I like the law. It leads you down some strange paths."

She rose, shivered slightly in the air-conditioning, put her beer down, and slipped on the sheer white robe. Dill continued to lie on his side, propped up on his left elbow. Singe sat down on the couch and picked up her beer.

"Well," she said, "what d'you think?"

Dill lay back down on the carpet and stared at the ceiling. "Felicity wasn't on the take."

"No, I don't think so either."

"She got the money someplace, though."

"I wonder where."

"Who knows?" Dill sat up without using his hands, reached for his shirt and shorts, and started putting them on. "What d'you do—keep it around sixty-eight or sixty-nine in here?"

"I like it cool," she said. After a swallow of beer, she used a musing tone to say, "Jake Spivey."

"Old Jake."

"Clay Corcoran was going to tell us something about him."

"Whoever shot Corcoran didn't shoot him just to keep him from talking to us."

"How do you know?" she asked.

"Too pat, too neat, too..."

"Convenient?"

"That, too," he said.

"But there's that other link between Jake Spivey and Corcoran," she said.

"If you can believe Harold Snow. Maybe I'll ask Jake tomorrow."

"Think he'll tell you?"

"He might." Dill picked up his pants, rose, and began to put them on.

"My God!" she said. "One leg at a time—just like everybody else."

"What'd you expect?"

"After this afternoon, something—well, different."

Dill smiled. "I'm going to take that as a compliment."

"You should."

Dill turned to examine the Maxfield Parrish print again. "Girls," he said finally. "Definitely girls." He turned back to Singe. "That old guy at the church."

"The reporter?"

"Yeah. Laffter. I think I'd better talk to him."

"Call him."

Dill shook his head. "Somebody leaked Felicity's money problems to him right after she died. He sat on the story until today, but now he's going with it because somebody else told him to. I'd like to find out who all those somebodies are."

"You know where he lives?"

"Laffter? I know where he hangs out. You like steak?"

She shrugged. "I'll eat it. Where d'you have in mind?"

"Thc Press Club."

"When?"

"Around eight."

"What'll we do till then?"

Dill grinned. "We can go try out your bed."

She returned his grin. "You'd have to take off your pants again."

"I can manage that."

They didn't make it to the Press Club that Saturday night until 8:35 because Dill decided he wanted to stop by his hotel to change his shirt and see if there were any messages. There was one in his box to call Senator Ramirez in Tucumcari, but when Dill called all he got was the answering machine's polite bilingual apology.

The temperature had dropped to 92 degrees when they entered the Press Club, Dill in a fresh white shirt and the blue funeral suit, and Anna Maude Singe in a sleeveless yellow dress that he thought was linen, but which she said was some kind of wrinkle-resistant synthetic.

He rang the Press Club bell. Inside, Levides the Greek watched them approach the L-shaped bar. There were two spaces open at the small end of the L and Levides jerked his head toward them. When they were settled onto the stools, Levides said to Anna Maude Singe: "You used to come in here sometimes with AP Geary, didn't you?"

"As opposed to?"

"UPI Geary."

"I don't know UPI Geary."

"He's a slob, too. Singe, isn't it?"

"Anna Maude."

"Right." Levides nodded at Dill, but kept his eyes on Singe. "You're not doing a whole hell of a lot better."

"He's all I could scrape up," she said.

Levides turned to Dill. "Hell of a funeral, I hear. One guy gets killed. A thousand cops standing around and somebody shoots some poor sap and nobody sees anything. I started to come. I wish I had now."

"Scotch," Dill said.

"What about you?" Levides said to Singe.

"White wine."

After he served Singe her wine and Dill his Scotch and water, Levides said, "You see the paper?"

"Tomorrow's?" Dill said.

Levides nodded, reached underneath the bar, and came up with an early edition of the Sunday *Tribune* folded to page three. "Chuckles claims your sister got rich."

It was a two-column bylined sidebar tucked beneath the three-column story that reported the murder at the cemetery. The two-column headline read:

POLICE PROBE SLAIN
DETECTIVE'S ASSETS

The story was written in what Dill always thought of as the *Tribune's* patented dry-as-dust style, which it used to recount rape, murder, child molestation, treason, Democratic sweeps, and other assorted calamities that would be read over the family breakfast table. The story contained nothing Dill didn't already know. He himself had been quoted by Laffter in the final paragraph as having no comment.

Dill passed the newspaper to Singe and asked Levides, "Is Laffter here yet?"

"He's back in his corner, drunk as a bear, and spooning up his chili and whatever."

"Ask Harry the Waiter if he can get us a table next to him."

As he considered Dill's request, Levides used a knuckle to brush his mustache thoughtfully. "Why the hell not?" he said finally and went in search of Harry the Waiter.

It took Singe only another thirty seconds to finish the story. She put the newspaper back on the bar and said to Dill, "Nothing new in any of that; nothing even faintly libelous. I think I counted five uses of 'alleged.' Everything except her death is alleged. They come right out and admit she's dead."

"I noticed," Dill said and drank some more of his Scotch. "I'm going to get nasty with the old guy."

"Laffter?"

He nodded.

"Nastier than you were with Harold this afternoon?"

Again, Dill nodded.

"This I've got to see."

"I want your cold approval."

"Cold, clipped, and lawyerly."

"Right. And no matter what I say, don't look surprised."

"Okay." She sipped her wine and then examined him curiously. "Where'd you learn to do this?"

"Do what?"

Before Singe could reply, Levides returned to the small end of the bar. "Harry the Waiter says he can put you next to Chuckles in about five minutes. Okay?"

"Fine."

"He wants to know what you wanta eat."

Dill looked at Anna Maude Singe and asked, "Filet, baked potato, and salad?"

She nodded. "One rare."

"And one medium rare."

Levides nodded and went away again. And again Anna Maude Singe turned to Dill and asked, "Where'd you learn to do what you did to Harold this afternoon?"

"I don't know," Dill said. "I think I've always been that way."

"But it is an act, isn't it?"

"Sure," Dill said, "it's an act," and wondered if it really was.

CHAPTER

25

THE old man had spilled some chili-mac on his yellowing pongee shirt. He was trying to mop it off with the napkin he had dipped into his water glass when Dill and Singe sat down next to him. Laffter looked up at them and then went back to work on the chili stain. The padded bench that ran along the wall ended in the corner where the old man sat. Singe also sat on the bench, Dill in a chair across the table from her. Without looking up at Dill, the old man said, "Like my story?"

"I think I counted alleged thirteen times."

"I used it four times, but some shit on the desk stuck in another one." He looked up then. "What's on your mind?"

"You want a drink?"

"If you're buying, sure." He nodded at Anna Maude Singe. "Who's she?"

"My lawyer," Dill said. "Miss Singe, Mr. Laffter, who some call Chuckles."

Singe turned her head and nodded at Laffter cooly. "Do you chuckle a lot, Mr. Laffter?"

"Hardly at all," the old man said.

Harry the Waiter appeared at Dill's table with napkins and silver. As he laid them out, he asked if Dill and Singe would like fresh drinks. Dill told him they'd stick with the ones they'd brought from the bar, but added, "You can bring Chuckles a drink."

"The old goat's had enough," Harry the Waiter said.

"I'll have a cognac, old blackamoor buddy," Laffter said. "A double."

Harry the Waiter inspected him. "Spilled chili on your shirt, huh? Well, shoot, you only been wearing it four days now. Could've got another two days out of it at least, if you hadn't spilled stuff on it."

"Step and fetch the drink, waiter," the old man said, his voice loud enough to make heads turn.

"I got a good mind to eighty-six you right here and now," Harry the Waiter said.

The old man glared up at him. "A good *mind? You?*" He shook his head in well-feigned disbelief.

"Old broken-down reporter," Harry the Waiter said, and clucked sympathetically. "No sadder sight in the world. Used up. Worn out. Never was. Half drunk most of the time." He turned to Dill. "You sure you wanta buy this old fool a drink?"

"I'm sure," Dill said.

Harry the Waiter shook his head and turned away. As he moved off, the old man spoke in a loud voice of mock apology: "Misses the jungle, you know." He grinned without mirth at Dill. "What d'you think a double cognac'll buy you?"

"I need to find out who wanted that story about my sister printed." Dill smiled, but it was a cold and even heartless smile just as he had intended it to be. "That's one," he said. "Two, I need to find out who leaked it to you."

"Do you now?" the old man said.

214

"And three, if you don't tell me, then I'll make you wish to hell you had."

The old man snorted. "What d'you think you can do to me, Dill? I'm seventy-three fucking years old. It's all been done to me already. You gonna beat the shit out of me? One knock and I'm dead and you wanta know what my last words would be? 'Thanks very much,' that's what. Get me fired? I'd move to Florida and fry in the sun like I shoulda done five years back. You can't make me wish I'd done one goddamn thing."

Dill smiled his smile again. "My sister had an insurance policy, Chuckles. I'm the sole beneficiary. The amount she left is a quarter of a million dollars. Are you indigent?"

Laffter's washed-out blue eyes turned suspicious. "What d'you mean, indigent?"

"Are you without funds? Broke? Busted? Flat? Tapped out?"

The old man shrugged. "I got a few bucks."

"Good. Then you can afford a lawyer."

"For what?"

"You'll need him when I sue you for libel. Not the *Tribune*. Just you. I know my sister wasn't on the take, Chuckles, but your story says she was. I don't think it'll be too hard to prove malice—do you, Miss Singe?"

"I think you've got an excellent case," Singe said.

"And how much will two hundred and fifty thousand dollars buy in legal services?" Dill asked her.

Singe smiled. "Years. Simply years."

"Now if I sue you, Chuckles, do you think the *Tribune's* going to pick up your legal fees?"

"You haven't got a case," the old man said with a sneer. "You don't know anything about libel, either one of you. I know more about libel than both of you put together. They'll laugh you outa court."

"Then we'll appeal," Anna Maude Singe said with another smile.

"Appeals cost money," Dill said. "I've got two hundred and fifty thousand to spend, Chuckles. How much've you got?"

"You got shit," the old man said, as Harry the Waiter appeared and put a balloon glass of cognac in front of him.

"Who's got shit?" Harry the Waiter said.

"This fuck says he's gonna sue me for libel."

Harry the Waiter grinned at Dill. "You need a witness? You need somebody to stand up in court and say how nasty this old fool is? You do, I'm your man."

"Go away," Laffter said.

Harry the Waiter went away, grinning. Laffter watched him go. He remembered his cognac then, picked it up, and drank. When he put it down he smacked his lips and lit one of his Pall Malls.

"There was no libel in that story," he told Dill. "You think I don't know when I'm skirting the edge?"

Dill shrugged and looked at Singe. "Libel trials can be long drawn-out affairs, can't they?"

"They can go on forever," she said.

Dill looked back at Laffter. "You know what old man Hartshorne'll do when I sue? He'll hang you out to dry, Chuckles, especially if the *Tribune* isn't a defendant. He won't even remember your name. He might even fire you, but that won't stop the suit. I've got both the money and the time. I don't think you've got enough of either."

Laffter finished his cognac in a gulp. "Blackmail," he said.

"Justice," Dill said.

"I didn't say she was on the take."

"You implied it. You told me you wrote another story about her once before, a feature, but they didn't print it. It'll be interesting to find out why."

"They killed it, that's all."

"But why?" Anna Maude Singe asked. "Did they kill it—if they did—because it was inaccurate, malicious, unfair—libelous? What?"

"It was a fucking feature, lady, that's all. It was cute, if anything. You can't sue for cute."

"Today's story wasn't cute, Chuckles," Dill said.

The old man stared at Dill for long moments. Finally, when he sighed and said, "You really would, wouldn't you?" Dill knew he had won and almost wished he hadn't.

"Count on it."

"Five years ago I'd've told you to go fuck yourself."

"Five years ago you were only sixty-eight."

"So what d'you want?"

"Who leaked you the stuff on my sister's finances?"

"*Leaked?*" Laffter said. "How do you know it was a leak? I got taps down there I turn on and off like a faucet. You know how long I've been on police?—fifty years, that's how long. Think about it. Fifty years—except during the war. I've seen rookies come on the force, grow old, and retire. Christ, I've even seen rookies have kids who're damn near ready for retirement themselves. I'm a fuckin' institution down there, Dill. Leaks!" He almost spat out the last word.

"Who'd you get it from, Chuckles?" Dill said.

The old man sighed again, picked up his empty glass, and drained the last few drops. "The chief," he said in a resigned voice.

"You mean the chief of police—Rinkler?"

"The chief of detectives, asshole. Strucker."

"Why?"

"*Why?*" the old man said, his tone incredulous. "Did you ever ask somebody why they told you something? Is that how you used to do it for UP, Dill? Somebody out at the statehouse'd let something drop and you'd say, 'My goodness, why are you telling me all this?' Is that how you used to work it, fella?"

"No."

"Then don't ask me why."

"What'd he say to you?"

"Strucker? He said, You might find this interesting. He

reeled it off and I wrote it down. And sat on it—until today when the word came down and they said, Let's go with that Felicity Dill stuff you've got. It was a story, that's all—news—and I wrote it straight as a string because that's how I do it. And there wasn't one word of libel in it. You know it and I know it."

"The word came down from where—old man Hartshorne?" Dill asked.

"I don't know," Laffter said. "Either him or junior. What the fuck difference does it make?" He paused and then said, "That's it! That's all, by God!" He shoved the table away and rose. "You still wanta sue, Dill, well, you just go ahead and goddamn well sue."

Laffter started around the table, but stopped. His pale-blue eyes bulged and a dark-red flush spread across his face and it twisted itself into pure pain. He clapped his right hand to his chest and bent forward. He began to sag then and tried to support himself on the table with his left arm and hand, but they refused to cooperate. He crumpled and would have fallen if Harry the Waiter hadn't rushed over, caught him, and lowered him gently to the floor.

Harry the Waiter looked up at Dill. "Tell the Greek to call the paramedics for the old fool," he said.

"I'll do it," Anna Maude Singe said. She rose and hurried toward the bar.

"You ain't gonna die on me, old man," murmured Harry the Waiter, as he ripped off Laffter's greasy gray tie. "You ain't gonna die in my place."

Harry the Waiter shook the old man's shoulder and yelled, "You all right?" at him. There was no response, but he seemed to expect none. He put his left hand under the old man's neck, lifted up, and pushed down on the now sweaty forehead with his right hand. The old man's mouth came open. Harry the Waiter bent to listen and then shook his head, almost in disgust.

"I'm gonna have to kiss you on the mouth again, old

man," Harry the Waiter muttered. He kept his left hand under Laffter's neck, still lifting it up, and with his right hand pinched Laffter's nostrils until they closed. Harry the Waiter took a deep breath, opened his own mouth as wide as it would go, placed it over the old man's mouth, and blew into it. Dill could see the old man's chest rise. Harry the Waiter removed his mouth, checked to see if the old man's chest was falling, and seeing that it wasn't, blew four full quick breaths into Laffter's mouth. This time the old man's chest rose, fell, and then stopped.

Harry the Waiter got to his knees and checked the carotid artery in Laffter's neck next to the voice box. "Goddamn you, old man," he said. He placed the heel of his left hand an inch or so down from the tip of the sternum at the xiphoid, interlocked the fingers of his hands, leaned over Laffter, and pressed down. The old man's chest seemed to sink two inches. Harry the Waiter rocked back, came forward, and repeated the process. He repeated it fifteen times and then bent down quickly and blew twice into the old man's mouth.

A woman's voice behind Dill said, "Isn't that disgusting?" He looked around and saw that a small crowd of curious diners had gathered.

Harry the Waiter looked up at Dill. "Can you blow in him?"

"Sure," Dill said and knelt beside Laffter. "Just tell me when."

"When I hit five again," Harry the Waiter said and began counting his compressions aloud. When the waiter reached five, Dill inhaled deeply, covered the old man's mouth with his own, and blew.

"Again," Harry the Waiter said.

Dill inhaled and blew again. The old man's mouth tasted of stale tobacco smoke and cognac. And probably Polident, Dill thought as he forced himself not to gag.

"Again on five," Harry the Waiter said.

"Right," Dill said.

219

After the waiter again made a fifth cardiac compression, Dill again blew breath twice down into the old man's lungs. They were both still at it a few minutes later when the fire-department paramedics arrived and took over. The paramedics put Laffter on oxygen, lifted him onto a gurney, and rolled him toward the front of the club. Dill and Harry the Waiter went with them. The onlookers went back to their drinks and dinners.

"He gonna make it?" Harry the Waiter asked one of the paramedics.

"Yeah, I think so. You hit him pretty good with your CPR again, Harry. Thanks."

When the paramedics were gone, Dill asked Harry the Waiter, "You did CPR on him before?"

"Twice."

"Jesus."

"I told the old fool time and again he ain't gonna die here in my place. He's gonna die at home in bed all alone. That's how and where he's gonna die. Not here in my place. You really say you were gonna sue him?"

Dill nodded.

Harry the Waiter shook his head and grinned. "That'd set him off. That'd set him off for sure. You know who the old fool's gonna leave all he's got to?"

Dill could only stare at Harry the Waiter with utter disbelief.

Harry the Waiter went right on grinning. "That's right. Me. Ain't that something?" He ran his tongue over his lips and grimaced. "And don't that old man taste bad?"

CHAPTER

26

DILL found Anna Maude Singe at the small end of the
L-shaped bar huddled over a glass of something that looked
like vodka on the rocks. He told the Greek he would have
the same, whatever it was. Levides poured the drink and
indicated the silent woman. "I told her it really wasn't
anything you two said or did, but she's not buying it."

Dill nodded and drank. It turned out to be vodka. He
looked at Singe. She continued to stare into her glass.

"I told her the old guy's seventy-three," Levides went
on, "and that he puts away at least a fifth a day and
smokes three packs of Pall Malls and eats grease and junk
and walks maybe fifty or sixty steps a week, if that, and
that's what did it to him before and that's what did it to
him tonight. Not anything anybody said." He paused.
"Christ, you and Harry the Waiter saved his life."

"If he lives," Dill said.

"So? He's seventy-three." Levides paused. "Damned
old fool."

"I want to get out of here," Anna Maude Singe said, still staring down into her drink.

Dill put a ten-dollar bill on the bar, picked up his drink, finished it in three swallows, shuddered, and said, "Let's go."

She silently got down from the bar stool and started for the door. Dill was picking up his change when Levides, looking somewhere else, asked in his too casual offhand voice, "What'd you say to old Chuckles anyhow?"

"I said I was going to sue him for libel."

"No shit," Levides said as Dill turned and went after Anna Maude Singe.

Dill drove south on TR Boulevard toward downtown. Anna Maude Singe huddled against the right-hand door. Dill glanced over at her and said, "I don't suppose you're hungry."

"No."

"Me either."

"I'd like to go home."

"All right," he said. "You mind if I stop at a drugstore?"

"For what?"

"Mouthwash. I can still taste him."

Dill stopped at a drugstore whose digital temperature and time sign said it was 9:39 and 89 degrees. He bought a small bottle of Scope, came out, uncapped the bottle at the curb, rinsed his mouth out, and spat into the gutter, which was something he could not remember ever doing before—at least not since he was a child.

He got back into the car, started the engine, and pulled out into the street. Singe said, "You couldn't wait to get home to do that?"

"No," he said, "I couldn't. I could still taste him."

"What'd he taste like?"

"Like old death."

"Yes," she said, "that's what I figured he'd taste like."

When they neared the Van Buren Towers Dill started looking for a place to park. "Don't bother," she told him. "Just let me out in front."

"Okay."

He pulled up in front of the building and stopped. Anna Maude Singe made no move to get out. Instead, staring straight ahead, she said, "I don't think I want to be your friend anymore. I'll be your lawyer, if you want, but I don't want to be your friend."

"I'm sorry," he said. "I don't have all that many friends."

"Nobody does."

"Was it the old man almost dying?"

She looked at him then and slowly shook her head. "You weren't trying to kill him."

"You're right. I wasn't."

"If I went on being your friend, and not just your lawyer, I'm afraid two things might happen."

"What?"

"I might fall in love with you—and I'd probably get into some kind of trouble I don't want to get into. Being in love with you—well, I could handle that. At least I think I could. The other, I don't know."

"What other?"

"The trouble."

"You mean like this afternoon with Harold Snow?" She nodded. "You liked that," Dill said, "I could tell."

"You're right," she said. "I did. I never thought I'd like something like that before. I thought I liked safe, polite things." She shook her head as if in wonder. "Even tonight I liked it, when we were only talking to that old man, to Laffter, and he didn't just lie down and take it. He gave as good as he got. In fact, he was better than you were—than we were—most of the time anyway and, well, I liked that, too. At least, until he keeled over. That shook me. Even Clay getting shot didn't hit me that hard. And poor dumb Harold Snow, well, that was just kicks. But I was involved with that old man. I helped make it happen. And that got to me because I finally realized it's not just let's pretend, is it?"

"No," Dill said.

"You remember my asking if you weren't just all act?"

"Yes."

"You're no act."

"I suppose not."

"It makes me afraid and I don't want to be afraid. And I don't want to be in love with you either. And I don't want to be your friend."

"Just my lawyer."

"If that."

Dill wasn't at all sure what he should say. So he said nothing. Instead, he reached over and drew her to him. She went unwillingly at first, but then all resistance ceased and their mouths were again mashed together in one of their long, almost angry kisses.

When it was over she half lay on the car seat with her head on his shoulder. "I wanted that," she said. "I wanted to see if I could taste old death."

"Did you?"

"If it tastes like Scope, I did."

He kissed her again, gently this time, almost lovingly, and said, "You don't really want to be just my lawyer, do you?"

She sighed. "I reckon not."

"You can be both my lawyer and my sweetie."

"Your *sweetie?* Good Lord."

"What's wrong with that?"

She raised up to look at him. "I don't want any more trouble."

Dill grinned. "You like it. Trouble. You said so yourself."

She put her head back down on his shoulder. "Sweetie," she said unbelievingly. "My God. Sweetie."

• • •

As he drove down Our Jack Street on his way back to the Hawkins Hotel, Dill saw that the First National Bank was proclaiming 88 degree weather at 10:31 P.M. He automatically looked for Clyde Brattle's blue Dodge van as he drove into the basement parking garage, but didn't see it. Dill got out of the Ford and hurried to the elevator, skirting carefully around the big square concrete posts. He rode the elevator all the way up to the ninth floor without bothering to stop by the desk for any messages.

Dill unlocked the door to 981 and shoved it open, but didn't go in. The only sound he heard was that of the air-conditioning. He went in quickly, closed the door, and looked in the bathroom, but found only a faucet dripping into the sink. He turned it off.

Back in the room, Dill crossed to the phone and called information. He asked for and was given the number of St. Anthony's Hospital. He called the hospital and after going through four different departments was at last connected with a Mr. Wade who sounded very young and very casual.

"I'd like to know how an intensive-care patient of yours is doing," Dill said. "Laffter. Fred Y."

"Laughter like in ha-ha?" Mr. Wade asked.

"Like in L-a-f-f-t-e-r."

"Lemme check. Laffter...Laffter. Oh, yeah, well he died. About twenty minutes ago. You a relative?"

"No."

"There's no relative listed in his admission. Who d'you think I oughta call?"

Dill thought for a moment and then told Mr. Wade to call Harry the Waiter at the Press Club.

Later, Dill telephoned room service and asked them to send him up a bottle of J&B Scotch, some ice, and a steak sandwich. When it came he ignored the sandwich and mixed a drink. He drank that one quickly, standing up, and then mixed a second one.

He carried the second one over to the window and stood there, sipping it, and staring down at Our Jack Street on Saturday night. There were few cars to be seen and even fewer pedestrians. Once, people had come downtown on Saturday night, but they didn't anymore, and he wondered where they went—or if they went anywhere. He thought about Clay Corcoran then, the dead football player turned private detective who had loved Dill's dead sister. The two deaths were connected somehow, Dill knew, but he soon tired of trying to understand what the connection was. He thought about the sheep-faced Harold Snow after that, but only briefly, and then his thoughts went in a direction he didn't want them to go and he thought about the irascible old police reporter who had died alone in the hospital, possibly of apoplexy. He thought about Laffter for a long time and stopped only because he noticed that his drink was empty. He looked at the First National Bank's time and temperature sign. It said it was two minutes past midnight on Sunday, August 7. It also claimed that the temperature was still 88 degrees.

Dill turned from his vigil at the window, went to the phone, and called Anna Maude Singe. She answered on the seventh ring with an almost inaudible hello.

"He died about two hours ago," Dill said.

She was silent for several moments and then said, "I'm sorry." She paused. "Is there anything I can do?"

"No."

"You're blaming yourself, aren't you?"

"Some, I guess. I made him pretty mad."

"Well, it's done now. It's over. There's nothing you can do unless you want to grieve for him."

"I didn't know him all that well."

"I'll give you some legal advice then."

"All right."

"Forget it, sweetie," she said and hung up.

AT shortly after nine on Sunday morning the telephone rang in Dill's hotel room. He had been asleep when it began to ring and he was still half asleep when he answered it with a scratchy hello and heard Senator Ramirez say, "This is Joe Ramirez, Ben. You awake?"

"I'm awake."

"We'll be coming in tomorrow around four o'clock. Could you rent a car and meet us at the airport by any chance?"

"Us?"

"Dolan and me. He'll be coming in from Washington. I'm still in Santa Fe."

"Around four," Dill said. "Tomorrow."

"If it's no bother, of course."

"I'll be there. Can you hold a second?"

"Of course."

Dill put the phone down, went into the bathroom, splashed cold water on his face, came back into the room, noticed the bottle of whisky, paused, tilted it up, took a quick swallow, and got back on the phone with a question: "Did Dolan tell you about Clyde Brattle?"

"Yes, he did, and it presents a problem, doesn't it?"

"I told Dolan you can have either Brattle or Jake Spivey—but not both."

"I'm not quite sure I agree, Ben. I think I'll need to talk to them both. Can you arrange it?"

"Spivey's no problem. I'm seeing him today. But I'll have to wait for Brattle to call me, although I'm pretty sure he will—unless the FBI's got him."

"You didn't tell them he's there, did you?" The Senator's baritone rose in what sounded very much to Dill like alarm.

"I haven't talked to the FBI, Senator," he said carefully. "I was going to call them, but Dolan said he'd take care of it in Washington. Did he?"

"I'm sure he must've."

"Maybe I'd better call their office here—just to make sure."

"I don't really think so, Ben," the Senator said in a tone that managed to be both reasonable and stern. "I'm confident Dolan's got everything worked out in Washington. A call from you might—well, confuse things and destroy whatever political advantage we might get out of this. I'm talking about political advantage in its broadest aspects, of course."

"Of course," Dill said, not bothering to hide his skepticism. "What d'you want me to tell Brattle when he calls?"

"Tell him I'm prepared for a completely off-the-record exploratory meeting either late tomorrow or early Tuesday." The Senator paused. "Just him, Dolan, me...and you, of course."

"What about Jake Spivey?"

"Make him the same offer, but don't let the times conflict."

"I'll set it up," Dill said.

"Good." The Senator paused again. "And Ben?"

"Yes."

"I read a brief wire story in *The New Mexican* this morning. It was about your sister's funeral. An ex-policeman was murdered at it?"

"Clay Corcoran."

"The same Corcoran who used to play for the Raiders?"

"The same. He also used to go with my sister."

"I'm—well, I'm not quite sure how to ask my next question."

"The best thing to do is just ask."

"None of what happened to your sister or to Corcoran has anything to do with you—or with us, does it?"

"Not that I know of."

"It could be awfully embarrassing if it did—although I don't see how it possibly could."

"Neither do I," Dill said.

"Yes, well, I'll see you tomorrow then—at the airport."

Dill said he would be there. After the Senator hung up, Dill called down for room service. In the bathroom he stood under the shower for five minutes, shaved, brushed his teeth for another five minutes, and dressed in his gray slacks, white buttondown shirt, and the polished black loafers. The coffee arrived just as he finished dressing. He tipped the same room waiter another two dollars and received a cheerful thank you, sir, in return. The waiter left, Dill poured a cup of coffee, hesitated, added a shot of Scotch, and sat down at the writing desk to drink it. He was on his fourth sip when the phone rang again.

After Dill said hello, Clyde Brattle said, "Have you spoken to our friend from the Land of Enchantment yet?"

"I just got through."

"And?"

"He wants a completely off-the-record meeting either tomorrow evening or Tuesday morning. Early. Just you, him, Dolan, and me."

"A bit stacked, isn't it?"

"What d'you suggest?"

"I'd like to bring Sid and Harley—just for a security check, of course."

"If you bring them, I name the meeting place."

There was a pause until Brattle said, "Providing it's some place neutral."

"My sister had a carriage house—back on an alley and across the street from a park. Very private. How does that sound?"

Brattle thought about it. "Yes," he said, "that might do nicely. What's the address?"

"Corner of Nineteenth and Fillmore—on the alley."

"What about six tomorrow?"

"Make it seven," Dill said.

"Until seven then," Brattle said. "By the way, I understand you didn't call the FBI after all. Why ever not, if I may ask?"

"How d'you know I didn't call them, Clyde?"

"What a peculiar question."

"Dolan's taking care of it up in Washington."

"Is he now? Well, that's fine. Yes, that's splendid. Until tomorrow then."

After Brattle hung up, Dill recradled the phone, picked it up again, and called information. He asked for and was given a number. He dialed the number and it was answered on the third ring by a woman's hello.

"Cindy," Dill said with faked good cheer. "It's Ben Dill."

"Who?"

"Ben Dill—Felicity's brother."

"Oh. Yeah. You. Well, I can't talk right now."

"I want to talk to Harold, Cindy."

"To Harold?"

"That's right."

There was a pause and Dill could hear Cindy McCabe's muffled voice calling, "It's Felicity's brother and he says he wants to talk to you."

Harold Snow came on the line with a snarling question: "What the fuck d'you want?"

"How'd you like to make a thousand dollars, Harold, for an hour's work?"

"Huh?"

Dill repeated the question.

"Doing what?"

"Just put back into place what you took out yesterday."

"You mean over there—across from the park and up in the attic?"

"But over the living room this time, Harold—for easier listening."

"When?"

"Either this morning or this afternoon."

"When's pay day?"

"You take a check?"

"No."

"Okay. Cash. Late today. This evening sometime."

"Where?"

"Your place."

"What's going on?"

"Believe me, Harold, you don't really care."

"You want me to set it all up just like before—except over the living room this time?"

"Right."

"And you'll be over with the whatchamacallit later today?"

"By seven at the latest. I take it you don't want Cindy to know about the whatchamacallit."

"I don't think that's really necessary," Snow said.

"I don't either, Harold," Dill said, and hung up.

• • •

When Dill picked up Anna Maude Singe at her apartment it was shortly before noon and the Ford's radio was predicting that Sunday, August seventh, might well set an all-time heat record. At 12 noon it was already 95 degrees. There was no wind, no clouds, and no relief in sight.

Singe was wearing white duck shorts, a yellow cotton shirt with the tail out, and sandals. When she got in the car she eyed Dill critically. "Where'd you say we were going?"

"To Jake Spivey's."

"For a prayer meeting?"

Dill looked at his white shirt and gray slacks. "I could roll up the sleeves, I guess."

"There's a TG&Y on the way that's open," she said. "We'll buy you a shirt and something to swim in. Then you can take off your socks and wear your loafers barefoot and everybody'll think you just flew in from Southern California."

"What's TG&Y stand for anyway?" Dill said. "I forget."

"Tops, Guns and Yo-Yos," she said. "At least, that's what Felicity always claimed."

They stopped at the large general-merchandise store in a shopping center that had been, the last time Dill saw it, a dairy farm. He bought a plain white polo shirt and a pair of tan swimming trunks. When he got back into the car he took off his buttondown shirt and slipped on the polo shirt.

"Now the socks," she said.

"Don't you think that's a little daring?"

"You're down home, not in Georgetown."

"They dress kind of weird in Georgetown, too," Dill said as he bent over and stripped off the calf-length black socks. They were the only kind he ever wore, primarily because they were all exactly alike and when he reached

232

into the sock drawer, he didn't have to worry about whether they matched.

"Well?" he said.

Singe again inspected him critically. "You still look like you're going to the office on Saturday, but I guess there's nothing else we can do about it."

"Where's your swimsuit?" he asked.

"I've got it on underneath—what there is of it."

Dill grinned as he started the engine and backed out of the parking space. "You advertising?" he asked.

She smiled. "I could use a rich client. That's who'll be there, isn't it—rich folks?"

"At Jake Spivey's?" Dill said and shook his head. "There's no telling who'll show up at Jake's."

CHAPTER

28

THERE was a young Mexican guard on the big iron gate at Jake Spivey's. The last time Dill had seen him, the Mexican had been helping dig something up in Spivey's backyard. Now he sat in a canvas director's chair beneath a Cinzano umbrella. Near his feet was a gallon Thermos jug of something cool to drink. Across his lap was a shotgun. On his right hip was a holstered revolver with a plastic pearl grip.

The Mexican rose as Dill drove the car halfway through the gate and stopped. The Mexican moved over to Dill's side of the Ford. He carried the shotgun across his chest. Dill noticed its safety was off. The Mexican bent down to peer carefully at Dill and Singe through dark aviator glasses. He nodded thoughtfully at what he saw and said, "You are?"

"I'm Ben Dill and this is Miss Singe."

With a forefinger still around the trigger of the shotgun, which Dill recognized now as a 12-gauge, the Mexican used his other hand to reach into a shirt pocket and bring out a three-by-five card that contained a list of typed names. He studied it for a moment, then nodded and said, "Dill," pronouncing it very much like deal.

The Mexican used his shotgun to point toward the house. "Drive to the house," he said. "Somebody'll park your car."

Dill thanked him and started up the curving asphalt drive. Once again, all the sprinklers were on and the grass looked cool and wet and very green.

"Beauchamp Lane," Singe said almost to herself. "My God, I finally made it out to old Ace Dawson's place on Beauchamp Lane."

"I was eleven the first time I was out here," Dill said. "At a Christmas party."

"You lied and hustled your way into that, you and Spivey. Felicity told me about it. I'm really invited—well, sort of anyway."

The asphalt drive ended just beyond the big oak front door, and then formed itself into a large square where a dozen cars were already parked. They were all new cars, mostly expensive domestic makes that included four Cadillacs, two Lincolns, one Oldsmobile 98, and a Buick Riviera convertible. But there were also two Mercedes, a Porsche, and one large BMW. Dill estimated that the small parking area contained three or four hundred thousand dollars' worth of automobiles—and a rented Ford.

"Looks like I was right," Singe said as another young Mexican started moving toward the car.

"About the rich folks being here?"

Singe nodded as the young Mexican hurried around the Ford and opened the door for her. He smiled politely as she got out. The Mexican then waited for Dill to get out from behind the wheel. When he did, the Mexican, still smiling, slid across the seat. He wore his squared-off white shirt outside his black pants. The sliding motion caused the shirttail to rise up just enough for Dill to see the holstered automatic. He thought it looked like a 9-mm of some foreign make. The Mexican noticed Dill's interest in the pistol. The smile went away, then came back almost instantly, more polite than ever, as he started the engine and expertly shot the Ford into a parking space between a Cadillac and the BMW.

Before Dill and Anna Maude Singe could ring the "How Dry I Am" doorbell, it was opened by a smiling Daphne Owens who wore even fewer clothes than she'd worn the first time Dill met her. This time she had on only a pale-green bikini bottom and a kind of sleeveless top with enormous armholes that looked as if it might have been made out of an old sweatshirt, although Dill knew it wasn't.

He made the introductions and for some reason felt gratified when the two women immediately despised each other. Although their smiles were polite, their greeting ritualistic, and their handshake casual, the encounter nevertheless produced two instant enemies.

"What should I call you," Daphne Owens said, "Anna or Maude or both?"

"Most folks just run it together and call me both."

"And so shall I. You must call me Daffy—as in Duck, right, Mr. Dill?"

"Right," he said.

"Now let's go back so you can get something to drink and meet everyone."

They followed her down the long wide hall and through french doors that led out onto a patio that was formed, jigsaw fashion, out of large irregular pieces of black slate. Carefully trimmed and cultivated grass grew in the cracks between the pieces. Dill suspected that if he were to go high enough, perhaps up on the roof of the house, the green grass might spell out a word or a name or even a picture. Probably something bawdy, he thought, and decided to ask Spivey about it.

As he glanced around he saw there were four people

splashing about in the big pool. Daphne Owens then introduced him and Singe to three different knots of guests who were in their thirties and forties. All were trim, well groomed, and held glasses of wine or Perrier in their hands, but no cigarettes. The men all looked as if they ran six miles a day; the women as if they were Jane Fonda Workout disciples. Dill immediately forgot their names.

He didn't forget the names of the next two persons he and Singe met. Both were men and both were older. The older one was so old he might not have been able to rise from his white iron lawn chair. The other one, who was only sixty-seven, rose easily.

"I don't believe you've met the Hartshornes," Daphne Owens said. "Mr. Jim Hartshorne and this is his—"

Before she could finish, the sixty-seven-year-old man who had risen stuck out his hand to Singe and said, "I'm Jimmy Junior."

She shook hands with him and said, "Anna Maude Singe and Ben Dill."

"Who's that, Junior?" the very old man said from his iron seat.

"Miss Singe and Mr. Dill, Daddy."

"Dill? Dill?" the very old man said in a cracked voice. "Have a drink with us, Dill."

Daphne Owens asked Dill and Singe what they would like. They told her. She said she would have it sent over and left. The older man patted the iron chair next to him and said, "You sit down here, young lady whose name I'm sorry I didn't catch."

"Anna Maude," Singe said, sitting down next to the very old man, who wore gray seersucker trousers that climbed halfway up his chest. They covered most of a blue short-sleeved pullover shirt that had a little alligator on it. On his feet were blue running shoes. Purple glasses covered his eyes. His left ear, the one next to Singe, contained a tiny hearing aid. There was a little hair left just above the ears, but the rest was long gone. It had left a dome that was smooth and tan until it reached where the hairline had once been. There the wrinkles began—ridge after parallel ridge until they almost reached his nose, where they changed direction and turned into small vertical gulches that ran into short tiny fine wrinkles and others, not so fine, that wandered off in all directions. The old man's lips were bluish in color and when he opened his mouth he revealed only a black hole. The nose was still sharp and inquisitive, but the once firm chin seemed ready to crumble. James Hartshorne Senior was ninety-seven years old.

"Dill, you sit down over here," the old man said, patting the chair on the other side of him. "Junior, you drag up another chair."

While his son dragged up another chair, the old man turned back to Anna Maude Singe. "I like women's bare arms," he said, giving Singe's right one a quick stroke. "They turn me on, as much as anything turns me on these days, which isn't a hell of a lot. But bare arms always did. Downed with light brown hair. Anybody read him nowadays?"

"Kids in college do, I hear," Singe said. "You knew him, didn't you?'

"Eliot?"

"I'm sorry. I meant Ace Dawson."

"Old Ace. Yeah, I knew Ace. The slickest article ever to come up the Yellowfork." The old man cawed like a crow and Dill assumed he was chuckling. "He came up from Texas somewhere and I came up from Shreveport. I used to think they don't make 'em like Ace anymore. I thought that until I met the boy who owns this place now. Where'd you ever meet Jake anyhow?"

"I haven't yet," Singe said.

The old man turned to Dill just as the Mexican gardener-houseman arrived with the drinks. "Spivey's your pal then, huh, Dill?"

"That's right," Dill said, accepting his drink.

"Known him long?"

"Forever."

"If you were me, would you do business with him?"

"What kind of business?"

"Politics maybe?"

"I think politics might be where Jake's been heading all his life."

The old man smiled his blue-lip smile. "That distant shore, huh?"

"Maybe."

"Daddy," Hartshorne Junior said.

"What?"

"I think we ought to thank Mr. Dill."

"Yeah, you're right." The old man cocked his head and examined Dill. "Both Junior and I want to thank you for last night."

"Last night?"

"For trying to save young Laffter's life—you know, blowing in his mouth and all, you and that Press Club nigger waiter, what's his name, Harry. I already called and thanked him. Seems the hospital made some damn-fool mistake and called the nigger after Laffter died. Well, it seemed like a mistake anyway until I heard Fred'd left the nigger everything." He looked at his son. "You sure Laffter wasn't a nancy boy after all?"

Hartshorne Junior frowned. "He left everything to Harry, Daddy, because Harry put up with him all those years. I told you that."

"Well, you oughta know—about nancy boys anyway." He turned to Dill and cackled again. "Junior never married for some reason. He's been the town's most eligible bachelor for about forty-five, forty-six years now. Right, Junior?"

Hartshorne Junior ignored his father and turned to Dill. "Anyway, Mr. Dill, we'd like to tell you how much we appreciate what you did."

"How much do you really appreciate it?" Dill said.

Hartshorne Senior slowly removed his purple glasses and slipped on a pair of round horn-rimmed ones. Trifocals, Dill noticed. The old man tilted his head back and examined Dill through all three focal planes. The eyes behind the glasses looked bright and black and curiously young.

"What's on your mind, Dill?"

"Why'd you run that story on my sister?"

The old man looked at his elderly son. "What story?"

The son frowned again. "Felicity Dill. Homicide detective. Murdered. Financial irregularities. Laffter's last story."

"Oh," the old man said and stared at Dill. "You're that Dill, huh? The brother. I should've added that up right away. But I still don't understand your question."

"Why did you run that story on my sister's finances?"

"You thinking of suing?"

"No."

"Wouldn't do you any good. Nothing libelous in it. We got lawyers who see to that. And why shouldn't I run it? You trying to say somebody tells me what to print and what not to print?" Before Dill could answer, the old man turned back to his son and said, "Why did we print that fucking piece anyhow?"

Hartshorne Junior was a plump man with a big round head and a small pink face. The fat on his right bare arm jiggled as he moved his glass up to his lips. His mouth was small and usually pursed as if it were about to say, "Oh-oh!" He wore yellow slacks and a bright-green short-sleeved shirt with the tail out. Except for his eyes, he didn't look very much like his father. Hartshorne Junior's eyes were also black and shiny, but they didn't seem curiously young. They seemed terribly old. He sipped from his glass of white wine. When he put it back down on a glass-topped table, the fat on his right arm jiggled again.

"We ran the story," he said slowly, "because we were

asked to by the police." He cleared his throat. "We frequently cooperate with the police, especially when they tell us it will aid their investigations. Almost every newspaper does."

"In their investigation of what?" Dill said.

"Your sister's death, of course," Hartshorne Junior said. "And also the death of the man who was killed yesterday—the ex-football player."

"Corcoran," Dill said.

"That's right. Corcoran. Clay Corcoran."

"Mr. Hartshorne," Anna Maude Singe said. Both father and son looked at her. "Jimmy Junior, I mean." He smiled. "May I ask you something?"

"Of course."

"Which cop told you to run it?" she asked in a cold flat voice.

Hartshorne Senior cackled again. "Now that's the kind of question I like. Straight out. Right to the point. No futzing around. A question like that deserves an answer. Tell her, Junior. Tell her which cop told us to run it."

Hartshorne Junior pursed his lips. "It was a request, not an order, Daddy."

"Tell her."

"It was Strucker," Hartshorne Junior said. "Chief of Detectives Strucker."

Hartshorne Senior looked at Dill. "You gonna take it up with him, with Strucker? Maybe ask him why?"

"I might."

"He's here, you know."

"Strucker?"

"Yep. Last time I saw him—wasn't more'n half an hour ago—he was heading for a parley with your pal, Jake Spivey. In the library." The old man looked toward the pool. "That's Mrs. Strucker over there," he said. "The one in the black suit."

Dill looked and saw a tall, dark-haired woman poised on the edge of the pool at its deep end. He thought she

241

looked about forty. She dived cleanly into the water. It was an expert dive.

"Fine-lookin' woman," Hartshorne Senior said. "Her husband and Jake're in there talking politics."

"We plan to join them later," Hartshorne Junior said.

"Talk about the chief's future," his father said and turned to watch Mrs. Strucker climb up out of the pool. He turned back to Dill. "What would you say is the most important thing a wife can bring to a man's political campaign?"

"Money," Dill said.

The old man nodded his agreement and again turned to look at Mrs. Strucker. "And she's got just about all there is."

"Some time back," Dill said, "maybe a year ago, you killed a story Laffter wrote about my sister. He said it was a harmless girl-detective feature. Why'd you kill it— if you did?"

The old man was still staring at Mrs. Strucker. "I reckon you'd better ask the chief about that, too, Mr. Dill."

29

THE foursome was broken up by the arrival of the Mexican houseman-gardener (and putative butler), who asked Dill if he would please join Señor Spivey in the *biblioteca*. The notion of Jake Spivey having a butler to send with an invitation for a meeting in Señor Spivey's very own library struck Dill as funny, but no one else even smiled, not even Anna Maude Singe, who said she thought she'd go for a swim and started unbuttoning her blouse. Hart shorne Junior said he thought he'd circulate. Hartshorne Senior cawed again and said he thought he'd take a nap as soon as Anna Maude got through shucking off the rest of her clothes.

Dill followed the houseman-gardener. They went past the spot in the garden where the three Mexicans had been digging Friday. Dill now saw that what they had been digging was an immense barbecue pit. A quarter side of beef was roasting over a bed of hickory coals. The spare ribs from at least three or four hogs were cooking on a grill. A big iron pot of sauce simmered off to one side. The chef was an elderly black with white hair who seemed to know what he was doing. The smell of the cooking meat made Dill ravenous.

Just before they entered the house, Dill looked back at the pool. He saw Anna Maude Singe chatting with Mrs. Strucker. A moment later, they were joined by Daphne Owens. Singe, laughing, said something to Mrs. Strucker and then dived into the pool. Dill, who knew something about diving, thought she dived very well.

The outside heat, which already had reached 100 degrees, made it seem almost chilly in the air-conditioned house. After the Mexican slid back the library's twin doors, Dill went into the room, where he found Spivey seated behind the desk and Strucker standing in front of it, as if about to leave. Spivey called to Dill, "How you, Pick?"

"Fine," Dill said.

"You know the Chief here."

Dill said yes, and nodded at Strucker, who nodded back and said, "I was just leaving."

"I'd like to talk to you later," Dill said.

"Fine," Strucker said, turned back to Spivey and added, "We can go over all that this afternoon."

Spivey rose. "We'll work something out."

"Guess I'd best go mix and mingle," Strucker said, grinned and left. Spivey thoughtfully watched him go. After Strucker closed the twin sliding doors, Spivey smiled at Dill. "Thinks he'd like to be mayor. That's for starters."

"What's for afters?"

"Congressman. Or governor. Or senator. One of 'em anyway. The vote bug's done bit him." Spivey smiled again. "Course, his wife's been egging him on some. You meet her?"

"I saw her."

"She's something. Rich as greases, like we used to say till you found out who Croesus was."

"Speaking of money, Jake, I need some. Today."

Spivey frowned. "Jesus, Pick, it's Sunday. How much you need?"

"A thousand in cash."

Spivey's frown went away. "Shit, I thought you said money." He reached into a pocket of his faded jeans and brought out a roll of bills that was bound with a rubber band. He snapped off the band and counted ten one-hundred-dollar bills onto the desk, picked them up, and offered the money to Dill. After Dill accepted it, Spivey snapped the band back around the roll. It was still more than three inches in diameter. Dill took out his checkbook, sat down at the desk, and started writing a check.

"You ain't short, are you?" Spivey asked. "If you're short, just mail it to me sometime."

"I'm not short," Dill said, tore out the check, and handed it to Spivey, who folded and tucked it away in the pocket of his blue chambray shirt without looking at it.

"Want a beer?" Spivey asked.

"Sure."

Spivey sat down, took two cans of Michelob from his desk refrigerator, and handed one to Dill. After opening his beer, Spivey drank several long swallows, smiled with pleasure, and said, "First one today, if you don't count the one I had with breakfast, which I don't."

"Who're all your pretty new friends?" Dill asked.

Spivey grinned. "You mean the young and the restless out there? Well, sir, lemme tell you who they are. They're all veterans of our recent turbulent past. In sixty-five you'd've found a couple of 'em out in Haight-Ashbury. Or down in Selma. Or in sixty-seven marching with Mailer on the Pentagon. But when all that shit ended they came back home and went back to school, or into daddy's oil company, or his bank, or his construction company, or married somebody who did, and registered independent and made a pot of money and voted for Reagan, or for old John Anderson anyway, and now that they're forty, or prid near, they figure they're ready to do some real moving and shaking. After all, they got their weight back down, and they're doing aerobics, and they don't smoke dope no more, except maybe a little on Saturday night, and they don't do coke hardly at all and never ever touch hard liquor. So now, by God, they figure it's time they went and did their civic duty and elected somebody to something. Well, I'm kind of their glorified political guru and precinct captain on account of I got the most money except for Dora Lee Strucker, who's got more money'n anybody."

"And Strucker's your boy?" Dill said.

"Providing the Hartshornes'll go along, which I reckon they will."

"A law-and-order mayor, right?" Dill said.

Spivey grinned. "You ain't for lawnorder?—which you notice is one word in this house."

Dill smiled, drank some of his beer, and then gazed up at the ceiling. "You might pull it off, Jake."

"What I figure I'm really doing is growing my own briarpatch. Grow it high enough and thick enough, there ain't nobody gonna come poking around in it." He paused. "Except maybe that kid Senator of yours."

"I talked to him," Dill said, still staring up at the ceiling.

"And?"

Dill shifted his gaze from the ceiling to Spivey. "I think he's going to fuck you over, Jake."

Spivey nodded calmly. "He's going with Clyde, huh?"

"I think he thinks he can nail you both."

"No way he can nail Brattle good without me, and he won't get me unless I get immunity." Spivey lit a cigarette, inhaled deeply, and blew smoke at the ceiling. "You see my boy on the gate?"

"I saw him."

"And the kid parking cars?"

"I saw him, too."

"I figure old Clyde's gonna come after me."

"Himself?"

"Lord, no. He'll get Harley and Sid to find somebody." Spivey chuckled. "Maybe they've already run an ad in *Soldier of Fortune*. Or maybe Sid'll try it himself. Old Sid likes that kinda shit."

"You want to talk to the Senator?"

"When?"

"Tomorrow. He and Dolan are coming in at four."

"When's he seeing Brattle?"

"At seven."

"What d'you think, Pick, should I go first or last?"

Dill didn't hesitate. "First."

"Why?"

"Because maybe I can get you some insurance."

"What'll it cost me?"

"How much leverage have you got with Strucker?"

Spivey shrugged. "Enough, I reckon. What d'you want?"

"I want him to sit down and tell me the facts." Dill paused. "Whatever they are."

"About Felicity?"

Dill nodded.

"I'll see what I can do," Jake Spivey said.

Dill did not meet Dora Lee Strucker until after he performed a not quite perfect half gainer off the twelve-foot board. As he went into the water he thought his back could have been a trifle straighter, but he also knew it was still a fairly good dive. Diving was the only sport Dill had ever participated in seriously—probably because it was essentially a solitary sport. He had pursued it through junior and senior high school, and well into his freshman year in college, when he realized he would never be any better than he was at that instant, which was not quite good enough. He had abandoned it without regret and even with some sense of relief. The only diving he did now was into the pool at the Watergate gym when the mood seized him, as it did fitfully every two weeks or so.

When he climbed out of the pool, Anna Maude Singe clapped mockingly three times and said, "Show-off." She was wearing a dark-red swimsuit consisting of two small triangles up above and a mere suggestion of something down below.

If she took everything off, Dill thought, she would look a lot less naked. He said, "I just wanted to see if the brain could still tell the body what to do."

"I don't think you've met Mrs. Strucker, have you?" Singe said and turned to the woman in the one-piece black suit. "Ben Dill."

Mrs. Strucker held out a hand. Dill found she had a firm strong grip and a firm strong voice that said, "I thought it was a beautiful dive."

Dill thanked her and sat down next to Singe, who was seated crosslegged on a large towel. Mrs. Strucker was in a chair made out of aluminum tubes and plastic webbing. She had long tanned solid-looking legs, not quite heavy hips, a very small waist, large firm-looking breasts, and magnificent shoulders. An abundance of ink-black hair was piled up on top of her head. Below it was a bold face: high-cheekboned and black-eyed and wide-mouthed. There was also a touch of the hawk in her nose, an attractive touch, and Dill wondered if she'd had some Indian ancestors and how she had come to be so rich. He guessed her age at forty-three, although she could easily shave five years off that should the need arise. Chief of Detectives Strucker, he decided, had married well.

Singe said, "I was telling Mrs. Strucker—"

Mrs. Strucker interrupted. "Dora Lee, please."

"Right. I was telling Dora Lee here how you and Jake Spivey go back years."

"Eons," Dill said.

Singe grinned. "How long's an eon anyway?"

"Two or more eras, I believe," Mrs. Strucker said, and since that had a faintly geological ring to it, Dill decided she must have made her money in oil. Or her ex-husband had. Or her father. Or somebody. She smiled and added, "Which is quite a while."

"That's about how long I've known Jake," Dill said. "Quite a while."

"Has he always been so—well, so damned optimistic?" Mrs. Strucker asked.

Dill made a small gesture that took in the pool and the house and the grounds. "Maybe he's got good reason to be," he said with a smile. "It's the Micawber syndrome. Something's bound to turn up, and for Jake it always does and always has."

"You don't sound in the least envious, Mr. Dill—or Ben, if you don't mind sudden old-pal familiarity."

"Not at all," Dill said. "I mean, I'm not at all jealous of Jake and I don't at all mind being called Ben."

"I've noticed," she said, "that one old friend's good fortune is sometimes another old friend's despair."

"You're probably right," Dill said. "When somebody you know fails, your immediate reaction is, Thank God it's him and not me. But when somebody you know succeeds, it's, Why him, Lord, and not me? But as for Jake—well, I think of Jake as sort of a walking miracle: you don't quite believe it, but you sure as hell hope it's true."

"You're very fond of him, aren't you?"

"Of Jake? Let's say Jake and I understand each other and always have. It goes a little beyond fondness."

"Johnny—that's my husband—says Jake Spivey's the smartest man he ever met."

"I'm not sure what your husband means by smart. I think Jake may be the shrewdest man I ever met, the most cunning, the most—"

"Wily?" Singe suggested.

"And the most wily."

Mrs. Strucker examined Dill carefully, a half-smile on

her lips. "I also have the feeling that you trust him implicitly."

Before Dill could tell her she was dead wrong, Jake Spivey's voice boomed from twenty feet away. "Who's that pretty little half-naked thing there that nobody's introduced me to yet?"

Dill turned and said, "She's not so little."

When Spivey reached them, he grinned down at Anna Maude Singe and said, "By God, you're right, Pick, she ain't."

"Jake Spivey," Dill said, "meet Anna Maude Singe, my sweetie."

"Sweetie!" Spivey said. "Damned if you don't use old-timey words." He was still grinning down at Singe. "You know what he calls me sometimes? He calls me a brick, except you gotta listen real close to make sure how he's pronouncing it." Spivey shifted his grin to Mrs. Strucker. "How you doing, Dora Lee?"

"Quite nicely, Jake; thank you."

"Well, that's fine. We're gonna eat in about thirty minutes so lemme know if there's something you all need."

"There is one thing," Singe said.

"What's that, darlin'?"

"If I stand on my head and eat a bug, will somebody give me a tour of your house?"

Spivey cocked his head and smiled down at her. "You grow up rich or poor, Anna Maude?"

"Sort of poor."

"Then I'll give you Jake Spivey's personally escorted poor folks, lawdy-lookit-that tour of the Ace Dawson mansion."

Singe rose quickly to her feet. "No kidding?"

"No kiddin." He turned to Dill. "By the way, Pick, that fella you wanted to see. I think he's waiting for you in the library."

"Thanks."

Spivey turned back to Singe. "Let's go, sugar."

. . .

Chief of Detectives Strucker didn't smile or even nod
this time when Dill, dressed again in shirt and slacks,
came into the library. Strucker was seated in front of
Spivey's large desk and Dill, for a moment, thought of
sitting behind it, but immediately discarded the idea as
silly. Strucker was also wearing casual clothes—an expensive dark-blue sport shirt, ice-cream slacks, and a pair
of new-looking Top-siders with thick-ribbed white socks.
Dill thought Strucker wore the outfit like a new and
uncomfortable uniform.

As soon as Dill sat down in the other chair in front
of the desk, Strucker said, "Your sister was on the
take."

Dill said nothing. The silence grew. They stared at each
other and the older man's gaze somehow managed to be
both impassive and unforgiving. It was the gaze of someone who had long ago determined the real difference between right and wrong—and who should get the blame.
It was a gaze without pity. It was the law's gaze. Finally,
Dill said, "How much?"

Strucker looked up at the ceiling as if trying to do a
difficult sum in his head. He also fished a cigar from his
shirt pocket. "In eighteen months," he said, and lit the
cigar with a wooden match. "Give or take a week." He
made sure the cigar was going well. "We figure ninety-
six thousand two hundred and eighty-three dollars passed
through her hands." He waved the match out and dropped
it into an ashtray on Spivey's desk. "About one-two-five-
o a week or a little less if you wanta average it out." He
paused to reexamine the cigar's burning tip. "We also
know where some of it went: on the duplex; on the insurance policy she took out; the rent for that other place
she had—the garage apartment—but there's still about
fifty thousand missing." He puffed on the cigar. "The fifty
grand's kind of interesting."

Dill nodded. "It's just about what she'd've needed for the balloon payment."

"Just about."

"Why'd you feed all that crap about her to the *Tribune* and then make damn sure they ran it?"

Strucker shrugged. "Publicity is often the most useful tool in any investigation. You know that, Dill."

"Old Fred Laffter told me he wrote a harmless cutesy feature about Felicity some time back. They say you killed it. Why?"

Again, Strucker shrugged. "We thought it was premature, that's all. That it might've done her more harm than good."

"Whose pad was she on?"

"We don't know."

"Why was she killed?"

"We don't know that either, and before you ask me who killed her, or what she was doing to earn her one-two-five-o a week, I've got to remind you this is an ongoing homicide investigation and there's not much more I can tell you than I've told you already."

"Tell me how Clay Corcoran's death is tied in with my sister's."

"It isn't."

"Bullshit."

"Bullshit," Strucker said thoughtfully, much as if he had just stumbled across a new and interesting synonym. "Well, here's some more of it: Corcoran was killed with a twenty-five-caliber softnosed slug at a range of approximately twelve yards. I'm surprised the hole in his throat wasn't bigger than it was. I'm even more surprised that whoever shot him hit him. He must've been the best fucking shooter in the world if, in fact, he was aiming at Corcoran."

"Who else would he be aiming at?"

"Well, there's you and there's Miss Singe."

"Nobody was shooting at me."

"What about Miss Singe?"

"Her either."

Strucker drew in some more cigar smoke, tasted it for a moment, blew it up in the air, and said, "I made some phone calls to Washington. Not many. Two or three at the most. It seems you're kind of well known up there, at least by some folks. From what I understand you're nosing around after some renegade spooks—and every last one of them a real honest-to-God hard case. Maybe one of them figured you were getting too close, dressed himself up in an out-of-state-cop uniform (that sounds like a spook, doesn't it?), took a shot at you, missed, and hit poor old Clay Corcoran instead." He gave his big shoulders a strange almost Mediterranean shrug. "Could've happened that way."

"No," Dill said, "it couldn't've." He paused then, partly because of Strucker's evasions, and partly because he didn't really want to say what he was going to say next. "I understand," Dill said, "that you'd like to be mayor."

Strucker waved his cigar deprecatingly. "Just talk."

"But if the talk turns into something else, Jake Spivey's going to be awfully useful to you, right?"

"Well, yes, sir, his help would be much appreciated, if he sees fit to give it."

Dill leaned forward, as if to examine Strucker more closely. "I can jerk the chain on Jake," he said. "I can send him down the pipes where he won't be of any use to anyone."

Strucker again sucked on his cigar, took it out of his mouth, looked at it, and said, "Your oldest friend."

"My oldest friend." Dill leaned back in his chair. His voice turned cold and distant and nearly uninflected. "She was my sister. The only family I had. I knew her better than I've ever known anyone in my life. She wasn't bent. She wasn't on anyone's pad. I know that. And I'm pretty sure you know it. I also think you know what happened to Felicity and why. I need to know what you know. So either you tell me or I flush my old friend and your political future right down the drain."

Strucker nodded almost sympathetically. "Must be kinda hard, choosing between a live friend and dead kin."

"Not all that hard."

"For you, maybe not." He drew in some more smoke, blew it out, and again examined his cigar thoughtfully. "How long can I have—a week?"

"Three days," Dill said.

"A week'd be better."

"I would say okay, but three days is all I've got."

Strucker rose, stretched a little, and sighed his heavy sigh. "Three days then." He stared down at Dill almost curiously. "You really would, wouldn't you—dump your old friend?"

"Yes," Dill said, "I really would."

Strucker nodded again as though reconfirming some expected, but nevertheless unpleasant, news, turned, and walked out of the room. Dill watched him go. When the sliding door closed, Dill got up and went behind Spivey's desk. He ran his hand beneath the well of the desk and eventually found the switch. He went down on his hands and knees to examine it. The switch was turned to "on." Dill left it that way, pulled out the top right-hand drawer of the desk, then the middle drawer, and finally the deep bottom one. The Japanese tape recorder was in the bottom drawer, turning slowly. It obviously had been installed by an expert. Dill closed the drawer gently and rose.

He looked around the room and then said in a firm loud clear voice, "I wasn't kidding him, Jake. I really would."

CHAPTER

30

THE party at Jake Spivey's began breaking up when the sun went down, and it was a little after 9 P.M. when Dill and Anna Maude Singe arrived at the yellow brick duplex on the corner of 32nd and Texas Avenue. Lights were on in the ground-floor apartment. The rented Ford's radio said the temperature had fallen to 93 degrees, but Dill thought it was still much hotter than that.

"Well, he's home," Singe said, looking at the lights in Harold Snow's apartment.

"Keep her in the living room if he and I go in the kitchen," Dill said. "If she goes in the kitchen, you go with her and make sure she stays there for at least two or three minutes."

"Okay."

They got out of the car and moved up the walk to the door with the blistered brown molding. Dill rang the bell. Seconds later, the door was opened by Harold Snow, who wore a T-shirt, tennis shorts, and a cross look. Before

Snow could say anything, Dill said in a too-loud voice, "We've come about the rent, Harold."

There was a brief puzzled look that lasted for less than a second until the coyote eyes signaled their understanding. Snow turned his head to make sure his voice would carry back into the living room. "Yeah. Right. The rent."

Snow led them through the small foyer and into the living room, where Cindy McCabe was applying pink polish to her toenails and watching a television program that featured elderly British actors. Dill introduced the two women and Cindy McCabe said, "Hi."

"Turn that shit off," Snow said. "They're here about the rent."

McCabe recapped the nail-polish bottle, rose, and in an effort to protect her freshly painted toes, walked awkwardly on her heels over to the large television set and switched it off. "What's with the rent?" she said.

"God, it's hot outside," Dill said, hoping he wouldn't have to add: It sure makes you thirsty.

He didn't. The cleverness again flitted across Harold Snow's face and he said, "You want a beer or something?"

Dill smiled. "A beer would be great."

"Get us four beers, will you, doll?" Snow said to Cindy McCabe. Before she could reply, Anna Maude Singe said, "Let me help, Cindy." McCabe nodded indifferently and started toward the kitchen, still walking awkwardly on her heels. Singe went with her.

"Where's my thousand bucks?" Snow said in a low hurried voice.

"Did you put it in, Harold?"

"I put it in, just like you said—in the living room. Where's my money?"

Dill took the ten folded hundred-dollar bills from his pants pocket and handed them to Snow, who counted them quickly. "Jesus," he said, "couldn't you even've found an envelope?" He counted the bills a second time and then stuffed them down into the right pocket of his tennis shorts.

"You're sure it works, Harold?" Dill said.

"It works. I checked it. Voice-activated, just like before. Funny thing is, though, I found something else."

"What?"

"What comes extra."

Dill shook his head wearily. "The rent, Harold. You don't have to pay this month's rent."

"What about next month?"

Dill scowled. "Remember your knee, Harold."

The warning made Snow take a quick step back. It was almost a skip. "But I don't have to pay this month's rent, right?"

"Right."

"Well, what I found was that somebody else'd wired the place. The living room, I mean. Looked like maybe a cop job."

"What d'you mean, cop job?"

"I mean a pro did it. Not as slick as me, but he still knew what he was doing. So I left it in place, but what I did was, I squirted some piss into the mike. It'll still pick up sound, but it'll take a week to get the distortion out. If they can't, all they'll have is funny noise." He frowned. "You don't look too surprised."

Dill assumed that Clyde Brattle had ordered the wiring of the place where the meeting with Senator Ramirez would take place, and nothing Brattle might do would ever surprise Dill. He smiled at Snow and said, "Harold, just to show how much I appreciate your efforts, you don't have to pay next month's rent either."

Instead of looking pleased, Snow again frowned. He has to work the angle, Dill thought. He has to give it another twist. "Don't tell Cindy," Snow said. "I mean, we'll tell her about not having to pay this month's rent, but not about next month's. Okay?"

"Fine."

"Well, I guess we might as well sit down," Snow said and waved Dill to the cream-colored chair where Cindy McCabe had sat painting her toenails. After Dill sat down, Snow sat on the couch opposite. The couch wore a slipcover patterned with monarch butterflies. Snow leaned forward, his elbows on his bare knees, his expression and tone confidential. "All this has got something to do with your sister, right?"

"Wrong," Dill said.

Snow's expression went from confidential to skeptical. But before he could outline his doubts, Cindy McCabe came back, carrying a tray with four open cans of beer. Anna Maude Singe followed with two glasses in each hand.

"I brought glasses, if anybody wants one," she said.

Nobody did. McCabe served the beer and sat next to Harold Snow on the couch. Singe sat in the room's only other easy chair. Cindy McCabe looked at Snow. "What about the rent?" she said.

"We don't have to pay this month's."

"No shit. How come?"

She asked the question of Dill, but Harold Snow answered. "He wants us to sort of look after the place until he decides what to do with it. Even show it maybe, you know, to people who might wanta buy it." He looked at Dill. "Right?"

"Right."

"Hey, that's okay," Cindy McCabe said and smiled.

"But we gotta pay next month's," Harold Snow said.

"Well, sure, but one month free's nothing to sneeze at." Something else occurred to her. "You thank him?"

"Of course I thanked him."

"Well, sometimes you forget."

The doorbell rang and Harold Snow said what everyone says when the doorbell rings after the sun goes down. He said, "Who the hell can that be?"

"Bill collectors maybe," Cindy McCabe said and tittered.

Snow rose, holding his beer, crossed the living room, and disappeared into the small foyer. They could hear him opening the front door. They could also hear him say, "Yeah, what is it?"

Then they heard the first shotgun blast. Then the second one. After that, it was absolutely quiet until Cindy McCabe began to scream. She didn't get up off the couch. She simply sat there, slowly crushing her beer can with both hands, and screamed again and again. The beer spilled out of the can and onto her bare legs. Anna Maude Singe rose quickly, hurried over to McCabe, and slapped her across the face. The screaming stopped. Singe knelt by McCabe, pried away the crushed beer can, and held the now sobbing woman in her arms.

Dill was up. He moved slowly to the foyer. I don't want to look at him, he thought. I don't want to see how he looks. He swallowed when he saw Harold Snow and then took four very deep breaths. Snow lay on his back in the foyer. The beer can was still in his left hand. The right side of his face was gone, although the left eye remained, still open. But it no longer looked clever. Much of Snow's upper chest was a red wet depression. The blood, bone and flesh had splattered the walls and the mirror that hung on the farthest one. Dill knelt by the body and tried to remember which pocket Snow had put the thousand dollars in. He decided it was the left one. But after he put his hand into it, he discovered he was wrong, tried the right pocket, and found the money. He put it into his own pocket and rose, realizing he had not breathed once since kneeling by Harold Snow. You didn't want to smell him, he thought. You didn't want to smell the corruption and the blood. You didn't want to smell the death.

Dill went back into the living room. Cindy McCabe, still sobbing, lifted her head from Anna Maude Singe's shoulder. "Is...is he..."

"He's dead, Cindy," Dill said.

"Oh shit, oh God, oh shit," she wailed, dropped her head back down on Singe's shoulder, and started sobbing again.

Dill looked around the room and spotted Cindy McCabe's purse on top of the television set. He walked over, opened the purse, took the ten hundred-dollar bills from his pocket, made sure there was no blood on them, and tucked them down into the purse. Then Dill went to the phone and called the police.

First to arrive were two young uniformed officers in a green-and-white squad car. They arrived with siren blaring and bar lights flashing. Neither was much over twenty-five. One of them had a large handsome nose. The other had an out-sized chin. They told Dill their names, which he promptly forgot, and thought of them as the Chin and the Nose. The Chin took one glance at Harold Snow's body and then looked quickly away—as if for a place to vomit. The Nose stared at the body with fascination. He finally looked up at Dill.

"Sawed-off, huh?"

"Sounded like it," Dill said.

"Gotta be," the Nose said and turned to his partner, who now seemed extremely interested in the small crowd of neighbors who had gathered outside at a safe, respectful distance. "Go talk to 'em," the Nose told his partner. "Get their names. See if they heard or saw anything—and check around in back, too."

"What for?"

"Maybe the whoever with the sawed-off's still back there."

"The whoever's long gone."

"Check anyhow."

After the Chin headed for the neighbors, the Nose

looked at Dill. They were still standing in the foyer. "Who're you?" the policeman asked.

"Ben Dill."

"Bendill?"

"Benjamin Dill."

"Right," the Nose said and wrote it down. "Who's he?"

"Harold Snow."

After he wrote that down, the young policeman indicated the living room. "Who's in there making all the noise?"

"His girl friend and my lawyer."

"Your lawyer?" That made the Nose suspicious momentarily, but he passed over it and turned his attention back to the body of Harold Snow. It still seemed to fascinate him. "What'd he do—the deceased?"

Dill shook his head. It was a small commiserative gesture. "He answered the doorbell after dark, I guess."

The real questioning didn't begin until the homicide squad arrived, headed by Detective Sergeant Meek and Detective First Grade Lowe. After Dill identified himself, Meek looked at him quizzically. "Felicity's brother?"

Dill nodded. "You knew her?"

Meek stared thoughtfully down at the floor before answering. Then he looked up at Dill and said, "Yeah, I knew her pretty good. She was—well, Felicity was okay."

It was Meek who took over the interrogation and Detective Lowe who handled the technical side. Meek was a tall, almost skinny man in his late thirties. Lowe was not much more than thirty-one or thirty-two, of a bit more than medium height and weight, and if he had one distinguishing characteristic, it was his completely bored expression—except for his eyes. His gray-blue eyes seemed interested in everything.

The medical examiner had come and gone, the photographer had finished, and they were about to cart away the body of Harold Snow when Homicide Captain Gene Colder came into the living room dressed in a navy-blue jogging outfit and Nike running shoes and carrying a pint of ice cream that he said was fudge ripple. He handed the sack to Detective Lowe and told him to put it in the freezer. The Chin volunteered to do it and Detective Lowe looked grateful.

Cindy McCabe had at last stopped sobbing. She sat on the couch with her hands in her lap and her knees primly together. She spoke only when spoken to. Her voice was low and almost indistinct. Once again, for the benefit of Captain Colder, she told her story. Dill then repeated his, and Anna Maude Singe hers. Colder looked questioningly at Sergeant Meek, who by then had already heard the same stories three times. The Sergeant gave the Captain a small nod.

Colder looked thoughtfully at Dill. "Let's you and me go in the kitchen."

"Officially?" Dill said.

"What d'you mean, officially?"

"If it's official," Dill said, "she goes with me." He nodded at Anna Maude Singe.

"You want your lawyer along, bring her along," Colder said and started toward the kitchen. Dill and Singe followed. They stood and watched Colder open the freezer, remove his pint of ice cream, find a spoon, sit down at the kitchen table, twist the top off the pint, and begin eating the fudge ripple, offering them only the explanation "I didn't have any dinner."

They also stood and watched as Colder finished almost half the pint, rose, put the top back on, and replaced the container in the freezer. As he sat back down at the table, he looked up at Dill and asked, "What d'you know about Harold Snow?"

"Not much."

"Felicity ever write you about him?"

"No," Dill said and turned to Singe. "You want to sit down?"

She shook her head. "I'd just as soon stand."

Colder pushed a chair out from the kitchen table, but neither Singe nor Dill sat in it. "We started checking into Harold right after Felicity died," Colder said. "And guess what we found?" He answered his own question. "Harold was all bent out of shape."

"Dishonest, you mean," Singe said with a small polite smile.

"Very," Colder said.

Dill shook his head in apparent disbelief. "He told me he was a home-computer salesman."

"He was, part of the time," Colder said, "but he worked strictly on commission, and if he didn't feel like working some days, well, he didn't have to. He could stay home. Or go somewhere else and be what he was really good at, which was a thief."

"What'd he steal?" Dill said.

"Time."

"Time?"

"Computer time," Colder said, "mainframe, which is pretty valuable."

"So I understand," Dill said.

"Well, Snow would locate it, figure out how to steal it, and sell it. He was sort of a computer and electronics genius. Some people are like that. They might not be too bright about most things, but they're real technical geniuses. You've known guys like that, haven't you, Dill?"

"I don't think so," Dill said.

"What about you, Miss Singe?"

"I haven't either."

"Huh. I thought everybody had. Well, when Snow wasn't stealing and selling computer time, he was doing something else that wasn't too nice either. He was tapping people's phones and bugging their offices and bedrooms and stuff like that, although I doubt if we could really prove it now. But guess who his last customer was?"

"You don't want me to guess," Dill said.

"You're right. I don't. Well, his last customer was Clay Corcoran—who dropped dead at your feet yesterday in the cemetery. And now poor old Harold drops dead at your feet here tonight. How's that for coincidence, Mr. Dill?"

"Strange and rare," Dill said. "But let me ask you this: what the hell've Snow and Corcoran got to do with who killed Felicity?"

Colder stared for several seconds at Dill. It was a stare that Dill felt contained nothing but distrust and dislike. "We're working on that," Colder said finally. "In fact, we're working on that very, very hard."

Colder rose from the table, took his pint of fudge ripple out of the freezer, and headed back toward the living room. Dill and Singe followed. Cindy McCabe was still seated on the couch, her hands in her lap, her knees pressed tightly together. Colder went over to her.

"Miss McCabe?"

She looked up at him. "Yes?"

"Is there anyone we can call for you—about Harold?"

She dropped her eyes. "There's his brother," she said.

"What's his name?"

"Jordan Snow."

"Do you have his number?"

"No, but you can get it from long-distance information. Back home, he's the only Jordan Snow in the book."

Colder turned to Sergeant Meek. "Have somebody call the brother and tell him what happened."

"Where's back home?" Sergeant Meek asked.

"Kansas City," Colder said.

"Right," Sergeant Meek said.

CHAPTER

31

THEY argued all the way to the Hawkins Hotel. It turned nasty as they got out of the rented Ford in the hotel basement garage and headed toward the elevator. They fought in the elevator. They were still fighting when Dill unlocked the door to room 981 and held it open for Anna Maude Singe, who sailed into the room, trailing the accusation "goddamned fool" behind her.

"It'll work," Dill said, closing the door.

"Never," she snapped.

"Watch," he said and crossed to the phone. After picking it up he looked at her questioningly. "Well?"

"What is it with you anyway?" she demanded, her tone furious, her face pink and angry beneath the tan. "Do I owe you something? For what? Because we fooled around a couple of times? I don't owe you anything, Dill. Not one damned thing."

Dill was dialing now. "Sure you do," he said. "You're my sweetie."

"Your *sweetie!* Christ, I don't even like you anymore. I'm your lawyer. That's all. And all I have to do is give you sound advice. Well, here's some: don't make that call. You want to call somebody, call the FBI."

"Somebody's already called them," Dill said as he listened to the phone ring. "In Washington. If I called them and I'm wrong, it would just screw up the deal the Senator's got with them. This way—well, if I'm wrong, nothing happens."

"Nothing good," she said as Daphne Owens answered the phone on its fifth ring. Dill identified himself and a few seconds later Jake Spivey came on with "I got your message, Pick, there at the tail end of the tape. I think you kinda shook old Chief Strucker up some. You really think he knows who killed Felicity?"

"He thinks he does."

"So what's on your mind?"

"How would you like to get Clyde Brattle off your back for good?"

Spivey didn't answer immediately. When he did, it was with a cautious question: "Do a deal with him, you mean?"

"Something like that."

"What kind of deal?"

"Not over the phone, Jake. But I think I've got an idea you two should sit down and talk about—just you, him, and me."

"When?"

"Tomorrow night after you're both through with the Senator."

"Where?" Spivey said. "Where's gonna be important, Pick. In a sitdown with Clyde, where's gonna be almost as important as what we're gonna talk about. So where's where gonna be?"

"Just a second," Dill said. He pressed the phone against his chest and looked at Anna Maude Singe, who was now

266

lying on the bed, staring up at the ceiling. "Well?" Dill said.

She didn't look at him. She was still staring at the ceiling when she said, "Okay. My place."

Dill put the phone back to his ear. "I'm thinking of Anna Maude's place in the Old Folks Home, but there're still a couple of details to work out. Let me call you back in fifteen or twenty minutes."

"I'll be here," Spivey said and hung up.

After Dill put down the phone, he turned to Singe and said, "Let's go."

She asked the ceiling, "I wonder why I said yes."

Dill unlocked the door to the narrow stairway that led up to his dead sister's apartment in the carriage house. The airless stairway was at least ten degrees hotter than the outside temperature, which seemed to be resting for the night at 91 degrees.

Followed by Anna Maude Singe, Dill went slowly up the stairs, unlocked the door on the small landing, went inside, and turned on the brass reading lamp. When Singe started to close the door, he said, "Leave it open."

He went to the telephone, picked it up, and again called Jake Spivey. When Spivey himself answered, Dill said, "It's me."

"You get it worked out?"

"Well, I think it's both neutral and reasonably secure."

"Reasonably don't cut it, Pick, but I've been thinking and, well, the Old Folks Home just might do. All we'd have to have is somebody on the stairs and at the elevator. My Mexicans can handle that. And I expect old Clyde'll want Harley and Sid along, so what we'll have is kind of a Mexican standoff, which'll suit me just fine. What time you aiming for?"

"Ten tomorrow night."

"When we gonna meet with the Senator?"

"He gets in at four tomorrow afternoon," Dill said. "Why don't you go out to the airport with me? I'm reserving them a suite at the Hawkins. We can all ride back together and talk in the car and then up in the suite."

Spivey made a counterproposal. Dill had known he would. "Tell you what," Spivey said. "Why don't I come down at three and carry you out to the airport in my Rolls-Royce automobile? I've never known fancy to hurt none when you're doing a deal like this."

"Okay," Dill said, "but no driver."

"Boy, you sure like to explain things to us dumb ones, don't you?" Spivey said and hung up.

Twenty-five minutes later they were in Anna Maude Singe's living room, seated on the couch. She held a glass of Scotch and water and looked around the room as though seeing it for the very first time. "So," she said, "this is where you're going to do it—in the only home I've got."

From the other end of the couch, Dill said, "Right here."

"You still think those phone calls worked? What if neither of them were tapped? Where does that leave you?"

"I think my phone at the hotel is tapped," Dill said. "And Jake's is, I'm pretty sure. I'm positive—well, almost—that the phone in Felicity's alley place is tapped. It must be by now. So whoever's reading those taps will know Jake Spivey's meeting here tomorrow night with Clyde Brattle. I don't think they want that meeting to happen."

"Why not?" she said.

"I think that's what Corcoran found out. The why. I think that's why he got killed."

"But you're not sure, are you?"

"No."

She looked around the room again. "Something rotten's going to happen, isn't it?"

"Yes. Probably."

"Here. I mean here in this room."

"Yes."

"What're you going to do when it does?"

"I don't know yet," Dill said.

"Maybe you'd better start thinking about it."

"Yes," he said. "Maybe I'd better."

Dill was up by seven the next morning, boiling water for instant coffee in Anna Maude Singe's kitchen. He carried two mugs of it into her bedroom. She opened her eyes and sat up in bed, barebreasted. Dill sat down on the edge of the bed, handed her one of the mugs, bent down, and kissed her right breast. She jerked the sheet up to her neck, sipped the coffee, and stared at a still life print on the far wall. Then she said, "I wonder what I'll do when I'm disbarred."

"You can come live in Washington for a while and when you get tired of that, we can go live somewhere else."

She stared at him with amazement. "Why do you think I'd want to do that?"

"Because you're my sweetie."

"Don't bank on it, Dill."

At 7:49 on that morning of August 8, a Monday, Dill got stuck in the traffic near the intersection of Our Jack and Broadway. As he waited, he watched the digital time and temperature sign on the First National Bank go from 7:49 and 91 degrees to 7:50 and 92 degrees. The radio newsreader in a tired voice was predicting 106 degrees by 3 P.M.

After parking the Ford in the basement, Dill rode the elevator up to the lobby and stopped by the desk to see whether he had any mail or messages. He didn't. The elderly woman he had taken for a permanent hotel guest was also at the desk. As she turned, she looked at him, hesitated, and then spoke.

"You're Henry Dill's boy, aren't you?" she said in a soft voice.

"Yes, I am. Did you know him?"

"A long time ago," she said. "I'm Joan Chambers." She studied Dill for a moment or two. "You look like your father, you know. The same nose. The same eyes. He and I had a summer together once. It was 1940—the next to last summer before the war. I sometimes think it was the last good summer ever." She paused and then added, "I read about your sister. Felicity. I'm very sorry."

"Thank you," Dill said.

"Excuse me, ma'am," a man's voice said. The Chambers woman stepped back. Dill turned. The voice belonged to Captain Gene Colder. He was no longer wearing his blue jogging suit or his Nike running shoes. Instead, he wore a nicely pressed tan mohair suit, a foulard tie, and a blue shirt whose tab collar was held together by a gold pin. Colder was also freshly shaven, but there were circles under his eyes, and the expression around his mouth was grim.

"I've been waiting for you," he said, apparently indifferent to the still-listening woman.

"Why?" Dill said.

"We know who killed your sister," Colder said.

"And high time, too," said the woman who had spent her last good summer with Dill's father. Then she turned and walked away.

CHAPTER

32

At a corner table in the coffee shop of the Hawkins Hotel, Colder explained how it wasn't his idea to inform Dill of the department's findings. He had come, he said, only at the insistence of the chief of detectives, John Strucker. "I've been here since seven," he added.

"Who killed her?" Dill said.

The waitress arrived at that moment and Colder ordered coffee, orange juice, and rye toast. Dill said he wanted only coffee. When the waitress left, Colder brought out a small flipback notebook and began to talk, not quite reading from his notes.

"A warrant was obtained from District Judge F. X. Mahoney at 11:57 P.M., Sunday, August 7. The warrant was served and a complete search was made of the premises at 3212 Texas Avenue, which are owned by Felicity Dill, deceased, and occupied by Harold Snow, deceased, the tenant, and by Lucinda McCabe, also a tenant and the deceased Snow's common-law wife. The search was conducted by Detective Sergeant Edwin Meek and Detective Kenneth Lowe under the supervision of Captain Eugene Colder. Chief of Detectives John Strucker was also present."

"Who killed her?" Dill said.

Colder didn't reply. Instead, he started to read from the notebook again, but was interrupted by the waitress, who placed coffee in front of Dill and coffee and juice in front of Colder, informing him the toast would be along in a jiffy. Colder picked up the glass of orange juice and drank it down. Then he went back to the notebook.

"At approximately 12:41 A.M., a gray steel locked toolbox was discovered. The toolbox was hidden under and behind two bedspreads and three suitcases in the closet of the bedroom occupied by the deceased Snow and his common-law wife, McCabe. Upon questioning, McCabe insisted she had no idea how the toolbox had got in the closet."

Colder stopped his recitation because the waitress arrived with the rye toast. He put the notebook down to butter the toast. He ate one piece, drank some coffee, and picked up the notebook again. Dill watched him silently and wondered what had taken place between Colder and Strucker, and how nasty the argument had been.

Colder again read from the notebook. "The toolbox lock was forced by Sergeant Meek, who then opened the toolbox in the presence of Chief Strucker, Captain Colder, Detective Lowe, and Lucinda McCabe." Colder looked up at Dill. "Then there's a whole list of things we found in the top tray, but I'm not going to read those."

Dill nodded.

"In the lower compartment of the tray, the following items were found, removed, and tagged by Sergeant Meek:

"One—Ten thousand two hundred dollars in one-hundred-dollar bills.

"Two—four fulminate of mercury blasting caps.

"Three—a .25-caliber Llama automatic pistol, serial

number—" Colder broke off and looked up at Dill again. "You want the serial number?"

Dill shook his head no.

Colder closed the notebook. "Well, that's it. The Spanish piece is at ballistics. They're checking whether it's the one that killed Clay Corcoran. If it is, then it means Snow wired up Felicity's car for a price, and then killed Corcoran, who must have been on to him. Your next question is going to be, who killed Harold Snow? We don't know yet. And that's why I argued against telling you what we'd come up with. You've got a loose mouth, Dill, and you move around in pretty funny circles. I told Strucker I didn't think you'd keep your mouth shut about this, but he told me to tell you anyway. Maybe he figures you can swing him a few votes when he runs for mayor. But that's none of my business either. So. Any questions?"

Several seconds went by before Dill shook his head and said, "I don't think so."

"I don't know if knowing who killed Felicity makes you feel any better or not. I hope it does."

"I guess I feel about the same."

"So do I. Snow was just hired help. Nailing the bastard who hired him is the only thing that'll make me feel any better."

"Harold Snow," Dill said thoughtfully.

"Harold Snow," Colder agreed.

"Ten thousand bucks."

"Ten thousand two hundred."

"Somehow," Dill said, "I thought killing Felicity would've cost a whole lot more."

Dill rode up to his room in the elevator alone. Just as he passed the sixth floor he smiled a wry, almost sad smile and said aloud, "Well, Inspector, I guess that wraps this case up."

In his room, he showered and shaved. Wearing only his shorts, he lay on the bed, his hands folded behind his head, and stared up at the ceiling. At ten o'clock, he ordered a pot of coffee. At one, he had them send up a ham sandwich and a glass of milk. When he finished his lunch, he put the tray out in the hall, sat down at the desk, and outlined the facts as he knew them. When he was done he tossed the ballpoint pen onto the desk, almost certain he would never know who had actually had the bomb wired to his dead sister's car.

At 2:30 P.M. he picked up the phone and called information for the number of the police department. He then dialed the number and asked for Chief of Detectives John Strucker. Dill had to identify himself to two officers, one male and one female, before he was put through.

After Strucker said hello, Dill said, "It wasn't Harold Snow, was it?"

"Wasn't it?"

"No," Dill said. "Harold was from Kansas City."

"Kansas City," Strucker said.

"It hadn't occurred to you—Kansas City?"

Strucker produced one of his sighs—a long mournful one that seemed to go on forever. "It occurred to me."

"When?"

"About eighteen months ago."

"You're away ahead of me, aren't you?"

"It's what I do, Dill. It's what I'm good at." Strucker sighed again, wearily this time. "Don't fuck it up for everybody, Dill," he said, and hung up.

Dill rose from the desk, took his blue funeral suit from the closet and laid it on the bed. From the bureau drawer he took his next to last clean white shirt. He dressed quickly, mixed himself a Scotch and water with no ice, and drank it standing by the window, staring down at Broadway and Our Jack Street. When he finished the drink it was five minutes till three. He turned and started for the door. He passed the bureau, stopped, and went back.

After a moment's hesitation, he opened the bureau drawer and from beneath the wad of soiled shirts took out the .38 revolver that had once belonged to Harold Snow. Dill stared at the revolver for several seconds. You don't need it, he told himself. You wouldn't use it even if you did need it. He put the pistol back beneath the soiled shirts, closed the drawer, stood there for a second or two, opened the drawer again, took out the pistol, and shoved it down into his right hip pocket. There was a full-length mirror on the door that led out into the corridor. Dill noticed the pistol made almost no bulge at all.

When Jake Spivey's gray Rolls-Royce Silver Spur sedan pulled up in front of the Hawkins Hotel, it was, according to the First National Bank's sign, 3:01 P.M. and 105 degrees.

Dill got into the air-conditioned car and waited until Spivey had pulled out into the traffic before he said, "How long've we known each other, Jake?"

Spivey thought about it. "Thirty years, I reckon. Why?"

"In all those thirty years, did you ever imagine that one day you'd be picking me up in front of the Hawkins in a Rolls-Royce?"

"Wasn't ever a Rolls," Spivey said. "Back then I always thought it'd be a Cadillac."

They drove west on Forrest, which had been named after the Confederate general Nathan Bedford Forrest. Some old-timers, mostly from the deep South, had once called it "Fustest Street" in honor of the general's strategy—or tactics—which had been to get there fustest with the mostest. Dill had heard the story from his father, although he himself had never heard anyone call it Fustest Street. When he asked Spivey about it, Spivey said his granddaddy had called it that, but his granddaddy had been a real old geezer who'd been born in 1895 or thereabouts.

As they drove through the rebuilt downtown area they tried to remember what had once stood on the sites of the new buildings that had gone up—or were still going up. Sometimes they could remember; sometimes they couldn't. Spivey said it made him feel old when he couldn't.

"Why'd you come back here, Jake—really? It wasn't just to grow yourself a briarpatch. You could've done that anywhere."

Spivey thought about it for a while. "Well, hell, I guess I came back for the same reason Felicity never left. It's home. Now you, Pick, you always hated it. I never did. I remember that summer you were eleven and your old man took you up to Chicago and you saw the first body of water you couldn't see all the way across. I thought I'd never hear the end of it. Chicago. Jesus, you made it sound like a fuckin' paradise. But I got up there when I was seventeen or eighteen and all I saw was one big horseshit town that some folks who talked funny'd built on a big old dirty lake."

"I still like Chicago."

"And I still like it here because I understand the sons of bitches here and, like the fella says, that means it's home. And I guess home is where I wanted to grow my briarpatch and show off how rich poor little old Jake Spivey done went and got." He grinned. "That's part of it. Showing the sons of bitches how rich you got."

"Revenge," Dill said.

"Don't knock it."

"I don't," Dill said. "I don't knock it at all."

When they were halfway to Gatty International Airport, Dill asked a question whose answer he thought he already knew. It was the first of a series of questions whose answers might decide who lived, who died, and who wound up in jail.

Dill made the first question as casual as he could. "When'd you say you saw Brattle last?"

"About a year and a half ago—in Kansas City."

"You said you went up there just to sign some papers."

"Well," Spivey said, drawing the word out, "it might've been just a little more'n that, Pick."

"How?"

"Clyde was pretty pissed off at me. He thought I owed him—owed him enough to lie for him to the Feds. I had to tell him I didn't owe anybody that much. Well, we'd had a few drinks and he started rantin' and ravin' about how if I wouldn't testify for him, I sure as hell wouldn't ever testify against him. So I told him to take his best shot. And he told me I could count on it. So I popped him one, and he popped me back, and about that time Sid and Harley rushed in and broke it up before we both had heart attacks. And then old Clyde looked at Harley and Sid and pointed at me and said, 'See him?' And they said, yeah, they saw me all right. Then Clyde gets all dramatic and says, 'Well, take a good look at him because he's a dead man, you understand what I'm saying?' Then it was either Harley or Sid, I don't remember which now, who said something like Sure, Clyde, we understand all right. I guess it must've been Harley who said it. Well, our business was all done, the papers all signed, so I got out of there and flew back home and hired me a mess of Mexicans."

"Has Brattle ever tried anything?" Dill asked.

"I'm not sure. About a year or so after I hired my Mexicans, I also hired a guy called Clay Corcoran—the one who got killed out at Felicity's funeral?"

Dill nodded. "Hired him to do what?"

"See if he could get past my Mexicans."

"Could he?"

"He said he couldn't, but that he'd like to take it one more step and hire another guy who was supposed to be tops at tapping phones and planting bugs and shit like that. So I said go ahead. Well, about a month or so before he got killed, Corcoran called and told me this guy he'd hired said it was impossible to get near my place. Now that made me feel some better, but then Corcoran got killed and I stopped feeling that way."

"Did Corcoran ever mention the name of the guy he hired?"

"He didn't mention it and I didn't ask. Why?"

"It's not important," Dill said. "Who picked Kansas City to meet in—you or Brattle?"

"Brattle."

"Why?"

"Why? Hell, Pick, Clyde was born there. It's his briar-patch, his hometown."

"I didn't know that," Dill lied. "Or if I did, I must've forgot."

CHAPTER

THE subcommittee's minority counsel, Tim Dolan, and Jake Spivey had never met. When they shook hands in front of the bronze statue of William Gatty, Dill was struck by the pair's resemblance. Their clothes helped. Both wore creased and wrinkled seersucker suits (one blue and the other gray) with shirts open at the neck from which loosened ties dangled like afterthoughts. Both were fifteen to twenty pounds overweight and most of it had gone to their bellies. Both were sweating heavily despite the air-conditioning. Both looked thirsty.

Yet the resemblance was more than physical. As they shook hands, Dill sensed that each recognized in the other a kindred spirit with a commonness of attitude, approach, and flexibility. Instinct seemed to tell them that here a deal could be cut, an accommodation reached, a sensible compromise negotiated. Here, both seemed to think, is somebody you can do business with.

The banalities had to be got through first. When Spivey

asked if Dolan had had a good flight, Dolan said he wasn't quite sure because he had slept all the way from Herndon, Virginia. When Dolan asked Spivey if the weather down here was always like this, Spivey said it was, as a matter of fact, just a touch cool for August, but it'd probably hot up some toward the end of the month. Each chuckled as he recognized a long-standing fellow member of Bull-shitters, International.

Dolan then turned to Dill and, after inquiring about his well-being, informed him the Senator's flight would be twenty or twenty-five minutes late. He suggested that they all repair to the airport bar for something cold and wet. Dill said fine, and Spivey said he thought it sounded like a hell of an idea. At no time did Dolan display the slightest surprise at Spivey's unexpected presence.

They sat in a round corner booth and ordered three bottles of Budweiser. Jake Spivey paid. Nobody objected. They all raised their glasses, said cheers or something equally meaningless, drank deeply, and then talked base-ball, or rather Spivey and Dolan talked baseball as Dill pretended to listen. Dolan seemed impressed by Spivey's acute analysis of how the Red Sox just might make it into the playoffs. Still thirsty, they ordered another round of beer and just as they finished that, the Senator's plane was announced. It was then that Dill made his second move.

He turned to Spivey and said, "Jake, I've got a couple of things I need to talk over with Tim here and I wonder if you'd mind meeting the Senator when he comes off the plane?"

Spivey hesitated for only a moment. "Sure," he said. "Be glad to. I've never met him, you understand, but I've seen his picture in the paper and on TV, so I reckon I'll spot him okay."

"Just look for the youngest kid off the plane," Dolan said.

Spivey chuckled, said he'd do that, and left. Dolan

turned to Dill and let the surprise creep into his tone, if not into his expression. "What the fuck was all that about?"

"Tell me about you and the FBI first. What kind of deal did you make with them?"

"No deal, Ben."

"None?"

"None."

"Why in hell not?"

Dolan frowned thoughtfully, perhaps even judiciously. Comes now the Boston dissembler, Dill thought. Dolan said, "Two reasons. One, leaks."

"From the FBI?"

"Like a wet brown bag."

"What's two?"

"Two. Well, two is political leverage. If the kid brings this off all by himself, he'll be in deep clover."

"And if he doesn't," Dill said, "he'll be in deep shit—and you with him."

"We discussed it," Dolan said. "We both agreed the risk is acceptable."

"Hear me, Tim. For the record I think you both made a mistake. A bad one. I think you should've called in the FBI—for the record."

Dolan shrugged. "Okay. You're on record. Now tell me why you sent Spivey to meet the kid."

"You notice how willingly he went?"

Dolan nodded.

"That means he's not worried about passing through the metal detector."

This time both surprise and shock spread across Dolan's plump handsome Irish face. And fear, too, Dill thought. Just a trace. "Jesus," Dolan said. "You mean it's gonna be like that down here?"

"Exactly like that," Dill said.

• • •

The Senator and Jake Spivey seemed to be chatting amiably as they rode the passenger conveyor belt down the long corridor to where Dill and Dolan waited. Spivey was carrying the Senator's garment bag; the Senator carried his own briefcase.

After the Senator greeted Dill and Dolan, Spivey turned the garment bag over to Dill and went to fetch the car. The three men waited for it just inside the airport's main entrance. "Looks hot out there," Senator Ramirez said.

"It is," Dill said.

Ramirez turned to Dolan. "Well?"

"Ben's put himself on record. He thinks we should've gone with the FBI."

The Senator nodded as though Dill's attitude was expected, if not altogether reasonable. "No gain without risk, Ben," he said, and turned to survey the less-than-two-year-old airport. "Who was Gatty anyway?" he asked.

"He flew around the world with Wiley Post in thirty-one," Dill said, not caring whether the Senator knew who Post was.

He apparently did, because he said, "Oh," in an appreciative tone, gave the airport another sweeping glance, added, "Nice airport," and again turned to Dill. "What's Jake Spivey's last price?"

"Immunity."

"What d'you think?"

"Take it," Dill said.

"Tim?"

"Take it under advisement."

Again, the Senator nodded, thoughtfully this time, and said, "At least until we find out what Clyde Brattle's got to say for himself."

"Right," Dolan said. "Never let the contract till you know what Paddy will pay."

One of the Senator's elegant eyebrows went up. "Boston folklore?"

"It's in the catechism."

"Well," the Senator said, "what we'll do is talk to them both and then make up our minds." He turned to give the bronze statue another inspection. "William Gatty, huh? He looks like quite a guy."

As they stood waiting for Jake Spivey to bring his car round, Dill examined the Senator, who was still examining the statue. You come, young sir, Dill thought, unfettered by either compunction or conscience, not to mention common sense. You come armed only with ambition of the ruthless and burning kind, which may or may not be enough. It'll be interesting to see the battle joined. It'll be even more interesting to see who wins.

"Jesus," Tim Dolan said, as Spivey pulled his hundred-thousand-dollar machine to a stop in front of the airport entrance.

The Senator smiled slightly. "Somehow," he said, "I knew it would be a Rolls."

It wasn't really a suite that Dill had reserved for Senator Ramirez and Tim Dolan on the sixth floor of the Hawkins Hotel. Instead, it was merely two connecting rooms— one of them with twin beds and the other with a single bed, a couch, and a few additional chairs. They had had coffee sent up. The empty cups now sat on the round low table along with the ashtrays and Tim Dolan's yellow legal pad on which not a word had yet been written. Spivey smoked a cigar; Dolan his cigarettes; the Senator and Dill nothing. They were all in their shirtsleeves, except for Dill, who still had the revolver stuck down in his hip pocket. The meeting, only forty-five minutes old, had already reached its impasse.

Jake Spivey settled back in his chair, put the cigar in the corner of his mouth and smiled cheerfully around it. "Tim, what you're asking me to do is climb up on the scaffold, stick my head in the noose, let you fellas give it a few yanks—just to make sure it's snug—and then

I'm supposed to say what an honor it is to be there on the occasion of my own hanging. Then, depending on how you all're feeling that day, maybe you'll spring the trap, and maybe you won't."

"Nobody's going to spring any trap, Jake," Dolan said.

Spivey looked at him quizzically. "You got the votes on the full committee?"

"We've got them," Senator Ramirez said.

Spivey turned to study the Senator with interest. "Well, sir, I'm sure you can add as well as I can, and probably better because I'm not real good at it. But I hired me some lawyers up in Washington who everybody says are damn good at their adds and takeaways. God knows they oughta be. They charge enough. Well, these lawyers up there— after they got through adding this and subtracting that— well, they say you're gonna be between two and three votes shy. Probably three."

"Then I suggest you retain different counsel," Ramirez said.

"Senator, lemme ask you one simple question."

"Of course."

"What you want me to do—when you boil it all down— is help you hang Clyde Brattle, right?"

The Senator nodded.

"So what's in it for me?"

"You're asking for total immunity."

"That's what I'm asking for. But what am I gonna get?"

"Immunity is a distinct possibility," Ramirez said.

Spivey smiled. "Possibility don't quite hack it, distinct or otherwise."

"It would be premature for us to say anything else at this stage, Mr. Spivey. You know that."

"Jake," Tim Dolan said.

Spivey turned to look at him. Dolan leaned forward, selling. "Let me put it this way, Jake. Brattle's bad and we want him bad. You're, well, you're only half bad, or maybe even only one-quarter bad, so if we have to choose between you and Brattle—choose who we're going to put the blocks to—then we'll go for real bad and Brattle and so will Justice and I can almost damn near guarantee you total immunity."

Spivey smiled once again and Dill noticed that each time the smile grew colder. "There's that 'almost' again," Spivey said, "which is almost as bad as 'distinct possibility.'" The cold smile grew icy. "You know what I think you guys are really trying to do?" The cold smile was still there as he looked first at Dolan, then at the Senator, and then back at Dolan. His glance slid over Dill.

It was the Senator who finally said, "What?"

"I think you're trying to jug both me *and* old Clyde. I think you're fixing to do a deal with Clyde where he'll go rest up in one of those federal country clubs for a year or two and, in exchange for that, he'll give you me—and maybe a couple of other guys I can think of. Or he says he'll give us to you. Clyde lies a lot, you know. Thing is, he lies all the time—morning, noon, and night. But I'm gonna give you the facts: Clyde can't hand you me—no matter what he claims."

"What about all that stuff in Vietnam, Jake?" Dill said.

Spivey seemed grateful for the question. "Well, all that happened a long time ago, didn't it? And nobody gives a shit anymore anyhow. But what I did there I did as a contract employee of the United States Government. And while what I did wasn't pretty, it wasn't any worse'n what some of the rest of 'em did. So if you think you can scapegoat me on that, you're flat wrong. To do that you'd have to have more'n Clyde Brattle. You'd have to have Agency backing and that you're just not gonna get."

"And afterward?" Dill said.

"You mean after the last chopper took off from the top of the Embassy and we lost and went home? Well, after that I bought stuff and sold it. That's all."

"Trading with the enemy is what some might call it, of course," the Senator said.

The small half-smile that appeared on Spivey's face was mean for its size. Here it comes, Dill thought. The one he's been saving. He looked at Dolan and Ramirez and saw that they, too, had sensed it.

Spivey's voice was low and almost gentle when he said, "They haven't called it trading with the enemy yet—and you wanta know why?"

Dill didn't think anyone really did. Finally, it was the Senator who quietly asked, "Why?"

"I was told to," Spivey said.

"Who told you to?"

"Langley." The half-smile was back now, no longer mean, but triumphant. Or vindictive, Dill thought. "It was a long time ago, Senator," Spivey went on, "almost ten years ago and maybe you don't remember, but—"

The Senator interrupted. "I remember."

"—we bugged out and left it lying around. Tons and tons of it. Heavy stuff, light stuff, you name it—just lying around. The spoils. Well, it was over and old Ho's folks'd finally won just like everybody with a lick of sense knew they would. They didn't need *all* that stuff though. Some of it, of course, but not all. But Langley knew folks who did. Folks in Africa and the Middle East and South America and Central America and you name it. So our job, me and Clyde, was to buy it from Ho's people for cash money and sell it for cash money to those folks who had their own little insurrection going—or counterrevolution or half-ass uprising or what have you. These were all folks that Langley was sort of looking after and encouraging. So that's what we were told to do, and that's what we did, and that's how we by God got rich. So if you wanta indict me for that, you're gonna have to indict half of Langley and a whole bunch of other people, and to tell the truth, Senator, I don't think you got the git to make it go."

"But after that, Jake?" Dill said. "After Vietnam?"

"After, huh? Well, after that Clyde got greedy, and went

bad, and got even richer, and I got out. I had nothing to do with later, but I know what happened. So if all you wanta do is hang old Clyde Brattle—well, shit, fellas, I'll furnish the rope." He paused and added in a low hard voice, "But you don't touch me."

There was a silence until the Senator smiled and said, "So. I'd say we've arrived at an understanding of our respective positions at least, don't you, Tim?"

Dolan looked at Spivey and grinned. "I'd say we know where Jake stands pretty well."

The Senator rose. The meeting was over. After Spivey rose, the Senator held out his hand. "You've been frank with us, Jake—you mind that? The Jake?" Spivey shook his head. "And we appreciate it. We'll discuss it among ourselves and I'm sure something can be worked out that'll make us all reasonably content." The Senator was smiling as he shook Spivey's hand. It was a pleasant smile, even warm, but not warm and pleasant enough to guarantee anything.

Spivey smiled back—his quick, brief half-smile— turned, picked up his seersucker jacket, slung it over his shoulder, and headed for the door. He stopped at the sound of Dill's voice. "I'll ride with you, Jake."

As they waited for the elevator, Spivey said, "I think I'd better cut myself that deal with old Clyde."

"I think you'd better," Dill said.

CHAPTER

34

AT 6 P.M. on that Monday evening, that hot August 8, the outside temperature was still 101 degrees. At a little past six they made love on the large old oak desk. The desk was in her office in the suite Anna Maude Singe shared with a certified public accountant. The CPA had given up and gone home shortly after four o'clock on what had turned out to be the hottest day of the year. The secretary he and Singe also shared lasted until four-fifteen before she, too, gave up and went home.

Dill had signed the papers first. They gave Singe his power of attorney and enabled her to collect on his sister's life-insurance policy and, if possible, sell the yellow brick duplex. After scrawling his name for the last time, Dill put the ballpoint pen down and touched Singe on her bare tanned arm. Suddenly, they were up and kissing frantically, she working on his belt, he on her panties, sliding them down over her hips and bare legs. She got his belt undone and he paused long enough to shrug out of his jacket. His pants and shorts dropped to the floor with a clank and the pistol fell out of his hip pocket. Neither of them noticed because they were too busy with the mechanics of the thing. But they soon worked that out, and then it was all lunge and thrust and small cries and finally joint explosion and sweet release.

Dill stood up after a while, his pants and shorts still around his ankles. Anna Maude Singe sat up on the edge of the desk, tugging her skirt down over her knees and smiling, obviously pleased with herself. She looked down, prepared to laugh at the pants and shorts puddled around Dill's ankles. But when she saw the pistol lying on the hardwood floor, her smile went away and she didn't laugh. She said, "Aw shit," instead.

Dill reached down and pulled up his shorts and pants, buckled his belt, bent back down, picked up the revolver, and jammed it into his right hip pocket. He then picked up his jacket from where it had fallen and slipped it on.

"Just who're you going to shoot?" she said.

"Who do you suggest?"

"That's smartass," she said, sliding off the desk and moving to a window that looked down on Second and Main six floors below. "I don't want smartass right now. What we did on that desk top there for five or ten or fifteen minutes, or whatever it was, well, it was the most erotic and satisfying fucking I've ever done, which, you might've guessed, is considerable." She paused. "I don't know why it was, but it was."

Dill nodded, almost gravely. "I thought so, too."

"Then I saw the gun lying there and it went away. The afterglow—or whatever. I'll look at that desk now, and I'll remember making love to you on it, but I'm not going to remember how tremendous it was. All I'm going to remember is that goddamn gun."

"I'm sorry," he said. "About the gun."

She turned, sat down at the desk, and opened a drawer. She took out her purse, removed a set of keys, and offered them to Dill. "The one with the dot of red nail polish opens my door." He took them, examined the one with the red dot, and slipped them into his pocket. She looked at her watch. "You'd better go."

"I've still got a few minutes," he said.

"You'd better go."

"All right."

She frowned. "When can I come home?"

Dill thought about it. "Eleven-thirty, I'd say. No later than that."

"Will you be there?"

"Sure, if you want me to."

She was still frowning when she said, "I don't know whether I do or not."

"If you don't, you can throw me out."

She nodded and said, "You'd better go."

"Right," he said, turned, and moved to the door.

"Dill," she said.

"Yes?"

"I wish you hadn't had the gun."

"So do I," he said, opened the door, and left.

By five minutes before seven that evening the temperature had dropped to 98 degrees. The rented Ford sedan with Dill at its wheel was parked some forty feet from the alley that ran behind the large old house at the corner of 19th and Fillmore. On the alley was the garage apartment or carriage house where Dill's dead sister had sometimes lived and where he had made the appointment with Clyde Brattle for seven o'clock.

Seated next to Dill was Tim Dolan. In back was Joseph Luis Emilio Ramirez, the Child Senator from New Mexico, whose black eyes glittered with what Dill supposed was excitement.

"What did you say their names are?" the Senator asked, staring at the dark blue Oldsmobile 98 that was parked the wrong way just up the street and on the other side of the alley. Two men were seated in the front seat of the Olds. Their faces were indistinct.

"Harley and Sid," Dill said. "They work for Brattle. As far as I know, they always have."

"What do they do?"

"Whatever he tells them to do. Right now, I think they're making sure the FBI hasn't been invited."

"Where's Brattle?" Dolan said.

"He'll be along."

They sat in silence for a minute or two. A taxi turned the corner at 20th and Fillmore and drove toward Dill's Ford and parallel to the brickyard turned park across the street.

"I'd say that's Brattle in the taxi," Dill said.

Just before it reached the Oldsmobile, the taxi speeded up. By the time it passed Dill's parked Ford it was moving at fifty miles per hour at least. "That was Brattle all right," Dill said.

"Why didn't he stop?"

"He'll be back. Harley and Sid probably signaled him with the brake lights." Dill looked at his watch. "Well, it's one minute till. I guess we'd better go."

He got out and went around the car. The Senator slid over and got out on the right-hand side, carrying his brief-case. "Put it back," Dill said, "unless you want Harley and Sid to paw through it."

"Oh," the Senator said. "Yes. I see." He put the brief-case in the Ford's back seat. Dill checked to see that all four doors were locked. They started for the carriage house. The Oldsmobile blinked its lights on and off. Dill waved.

"Brattle will want to make sure that none of us is wired," Dill said as he put the key into the lock of the door that led to the airless stairway. Before he opened the door, he turned to look at Ramirez and Dolan. "You're not, are you?"

The Senator shook his head. Dolan said, "Shit, no."

"We'll probably have to unbutton our shirts anyway."

"What about him?" Dolan asked.

"Brattle? We'll make him unbutton his, too."

It was five minutes past seven before Clyde Brattle arrived, accompanied by Harley and Sid. Dill had turned the air-conditioning on and the temperature was down to an almost comfortable 80 degrees. The Senator and Dolan had their jackets off. When Tim Dolan asked Dill why he didn't take his off, Dill said he didn't feel all that warm. Dolan looked at him curiously, but said nothing because of the knock at the door.

It was Dill who opened it. The knocker was the big man, Harley. Behind Harley was Sid and behind Sid, farther down the stairs, was Clyde Brattle.

"Just the three of you?" Harley said.

Dill nodded. "Just the three of us."

"You don't mind if Sid and me make sure."

"I don't mind."

Harley and Sid came in, slowly followed by Clyde Brattle, who nodded at the Senator and Dolan, but ignored Dill. Harley headed for the rear of the apartment and its bedroom and bath. Sid went over the living room and kitchen. Dill went with him and watched him work. He decided Sid was very good. He knew where to look and what to look for and also where not to look. He wasted no time. In less than five minutes Sid was back in the living room. He shook his head at Brattle. Harley arrived a moment later and did the same thing.

Brattle smiled almost apologetically to Ramirez and said, "Senator, if you don't mind we'd like you and Mr. Dolan to unbutton your shirts—just to avoid any unpleasantness later."

"Of course," Ramirez said, and started unbuttoning his shirt, which, Dill noticed, was custom-made. The Senator, his shirt unbuttoned, revealed a flat tanned chest and belly. Dolan's unbuttoned shirt revealed a soft, white, strangely hairless body.

"You, too, Clyde," Dill said, starting to unbutton his own shirt. Brattle smiled, took off his jacket, and unbuttoned his shirt. His stomach was flat and untanned. Dill kept his jacket on, but pulled his shirttails out and held the shirt wide open for all to see.

Brattle smiled at Sid and nodded at Dill. "Pat him down anyway, will you, Sid?"

Sid found the pistol almost immediately and showed it to Brattle. "He's got this piece is all," Sid said.

After seeming to consider the find, Brattle shrugged and said, "I think everyone can get dressed now."

Sid gave the pistol back to Dill, who put it away and started stuffing his shirttails back down into his pants as he turned to Harley and Sid and said, "So long, guys." They looked at Brattle. He nodded. Harley and Sid left. For some reason no one said anything until their footsteps could no longer be heard on the stairway.

The Senator took over then. He placed Brattle in a chair, and himself and Dolan on the couch. He asked Dill if there might be something cold to drink, water if nothing else. Dill said he thought there might be some beer.

Dill came back from the kitchen with the last four bottles of Felicity's beer and four glasses. He put them on the coffee table and let everyone help himself. Brattle poured his beer, tasted it, smiled his appreciation, turned to the Senator, and said, "So. I presume you've already talked to Jake."

"Today, you mean?" Ramirez said, not giving anything away.

"How is he—still protesting his innocence?"

The Senator smiled. "At least he's not a fugitive."

Tim Dolan leaned forward, both hands wrapped around his glass of beer. "You're here to plea-bargain, Mr. Brattle. Let's hear what you've got to offer."

Brattle made a small deprecatory gesture. "I offer myself, of course. A plea of guilty to certain indiscretions in exchange for a certain amount of leniency."

"How much leniency?" Dolan asked.

"Say, oh, eighteen months?"

Dolan smiled, although in it there was nearly as much sneer as smile. "Instead of ninety-nine years, right?"

"I haven't quite finished," Brattle said.

"Go on," the Senator said.

"In addition to myself, I can also give you Jake Spivey, whose culpability in this business is only a shade less than my own."

"Spivey," the Senator said. "Well, Spivey is, I think, already hooked. We can reel him in, take a look at him, and either keep him or throw him back."

"Spivey is part of my package," Brattle said. "I'm afraid you'll have to keep him—small fry or no."

The Senator looked at Tim Dolan, who made the corners of his mouth go down in an expression that said, So what if Spivey does a year or two—who cares? The Senator's small nod replied that he didn't.

"So far, Clyde," Dill said, "you've offered us yourself and Jake. I don't know if Jake's a keeper or not. But you're the real prize. The big fish. The trophy winner. Still, all we really have to do is get up, walk over to that phone there, call the FBI, tell them you're here, and ask them to bring along the net. And that doesn't require any bargaining or deal. Just a phone call."

"That occurred to me," Brattle said.

Dill smiled. "I'll bet it did." He turned to the Senator. "I think Clyde has something else to offer. Something irresistible."

"An inducement," Brattle said with a pleasant smile.

The Senator didn't return the smile. He asked, "What?" instead.

Brattle reached into his jacket pocket and brought out a three-by-five card. He passed it first to Dolan, whose eyebrows shot up after he read what was written on it and whose surprise made him say, "Mothera God." He handed the card to the Senator, who read it without expression and started to put it away in his pocket until he saw Dill's outstretched hand. After only a slight hesitation, the Senator passed the card to Dill, who read the four names on it in a clear loud voice.

Two of the names were household words, providing the household listened occasionally to the evening network news, read the hard-news section of at least one daily paper, and bought or subscribed to almost any magazine other than *TV Guide*. The two other names were less well known, but still familiar and much respected by those who thought of themselves as Washington power brokers. The first less well-known name belonged to a man who was still an extremely high-ranking CIA officer. The second not so well-known name was that of another man who also had been a top CIA officer, but was now an expensive Washington lobbyist. The first household name was a White House deputy chief of staff. The second household name was the real prize: it was that of a former CIA superstar who had since gone on to become a U.S. Senator.

"What you're saying, Clyde," Dill said, "is that you've got the goods on all these guys." And again, Dill read the four names, but this time in a normal, almost indifferent voice.

"I made all four of them rich," Brattle said. "Wealthy, anyway."

"You can prove it, of course," the Senator said.

"I can prove it."

Dill especially was surprised by Tim Dolan's next question. And he felt the lads up in Boston would not only have been surprised, but also disappointed. Dolan's question was: "And now you want us to help you jug these four guys?"

The Senator couldn't quite keep the exasperation out of his voice as he turned to Dolan and snapped, "For God's sake, Tim!"

Dolan stared at the Senator. And then a look of comprehension and deep appreciation spread across the handsome Irish face. Dill also thought there was a touch of awe in the expression when Dolan slowly turned back to Brattle and said, "Oh. Yeah. I see. You don't necessarily want 'em in jail. What you're doing is offering us the opportunity to keep 'em out."

Brattle smiled at Dolan much as he might have smiled at a dim student who showed unexpected promise. "Exactly," he said and turned to Ramirez. "Well, Senator?"

Dill felt he knew which way the Senator would go. Nevertheless, he gave him some silent advice. Put important men in jail, young sir, and you gain but fleeting fame. Keep important men out of jail, and make sure they know it's you who're keeping them out, and you gain immense power. And power, of course, is what your chosen profession is all about: how to get it; how to keep it; how to use it.

Ten seconds must have gone by before the Senator replied to Clyde Brattle's question. "I think," he said slowly, "that we can reach some kind of accommodation, Mr. Brattle."

And it was then that Dill knew, providing the dead Harold Snow hadn't lied to him, that Jake Spivey need never spend a single day in jail.

CHAPTER

DILL walked Clyde Brattle down the stairs. When they reached the last step, Dill said, "Jake wants to meet. He wants to cut a deal with you."

Brattle turned and examined Dill carefully. He started with Dill's shoes and worked his way up to the eyes. He seemed to find Dill's eyes particularly interesting. "When?" Brattle said.

"Tonight at ten."

"Where?"

"My lawyer's apartment. Here's the address." Dill handed Brattle a scrap of paper on which Anna Maude Singe's name and address were written. Brattle didn't read it. He stuck it into his jacket pocket instead.

"What's it like?" Brattle said.

"The only way up are the stairs and one elevator. Jake's bringing two of his Mexicans. You can bring Harley and Sid. They can all stand around and glare at each other."

"Who else'll be there?" Brattle asked.

"Just you, Jake, and me."

"Why you?"

Dill shrugged. "Why not?"

After a moment or two, Brattle nodded his fine Roman head. "I'll think about it," he said, turned, and went through the door and out into the August evening.

It was not yet eight o'clock when Dill came back into his dead sister's living room. By walking Brattle down the stairs, he had given the Senator and Tim Dolan time to think up the plot that would enable them to accept Brattle's proposal. But first they would have to ease Dill out. He wondered how they would go about it. He knew they would be devious; he almost hoped they would be clever.

As he came back into the living room, Tim Dolan asked him a question and Dill immediately ruled out clever. Dolan asked, "D'you think he bought our act?"

"Brattle?"

"Yeah."

"He seemed to," Dill said.

The Senator smiled. "I think we all played him rather expertly, don't you?" Before Dill could answer, the Senator went on, "Especially when Tim here went into his dumb guy role."

Dill nodded. "That certainly was convincing."

"He bought it," Dolan said, his expression confident, but his tone a trifle dubious.

"He did that," Dill said and asked the Senator, "What now?"

"Now? Well, now we play him along for just a day or two and then we'll reel him in. I think, though," he added slowly, letting a wise, thoughtful look spread across that almost perfect face, "I think we should let Tim here handle all negotiations with Brattle from now on, don't you?"

"He's counsel," Dill said. "It should be his job."

"Good," Ramirez said. "By the way, Ben, I want to compliment you on the way you've handled everything down here. Really excellent. First class."

"Thank you."

The Senator had one more question. He asked it as casually as he could. "Do you think it's true?"

"You mean about those four names he gave you of the guys he made rich?"

The Senator nodded.

"Sure," Dill said. "It's true. If it weren't, why would Brattle bring them up? What good would it do him?"

"My thinking exactly."

"And mine," Dolan said.

"Well," the Senator announced in a too bright, too cheery voice, "I'm starved. Why don't we all go get a big steak somewhere?"

"I'll take a raincheck," Dill said and noted the small look of relief that appeared on the Senator's face, but which almost immediately changed into one of mild suspicion. Dill went quickly into his explanation. "I'll be going back to Washington tomorrow or the next day and this'll probably be the last chance I'll have to look around here to see if there's anything of Felicity's I want—family pictures, letters, stuff like that. Why don't you all take the car and I'll call a cab later."

After Dill handed the car keys to Dolan and asked him to leave them in his hotel box, the Senator took one last glance around the living room and said, "Your sister lived here quite a while?"

"No, not too long."

"Cozy little place, isn't it?"

After the Senator and Dolan left, Dill carried the kitchen stool back into the bedroom. He slid open the closet door, shoved Felicity's clothes to one side, and placed the stool in the closet beneath the ceiling trap that led up into the carriage-house attic—or crawl space.

Standing on the kitchen stool, Dill pressed his palms against the trap. It gave way easily. He shoved it over to one side. The kitchen stool was only three feet high and Dill's height brought the top of his head even with the nine-foot ceiling. He grasped the edge of the trap hole, jumped, got his elbows over the edge, and after some frantic scrambling, managed to get a knee up. After that it was relatively easy.

The ceiling joists were covered with pieces of scrap plywood that formed a kind of path. Dill took from a pocket the candle he had found in the kitchen and lit it with a wooden match. He followed the plywood path toward the area of the living-room ceiling. As he crawled along the plywood, he talked silently to the dead Harold Snow: You wouldn't have lied to me, Harold, would you? No, not you. Never. A thousand dollars for fifteen minutes' work. So why would you lie to me?

When Dill reached what he guessed was the center of the living-room ceiling, he stopped, held the candle up, and found that Harold Snow hadn't lied after all. The small voice-activated tape recorder was just where Snow had said it would be. Dill pushed the rewind button, removed the cassette, and put it in a pocket. He left the tape recorder where it was and backed his way along the plywood path to the trap hole. It was much easier going down than coming up. Standing on the kitchen stool once more, he put the trap lid back into place.

After he carried the stool back into the kitchen he stopped and listened. It was not any particular sound that caused him to listen, but the absence of one. He went to the kitchen window and looked out. The view was of the alley, and across it was a backyard that boasted six tall silver poplars. The poplars usually swayed, shivered, and trembled even in the slightest breeze. They were now perfectly still because there was no wind—none at all. Then suddenly it came, down from the north, down from Canada and Montana and the Dakotas. The poplars trembled at first, then swayed, and finally danced madly in the cool hard north wind.

By the time Dill turned off all the lights, made sure the windows were closed, and went down the stairs and out the door, it was 8:33 P.M. and dark. The temperature had dropped 31 degrees in the past thirty-five minutes and was now down to 64. The north wind was beginning to gust. There was the smell of rain. Dill shivered in the sudden chill and found it to be a curious sensation. But then, he thought, so is any cold day in August.

Dill cut diagonally across the old brickyard that had been transformed into a park. Just as he reached the municipal pool where he and Jake Spivey had learned to swim and Dill had taught himself to dive, the rain began—big fat splattering drops that hit the dust and sent up a sweet clean smell. Dill stopped and turned his face up to the rain. The pleasant sensation lasted only a few seconds before the chill set in. Dill hurried through the rain, trotting now. He got wet, then drenched, and by the time he came out of the park near 18th and TR Boulevard, he was soaked, shivering, and wishing it would stop.

There had been a drugstore on the corner of 18th and TR Boulevard for years, Dill recalled. He wondered if it was still there. The King Brothers, he remembered. We Deliver. It had kept its soda fountain even after all the other drugstores got rid of theirs. The King brothers had said they didn't think a drugstore was really a drugstore without a soda fountain. When Dill came out of the park he spotted the old neon sign with its economical abbreviation: King Bros Drugs. He trotted down the sidewalk and ducked into the store out of the rain.

It was a place that still offered a little of everything and the first purchase Dill made was a bath towel. He used it to dry himself off as he wandered down the aisles looking for a small tape recorder-player. He found one, a Sony Super Walkman, jammed in between the Mr. Coffee cartons and the sets of chrome socket wrenches. Dill took the Sony over to the counter. A man of about sixty stood behind the cash register. Dill thought he might be one of the King brothers, but wasn't sure, and blamed his faltering memory on approaching senility.

The man took the Sony, looked at its price, nodded his appreciation, and said, "Can't beat those Japanese," when Dill handed him a hundred-dollar bill.

The man put the Sony in a sack and slid it across the counter along with ninety-nine cents change. "I put it in an ice-cream sack," he said. "It'll keep the rain out."

"Thanks," Dill said. "Have you got a pay phone? I need to call a cab."

"You can call one, but it won't ever come. Not on a night like this."

"Then I'll call somebody else," Dill said.

"Phone's right back there," the man said, nodding toward the rear of the store. He stared at Dill for a moment. "Say, didn't you used to come in here when you were a kid?—hell, it must be twenty-five, thirty years ago—you and your buddy, who was kinda chubby back then."

"He still is," Dill said.

"I remember your nose," the man said. "Haven't seen you around lately, though. What'd you do, move out of the neighborhood?"

"Moved a little north and east," Dill said.

The man nodded. "Yeah, a lot of folks are moving out that way."

Dill dropped a dime into the pay phone and called Anna Maude Singe at her office. She answered on the second ring. He told her where he was stuck and she said she would come get him. Dill's second call was to Jake Spivey.

After Spivey said hello, Dill said, "It's on."

"Clyde say he'd be there?"

"He said he'd think about it."

"That means he'll be there. Who else?"

"Just me," Dill said. "Better make it nine-thirty instead of ten."

"Well, it's gonna be one real interesting night," Spivey said, and hung up.

Dill moved back to the front of the drugstore and took a stool at the soda fountain. He wondered if they still called them soda jerks. Whatever they called them, Dill asked the one behind the counter for a cup of coffee. While he waited, he checked the Sony to see if it had batteries. It didn't, so he bought some, put them in, inserted the end of the earplug into its proper socket, slipped in the cassette, held the earplug up to his ear, and pressed the play button.

The first thing he heard was "Sixty-nine is very fine, testing, testing. Ten, niner, eight, seven, six, five, four, three, two, and we've got ignition. Testing...testing ...testing...and fuck you, Dill." It was the voice of the dead Harold Snow, sounding very much alive. There was a brief silence. Then Dill heard Tim Dolan's voice: "Don't you wanta take your coat off?" And his own reply: "I'm not all that warm." This was followed by the voice of Harley saying: "Just the three of you?" And again Dill: "Just the three of us." Thank you, Harold, Dill thought, and pushed the button for stop and then the one for fast forward.

With a judicious amount of backing and filling, Dill soon found the place on the tape he wanted—the one where the conversation between Senator Ramirez and Tim Dolan took place while Dill was walking Clyde Brattle down the stairs of the carriage house. Afterward, Dill could never remember the conversation without one word popping unbidden into his mind: illuminating.

Dolan spoke first: He gone?

Then the Senator: Yes. Well?

DOLAN: Jesus.

SENATOR: You understand it now?

DOLAN: Sure I understand it now. A kid could understand it.

SENATOR: I want those four guys, Tim.

DOLAN: Christ, I don't blame you. You'll get all the ink for handing Brattle and Spivey over to Justice, and those other four guys will be forever asking how high when you say hop.

SENATOR: There's Dill though.

DOLAN: You could fire him.

SENATOR: Not smart.

DOLAN: Find him a cushy job in Rome or Paris or somewhere. Make him grateful.

SENATOR: Better. I think I'll start easing him out tonight. Just follow my lead.

DOLAN: He's coming back.

SENATOR: Right.

There was the sound of the door being opened and closed and then Dolan asking, "D'you think he swallowed it?" and Dill replying: "Brattle?" After that, Dill pushed the stop button and then the one for rewind. He put the tape recorder and the earplug back into the ice-cream sack. Remembering his coffee, he picked up the cup and tasted it. He'd forgotten the sugar, so he put some in. He sat there at the marble soda-fountain counter, the same counter he had spent hours at as a child, and thought about the hole he had dug for himself. He marveled at its depth, and at the slipperiness of its sides, and wondered how he would ever climb out of it.

36

BACK in his room at the Hawkins Hotel, Dill showered and changed into his seersucker jacket and gray pants while Anna Maude Singe listened to the tape on the Sony. The tape was almost over when Dill slipped the jacket on, moved to the writing desk, and started putting coins, keys, airline ticket, and wallet into his pockets. The last item was the .38 revolver. He again shoved it down into his right hip pocket. She watched, but made no comment, and went on listening to the last words on the tape as they came over the earphone. When the words ended, she punched the stop button, then the rewind one, and said, "It's dynamite."

"I know."

"Have you got a copy?"

"No."

"You should have copies made."

"I'll let Spivey do that."

"You're giving it to him?"

"I think so."

She nodded slowly. "Then you've made a pretty big choice, haven't you?"

"Have I?"

"Sure. You've had to choose between your friend and your government, and you've chosen your friend."

"That's not a very big choice," Dill said. "That's hardly any choice at all."

He picked up the phone and dialed information. When the operator finally came on—after a recorded voice first counseled him to consult the directory—Dill asked for the home number of John Strucker, the chief of detectives. The information operator told him a few seconds later that no such number was listed. Dill hung up.

"Unlisted?" Singe said.

He nodded.

"Let me try." She took an address book from her purse, flipped through it, found a number, and dialed it. When the call was answered, she said, "Mike?" and when Mike said yes, she said This is Anna Maude. They chatted for a few moments and then she said she needed to get in touch with John Strucker at home. Mike apparently had the number handy, because she wrote it down on the back of a hotel envelope she took from the desk. She then thanked Mike, said goodbye, and hung up.

"Who's Mike?" Dill asked.

"Mike Geary as in AP Geary."

"The one you used to go to the Press Club with."

"Right."

"I'm jealous," Dill said as he picked up the phone and dialed the number she had written on the envelope.

"No, you're not," she said.

The phone rang three times and was answered by a woman's voice. Dill assumed it was Dora Lee Strucker, the rich wife. Dill identified himself, apologized for calling so late, and asked if he could speak to her husband. She said it was nice to hear from Dill at any time and that Johnny would take the call in the study.

Strucker came on with a noncommittal "Yes."

"How would you like to collar Clyde Brattle?"

"Brattle, huh?"

"Brattle."

Strucker sighed. It was the most sepulchral Strucker sigh Dill had heard yet. "From Kansas City?" Strucker answered, almost as if he were hoping Dill would say, No, this particular Brattle is from Sacramento or Buffalo or Des Moines.

"From Kansas City," Dill said. "Originally."

"Where?" Strucker said.

Dill gave him Anna Maude Singe's apartment number and address.

"When?"

"Ten sharp."

"Ten, huh?"

"Ten."

"I'll think about it," Strucker said, and hung up. It wasn't quite the reaction Dill had been expecting. By rights, he thought, Strucker should have jumped at it. Unless, of course, he needed to check with someone else. Dill dialed Strucker's number again. It was busy. He cut the connection and dialed Jake Spivey's number. It, too, was busy. Dill put the phone down slowly. They could be talking to each other, he told himself, or to any of a million other people.

"You look funny," Singe said.

"Do I?"

"You look like he said no."

"He said he'd think about it."

"That's not what a cop's supposed to say. He's supposed to say, Stall Brattle till I get there and don't let him out of your sight—or something like that."

"Unless he..." Dill let the thought die because it was only half-born and extremely ugly, even grotesque.

"Unless he what?" Singe demanded.

"He already knew Brattle would be there."

Her eyes opened very wide and Dill again noticed how pretty they were. Concern makes them even darker, he thought. Almost true violet.

"If he knew about Brattle before you called," she said, "that means somebody's about to get shafted. You, probably."

"Maybe," Dill said. "Maybe not."

It was then that the new fight began. Anna Maude Singe insisted on going with Dill. He refused. She asserted it was her goddamned apartment and she could go there any goddamned time she pleased. Dill replied she goddamned sure wasn't coming with him. She threatened to phone the Senator and tell him about the tape. Dill offered her the phone. She took it, dialed 0, and asked for Senator Ramirez' room. Dill snatched the phone from her and slammed it down. A few moments later they reached the compromise: she would come along, but she wouldn't go inside. Instead, she would wait in Dill's car and watch who went in and came out. She said she thought that sounded goddamned silly. Dill said if he didn't come out in an hour, it wouldn't be goddamned silly, it would be a goddamned shame. She wanted to know what she was expected to do if he didn't come out in an hour. He told her she should call someone, but when she asked who, he said he didn't know. Someone. They left it at that.

It was still raining when they pulled up across the street from the Van Buren Towers in Dill's rented Ford. He suddenly realized he always thought of the apartment building as the Old Folks Home first, and then consciously translated that into its proper name. The rain was steady and unrelenting and, like all steady and unrelenting things, boring. Dill found a parking space directly across from the apartment-building entrance, but Anna Maude Singe said, "You can't get this thing in there."

"Watch," said Dill, who prided himself on his ability to jockey large cars into impossible places. He parked the Ford with dispatch and even with a bit of a flourish. When done, there was only six inches or so of space left at either end of the car. Singe remained unimpressed. "What if I have to get out of here in a hurry?" she asked.

"I guess you can't," he said.

She looked at her watch. "Nine twenty-five."

"I'd better go."

"Have you got a raincoat?"

"No."

"You ought to have a raincoat."

"Well, I don't."

She frowned. "I don't want you to go in there."

"Why not?"

"Aw, for God's sake, guess."

He smiled and put an arm around her and gently pulled her toward him. She went willingly. They kissed a long and somehow anxious kiss and when it was over she sat back and examined him thoughtfully.

"I don't know, Dill," she said.

"What?"

"Maybe I am your sweetie after all."

Carrying the Sony player-recorder in its King Brothers ice-cream bag, Dill ran across the street through the rain and into the Van Buren Towers. In the lobby he discovered he had got damp, but not wet. He rode the lone elevator up to the fifth floor, walked down the corridor, unlocked Anna Maude Singe's apartment door, and went in. After switching on two lamps, he looked at his watch and saw it was 9:29. He started toward the bathroom, but stopped to give the Maxfield Parrish print a brief inspection. He again concluded the two figures in the print were girls.

In the bathroom, he used a towel to dry off his hands,

face, and copper-colored hair. He looked in the mirror and saw a trace of lipstick on his mouth. He scrubbed it off with the towel, staring at his reflection. You look tired, old, scared, and your nose is too big, he told himself, and went back into the living room.

He was examining the Maxfield Parrish print again when he heard the knock. He went to the door, opened it, and Jake Spivey came in, wearing a Burberry trench-coat.

"Jesus, Jake, you look like something right out of *Foreign Intrigue.*"

"No, I don't" Spivey said. "I look like a fat guy in a trenchcoat, and the only thing that looks dumber's a sow in a white shirt. But Daffy bought it for me and well, what the hell, it was raining, so I wore the fucker."

Spivey was already unbuttoning the wet trenchcoat and turning to give the living room an inspection. "Damned if this don't look like nineteen-forty-something-or-other. She wasn't on this floor, was she?"

"Who?"

"Aunt Louise. You remember Jack Sackett's Aunt Louise."

"I remember."

Spivey closed his eyes and smiled. "July 19, 1959. About two-thirty in the afternoon." He opened his eyes, still smiling. "I can remember all that but I can't remember what floor she was on."

"The fourth," Dill said, suddenly remembering. "Number four-two-eight."

Spivey nodded. "Believe you're right." He held up the wet trenchcoat. "What d'you want me to do with this?"

Dill took the coat and said he would hang it up behind the bathroom door. When he came back, Spivey was seated on the couch staring at the Parrish print. Dill asked him if he wanted a drink. Spivey shook his head and said, "Liquor and Clyde Brattle don't mix." He turned from the print to Dill. "Clyde sound like he's willing to cut a deal?"

"He might—depending on what you've got to offer."

"I've been thinking about that, Pick, and I haven't got a whole hell of a lot. What I've got might get Clyde twenty-five years, but, shit, what's twenty-five years when you're looking a hundred in the face?"

Dill took the King Brothers ice-cream sack from the top of the old record player and handed it to Spivey, who asked, "What's this?" Both his tone and expression were totally suspicious.

"Fudge ripple."

Spivey stared at Dill for several seconds, and then opened the sack, much as if it might have contained either a bomb or a snake. He brought out the small Sony player-recorder. "I always did like Sony fudge ripple." He again looked at Dill. "Want me to go ahead and play it?"

"That's right."

Spivey studied the controls briefly, put the player-recorder on the coffee table, and pushed the play button. The sound this time came from the machine's small one-inch speaker. The voices were clear but tinny. Dill watched Spivey listen. And Spivey listened with total absorption and concentration, asking only two one-word questions and they were, "Ramirez?" and "Dolan?" when the voices of the Senator and the minority counsel were heard for the first time. There's no surprise on his face, Dill noted. No surprise, no elation, no appreciation. Nothing but that curiously blank and neutral look that comes when the mind is absolutely concentrated.

But when it was over the smile came—the Spivey smile: full of villainy and cheer, malice and humor. A rogue's smile, Dill thought.

With the smile still beaming, and an expression of mild wistfulness added, Spivey said, "You wouldn't wanta sell me that little old tape there, would you, Pick?"

"I might."

"How much you asking?"

"How much're you willing to pay, Jake?"

"About every dime I've got—and I'll throw in Daffy and the pickup, too."

"With that tape," Dill said, "you won't have to go to jail."

"You don't know what that tape really is, do you, Pick?"

"What?"

"Why it's the ultimate briarpatch, that's what. Shit, with that, I won't even have to *think* about going to jail." The smile appeared. "C'mon, Pick, how much you really asking?"

"My don't-fuck-around-anymore price?"

"Just name it, I'll pay it."

Dill felt the tension come then. It started in his shoulders, shot up to his neck, and fastened around his mouth. His lips felt stiff; the inside of his mouth dry. Go ahead, he told himself. Spit it out, and if you're too dry to spit, write it down.

"What I want, Jake," Dill said slowly, surprised at how calm and reasonable he sounded. "What I want is whoever it was who killed Felicity."

The Spivey smile went away. A grimace took its place. It was a grimace of regret. Spivey looked to his left at the Parrish print. He studied it for several moments, then looked down at the tape recorder and chewed on his lower lip at least three or four times. Finally, he looked back up at Dill. The grimace was gone. The smile was back and the eyes were brimming with what Dill took to be both guile and good will.

"Well?" Dill said.

"No problem," Jake Spivey said.

CHAPTER

37

AN almost ebullient Jake Spivey changed his mind about having a drink. Dill went into the kitchen and poked around until he found Anna Maude Singe's limited liquor supply. He poured two glasses of vodka on the rocks and carried them back into the living room. He handed one of the glasses to the seated Spivey and said, "Let's hear it."

Spivey took a big gulp of the drink, wiped his mouth with the back of his hand, shook his head and—smiling all the while—said, "You just sit back and let me handle this, Pick."

"Trust you." Dill didn't make it a question.

Spivey nodded. "Trust me."

"I don't trust anybody, Jake."

"Must be lonesome," Spivey said and started to say something else, but broke off at the sound of the knock at the living-room door. Dill looked at his watch. It was exactly 10 P.M. Spivey rose and said, "Why don't you let old Clyde in?"

Dill went to the door and opened it. Standing in the corridor, wearing a slight bemused smile, an oyster-white raincoat, a matching rain hat, and carrying a wet umbrella, was Clyde Brattle. Dill thought Brattle resembled some long-vanished Roman consul more than ever. Perhaps it was the way he wore the raincoat draped carelessly over his shoulders. Few men could wear a coat like that and not look silly. Dill didn't think Brattle looked at all silly. If anything, he looked a bit like some patrician forced by fate to the moneylenders and determined to make the best of it.

"Come in," Dill said.

Brattle came into the room then, and just as he entered, Spivey stepped from behind the open door and jammed an automatic pistol into the small of Brattle's back. Brattle smiled and stopped. "Well, Jake, how nice to hear from you again."

"Over there next to that pretty picture, Clyde," Spivey said.

Brattle glanced around. "The Parrish, you mean?"

"The one with the two fags."

"I think they're girls, actually," Brattle said, moved to the wall, and leaned against it with both hands, the umbrella still clasped in his right one.

"Take the coat and the hat and the umbrella, Pick," Spivey said. "Slow and careful. When you've got 'em, put 'em all in the closet over there."

Dill did as instructed, returned to Spivey's side, and asked, "Now what?"

"Now pat him down real good. Ankles, crotch, everywhere. We might even make him open his mouth and take a look in there."

Brattle shook his head and sighed. "Sometimes you're such a boor, Jake."

"Bad manners make for a long life, Clyde."

"An aphorism, by God. Well, almost anyway."

Dill found the small Walther automatic when his search reached Brattle's waist. The pistol was in a leather holster clipped to the waistband of Brattle's beltless trousers. He'd never wear a belt, Dill thought, as he examined the weapon. Braces, perhaps, with a three-piece suit, but never a belt.

"I'll take that," Spivey said. Dill handed him the Walther. Spivey dropped it into his left jacket pocket.

"You can straighten up and turn around now, Clyde," Spivey said. "Take a chair. That one over there looks comfortable. Pick here'll even get you a drink. I know there's vodka, but I don't know what else he's got."

"Vodka will do nicely," Brattle said as he straightened, moved over to the armchair, and sat down. Spivey resumed his seat on the couch. He put his own automatic down on the coffee table next to the Sony tape player. Dill noticed the automatic was a .38 Colt.

"On the rocks?" Dill asked Brattle.

Brattle smiled. "Perfect."

As he poured the drink in the kitchen, Dill could hear no voices coming from the living room. When he came back with Brattle's drink, he thought the silence seemed like that between two old, old friends who long ago had exhausted all topics of mutual interest and whose only bond now was a numbing familiarity.

Brattle raised his glass to his lips, sipped almost delicately, lowered it, and said, "Well, the rain was certainly welcome, wasn't it?"

"Clyde," Spivey said.

Brattle turned his head fractionally to look at Spivey. "Yes?"

"We're gonna do a deal here tonight, you and me, but first I want you to listen to something."

"Something interesting?"

"I think so," Spivey said, and pushed the tape recorder's play button. Dill watched Brattle listen—just as he had watched Spivey. At first, a slight brief frown crossed Brattle's face, but then it vanished and his expression relaxed as though he had just identified and was listening to a piece of music, perhaps a sonata, certainly an old favorite, that he had last heard long ago. Brattle leaned his head back against the chair. He closed his eyes. He smiled slightly. He listened to every word.

When it was over, Brattle opened his eyes, looked at Dill, and asked, "Your work?"

"Yes."

"Ingenious." Brattle turned his gaze on Spivey. "Well, Jake, congratulations. Now let's see what kind of deal we can work out. What're you asking?"

"Couple of things," Spivey said. "First, we're gonna have to forget all about me and what I might or might not've done during those years you and me messed around together."

"Of course. That's obvious. What else—money?"

"By God, I didn't even think of that. But no, not money. I got enough money."

Brattle's left eyebrow moved up to form a delicate arc. "You know something, Jake? I don't believe I've ever heard anyone say that before in my life. Not and mean it anyway. But all right. I accept that. Now what is it you do want?"

"I want the name of the dumb fuck who went and killed Pick here's sister."

Both of Brattle's eyebrows went up this time. He looked genuinely puzzled as he turned his head to inspect Dill. "Your sister?"

"Felicity Dill. Homicide detective second grade."

"As I told you. I read about it. Then there was that large funeral. Someone killed at it. But aside from that, I'm totally ignorant." He paused. "Sorry. But I am."

"What you are, Clyde," Spivey said, "is the best fucking liar who ever breathed."

"You *want* somebody for it, Jake? Is that it? Do you

need somebody? If so, you can have Harley. Or Sid. Or both. They didn't do it, of course, but take them with my blessing. Maybe they could even leave a joint suicide note confessing all. You used to be fairly good at suicide notes, Jake."

Spivey shook his head and smiled. "By God, you're something, Clyde, you really are. Now lemme tell you what I think. You sent somebody after me about—oh, I'd say a year and a half back. How do I know? I know just the same way you'd know if somebody came after you. You can feel it. Smell it. Sense it. Taste it almost. Whoever you sent was taking their time, not hurrying none, waiting for the perfect spot, the right moment and all that. I kind of sensed that, too. But then Pick here's sister stumbles on to it somehow, and she gets blown up in her car. So tell me who you hired to whack me out, Clyde, and I can tell Pick here who killed his sister."

Brattle took another small delicate sip of his drink. As he lowered the glass, he shook his head regretfully. "I don't know quite what to say, Jake, other than to simply deny—"

The hard knock at the apartment door interrupted Brattle. No one moved. Spivey and Brattle stared suspiciously at each other for a brief second and then, almost in unison, shifted their twin suspicious stares to Dill. The knock came again, although it was more than a knock this time, it was a loud pounding and over the pounding came a harsh voice that cried, "Police! Open up!"

It was Dill who went to the door and opened it. Gene Colder, the homicide captain, rushed through the door, his gun drawn. "Nobody moves!" he snapped. "Everybody freezes."

No one moved. Colder was in a half crouch, both hands wrapped around the revolver. He wore a short rain jacket and brown gabardine slacks that Dill thought looked expensive. The rain jacket was damp and so were the slacks, but not wet. On Colder's feet were lace-up brown shoes.

They were partially covered by half-rubbers. Dill couldn't remember when he had last seen someone wear rubbers in a summer rain.

Colder glanced at Dill. "Back up against that wall," he ordered.

"Want me to put my hands up?" Dill said.

"Just keep 'em in sight." Colder looked briefly at Jake Spivey, who was still seated on the couch. "And you, fats, you just keep sitting there. Spivey, isn't it?"

Spivey nodded. "Jake Spivey."

Still in his crouch, still holding his pistol with both hands, Colder turned his attention and his body toward Clyde Brattle. "And just who the hell are you?" he demanded.

Brattle was still seated in the chair, his legs crossed. He smiled and put down his drink. His left hand moved toward the inside breast pocket of his jacket as he said, "If you'll permit me to show you some ident—"

He stopped talking when Captain Gene Colder shot him through the forehead, just above the left eye. The impact of the round slammed Brattle back against the chair. As he started to sag, Colder shot him again, this time in the chest.

No one moved for a second or two. No one said anything. Slowly Captain Colder straightened up from his crouch and put the revolver back in its belt holster under the rain jacket. He turned to Dill. "I didn't have any choice," he explained. "He was going for his piece."

"Sure," Dill said. "Absolutely."

Spivey rose and slowly moved over to the dead Clyde Brattle. He stood looking down at him for several moments, then shook his head, and said, "Well, shit, Clyde, what'd you expect?"

He knelt down beside the body and looked from the dead Brattle to the standing Captain Colder, as if measuring distance and angle. Spivey then reached into the left-hand pocket of his jacket. He brought out the Walther automatic that had been Brattle's. He pointed the automatic at Colder and shot him an inch or so above where the short rain jacket ended.

Colder staggered back one step, then two, pressing both hands against the wound. He sank to his knees and stared down at the blood seeping through his fingers. Slowly, he lifted his head to look at the expressionless Jake Spivey. He seemed to be searching Spivey's face for an answer to an important question, but finding none, turned his head as far left as it would go and screamed a name. The name he screamed was Strucker.

Chief of Detectives John Strucker, looking neat and dry, strolled through the apartment's still-open door a second later. He had a lighted cigar in his left hand. He was dressed in a gray silk suit that Dill, for some reason, put an eight-hundred-dollar price tag on. Strucker turned, closed the door, nodded at Dill, and walked over to the still-kneeling Captain Colder.

Colder stared up at him. "Spivey...it was Spivey," he whispered.

Strucker shook his head sadly. "You know what you are, Gene? You're a fucking disgrace."

Strucker turned, moved over to Spivey and held out his hand. Spivey put the Walther automatic in it. Strucker removed his display handkerchief and carefully wiped off the pistol.

"This was Brattle's?" he said to Spivey.

Spivey nodded.

"Was he right- or left-handed?"

"Right," Spivey said.

The still-kneeling Colder groaned and muttered, "Goddamn you, Strucker, do something."

"I'm fixing to," Strucker said, sighed one of his heavier sighs, stuck the cigar between his teeth, and bent over the dead Clyde Brattle. He wrapped Brattle's right hand around the Walther and inserted Brattle's right forefinger through the trigger guard and around the trigger. He looked from the Walther automatic to the still-kneeling, staring Captain Colder. Strucker fired the automatic with the dead man's finger and shot Captain Gene Colder through the chest, just about where the heart would be. Colder jerked back with the impact, then came forward, and fell over onto his left side. A tremor ran through his body. Then he was still.

Strucker took the cigar from his mouth and moved over to the body of the dead police captain. He stared down at it for a moment, knelt, and carefully lifted Colder's revolver from its holster and placed it next to the lifeless right hand. Strucker rose, turned to Dill, and said, "Satisfied?"

"I don't know," Dill said. "Tell me about it."

38

STRUCKER looked at his watch. "You're gonna get the two-minute version," he said, "because when homicide comes through that door, I'm turning Colder into a brave and dedicated cop who shot it out with the most wanted fugitive in America." He turned to Jake Spivey. "How's that sound?"

"Just fine," Spivey said.

Strucker turned back to Dill. "She worked for me, your sister. For me and nobody else. Six months after they brought Colder down from Kansas City, he didn't feel right. He changed. His attitude shifted. His interest wasn't the same. That's hard to explain to a civilian, but I knew he had something going. He bought a house that was just a tad too nice. His suits were a hundred dollars too expensive. He wasn't dumb enough to buy himself a Mercedes, but he did pop for an Olds Ninety-Eight. Then there was that lousy business with his wife. You heard about that."

Dill nodded. "He committed her."

"So it was around in there that I called Felicity in and told her what I thought and felt and what I wanted her to do about it. Well, your sister was one brilliant woman, and beautiful, and if I wasn't so old and so happy with Dora Lee—well, I might've gone courting myself, even if Felicity was poor as Job's turkey. But she told me that was a Dill tradition—being poor."

"She was right," Dill said.

"So she turned herself into a honey pot and Gene Colder fell right into it and, shit, who could blame him? I couldn't. But what I wanted to know was how much money he had, and where it was coming from, and what he was doing to earn it. It took Felicity damn near six months just to find out how much he had, and it was around seven or eight hundred thousand. He gave her the money to make the down payment on the duplex and a lot more besides, but I guess you'd already figured that out."

"Some of it," Dill said.

"But what your sister couldn't find out was where the money was coming from because it wasn't. I mean, Colder just had it, you understand?"

"Yes," Dill said. "I understand."

"And then, one day, she mentioned you and Jake Spivey to him and how you two had grown up together and all. Well, Colder couldn't hear enough about that. Then, a few months later, they were at his place, Colder's, and it was a Saturday afternoon, as I remember, and he went down to the store for some beer or something, and Felicity started snooping around. She found a ledger about so big." Strucker's hands measured a small seven-by-nine-inch ledger. "So she read it and what she read was everything she'd told him about Jake. Not you. Just Jake. So I went calling on Jake out at the old Ace Dawson mansion."

"It was love at first sight," Spivey said with a grin.

"And you two figured it out, right?" Dill said. "The

322

Kansas City connection between Colder and Clyde Brattle."

Strucker nodded.

"How much do you think Brattle paid Colder to kill Jake?" Dill asked. "A million?"

Strucker nodded. "At least. Well, we—Jake and I—we decided if we could just keep Jake alive, Brattle'd show up sooner or later to find out how come he wasn't getting what he paid for. And when he showed, well, I'd collar him and that sure wouldn't hurt my political future any. Jake and I'd already talked some about that."

"And you just let Felicity dangle," Dill said.

"Colder hadn't done anything yet," Strucker said. You've gotta keep that in mind."

"And you're saying he killed Felicity when he found out what she was up to."

Strucker nodded somberly. And after the nod came another of his long sad sighs. "We couldn't prove it though. We had no case."

"Bullshit," Dill said. "You could've nailed Colder for Felicity. Or for what's his name, her ex-boyfriend, Clay Corcoran. Or for poor old Harold Snow. Jesus. Harold was the real easy one. But you didn't, did you, because you were still waiting for Brattle. You guys traded my sister for Clyde Brattle."

Strucker in two quick strides was at Dill's side. He grabbed Dill by the left arm and spun him around. The chief of detectives pointed down at the floor. His face was an angry wrinkled knot. His voice a rasp. "Who's that lying down there in his own blood and piss and shit? That's Gene Colder, *Captain* Gene Colder, who was the best fucking homicide cop I ever knew. He killed your sister without leaving a trace and then preached at her funeral. He shot Clay Corcoran through the throat from thirty-six feet away with a twenty-five automatic and six hundred other cops standing around with their thumbs up their ass. He used a sawed-off on Harold Snow and then waltzed back in carrying a pint of ice cream, took over the investigation, and planted the evidence that would prove Snow killed Felicity. You think he didn't know what he was doing? Why the fuck d'you think a guy like Clyde Brattle'd pay him a million dollars? And if Gene'd been just a little luckier tonight, he could've nailed Brattle, kept the money, and the law'd never touch him. But there he is. On the floor. Dead."

Dill reached over and removed Strucker's grip. He then stepped over to the coffee table. "What if he didn't do it?" Dill asked.

Strucker glanced quickly over at Jake Spivey who seemed puzzled. "What's he getting at?" Strucker said.

"Something," Spivey said.

"You say you can't prove he killed Felicity—or Corcoran, or even Harold Snow. So if you can't prove he killed them, he's innocent."

"He killed them," Strucker said. "All of them."

"You think he did."

"So do you, Pick," Spivey said.

"Maybe," Dill said, reached down, picked up the tape player, snapped out the cassette, and put it away in a pocket.

Spivey rose. "You ain't fixing to walk out the door with that tape, are you?" he said.

"It was supposed to be your briarpatch, Jake. The ultimate one. But now it's mine." Dill looked at Strucker and then back at Jake Spivey, who reached down and picked up the .38 Colt automatic from the coffee table. "I worry about you two," Dill said. "I worry about how high you'll rise and what you might do when you get there. And if you go far enough and high enough, then someday you might start remembering me and how I was here in this room on the night you did what you did. And then maybe you might start wondering if maybe you shouldn't do something about me. So when you start thinking like that, remember this: I've got the tape."

Spivey shook his head sadly and brought the automatic up until it was aimed at Dill. "Pick, I can't let you go through the door with that tape."

"What's on it?" Strucker said.

"Everything we need to keep me out of jail and make you mayor and then senator."

"Well, now," Strucker said.

Dill said, "I'm leaving, Jake."

"We're just gonna have to stop you one way or other," Spivey said, his voice sad and troubled. He looked over at Strucker.

The chief of detectives slowly shook his head. "No."

"What d'you mean no?" Spivey said.

"If we take that tape away from him, he'll talk," Strucker said. "About tonight. If we let him walk, he won't." He looked at Dill. "Right?"

"Right."

"Unless, of course," Strucker said to Spivey, "you want to plug him and get it over with. We could fix it up somehow."

Dill waited for Spivey to say or do something. Spivey again looked down at the automatic and again aimed it carefully at Dill. As he aimed it, an expression of genuine sorrow spread slowly across his face. Dill wondered whether he would hear the gun fire. The sorrow then left Spivey's face and regret seemed to replace it. He slowly lowered the automatic and said, "Shit, I can't do it."

Dill turned, opened the door, and left.

CHAPTER
39

As he strode down the corridor toward the elevator, doors opened cautiously and frightened middle-aged faces peered out. Dill glared at the faces and snapped, "Police." The doors slammed shut.

In the lobby there were only the two Mexicans who worked for Jake Spivey. Both wore neat, very dark-gray suits. They looked at each other as Dill came out of the elevator and the older of the pair shook his head, as if to say, Don't bother. Dill went up to him and said in Spanish, "Where are the other two men—the big one and the thin one with the dead eyes?"

The Mexican smiled. "When we arrived we persuaded them they had important business elsewhere. They left to attend to it."

The Mexican was still smiling contentedly as Dill went through the lobby door and out into the rain. He ran across the street, edged through the narrow space at the

Ford's rear, and opened the front passenger door. "You drive," he told Anna Maude Singe.

She slid over behind the wheel as Dill got in. "If this is the getaway," she said, "it's going to take an hour just to get unparked."

"Slam into the car behind you, cut the wheel all the way to the left, hit the car in front of you, and keep doing that till you clear your right front fender."

"You mean do it the way I always do it," she said.

It took her only twenty seconds and five bumps to work the Ford out of the confined space. She sped down Van Buren until she came to 23rd Street, heard the siren, pulled over to the right, and stopped. A green-and-white squealed around the rain-slick corner, siren screaming, bar lights flashing. Singe took her foot off the brake and once more started cautiously around the corner. But again she hit the brake at the sight of a dark unmarked sedan that came speeding down the opposite side of the street, a red light flashing from behind its grille.

Singe sat behind the wheel without moving until Dill said, "Let's go." The car slowly moved off.

"The cops," she said. "They're going to my place, aren't they?"

"Yes."

"I saw Jake Spivey and those two Mexicans of his go in. Then three more men went in and a few minutes later two of them ran out."

"That was Harley and Sid. They worked for Clyde Brattle."

"Then Strucker and Gene Colder went in together."

"Yes."

"What happened?"

"Brattle and Colder are dead."

"Where?"

"In the living room."

"*My* living room?"

"Yes."

"Aw damn, damn, damn." She automatically speeded up. "Don't tell me about it. I don't want to know. Why should I? I don't even know where I'm going."

"The airport."

"What about your stuff at the hotel?"

"It'll keep."

He reached into his pocket and brought out the cassette. "See this?"

She glanced at it and nodded. "You didn't give it to Spivey then?"

"No. I'm putting it in your purse." She saw him do it and then went back to her driving. "You know where you can get copies made?" he asked.

She nodded.

"Get six copies made tomorrow."

"Tomorrow?" she said. "What about tonight? Where the hell do I sleep tonight?"

"There's a Holiday Inn near the airport, isn't there?"

"Yes."

He took out his wallet, removed three one-hundred-dollar bills—almost the last of them, he saw—and tucked the money down into her purse next to the tape. "Pay cash for your room. Use an assumed name—Mary Borden."

"I don't look like a Mary Borden."

"Use it anyway. Keep the Ford and tomorrow go out only to get the tapes copied. Then go back to your room. I'll call you by noon."

"Noon."

"Yes."

"What if you don't?"

Dill sighed. "If I don't, take the tape and go to the FBI."

At the entrance to Gatty International Airport, Benjamin Dill and Anna Maude Singe kissed goodbye. It was a brief kiss, hurried, and almost without tenderness. She watched him get out of the car. "Call me, damn you," she said.

In the airport Dill walked around studying the scheduled departures. He finally picked a Delta flight that would be leaving for Atlanta in forty-five minutes. He bought a one-way first-class ticket, paying cash and using the name F. Taylor. In Atlanta, he knew he would be able to get a flight into Washington's National Airport.

Dill spent most of the time before the flight in a stall in the men's room. There he carefully wiped off Harold Snow's revolver with a handkerchief, wrapped the gun up in a newspaper he had bought, and dropped it in a trash can on his way out of the men's room. On board the plane, he found himself seated on the aisle next to a cheerful-looking man of about fifty. The man looked like a talker. Dill hoped he wasn't. The plane took off, banking over the city. The man stared down at the lights through the rain and then turned to Dill.

"Now that's one hell of a sight," the man said. "Wanta take a look?"

"No," Dill said. "I don't think I really do."

At 9:46 A.M. on Tuesday, August 9, the taxi let Dill out in front of his apartment building on the corner of 21st and N Streets, Northwest. He glanced around and saw them, two Mercury sedans, plain and unmarked, that might as well have had U.S. Government stenciled across their doors. One of them, dark blue, was parked on N Street. It had two men in it. The other one, dark gray, was parked in the No Parking zone in front of the old man's bile-green apartment building on 21st. There were also two men in it.

Dill entered the apartment building and checked his mailbox. There were three bills, nine pieces of junk mail, a copy of *Newsweek*, and a letter from his dead sister.

Dear Picklepuss:

The only real juicy item I've got for you this week involves your old high school flame, the very snooty, very stuck-up Barbara Jean Littlejohn (née Collins). And if you don't quite recall what she had to be snooty about, you need only remember she was president of her high school sorority, the *Tes Trams*. For God's sake, Pick, spell it backward! Now married to Art Littlejohn, manager of the city's *largest* TG&Y, lovely Barbara Jean was picked up for shoplifting last week at—are you ready?—Sears! She was trying to walk out the front door with a fake marten stole she'd slipped on. Now who would ever notice that in July with the temperature 101°?

As for your little sister, the ace detective, she's coming to the end of a long and rather sordid escapade that some day I'll tell you about in detail. Tomorrow morning I go down and reveal all to the cleancut & boring FBI. Why don't I, you may well ask, reveal all to my top cop boss, Honest John Strucker, chief of detectives and wedder of a rich widow? Well, I no longer trust old Honest John, or his newly acquired best friend, who is none other than your old asshole buddy, Jake Spivey, who now dwells in marbled halls. Can you imagine raggedy-ass Jake rattling around in the old Ace Dawson manse?

For the past year and a half I've been either a double or a triple agent of the down-home variety. I have trouble with the triple-agent concept because it's a mathematical abstraction and I, as you well know, am of an intuitive bent that simply abhors abstractions, especially Algebra 3, which I flunked twice.

The major players in this unsavory melodrama have been me (starring, of course), Honest John

Strucker, Jake Spivey (in the wings so far), and my current paramour, Captain Gene Colder of Homicide, who—although fearful of mien—is actually a real domp, which down here is what they call a cross between a dope and a wimp. Money's involved. Tons of it. And politics. And some mysterious international misterioso called Clyde Brattle who you must've heard of. I've learned just enough to get scared and maybe just enough to land Colder the domp in jail. Maybe. So this evening I mail this and tomorrow I rise bright and early and head for the FBI where I shall Tell All.

By the way (which is easier to spell than incidentally), I have taken out a $250,000 life-insurance policy naming you as sole beneficiary. If anything happens to me, call my lawyer, Anna Maude Singe, who has both looks and brains and you could do worse, which, as we both know, you often have.

Oh. One more thing. If anything does happen to me, don't believe one goddamn word they tell you down here. And now that I've cheered you up and got you interested, I'll say goodbye and also send you—

—all my love,
Felicity

The letter had been written on his sister's favorite stationery: ruled sheets from a yellow legal pad. The two sheets were not quite filled with the beautiful copperplate she had taught herself from a book during that summer vacation when she was twelve years old. Before that she had printed everything. Or almost everything.

Dill read the letter as he stood at his tall, almost floor-to-ceiling windows that gave out on the old man's apartment building across the street. When he looked up, he saw the old man was outside with his Polaroid, taking a picture of the dark-gray government Mercury that was parked in the No Parking zone. Two men got out of the Mercury and moved toward the old man. They seemed to be protesting. The old man yelled at them and pointed at the No Parking sign. The two government men pointed at the old man's camera and said something else. He quickly hid the camera behind his back and again yelled at them. Dill couldn't hear what he was yelling. Threats and curses probably.

A Metropolitan Police car pulled up and two black-uniformed cops got out to see what the trouble was. The uniformed cops blurred and Dill realized his eyes were wet. He turned from the window and wiped away the tears.

They all killed her in a way, he thought, and now all will pay just a little something on account. Otherwise, the preacher was wrong and she will have died in vain, although dying in vain isn't really all that bad since nearly everyone does it. It's the living in vain you really have to watch out for, and Felicity never wasted a day doing that.

He decided he had about five or ten minutes before the government agents, whoever they were, came knocking. He went to the wall phone in the kitchen and called long-distance information for the number of the airport Holiday Inn where Anna Maude Singe was waiting. As the phone rang, Dill wondered how good a lawyer she really was, and whether she would like Washington. Most of all he wondered whether she could keep him out of jail.